LETTERS FROM THAILAND

LETTERS FROM THAILAND

BOTAN

TRANSLATED BY

SUSAN F. KEPNER

For Barbara
from
Susan
3/8/03

SILKWORM BOOKS

For our daughters
Suweeriya and Pawasu
Julia and Anne

จดหมายจากเมืองไทย โดย โบตั๋น
Original Thai text © 1969 by Supa Sirisingh
English translation © 2002 by Susan F. Kepner

ISBN 974-7551-67-5

This edition is published in 2002 by
Silkworm Books
104/5 Chiang Mai–Hot Road, M. 7, Suthep, Muang, Chiang Mai 50200, Thailand
E-mail: silkworm@loxinfo.co.th

Cover photograph: Pandit Wattanakasiwit
Set in 10 pt. Garamond by Silk Type

Printed in Thailand by O. S. Printing House, Bangkok

10 9 8 7 6 5 4 3 2 1

TRANSLATOR'S INTRODUCTION

It is amazing to realize that this wonderful novel has been a part of my life, and of the lives of so many readers, for thirty years. I began the English translation of *Letters from Thailand* during the summer of 1971; it was first published in 1977, and then reprinted six times. During the summer of 2001 I returned to it, to make substantial revisions for this much-improved edition from Silkworm Books.

Letters from Thailand is the kind of novel one reads straight through, and then reads again, a year or five years later. Many readers have written to tell me so, and surely, that is the test of a great story. One reader went so far as to say that returning to the family of Tan Suang U and Lo Mui Eng, their friends and relatives, was like attending a family reunion. If it seems like a real family, that is because it is based upon a real family.

AN AWARD-WINNING NOVEL

When "Botan" (the pseudonym of Supa Sirisingh) was a graduate student at Chulalongkorn University during the 1960s, she ran out of money and had to leave the treasured privacy of her apartment and move back to her parents' home. Her father was a Chinese immigrant; her mother was also Chinese, but born in Thailand. Botan had already written and published one novel, an undistinguished (in her opinion) romantic tale. Now, she needed to write another book in order to reestablish her independence. Lying on her bed one evening, trying to map out the plot of the new book, she struggled in vain to ignore the noise in the next room: her parents were arguing, again. Exasperated, she took a fresh piece of paper and began jotting down the details of the argument—and that was how *Letters from Thailand* began, a novel about twenty years in the life of a Chinese family in Bangkok. The protagonist, Tan Suang U, is a composite of Botan's father and uncle, both of whom emigrated from southern China to Thailand after World War II, settling in Bangkok and Thonburi, cities of nearly equal size that face each other across the Chao Phraya River. Botan admits that Tan Suang U's youngest daughter in the novel, Meng Chu, is very like herself, a girl determined not only to succeed but to excel despite the limitations imposed upon her by a father who could see no point in educating girls. All of Botan's own education, after the compulsory four years of school (since increased to nine years), through her master's degree in Thai Literature at Chulalongkorn University, was made possible by scholarships, the first of which she earned at the age of nine.

In 1969, *Letters from Thailand* was named "best book of the year," and awarded the SEATO literary prize.[1] At twenty-one, Botan was by far the youngest author ever to be so honored. The novel was very popular with critics and readers alike, and also very controversial. It was a great departure from the typical Thai novel. No one had ever written such realistic, earthy fiction about people who said what they thought about anything and everything. Many people of Chinese descent complained that Botan presented them as greedy, predatory, and unwilling to assimilate into Thai society, while an equal number of Thais claimed that she depicted them as shallow, vain, not very bright, and hypocritical. These readers ignored the fact that the attitudes and prejudices that offended them were endlessly pondered, examined, and discussed by characters in the novel

1. This regional award has since been replaced by the SEAWrite Award.

who represented all vantage points. Eventually, these complaints ended, and within three years the novel had become assigned reading for all high school students.

The world of Botan's tale is entirely limited to the environs of Bangkok, Thonburi, and, briefly, the seaside town of Hua Hin. One critic has described the novel as "claustrophobically preoccupied with the small world of Bangkok's 'Chinatown'" (Anderson and Mendiones 1985:10). While this observation is correct, the "claustrophobic preoccupation" is not a flaw, but a key ingredient in the novel. The reader is swept into the narrow, teeming, claustrophobic world of Sampheng Lane, with its rows of shops owned by Chinese families who live above or behind them, and into the modest house in which Tan Suang U, his wife Mui Eng, and their four children eat, sleep, work, argue, and occasionally grieve. This was the world in which Botan herself had grown up, a world in which even the most successful merchants never seemed to think of moving to the suburbs.

The life of the individual, in this world of which Botan writes, is defined first by responsibility to one's family (including, of course, one's ancestors), second by one's gender, and third by one's occupation. For the adult characters in the novel, work consumes at least sixteen of every twenty-four hours, six or seven days a week, every week of the year, except for brief holidays such as the New Year, or the Moon Festival. Tan Suang U is consumed by the desire to build his family's fortune, yet he lacks any clear idea of what "success" might ultimately mean to himself, his wife, or their children. He is determined that his family remain Chinese and he knows intuitively what this means, but he cannot explain it in any way that makes sense to them, much less inspires them. The children study to their capacity—or, in the case of Tan Suang U's only son, the sad, weak Weng Khim—somewhere beyond it.

The original novel comprises two volumes, totaling 1,053 rather small pages (not a huge novel, by Thai standards). After lengthy discussion, Botan and I decided to delete a couple of repetitive letters and, in one case, we combined two unusually short letters into one—decisions which were to have unexpected consequences.[2]

The reader who is able to read the original Thai novel will observe that the translation does not match Botan's original text line for line, or even paragraph for paragraph. Nevertheless, as Botan commented about the final draft, "Although it is not every-word-every-word (*thuk kham thuk kham*), everything I wrote is in there."

Arguments for the value and importance of "close" literary translation always come down to the issue of degree. From a literary standpoint, an absolutely "literal" translation of any work of fiction would amount to gibberish. No one champions an approach this slavish. It is in the middle ground where the battles rage. At one end of the spectrum was the implacable Vladimir Nabokov, whom George Steiner describes as regarding "all but the most rudimentary of interlinear translations as a fraud, as a facile evasion of radical impossibilities" (Steiner 1975:74). Nabokov summed up his distaste for translation in his poem "On Translating 'Eugene Onegin'":

> What is translation? On a platter
> A poet's pale and glaring head,
> A parrot's screech, a monkey's chatter,
> And profanation of the dead. (Quoted in Steiner 1975:240)

Steiner himself, on the other hand, invokes John Dryden to offer a far more permissive view, and one that I find reasonable:

2. For years I was curious as to why translations of the book into several other languages appeared so soon after the first printing of my English version. Then, one day in a bookstore in Bangkok, I leafed through a few of these foreign cousins, and found that every one of them contained ninety-six chapters—just as in my English translation—and not the one hundred of the Thai original. Clearly, the English version had become the "original" from which these other translations were made, although, to be sure, each translator had included his or her own introduction, in place of mine.

The true road for the translator lies neither through metaphrase nor imitation . . . [but through] paraphrase "or translation with latitude, where the author is kept in view by the translator, so as never to be lost, but his words are not so strictly followed as his sense . . . Through paraphrase the spirit of an author may be transfused, and yet not lost. Right translation is a kind of drawing after the life." (Steiner 1975:255–56)

Such are the sentiments that cause heads to nod in agreement in some circles and necks to stiffen in others, and serve very well to delineate the controversy inherent in translation. My chief goal in translating this novel was to provide the reader with a literary experience as close as possible to that enjoyed by readers of the original text. There is more to literary translation than just getting the words right. We are always striving for accuracy, but accuracy alone is not enough.

DISCOURAGING YEARS

Six years passed between the day I finished the translation, and its initial English publication by Duang Kamol, in Bangkok. One of the reasons I had sought Botan's permission to translate the novel was its universal theme: the main character was an immigrant in a new land, determined to build a better life for himself yet fearful of losing his identity. I thought—wrongly, as it was to turn out—that this "universality" would appeal to a U.S. publisher. After all, my American and European friends who read the first fifty pages of the translation all expressed their astonishment at finding Tan Suang U to be "just like" their Jewish/Italian/Mexican father, or grandfather. But U.S. publishers saw the book only as the story of a family in a small Asian country that was unfamiliar (*The King and I* notwithstanding) to most Americans.

Even university presses were not, at that time, much interested in "third world" fiction, much less Southeast Asian fiction, which was tainted, in the early 1970s, by the traumatic experience of U.S. involvement in the war then being fought in Vietnam, Cambodia, and Laos (and experienced in other ways in Thailand). Other scholarly endeavors related to the Southeast Asian mainland also were affected. Another problem, thirty years ago, was that few university presses published any kind of fiction; and, as far as Asia was concerned, only translations of Chinese and Japanese "classical works," or the work of famous modern writers, were considered. Thai novels fell into the category of "minor literatures."

Botan and I grew discouraged. At one point, after yet another rejection, we came up with the idea of cannibalizing the novel, using it as the core of a new project based upon Botan's original text but set in both China and Thailand. (After all, Pearl Buck had done well enough with all-Chinese casts of characters.) The new book was to be called "The Bee and the Butterfly," a title suggested by a comment of Tan Suang U's about the differences between Thais ("butterflies") and Chinese ("busy bees"). In a box in the back of a closet somewhere I still have a couple of chapters set in China, and today Botan and I find it hard to believe that we could ever have considered this a reasonable idea.

In 1977, Duang Kamol published the translation in Bangkok. It was not available in the United States, and it is surprising that over the next decade, word of mouth sold out six printings. Every year, I would get enthusiastic letters from Americans and Europeans who had bought the novel in a hotel shop or bookstore in Thailand. American professors teaching various Southeast Asian subjects made copies for their students. I did this myself, for my Southeast Asian Cultures and Literatures courses at the University of California, Berkeley.

In the past thirty years, I have translated thousands of pages of Thai fiction and poetry. Botan has written many more novels. But there has been no experience quite like the writing and the translating of *Letters from Thailand*. When Botan and I began to work together, in Bangkok in 1971, she was single, and in her mid-twenties. I was thirty years old, married, and had just adopted the fourth of my children, who happened to be Chinese, and a girl. My friends promptly gave her the nickname "Meng Chu," after the youngest daughter in the novel. Annie/Meng Chu is now thirty herself, and uncannily like the outspoken and business-minded young woman of the novel. Botan and I each have two grown daughters, and each time we meet, we marvel that we have known each other so long, and through so many changes in our own lives, and those of our families. The opportunity to revise *Letters from Thailand*, and to see a new edition that will be widely available, is one for which we are both grateful. It also has added yet another chapter to our own tale.

As I worked on the revisions, I marveled at how well this novel has held up. It still seems "contemporary," which cannot be said of many of the other successful novels of its era. *Letters from Thailand* provides a unique glimpse into the particular world of the Chinese in Southeast Asia, as well as an unparalleled view of Thai urban society at mid–twentieth century. But the reason new readers come to love this book, year after year, is the family of Tan Suang U, with all of its high hopes, bitter disappointments, and occasional joys.

Welcome to the family.

Berkeley, California
July 2001

REFERENCES

Anderson, Benedict R. O'G., and Ruchira Mendiones, trans. and eds. *In the Mirror: Literature and Politics in Siam in the Modern Era*. Bangkok: Duang Kamol, 1985.

Biguenet, John, and Rainer Schulte. *The Craft of Translation.* Chicago: The University of Chicago Press, 1989.

Botan (Supa Sirisingh). *Letters from Thailand.* 6th printing. Translated by Susan Fulop (Kepner). Bangkok: Duang Kamol, 1982.

———. *Chot mai chak muang Thai* [Letters from Thailand]. Bangkok: Phrae Phittaya, 1970.

Steiner, George. *After Babel.* London: Oxford University Press, 1975.

LETTERS FROM THAILAND

PROLOGUE

THE LETTERS you are about to read were originally written in the Chinese language. They were translated into Thai at my direction, and I have worked with them further. It is my sincere hope that this collaboration will distress neither eye nor ear.

I should warn you, dear reader, that you are about to be startled, perhaps even alarmed, for the view of our great nation expressed in the letters which follow cannot be entirely palatable to Thai people. Is it not true, however, that the clearest glass may not give the reflection we like best.

Two months ago, these letters were seized by the Thai National Police Department from a Chinese communist defector named Li Buan Sun. According to our investigation, Mr. Li is a member of the Chinese intellectual class, formerly an official censor at Shanghai. It has been the policy of that government, since its establishment in 1948, to control all personal mail from abroad which suggested that those citizens who had emigrated to other lands might have found a more satisfying way of life. But the censorship system, in the case of Li Buan Sun, proved a double-edged sword, for the man empowered to stop the treacherous flow was at last tempted to flee himself.

Of course, the true owner of the letters is the man who wrote them, a Chinese immigrant to Thailand whom I shall call "Tan Suang U." He is a well-known businessman of Bangkok whose name would be instantly recognized, and whose privacy we shall continue to protect. Suang U mailed all the letters to his mother in Po Leng village, Teo Chiu province, southern China—the first in 1945, the last in 1967.

In 1945, there was no communist government in China and Li Buan Sun was not a high official at Shanghai. He was a simple letter carrier in the district encompassing Po Leng village, and Suang U's mother lived on his route. Perhaps he was unable to locate her farm, or some other circumstance may have prevented his delivering the letters, but the fact is that he did not deliver any of them. (We may gather from the content of the letters that money was enclosed in most of them, but it would be fruitless to enlarge upon this aspect of the matter today, so many years hence and so far from Po Leng village.) What does matter is that Suang U's mother never knew the letters existed, and in my opinion the greater part of Li Buan Sun's crime may be considered to lie here. For all she knew, her son had left her forever, without a word beyond the note he left on the kitchen table the night he boarded a ship bound for Bangkok.

After the communists came to power, Li Buan Sun rose to prominence rapidly, but even after he became official censor at Shanghai, he never lost his love of letters. He loved to write them, to receive them, to collect them. He made arrangements to continue receiving all the letters of Tan Suang U, among others. These, as he told me himself, he had come to think of as his private collection, his chief form of relaxation. In the evenings, after tea, he read them over and over again, and year by year the life and fortunes of Suang U unfolded before his eyes.

The letters were in my hands for several weeks before it occurred to me to take this peculiar course of action. How did I come to this decision? Why do I invite numberless strangers to read the private letters of a man who is neither famous nor, even, unusual? I am well aware that the letters are often offensive, occasionally foolish, and certain to make Thai people angry. It is even possible that they may harm the cause of Chinese integration in our society, a process which in its continuing success has marked us favorably among the nations of Southeast Asia. Nevertheless, I am convinced that our people will profit by reading them, and that making them public is not only a service but a responsibility which I must not shirk.

I have met Tan Suang U. He is a man of unquestionable sincerity and integrity, and he made no excuses for his letters when, to his amazement, he saw them on my desk two months ago. His only reaction was grief—grief that his beloved mother had never read them. What he has to say about our people (and his own) is without doubt a far more honest statement about the experience of the Sino-Thai than any you might elicit from, say, a proper survey of the attitudes of the Thai-Chinese minority in Bangkok, the sort of thing our university students these days delight in.

Do not suppose, now, that I agree with his every opinion and observation! I am a Thai, a patriot, and a man concerned with the honor of the Thai people, as you surely are yourself. But I recommend that you read his letters with an open mind, and think fairly about what he has to say. I do not think you will be disappointed, and I am sure that you will not be bored.

Police General Sala Sinthuthawat
Thai National Police Department

LETTER #1
13 AUGUST 1945

THE SHIP HAI WANG
SUOTAO [SHAN TOU] TO BANGKOK
SEVENTH MONTH, SIXTH DAY
YEAR OF THE COCK

MY MOST Beloved and Respected Mother,

Before you read this letter, your son will already be in Thailand. I plan to write every few days while I am on the ship and mail all the letters when we arrive, in about two weeks. Each letter will be numbered, so that you may read them in the proper order.

I raised my head from the pillow on my cot only today. I've been terribly seasick. Seng is the least affected of all of us, and after the first day he was well enough to make fun of everyone else, especially me. You know how he is. How strange some people are, to laugh at others when they are miserable.

Poor Kim is the sickest—wouldn't you know it? He's sure he'll die before we reach Thailand, no one has ever suffered so before, and on and on.

When I was sick, memories of our family and the village kept spinning around in my head. I thought of you and Younger Brother constantly. I couldn't bear to say goodbye to you, but now I feel guilty about running off as I did. Can you forgive me? You have read the note I left for you on the kitchen table. Please try to understand my dream. I shall do my best always, as you have taught me, and send you the first bit of money I earn. You gave me so much, Mother. Henceforth I shall make my own way and strive to honor our ancestors by the conduct of my life.

The ship is as big as all of Po Leng village, and there are a thousand people on board! My friends and I sleep in the belly of the ship, stuffed in together like pigs in a pen. Not like the second or third group of

4

Chinese who went to Thailand with enough money for cabins and good food. We have nothing left over for such luxuries after paying our fare and the immigration fees, which rise each year. I pray that some day, when I return to Po Leng to fetch you, we will make this voyage together sharing a real cabin. You will have pork to eat every day, dear Mother, not dried pickled vegetables like they give us.

The air at sea is different from our mountain air, salty and bitter and not particularly pleasant. Today, the freight manager on the ship told me that salt water is the best medicine for skin ailments and cuts, and he also said that sweet foods are bad for you. What do you think of that?

"It is so, Little One," he said. "Sweets are no good. The Thai have a proverb, 'Sweet sickens, bitter heals.'"

"My name is Tan Suang U, not 'Little One,'" I retorted irritably. I was then still seasick.

"I beg your pardon, Suang U!" he said with a kindly smile. "That's a fine name. It means 'diamond.' May your fortunes follow your name!"

"I hope so, too," I replied, sorry that I had spoken disrespectfully to him. His name is Lo Yong Chua. He is a big man of about forty or so, with a square face and strong features. He's good natured in spite of his stern appearance, and when we boys were sick he gave us medicine. Everyone likes him.

"What are you going to do when you get to Bangkok?" he asked.

"I'm not sure. I left our farm and boarded this ship because of a letter my friend Seng got from his uncle in Bangkok. His uncle says that a man can start a vegetable farm or a small business, and if he's thrifty he can send money home to his family and still have enough left over to live on. So I decided to come along—" Suddenly, without warning, I felt as if I might begin to cry! For the words I had spoken to him were almost the same words I wrote to you when I left home . . . homesickness is worse than seasickness. I excused myself and hurried below deck to hide my shame. But later in the day Lo Yong Chua called out to me and waved cheerfully as I was going to eat supper with Seng and Kim, and after supper I felt brave enough to go up to the freight office and chat with him again. He made a friendly remark about my "seasickness," then invited me to sit down while he copied figures into a gigantic ledger.

5

"Have you been to school, Suang U?"

"I don't even know what a school looks like, sir."

"That's too bad. If you could read and write, I might be able to help you. I have a cousin in Bangkok who's looking for a boy to help with his bookkeeping chores. He imports dry goods and foods from China and sells them wholesale. I told him I'd keep an eye out for a sharp lad this trip, someone who might be able to fill the job. You know, Suang U, if you can't read or write, I'm afraid you'll only find work as a coolie."

"But I can."

"Can what?"

"I can read and write. My mother taught me."

"Your mother, indeed! I thought you said your mother was a farm woman. She teaches reading and calligraphy? What kind of peasants do you have in that village?"

"My father was a farmer—he's dead now. But before my mother married him, she was a companion to the daughter of a noble family. They allowed her to study with their own children, but when the daughter married and moved away, they didn't need my mother anymore. They married her to my father, and she's lived on the farm ever since. She started teaching me to read and write when I was five, and I've read many books, but I've never had a chance to use the education she gave me. Sir, that's why I've come to you. To seek your advice."

He looked at me curiously for a long time. Then he closed the ledger, stood up, and began to pace slowly back and forth behind his desk. At last he spoke. "A remarkable story," he said quietly, still regarding me with a peculiar expression. "Go get yourself a pen and some paper. I want to see what kind of job that mother of yours did."

I hurried off to do as he said. It seemed the worst thing that had ever happened to me when I discovered that my pen was missing. (Things get "missed" on this ship very easily.) Frantically, I gathered up some scraps of paper and hurried back to Yong Chua. When I began to apologize for having no pen, he waved his hand as if to dismiss my worry and presented me with the one I am using to write this letter. You can see what a fine line it writes. Inside it, there's a thin tube full of ink that leaks out just a little at a time. It is a wonderful pen, and I am going to keep it with me always. I know that if I ever lay it down while I'm on the ship, it will be "lost" instantly. I even sleep with it tucked under my arm!

Yong Chua dictated and I wrote. The first part of his dictation was hard, some passages he had memorized from *The Three Kingdoms*.* Then he dictated some business letters he made up about parcels of dried plums, almond candy, dried lychees, Chinese flowers, and all kinds of things. I had to add up all the prices at the end. It was so easy! You used to dictate the very same kind of thing to me in the evenings at our kitchen table, for calligraphy practice. It always seemed a game, nothing to do with real work.

"Fine hand!" he said, smiling as he checked my work. "If your calligraphy were any better than this, you could easily pass yourself off among Teo Chiu people as a graduate of the upper school."

How proud I felt, and prouder of you. Most of the boys on the ship can't read or write at all. Seng can write a little, but his calligraphy is poor—every line wobbles. Thank you, Mother.

A few days after Yong Chua's dictation, he came down to the boys' quarters looking for me. I was alone for a change, reading.

"Suang U, I've been thinking about that bookkeeping job with my cousin. His name is Lo Nguan Thong—a good man. I know you'd like him. If you wish, I'll write a letter of introduction for you. You deserve that job . . . unless, of course, you have relatives in Bangkok—"

"No sir, no one. Only my friend Seng's uncle, Tae Lim. If you would write that letter for me, I would be—extremely grateful, sir."

"You needn't be embarrassed, Suang U. You see, I have no family. That is why it is my pleasure to look after you boys. Allow me that pleasure, will you?" He smiled. "My—my wife and son died in Thailand after the great flood three years ago. No, no—don't look sad. I have had time to accept it, though I confess I could not when it

* *The Romance of the Three Kingdoms*, a fourteenth-century novel by Lou Guanzhong, was translated into several Southeast Asian languages as soon as printing presses were available (the late nineteenth and early twentieth centuries). This tale of adventure, love, war, bravery, betrayal, and virtue has been viewed by its readers as a kind of guide to life. Its characters and events are commonly cited in literature as well as in casual conversation to comment upon contemporary individuals and events (as in the present novel). At the beginning of the twenty-first century, video games based upon the story are extremely popular, as attested to by many websites. *Trans.*

happened. You see, when the flood waters receded, there was disease. For some of the survivors, drowning would have been a kinder death than—than typhoid." I opened my mouth to speak, but he raised a hand to silence me. "These days, I am beginning to feel like my old self again. Because of you, for one thing. Don't look so startled. I enjoy talking with you, teaching you. You're a smart boy, and you make me laugh, generally in spite of yourself. Not many boys who make this journey are like you—very few have both determination and ability, and only one of those is not enough. Those are things your excellent mother couldn't give you, but she didn't have to. Now—however am I going to say what I want to say to you? . . ." He frowned and rubbed his chin nervously. "You have no father, and I have no son. I want you to become my adopted son, Suang U. I want to help you make a good life for yourself in Bangkok." He turned away from me quickly then and said, "Think it over, please. Don't say anything now." Then he hurried off.

I was stunned. I never dreamed he was thinking of anything like that. He was good to me, it is true, and taught me many things, but he was good to everyone, and helped everyone who turned to him. I felt a great lump growing in my throat. When am I going to stop crying every time I'm very happy or very sad?

I have said yes to Lo Yong Chua, and hope that you will not be angry with me. I shall call him father, but I shall always use my own *sae* Tan, not the *sae* Lo, for I have ancestors of my own to revere and honor, and the memory of a real father whom I loved dearly.

Yong Chua is teaching me many things about life in Bangkok, and I am learning to call him father, which is less difficult than I feared.

One bright, breezy afternoon, we pulled a table and two chairs out onto the deck for my abacus practice. After an hour's work, we pushed our chairs back, relaxed, and Father began to talk to me about Bangkok, as he does everyday, one way or another. Everything we do or see reminds him of something about Bangkok that I ought to know.

"Don't tell anyone you haven't been to school," he said. "Just say that you can read and write, and let them guess. I'm teaching you how to use the abacus well, and you already know a fair amount of book-keeping. That's enough. Nobody will doubt you've been to some kind of school."

"Shouldn't I be proud that my mother educated me?"

"That isn't what I said. I said you shouldn't talk about it—there's a difference. You see, in Thailand they have more respect for diplomas than for skill. They like to see a piece of paper that states you've sat in such and such a school for so many years. With that, you can get a job anywhere, even if you can't count to five. Among the older Chinese, it doesn't matter so much, but the younger ones were educated in Bangkok—some of them have begun to think like Thais, heaven help them. There's something to be said for sending our children to Thai schools, that I don't deny. But when they start to look down on hard work, I say it's no good.

"And don't tell anyone your mother worked as a servant, either, because Thailand is full of people who'd rather steal than be servants. They don't want to feel 'inferior.' I want you to be able to get along with the Thai and with the Chinese—both the fathers and the sons."

The next day, a shameful incident occurred. I don't even want to tell you about it, but I am afraid Seng will write to his mother, and then you will hear only his version of it.

Kim and I had come up on deck for a breath of fresh air and a stroll. Seng approached us, followed by a group of tough Swatow boys he has taken up with. "Hey, Suang U!" he shouted, "I guess men who spend all their time at sea don't see many girls. You have such a pretty face—maybe 'Father' thinks you're a good enough substitute!"

He laughed and turned to his friends, who laughed too, like a bunch of trained monkeys. I tried to ignore him, though my head was pounding. Father was at work in the hold and Seng must have known it, for he never would have dared say such a thing otherwise.

"Seng, you know that's crazy," Kim said through clenched teeth. "Talk like that can only cause trouble, big trouble!"

Seng ignored him. "Hey, Cutie!" he persisted, "how's the abacus practice coming? When you get the right answer, does he give you a big kiss?"

That was when I ran across the deck and punched him in the face. Before I knew it, we were rolling around on the deck pummeling each other, surrounded by cheering boys.

"Get him, Suang U!" Kim shouted at the top of his lungs. "Show him who's the real man!"

I won the fight, but I'm not proud of it. Seng has always had a bad temper, but until now I managed to get along with him by ignoring it. I should have realized immediately that he was only jealous; perhaps in a day or so he would have got over it. But now we are enemies, and he's the only boy here from Po Leng, besides Kim.

He crouched on the deck with his face in his hands after the fight, the blood from his nose dripping though his fingers. "Go and die in Thailand!" he sobbed. "Go and starve there! I'm finished with you, and your friend Kim, too. My Uncle Lim won't help anybody who insulted his nephew, I promise you—"

"Keep your Uncle Lim to yourself, Seng," I said. "But don't expect me to bear a grudge about this. We're from the same village, and that matters more than your temper, more than a fight. We've fought before."

"You go to hell!" he bawled. "I'll never forget this! You sold yourself to Yong Chua like a crate of dried plums." The he struggled to his feet, wiped his bloody hands on his shirt, and lurched away.

Don't worry, Mother. I have Yong Chua's introduction to his cousin in Bangkok, and I'm not going to starve to satisfy Seng's wrath, not in Thailand or anywhere.

Father apparently hasn't heard about the fight, because he came by a few minutes ago to see what I was doing and never mentioned it. "Ah, writing to your mother again," he said. "Good, good—one must never neglect such duties. And don't forget," he added with an odd smile, "mothers like to hear all the little details . . ."

It is nine days since I last wrote. I am on deck this evening, watching the sun set. If I write for very long, I shall have to borrow an oil lamp. At sea, night is different. How shall I describe it? It is frightening to be surrounded so entirely by darkness. Back in Po Leng, even on a moonless night we could see the friendly glow of a neighbor's lamp shining in the distance. But here, there is nothing, and it is easy to imagine that we could sail around in the endless dark forever.

Many of the boys have had a vacant and anxious look the last week or so, and I think they feel the same kind of fear. They complain constantly about the length of the voyage. Those who left their wives back in China are sorry now, and those who brought theirs are smug.

This is the day of the Autumn Festival, and I have many interesting things to tell you. We didn't pay respect to ancestors, as we do at home. Instead, everyone got up just before dawn and gathered at an altar at the prow of the ship, where we paid respect to the Lord of the Sea, the Spirit of the Ship, and the spirits of those who died without descendants.

I noticed that only ducks and geese were placed on the altar, though there are huge baskets of chickens on board. When I mentioned this to Father, he chuckled. "Chickens, Suang U? Have you ever seen a chicken swim? Not much of an offering to the Lord of the Sea!" What a fool I am. They offered something else I had never seen before— pickled eggs! Father says this is an old Chinese custom. Perhaps we never had enough left over at home to pickle any.

Our New Year celebration in Po Leng seems just past, although six months have gone by since that wonderful day. I remember getting up very early, tiptoeing about the house so as not to awaken you, and preparing our morning tea. Then I prayed alone at our family altar, in the cool stillness of dawn. Later in the day, we made a rare trip to town together, a trip I shall never forget. I still have the money you gave me as a New Year gift, and I shall not spend it. For my fare to Bangkok, I used only the money I have earned helping our neighbors with the rice transplanting.

The lights of the ship are glittering on the sea as night begins to fall, but I think I will be able to finish my letter before darkness enfolds us once again. All the little waves below are shining like the scales of a fish as it leaps from water into sunlight, and I am reminded of the gigantic carp Younger Brother caught in our stream last spring . . . do you remember how he ran home across the field leaping and shouting? I'm willing to bet he will never eat a more delicious fish in his life, and each year that carp will grow a little longer, and a little fatter. (I can see him now, hopping with indignation.) I send my love to you both across the wide black sea, and suddenly I feel afraid, for all the things I have loved are beyond it. Shall they ever be part of my life again?

Shame on me! I must force myself to think of the future. It is exciting to realize that soon I will be a bookkeeper! (Well, anyway a clerk.) Who would have thought it? And you will be able to afford a few luxuries when I am able to send money home.

We Chinese carry our homeland with us in our hearts and minds. I have no reason to feel sad, for even if I should some day live among red-haired foreigners, I would still be Suang U from Po Leng village. When I feel lonely, that must be my first thought.

As I wrote the last few words, Father appeared beside me, told me that we are within sight of Thailand, and rushed off again. Is it possible?

"And we have had luck, too," he called back as he hurried away. "We're touching bottom—that means that until the water rises in the morning, we stay right here. The mosquitoes are going to be terrible!"

Suddenly I realized that mosquitoes were clustering on my neck and arms. Even before I came up here, other boys were complaining about them. How could I not realize we must be near land? So, this is the first sign of Bangkok—mosquitoes, clouds of them. If they were organized, they could carry us to shore one by one.

LETTER #2
25 AUGUST 1945

KHLONG ONG ANG
SAMPHENG LANE, BANGKOK
SEVENTH MONTH, EIGHTEENTH DAY
YEAR OF THE COCK

KIM AND I are already settled in the household of Lo Nguan Thong, in a Chinese neighborhood called Sampheng Lane. I'm going to write again tonight to tell you all about it, and something about my new job, but I shall send you that letter separately. I am anxious to mail this letter with the ones I wrote on the ship, and Father has offered to take them to the post office on his way back to the port.

I was up on deck at dawn this morning to admire the Thai sun. A fine, fat yellow sun that shines more brilliantly on Bangkok than on Po Leng. Its rays were like fiery tongues licking at my arms. Father says this is the rainy season, and Thai farmers will work in the fields planting rice every day. They also have a hot season and what is called a cold season, which Father says will seem to me only a little less hot than the hot season.

As the ship started to move with the rising water, people began dragging crates and bags and bundles up on deck—probably, for most of them, all that they own in this world. I passed Seng, who turned away abruptly. Kim tugged at my arm.

"What are we going to do now?" he whispered. "He's still mad at you, and mad at me because I'm your friend. How can we go to his uncle if he won't talk to us himself?"

"Of course we won't go to his uncle. I may have a job with a cousin of Lo Yong Chua—"

"But what about me?" he interrupted with a wail. "Where do I go?"

"Will you let me finish? Do you think I'd desert you at the deck? Or grovel to Seng? At the worst, if you were really stuck in Bangkok, people of your *sae* would help you out. Father says there are *sae* organizations in all the Chinese neighborhoods that help people when they need a job or get into trouble . . ."

"Where? Before they found me I might starve!"

"Stop this! Come along with me and I'll ask Father to talk to his cousin about you. They'll at least take you on until you get something else. Chinese people wouldn't turn their own away."

"What if he says no?"

"Worry about that when you have to."

"Sure, you already have a job. But it's 'never mind, Kim' and 'worry about that when you have to, Kim.' It was your stupid fight, but who gets the worst of it? Old Kim, as usual."

"And who was yelling, 'Get him, Suang U!' when Seng was trying to gouge my eyes out? Ah, Kim, you should have stayed home hugging your wife. I told you I'd help you, so quit bawling, or everyone will think it's because you miss her. You'll shame yourself."

"Well, I do miss her, and I'm not ashamed. I've only been married a year, you know."

"Then why did you come?"

"Because I'd like to have a piece of pork in my mouth every day too—you're not the only one who wants to get rich in Thailand."

"As soon as you get rich you can send for your wife. But if I know you, you'll have a new wife before six months go by . . . maybe even a plump little Thai sparrow!"

He resented that and, for a change, was silent. We leaned over the deck rail and, shading our eyes with our hands against the fierce sunlight, looked out over the Thai coastline. The water is very high, and I should think the crops are good this year. There are a great many trees, some I've never seen before, and many coconut palms. I wonder what they do with so many coconuts.

Finally we were in Bangkok harbor, nearing the dock. The passengers—men, women, old people and babies, and boys like us—all began shouting and running up and down the deck, congratulating each other on a safe arrival, swinging laughing babies into the air, and stumbling over each other's bundles and boxes. Ducks quacked madly, beating their wings against the insides of great bamboo baskets. Little pigs snuffled and squealed and kicked the straw out of their crates. Even the animals seemed to know that a new life was beginning. One young woman sat on a dilapidated trunk, crying silently while she suckled her baby. I wondered why she came, why any of them came. How many separate dreams hovered over this noisy crowd? We have all come to seek our fortunes, no longer dreaming of opportunity in a new land, but here to seize it. The time has come to leave old dreams behind. Maybe that is why the woman suckling her baby was crying; it is sad to leave an old dream, especially when it has become the all-consuming force in one's life. For most of these people, the arrival of the ship Hai Wang in Bangkok harbor is the culmination of thousands of day's toil, of doing without much to save a little, year after year, in good years and bad. Imagine, then, the expectations with which they arrive, remembering all they have sacrificed for this day.

I had only one bag to carry, the heavy cotton cloth one I made the night I left Po Leng. There is another memory which will never fade, though even now, when I think of that night, I see myself as if I were a separate person. As if I watched Suang U, crouched behind his house sewing away by the light of an oil lamp, then writing a note to his mother (ten times, at least, before it was right), then tiptoeing into the house, putting the note and the lamp on the kitchen table, and tiptoeing back out again. Running, running in the darkness, under a pale moon that shone bleakly upon the sleeping village and on rice fields that shimmered in the chill night winds. Sobbing aloud as the first lights of town appeared, and Po Leng disappeared over the crest of a hill behind him.

"Good news!" Father said, hurrying toward us with outstretched arms. "I have the day off! As soon as we finish identifying the lots of freight I will take you to Lo Nguan Thong myself. It won't be long."

Kim jabbed me in the back.

"Father, do you think Nguan Thong might need an errand boy, or

14

someone who could do odd jobs around the store?"

"Well, I suppose he might . . . why?"

"It's my friend Kim. He doesn't have a job. He and—and his friend Seng had an argument." Kim's mouth fell open, and I flashed him a murderous look.

"I think it will be all right," Father said. "Well, well—an argument with your friend Seng, eh?" He scrutinized Kim's anxious face. "Will you work hard, if I recommend you?"

"Y-yes, sir!" he said, and bowed stiffly.

Then Father hurried away, grinning to himself. The crew made ready for the passengers' departure, and soon the gangway was lowered into place. Seng stood leaning against the rail some yards away, looking smug, waiting for us to beg his forgiveness so that he could humiliate us before his Uncle Tae Lim. Looking down the gangway, I saw a middle-aged, well-dressed man smiling and waving in our direction. Seng saw him then, quickly lifted his arm and shouted, "Uncle Lim! It's me, Tae Seng!"

He turned to us, and slowly the smug expression gave way to one of bewilderment, and finally of realization. He continued to stare at us for a few moments, then swung his bag up over his shoulder and trudged down the gangway. He approached Tae Lim, put down the bag, and bowed respectfully. Then he turned, pointed up at us, and began to speak in a loud voice. "There stand Suang U and Kim!" he pronounced. "I befriended them, but they have betrayed me—two dogs who run together! Let them return to Po Leng and work in the fields like oxen!" Then, smiling brilliantly, he turned his back on us.

Poor Tae Lim looked acutely embarrassed and glanced around quickly to see who had overheard this remarkable performance. Did he doubt the wisdom of importing his very odd young relative?

Father finished his work at least and, in high spirits, led us down to the dock while continuing to shout last-minute instructions to his crew. And then, suddenly, we stood on Thai soil, surrounded by hundreds of coolies who jostled us as they scurried everywhere, bent under heavy loads.

"Suang U!" Kim called in a frightened voice. "That work is harder than planting rice!"

"It may be hard work, but they get enough money doing it to send some home to their wives and children in China."

15

I did not want to hear any more of the cowardice of Kim. In this moment I had set my foot on the soil of Thailand. From the dock, I could see treetops, and the spires of *chedis* and temples. This is a Buddhist land. I hope that I shall find peace and happiness here, and prosper in business.

I KNOW you are anxious to hear all about my new surroundings, so I shall attend to describing the household of Nguan Thong and the neighborhood called Sampheng Lane before writing of anything else.

Nguan Thong, his wife, and their two daughters live in a store. That is, except for the kitchen and their bedrooms upstairs, every inch of the house is devoted to the storage of incoming merchandise. Their store stands in the center of a row of wooden houses. In every one, a family shares space with a business of one kind or another. The front of each store is open to the street, so that during the day all the neighborhood opens onto the busy life of Sampheng Lane and is absorbed by it. Then, there is little sense of the separateness of families one feels in the evenings, when the great wooden doors are pulled shut all along the row and across the street too.

Many of the families on Sampheng Lane are Chinese, but there are a few Thai families. In fact, there is one directly next door. Khlong Ong Ang is a canal which runs behind the row of houses, a different kind of avenue and one not less busy than the lane itself. Across the street from us the houses are identical, but they are less fortunate than we, for the *khlong* behind their row has been filled in, and another row of shops stands where it once flowed.

All day long, men and women paddle small boats back and forth on Khlong Ong Ang selling sweets, fruit, clothing, pots and pans; some sell *kuitieo*, noodles they ladle from great charcoal-heated drums. I saw many people taking their own bowls down to the water's edge at noon to wait for a *kuitieo* boat. When one does come in sight, the waiting customers cluster together and wave to it from one of the rickety piers that line the bank. The vendor paddles to shore and, after tossing a heap of steaming noodles into each bowl, garnishes them with peanuts, sugar, vinegar, and pickled vegetables, according to the taste of his chattering, gesturing customers. Then he hands up the bowls in exchange for a few coins, and paddles on to the next pier.

I noticed that the Thai boat vendors may be distinguished from the Chinese (of whom there are surprisingly many) by their hats—the Thai straw hat is not pointed like ours, but has a flat top and is raised off the head by some kind of band. It is surely cooler than the Chinese hat, more suited to this tropical land.

There are a few trees along the *khlong* behind the houses in Sampheng Lane, but most of them, and the grass too, must have been destroyed when the building went up. It is too bad. The other side of Khlong Ong Ang isn't built up yet, and many graceful coconut and banana palms still grow there.

Father told me that Nguan Thong's family moved here after a fire destroyed their first shop. The landlord in this neighborhood expects to begin construction of a new row of stores before long, on this site, and the new stores will be concrete and cement instead of wood. Nguan Thong will be assured of a place, so he doesn't mind putting up with cramped conditions for awhile.

We were greeted with excellent tea and urged politely to drink it. Later, Kim wondered aloud whether we'd get such tea every day. He is impossible, but I must say I wondered the same thing myself (silently).

Our *thaokae** seems to be a thoughtful, worried man, and he is most considerate of Kim and me. The office is crammed with imported merchandise, as I have already described, and he wasn't sure at first where Kim and I would sleep. He finally decided that we could make a bed by putting five or six boards on top of some large metal cans. Kim was very annoyed about these arrangements.

"Even some gunny sacks would be more comfortable than these stupid boards," he grumbled, "and they're a lot of trouble to set up every night. We'll be lucky if they don't break under us . . ."

I don't know if it's because they're protective of their daughters or not, but all the men eat together, boss and employees included, and the women

*A term used to refer to a Chinese boss or proprietor. His wife is known as the *thaokae nia. Trans.*

17

eat whatever is left. I don't like it. I think a family should eat together.

"The men work hard," Father said. "They need to eat first."

"But why must the women eat leftovers from a messy table? They work hard, too. They could take their own food out first, couldn't they? The men all put their chopsticks into the serving dishes and fish around in the soup tureen to get the best bits. By the time they finish eating it's—it's awful! Even the boss's wife has to eat those leftovers."

"Almost all the merchants handle it this way, Suang U, but in the stores where they don't have so many employees, the families do eat together." Then he laughed. "When you're the owner of a business someday, you can arrange things any way you like!"

The food today was wonderful. Boiled chicken—the whole chicken, too! Eggs, pork with vegetables, and enormous fried shrimps. I thought perhaps this feast was in honor of Father's visit, but he said, "No, this is the usual food. There are some places where they do give the employees the kind of food you were expecting, rice and a few vegetables. But they don't have to be stingy about food. Come outside with me—"

From Nguan Thong's small, fenced back yard we could see the masts of ships beyond our *khlong* and beyond the trees. The Chao Phraya River, where the ship Hai Wang docked, is not very far away. In the *khlong* before us, fat ducks and geese waddled along the bank or swam about lazily. Nguan Thong has a pen with six pigs in it and a large chicken coop which, judging by the noise emanating from it, promises many more chicken dinners.

"This is a rich land," Father said. "Food is abundant! There are many kinds of fruit growing all year, and what your friend's uncle wrote is quite true—"

If a man wants a garden, he can have his own mangoes and papayas and bananas. Anything will grow. Of course, we Chinese are not allowed to own land, but Thai landowners are always in need of money.

After a few hours, Father returned to the ship, assuring me he'd mail all my letters and scolding me for worrying about them. Then Kim and I were on our own.

Now I can see for myself exactly how Nguan Thong's business works. He imports food and merchandise from China and sends it out to retailers all over Bangkok. Then he buys Thai merchandise on order and puts it on ships returning to China. There were people in and out of the store all day because the ship came into port today. They brought samples of teak and sacks of Thai rice—so many things that I can't begin to describe them all. He needs so many delivery boys and coolies to haul boxes and crates and cans back and forth that finding work for Kim was no problem at all. Some of the coolies are Thai. I should think they'd be humiliated to do that kind of work for foreigners, but they don't seem to mind.

A while ago, as I was beginning my letter, Kim came by and asked if I had seen the boss's daughters yet—ah, Kim!

"No!"

"They're both pretty good—what are you frowning about?" He lowered his voice and said, "I hid behind the door when they were eating lunch. Even the old woman is still all right—she must have been something when she was young."

"Are you crazy? You can't go around spying on his women from behind doors! Why do you have to do something stupid the first day we're here?"

He shrugged and leaned over my shoulder to see what I was writing. "Another letter to your mother?"

"Yes. Have you written to your family?"

"I don't know how to write—you know that! Anyway, I don't have any money to send yet. How much do you think the old man is going to pay us?"

"Father says I'm to get twenty baht a month, and you'll get fifteen."

I waited for the explosion.

"You get more than me for what?"

"For working with the accounts. I'm going to help in the office, and you're not. You don't have a skill, Kim—you were only telling me that this morning, weren't you? So what do you expect? This is a lot better than a job at the docks."

He insists that he ought to get more than me, because he'll work harder while I'm "sitting around in the shade doing a few sums." And on and on. He has set up his boards and is now trying to fall asleep, but the griping goes on. The heat is unbearable, mosquitoes are biting his ankles, he's getting splinters from the boards that will probably get infected, the pigs outside are bumping into the house . . . eventually, he will grouch himself to sleep.

THIS WAS my second day in Bangkok and my first day of real work—there is so much to tell you!

At four o'clock this morning, when Nguan Thong called us, Kim groaned loudly. "What is this?" he muttered thickly. "Still the dark of night, and we're supposed to get up and work? I've hardly had any sleep yet . . ."

He slept like a stone all night, in spite of mosquitoes, pigs, and splinters, but I heard the striking of Nguan Thong's clock every hour until two. I was far too excited about the coming day to sleep.

"You must learn to rise and bathe at four," Nguan Thong said, materializing out of the darkness suddenly. "Go out back to the *khlong* and splash water over yourselves while you stand on the pier steps, but don't walk down into the water for the first few days. If you do as I say, heat will not remain in your bodies, and you will not suffer so much. But you cannot avoid the heat disease completely—all newcomers suffer from it. Here is a *phakhaoma* for each of you, and a bowl to use as dipper."

Then he showed us how to wear the *phakhaoma*, a simple length of cloth about a yard long. It is wrapped about the lower half of the body like a skirt and tucked in at the waist. Yesterday at the docks, I saw coolies wearing them, and some who wore ordinary pants wrapped their *phakhaoma* around their heads, because of the fierce sunlight.

Nguan Thong left us at the pier and went back into the house. When we had both made sure our *phakhaoma* was secure (we are not yet confident about keeping them up under all circumstances), we prepared for our first bath in Thailand. The world began to wake in the first pale light of morning, and up and down the *khlong* animals began squawking, cackling, bleating, and barking in celebration of the new day. I stepped carefully down the pier steps into the cool, green water.

"What an hour to be taking a bath," said Kim "and look at the lights going on all around us. People are up cooking breakfast already—everybody here is crazy!"

Obviously, it was going to be hot by eight o'clock, but Kim hadn't thought that far.

"Hey, the water's nice and cool!" he called out, wading from the pier and splashing about noisily. "I'll race you to the other side and back."

"Kim, didn't you hear anything Nguan Thong said?"

"Yeah, but we're not old men, you know."

"Father told me about the heat disease, and being young won't help you. If you get it bad, you won't be able to stuff yourself with fried pork like you did last night, because you'll have sores in your mouth." He waded cautiously back to shore, then, and threw a dipper full of water over his back.

Though I slept badly last night, the cool water refreshed me and I felt wide awake. A red moon hung over the tops of banana palms on the bank opposite and shone on the water before us, filling my eyes and heart. How lovely the *khlong* is at dawn! I'm surely not going to starve in this beautiful land.

In the few minutes it had taken us to bathe, the sky had turned from dark blue to gray, and Kim sniffed the air hungrily as we hurried toward the house. Suddenly, the kitchen shutters opened with a bang, and when I looked up, I found myself staring into the face of a girl. She dropped her eyes and popped back inside quickly, but not before I got a good look at her.

"That's one of the daughters," Kim said, "the older one."

The girl's face was like a pale and perfect moon. She had magnificent eyes, large and black and glowing. I don't know how to describe such beauty, except to compare her to you, dear Mother. Her hair is long and hangs straight beside her cheeks, as if to emphasize the paleness and clarity of her skin. I do not have unsuitable ideas, but anyone would be dazzled by that shining moon of a face.

Kim poked me in the back. "Nice, eh? The other one isn't bad either, but she's little and dark, like a Thai."

"Let's hurry and get to breakfast," I said, annoyed. "And please, don't complain, or talk too much around the other boys today. Especially about the daughters—don't talk about them at all."

21

"What's wrong with saying a girl is beautiful, if she is?"

"If someone else mentions her—that girl, says she's beautiful or anything, you can agree, but don't be the one to bring her up, understand? The boss wouldn't like it, you can be sure."

We discovered then that only lunch and dinner are served to the other employees. Since Kim and I live here, we have our breakfast with Nguan Thong and Thaokae Nia. I kept hoping their daughters would appear, but they never did. We had rice porridge for breakfast, with chopped pork, garlic, and scallions. Besides that, there were salty fried beans, dried shrimps, and pickled vegetables, and a delicious mixture of grilled pork with garlic and hot peppers. I suppose it must be a Thai dish, for I never ate anything like it before.

When she filled our bowls the first time with thick, fragrant rice porridge, Thaokae Nia smiled and said, "Eat as though it had to last you until next year!" Five minutes later, Kim had almost licked the bottom of the bowl clean, and she promptly filled it up again.

"Oh, no!" he protested insincerely. "I'll be eating this one for two years!" But before I had finished my first bowl, he was scraping the last grains of rice from his second.

"My, Kim," Thaokae Nia laughed, "how quickly the years pass!"

What a beautiful smile she has. It made me long to see her daughter's smile. If the girl looked that beautiful at four o'clock in the morning, what miracle of loveliness must she be at noon?

Kim's bowl was filled for a third time, and before long pork and shrimp and everything else had vanished from the serving plates, most of it into his bulging stomach. What can you do with him? He leaned back in his chair and burped cheerfully, his face glistening with sweat from hanging over the steaming porridge bowl. And then, for a fourth time, Thaokae Nia prevailed upon him to push his bowl toward the tureen and accept another ladle full.

"Don't worry," she said, noticing my embarrassment. "Even two more bowls wouldn't be too much. Big boys need big appetites when they have to work and grow at the same time."

After breakfast, Kim and I had a few moments alone before the rest of the employees arrived.

"They were laughing at me!" he said with an injured expression on his face.

"You're lucky they thought you were funny," I said.

The only nearly important work I did today was to check some figures Nguan Thong had prepared hastily once before. Then I had to make a clean copy for the ledger. I could see right away that the monthly profits must be very large. Nguan Thong could easily buy land and build his own store if he were allowed to. Perhaps the Thai know what they are about.

He passed by to observe my work and said, "You must have passed at least the intermediate level examinations . . . these characters seem to fly down the page!" He smiled. "Or was it the upper level examinations? No—I suppose you are too young."

My ears burned, and I remembered Father's words, "Don't tell anyone you haven't been to school!" "N-no, sir," I replied, swallowing hard, "I haven't finished the upper level. I—I was too young—"

"Well, it hardly matters," he said, then nodded quickly and walked off. At lunch, he told all the boys that I had passed intermediate level examinations in China, and I felt sure that my terrible guilt must show. I am not very proud of myself, Mother. Thank heaven Kim was across town making a delivery. He'd surely have blurted out the truth without thinking. Even imagining it makes me shudder.

I received my first month's salary in advance, but Kim did not; he doesn't know. I wrote before that I would send the first money I earned to you, but I am going to send only half, and give the rest to Kim so that he will not know I was favored. His family is so poor. Perhaps with this bit of money, they will suffer a little less. I know you will understand.

I almost forgot to tell you some news about Seng. Kim met him this afternoon when he was in Thonburi, across the river, where Uncle Tae Lim's store is located. It turns out that Tae Lim is an old friend of Nguan Thong's, and a customer too. Now Kim worries that Seng will use his influence to get us fired. I can't believe that—I mean, Seng might carry the grudge that far, but Nguan Thong seems too honorable a man to judge anyone by the spite of his enemy.

I did not see the face of the moon again today.

I CAN barely eat or sleep for excitement. Starting tomorrow, I shall be spending a whole hour every day with that girl, the face of the moon! I'm going to help both daughters study Chinese.

This morning the other daughter, the little dark one, ran into the office while Nguan Thong and I were working together. "Father, what does this phrase mean?" she asked, opening a book and putting it down directly on top of the papers we were studying. "Elder Sister and I don't agree."

Nguan Thong picked up the book and frowned at it, obviously annoyed at the interruption. I tried to keep my eyes on my work, but still I was able to observe her more closely than the sister who popped out from behind kitchen shutters for a fleeting second. She is about sixteen years old, and Kim was right—if she didn't wear Chinese clothes, she could pass as a Thai.

"I'm not sure myself," Nguan Thong said after staring at the page for a moment. "This is *Three Kingdoms*—I never quite finished it." He passed the book to me. "Suang U, are you familiar with this passage?"

"Of course," I lied. I have read some of the chapters, it is true, but I never knew anyone who owned them all.

"Then help the child with this phrase, if you don't mind." He shook his head wearily, and sighed. "These girls! Fighting over stories all day long. Why don't you fight over clothes like other girls?"

"Clothes!" The girl wrinkled her nose distastefully. "She has hers and I have mine—what is there to fight about? There's nothing else for us to do here but read. Now, if you'd let us go to school—"

"Enough!" He raised his hands as if fending her off. "I shall not change my mind about sending girls to school. You can read and write already, and that was a mistake. What more do you need?"

I looked hard at the phrase before me and, in answer to a hasty prayer, I was easily able to define it. It was underlined in red ink—perhaps the face of the moon herself underlined it. I had to restrain myself from touching the words with my fingers.

"What else have you read?" the girl asked, staring at me without a trace of shyness. "Do you know *Journey to the West*? Or *Uang Kim*

24

Leng? What about *The Bird Matchmaker*? My sister and I—"

"Ang Buai!" her father barked. "What is the matter with you?"

"Oh, Father, it's so lonely for us. We can't even go to the *ngiu** without Mother, and she's always too tired to take us. Now that you have someone here who knows about books, why can't he teach us?"

"Teach you? Why should he? He has to work all day, you know. He doesn't just fritter away his time like you do."

"What about early in the morning, Father?" she persisted. "Or in the evening after he finishes work? He doesn't work twenty-four hours a day, does he? And Elder Sister wants to study as much as I do!"

"You speak of him as if he were a slave, child! Do you think that would be fair to him?"

"That's all right, sir," I said, as casually as possible. "I could easily help them for an hour or so in the evening."

"It's a waste of your time, Suang U—teaching literature to a pair of girls!"

"Really, sir I wouldn't mind. It would be a good review for me, too. If you have *Journey to the West*, we could begin with that." It's one I know well. It wouldn't compromise the reputation for learning I have shamefully gained.

"How wonderful!" the girl cried, jumping up and down and clapping her hands like a child. "We have that book, we have it! Oh, I want to begin this very day!"

"It's up to you, sir," I said. "If you agree, I will be glad to help them." I tried to look sincere but not too interested.

"All right," he grumbled, looking at me carefully. "One hour a day, starting tomorrow. The girls can come downstairs to study in the office after dinner." He turned to Ang Buai. "Now don't go driving him crazy with all your damned questions!"

He sighed deeply. "What am I to do with such girls?" He looked at me as if I might have some idea. "I have no son, you know. It is a terrible disappointment—I don't pretend otherwise. No one to carry on the business, no son to honor me when I die, just two ill-mannered, demanding daughters with unsuitable ambitions, especially this one. The other one isn't so bad—stubborn, but at least she acts like a girl."

---

*Chinese opera. *Trans.*

"Father, you know I would give anything to help in the store," she piped up, holding her little chin high. "It's your idea to keep us in the kitchen all day long, and a bad idea it is!"

"Yes, and you'd better get back there before I change my mind about these foolish 'lessons' . . . Women and rice belong in the kitchen!"

"On, not that again!" she said, laughing, and skipped from the room with a grin of triumph.

I suspect that "women and rice in the kitchen" is an old joke between them, and that Nguan Thong is fonder of her than he would have anyone think. So her name is Ang Buai. I wonder what her sister's name is, and whether she too acts like a boy. "Stubborn," he said, but then added that "at least she thinks like a girl." Well, I shall soon find out for myself.

I am going to be a teacher! That must please you. The prospect of being in the same room with the face of the moon, at the very same table, one hour a day . . . it seems like heaven. I hope I don't make a fool of myself.

LETTER #6   EIGHTH MONTH, FIFTH DAY
10 SEPTEMBER 1945 YEAR OF THE COCK

YOU WILL probably think me disrespectful, but I am angry with my good employer, Nguan Thong! He paces the room while I teach the girls, or sits in the kitchen listening to every word we say. If he's busy, his wife takes his place. I have no right to be annoyed, of course, but I am.

Ang Buai chirps constantly, like a little bird, but the older girl is quite the opposite. She doesn't smile or frown, she never asks any questions, but slowly moves her large, magnificent eyes from the book to me, to her sister, to her father—without ever changing expression. I cannot begin to guess at her opinion of any of us, or even of the story we are reading. The only change of expression I have observed is a certain understandable impatience with Ang Buai's prattling. I suspect that the two girls do not get on well.

"Elder Sister thinks I talk too much," Ang Buai blurted out last night. "She always frowns at me when she thinks you aren't looking . . ."

26

"Please, Younger Sister," the girl replied quietly, "Our teacher will think you a rude child."

"No, he won't!" she snapped. "What does he care, anyway, if I'm a rude child?" She turned to me. "Teacher, don't you think it would be fun to learn Thai? I'd just love to study Thai! We can speak it, you know, but we can't read."

"I should say not!" their father shouted from the next room. "We have a higher language with a superior literature—what good is Thai?"

"I'm not criticizing our language," she answered, unperturbed. "But we could read so many more novels if we could read Thai—there are hundreds of them!"

"Trash!"

"How do you know that?"

"I see the covers. That's enough."

"Well, how can it be wrong to know another language? I was born here, and I can't even read the street signs. What sense does that make?"

"It is not necessary for you to learn Thai," he said, stalking into the room. "I forbid it. You start reading Thai, and before you know it, you'll be thinking like a Thai. That's all I need! Why can't you be more like your sister? She doesn't seem to feel that her life is wasted because she can't read street signs."

The older girl's face showed no reaction to this scene. Day after day, she sits and stares. If my eyes happen to meet hers, she does not look away. In fact, her gaze is rather bold. Or perhaps I should describe it as straight and simple, like that of a porcelain doll. At first, I feared she might have the mind of a doll, too, but it isn't so. She can read and understand the story quite well, and she answers questions intelligently, though as briefly as possible.

"Can you both write your names?" I asked last night, after waiting in vain for someone to call her anything besides "Elder Sister" or "Little Cat," her father's favorite nickname.

"Of course we can," Ang Buai answered at once, scribbling the characters of her name on a piece of paper. "That's the first thing we ever learned. Our names, then basic characters, then arithmetic, then stories!"

"Biggest mistake I ever made," Nguan Thong sighed as he paced by.

Then the older girl took up her pen and, slowly and gracefully, wrote the characters of her name. Mui Eng. The beautiful one. Even when she was a baby, they must have known.

Since Ang Buai mentioned it, I have been thinking about learning to read Thai (though I cannot see what good it would be to a girl). Father told me that the Chinese sons here have attended Thai schools, and I can see the advantage in that—providing, of course, that Chinese studies are not neglected. Ang Buai often stops by to talk to me while I work, but she seems more interested in the business than in the novel we are supposed to be studying.

"Before you came," she said the other day, "Father used to let me help with the books every day. Now that he's got himself a real live man who can read Chinese, he expects me to be an old-fashioned girl again. Well, I'm not."

Nguan Thong had gone to the docks on business, and his daughter took this opportunity to settle herself comfortably on a crate next to my desk. She ripped a banana off a bunch she had brought in with her, offered me one, and began to peel one for herself.

"I can't curl up in a chair like a cat and lick my paws. Like my sister, for instance. She never goes out, and she doesn't even want to. She says she hates being stared at by a bunch of coolies. Well, if you're pretty," she sighed, "I guess you have to get used to being stared at. Do you think she's pretty?"

"I suppose so. You're pretty yourself."

"Bah!" She swallowed a huge mouthful of banana, then laughed. "I'm as dark as a cup of old tea, but I don't care. I know I don't even look like a Chinese—everyone says so." She looked down at her small brown arms. "You should see the Thai farmers who come in here sometimes. They're almost black, from working out in the fields. I stay indoors all day, and look at me!"

"There are lots of dark Chinese people."

"Not lots . . . a few, and no dark Chinese girl is thought to be pretty, you know that. 'The whiter the prettier'! My sister has had men admiring her since she was twelve. She's a regular little white pussy cat, all right."

"Is—is she promised?"

Ang Buai looked up sharply and scrutinized my blushing face for a moment. "No. Even some Thais have wanted to marry her, but Father would never allow that. There was one who was rich and titled, and he had a houseful of wives. He saw Mui Eng at a temple one day and came to ask Father for her. His major wife was dead, and he promised he'd make Mui Eng the most important wife in the household. But even if he hadn't been a Thai, he was too old—and she doesn't even like the young ones, Thai or Chinese! Father can't make her do anything, and everyone thinks I'm the stubborn one. Hah! They should only know . . . She paused then, and sighed softly. "But I don't blame her. If I didn't like a man, nobody could force me to marry him, either."

"What if your father made the arrangements and told you later?"

"He'd never do that."

Have you ever heard such a thing in your life, Mother? I am amazed at the boldness of these girls. In Po Leng, parents did the choosing and children the marrying. I think that is still the best way.

Ang Buai's attentions to me, however innocent, are the subject of gossip around the store. I can't speak much Thai yet, but I understand enough to have guessed what two Thai coolies were saying yesterday. They were directly outside the office, squatting on their haunches in the dust, waiting for a truckload of rice to arrive.

"The new Chinese kid, the one in the office, he's pretty thick with the *thaokae*'s daughter," one of them began.

"The pretty one?"

"Naw—the younger one, Ang Buai. She's in the office every time the *thaokae*'s back is turned. But maybe he doesn't care—she won't be so easy to marry off."

"I thought Chinese people couldn't marry if they belonged to the same *sae* . . . Isn't he Lo Yong Chua's adopted son? That would make him a 'Lo' just like her."

"He kept his own *sae* name—I forget what it is, but not 'Lo.' He could marry her."

Ridiculous! Ang Buai is a child and has probably never thought of such things in her life. There is nothing I can do but keep quiet and hope they'll get bored with their gossip after a while, when nothing happens. I haven't been in this house long, and I don't want the family to lose face because of me. Nguan Thong has been good to me, and a rumor about either of his daughters falling in love with a clerk would be shameful. Even if Ang Buai thinks like a child, she is of marriageable age—perhaps her mother should have taught her better.

Naturally, Kim hears all gossip (and is forced to learn Thai lest he miss anything). When I answered his suspicions about Ang Buai by telling him I'm only helping her with lessons (not really a lie), he laughed. "You, who never set foot in a school? You must be some teacher."

"Study is a school, too. Look at the iron workers across the street. They're all first-rate at their work, and do you suppose they went to engineering school? They depend on their wits and learn from each other."

"Book learning is different from pounding iron," he insisted.

"No, it isn't."

"Yeah, well your face doesn't do you any harm either. If you didn't look like his own son, Yong Chua probably wouldn't have adopted you. And you're a real ladies' man . . ." He laughed. "Both the girls have their eyes on you—everybody knows it."

"Who's everybody?" I asked angrily. "That bunch of old ladies you tittle-tattle with all day? You know, it's funny that you're gossiping about me, Kim . . . if you want me to think you still miss your wife, you'd better stop talking in your sleep about Miss Kha Hieng over in Thonburi."

I thought he'd be dumbfounded, but he only shrugged. "So what? She works for one of Nguan Thong's customers. And she's a nice girl, too. It's not what you think. Suang U. How do I know I'll ever see my wife again?" Then he thrust his jaw out stubbornly and said, "I think I deserve a little happiness in this life!"

I almost laughed, but I said, "I don't think I deserve happiness yet. I can't afford a wife, and I don't know how you think you can."

That was dishonest of me, for Mui Eng has captured me with those strange, quiet eyes, and I do dream of such things. (Thank heaven I don't talk in my sleep.) That one hour a day we spend poring over an old novel keeps me alive the other twenty-three. What a hopeless dream, Mother! Kim has more sense, dreaming of his shop girl.

TODAY WE celebrated the Moon Festival. Unfortunately, the moon was not very beautiful, for it was a cloudy day and, toward afternoon, it even rained a little.

I'm sure the festival in Po Leng must have been as beautiful as ever. All the village girls entering the temple grounds together, carrying their offerings and their prayers to the moon, our goddess of love. It is almost unbearable to be away from home on a holiday, but the same moon shines on us both, Mother, the same sun and sky are above us, and these we may still share.

In Bangkok, each family has its own celebration. Up and down Sampheng Lane, families set up tables outside their stores and shops. Each table is laden with fruit, almond confections, sweets of all kinds and, of course, moon cakes. Ang Buai told me this morning that Thai people make fun of our Moon Festival. They say that the moon isn't really alive, or a goddess, and that according to science books the moon is a lifeless star, cold and dead. Even if all that is true, I think the festival is a lovely and important tradition. And, after all, the moon is so very far away—who is to know what it really is? Such traditions are especially important to people like me who are far away from home. Why is it that every nation considers its own customs reasonable, and those of other nations amusing?

Ang Buai also told me that Thais cremate their dead instead of burying them. They believe that a man's spirit cannot be released and reborn unless the body is cremated. What do you think of that? I think it is more reasonable to respect other people's beliefs than to argue on behalf of one's own.

Toward evening, the rain diminished and many Thais came into the lane to watch us celebrate our festival. Whether they were laughing at us or not I did not notice, but they certainly seemed to be enjoying themselves. Kim and I were sitting in the doorway of Nguan Thong's store watching the neighbors put the finishing touches on their decorations when, suddenly, we saw Seng standing across the street.

When he saw us, he leaned casually against a table loaded with fruit and moon cakes. The old lady who had just finished carefully arranging them glowered at him. He ignored her. At last she slapped his hand and began to cackle angrily at him, and he shuffled off to slouch against the table at the next shop, where two or three giggling young girls teased him and covered their laughing mouths with their hands. But Seng had no eyes for them. He was staring beyond us, and when I turned around I saw Mui Eng hurrying through the office, her arms laden with fruit. I moved aside quickly, and she stepped outside to help her mother without so much as a glance at Kim or me.

What was he doing there? Why did he come to Sampheng Lane on this night? I could tell myself that he was here to observe the celebration, like the hundreds of other people who wandered gaily up and down our street. But I would be fooling myself. Seng's Uncle Tae Lim is a good friend of Nguan Thong, and I believe that Seng came here to see the girls—to see Mui Eng, let me be honest. What could be more reasonable than a match between the two families? Having written the terrible words, I read them over and over, hoping that I can dull the pain by forcing the truth on myself. But it doesn't work. My only hope is that Mui Eng and I may have been together in a former life. If that is so, there may be the chance of a miracle in this life. I have prayed to the moon to intercede on my behalf, if I am at all worthy. I could almost accept losing her, knowing how far above me she is. But Seng! He has nothing I don't have except a rich uncle.

I am sure he saw me—our eyes met briefly. But his neck is stiff with pride, and now that he's dressed up like a rich boy, he needs my friendship even less. If we human beings did not measure ourselves in terms of our possessions, we would all be equal.

Because of the festival, our Chinese lesson began an hour later than usual this evening. Neither parent had time to stand guard, so Ang Buai's speech was even bolder than usual.

"Teacher, do you want to know what my sister prayed for?" Her eyes sparkled in anticipation of embarrassing her silent, proud elder sister.

"Most girls," I said, sensing trouble, "pray for beauty and—and for happiness."

"Not her," Ang Buai said. "She doesn't have to waste her prayers on beauty. She prayed for a husband who could suit her—he has to be handsome, good-hearted, and a good person, too!"

Mui Eng's face turned slowly scarlet, and she bowed her head. How lovely a beautiful woman is when she blushes! But most of us show anger when we have been humiliated, and Mui Eng was no exception. Suddenly Ang Buai let out a yelp of pain.

"Ooh! A big ant under the table just bit me!" she giggled.

"Ang Buai," I said quickly, "what did you ask of the moon?"

"Well what do you think?" she asked, looking at me sideways and smirking. "I asked the moon to do something about my looks, that's what. Maybe it is just a burned-out old star, but I'll try anything. If things don't get any better, I'll be an old maid."

"Younger Sister," Mui Eng said quietly without looking up, is there nothing you are ashamed to say?"

"We're all sick of this book," Ang Buai announced suddenly, as if Mui Eng hadn't spoken. "Let's start another one."

"What would you prefer?" I asked, looking directly at Mui Eng's bowed head.

"I'll get one from Father's room," she said, and left the room quickly, obviously glad of the excuse to regain her composure in privacy.

In a few moments she returned with a new book. I picked it up and was amazed to see what she had chosen. She had brought a love story for us to read. It is about a girl of good family who falls in love with a poor boy. She had met him only once when she showed her love for this boy by tossing a bracelet to him, wrapped in a handkerchief. And after that, she hid him in her room. Her older brother found out about it, and let her go away with the boy she loved. They had many adventures while trying to get away from a rich man who also loved her.

I could not understand why she would chose a story like this to read, but then I thought that perhaps this is the sort of tale young girls like. They may behave properly in real life, but in stories they can experience their emotions. What kind of man does she hope for? Only she knows. She and the moon.

If only the man she hopes for could be your son. I must write no more. I say goodnight to you now, dear Mother, and go off to my sweet dreams. I hope that you may give me your blessing, that I may be successful in love.

33

PLEASE FORGIVE me if I say that women are impossible to understand. Why would a girl whose behavior has always been correct suddenly conduct herself without propriety?

Yesterday morning, Kim refused to get up, so I went outside alone to bathe. It was very hot even at that early hour, and I couldn't bear to stay indoors another minute while the cool waters of the *khlong* lapped invitingly against the pier outside. I glanced at the kitchen window, as I always do, and Mui Eng was there, as she usually is. But today, she didn't pop back inside after a moment as she had always done before. She continued to stand at the window, like a lovely picture in a frame, and then she smiled. A smile brighter than the new sun.

"Here's something to wipe your face dry," she said shyly, and tossed a pink cloth to me. I caught it and saw at once that a bracelet was pinned to one corner of it, a lovely pale jade one I have often seen her wear. When I looked up again, Mui Eng was gone. Is it believable?

Your name is Jade Bracelet, and to me it is a sign. Perhaps my hopes may not be futile after all. And now I know why she chose that novel.

But what kind of behavior is this for a girl? Throwing love stories and bracelets in the path of a man! As soon as I recovered my senses, I began to feel angry. It is unsuitable for a girl to show her feelings.

I don't know what to think. I love her—I can't help it. And why should I complain? After all, I could hardly have raised my face from the bowl of rice my employer provides to ask for his daughter's hand. For that matter, what makes me think I can do so now? I have never been so confused in my life.

I was still staring at the bracelet when Kim shuffled through the door, yawning groggily and tucking in his *phakhaoma*. I hurried past him into the house, and he didn't notice anything, I'm sure.

I am keeping Mui Eng's bracelet in the box where I keep the money you gave me on New Year's Day and the pen Father gave me on the ship. Do girls always imagine themselves the heroines of novels, Mother? Forgive me, but did you too, once? It is difficult to believe that!

She loves me—me, Suang U! Whatever may happen, and even though I disapprove of her conduct, tonight I am proud. Just for tonight. I shall not worry about the future. Or I might be more truthful and say that I can't bring myself to think about it.

LETTER #9   NINTH MONTH, FOURTEENTH DAY
19 OCTOBER 1945   YEAR OF THE COCK

Please forgive the long delay between letters, It has been a very busy month, and I am learning, learning all the time.

This month I know you will observe a vegetarian diet.* Thaokae Nia does too, but the rest of us are not able to gain this merit because we must occasionally eat out with the other merchants and our customers. Even if we order vegetables at a restaurant, they're sure to be prepared with pork fat. I don't believe in going halfway in such things. To go to the temple and make a vow about it, then pick the meat out of the soup—what kind of piety is that? It is foolish to attach needless sins to the soul attempting to trick the gods.

Seng's uncle brought him here recently. Nobody told me why, but I can guess.

"This boy," Nguan Thong said, pointing to me, "can transact business for me if you come by and I'm not in. He's my lucky find!" He smiled at me in his kindly way, then turned to Tae Lim, who apparently did not remember me as the boy Seng cursed and raved at up the gangway of the ship Hai Wang. "So!" he continued, "I hear you're sending your Seng out to do business for you these days."

"Yes," Tae Lim replied with a smile. "I'm getting old, ready to sit in front of the store in a comfortable chair while the young ones do the running. My own children are too young to do more than sell over the counter, of course, but until they grow into the business I can rely on my nephew."

"Good. These two young men should get to know each other better." Then Seng smiled at me, and I smiled at him, smiles such as you

---

*Mahayana Buddhists observe at least ten meatless days, if possible, beginning the last day of the eighth lunar month.

have never seen. I'm only the hired help, though I'm an adopted cousin, and that doesn't go far. Not as far as being a blood nephew, certainly. I was immensely grateful, on this occasion, for not having been born a Thai, or I'd have had to *wai* him. That is the Thai greeting—you place your palms together before your face and incline your head slightly. If you're older or more important than the other person, you return the greeting only superficially. We Chinese have no such custom.

A change of subject. As I write, there's a lot of noise in the background, and I must explain. The Thai couple next door are having one of their arguments, screaming and cursing at each other. I can understand enough of what they're shouting to piece together the situation, It seems that he comes home drunk every night. The more money he has, the drunker he gets, and on payday (today) he can barely crawl home.

A little liquor is beneficial and stimulates the appetite, but the way they drink here it is nothing more than poison. Most of the Thai coolies in Nguan Thong's store are addicted to alcohol and never get out of debt because they drink up their wages instead of buying food and clothing for their wives and children. Pitiful, isn't it?

Someone who lives on the other side of the battlers just threw a rock up onto the roof of their back porch as a suggestion, and now they are both outside and, together, reviling the neighbor who interrupted them. I am willing to respect the Thai, but so far I haven't seen much to respect.

Well, I have strayed far from the subject once again, haven't I? I can't help but notice all the new and strange things happening around me, and even when they're not pleasant subjects to write about, I want to share them with you, along with everything else. I hope I haven't worried you. I am well able to take care of myself, thanks to you.

This evening, at our Chinese lesson, I began to fear that the jade bracelet may be the cause of trouble.

"Teacher, Elder Sister is too mean . . ." Ang Buai said petulantly.

"What nonsense must you bring up now?" Mui Eng asked irritably, tapping her pen on the table.

Ang Buai ignored her. "It's true," she continued. "She has a jade bracelet that she keeps locked in her jewelry box. She hasn't worn it for a week, but just because I asked her if I could trade my ring for it, she says it's her favorite, and she won't."

"Why should I?" Mui Eng retorted impatiently. "We aren't children any more, to be trading things."

"Well, I'm going to tell Mother," Ang Buai said, scowling darkly into her notebook.

"Tell her, then!" Mui Eng said. "I don't care if you do—she can't do anything about it and you know it."

She looks like an angel, that girl, but sometimes those star-like eyes have a cold, hard brilliance that almost frightens me. Maybe your son has fallen in love with the wrong girl, Mother, but I couldn't help myself. I saw her once, and I loved her, and I shall always love her.

—

LETTER #10   TENTH MONTH, SECOND DAY
6 NOVEMBER 1945   YEAR OF THE COCK

I EXPECTED to have a letter from you by now, and I'm beginning to get worried. Are you so busy on the farm? Or are you angry with a son who ran off, leaving only a note on the kitchen table? I pray that I may hear from you before long. But, whether you answer my letters or not, I shall never fail in my duty to you, a duty which I enjoy. When I lived at home, it was my habit to read before going to bed, or chat with you and Younger Brother about the happenings of our day. Now I am making a new habit for myself. On the evenings I am not too tired, I find it relaxing to write to you, and something of the mood of our old evenings together steals over me. Perhaps we can no longer talk of an evening, or laugh together as we once did, but I can bring you close to me by sharing my new life with you. It already seems such a long time since I saw your beloved face. Well, enough of that. I shall try to be a little more patient.

There is trouble in the household of Nguan Thong, and I fear I am the cause of it. Ang Buai is making much of the jade bracelet . . . I'm not sure she knows who has it, but I wouldn't be at all surprised if she saw Mui Eng toss it to me and is amusing herself at our expense. Yesterday I overheard Mui Eng and her mother arguing in the kitchen.

"Why don't you sell her the thing, then!" Thaokae Nia cried, exasperated. "What can it matter to you?"

"Why should I!? Sell, trade—what's the difference? I don't want to."

"Mui Eng, why are you so selfish? I'll buy you another just like it. You are of an age to marry now, and when you do there will be plenty of jewelry coming to you . . . please, think of your little sister's feelings! What can it hurt to do something, just once, to please her?"

"I like my own things."

Her mother left the kitchen and passed me hurriedly as she crossed the office, then climbed the stairs without so much as a glance at me. Mui Eng followed her after a few moments, her eyes fixed straight ahead and her mouth set in a firm, stubborn line. Nguan Thong, who sat nearby at his desk, glanced up briefly, shook his head, and returned immediately to his work without commenting. I think such scenes have not penetrated his concentration for years. A moment later the procession of two descended the stairs again, Thaokae Nia still in the lead.

"The jade bracelet is gone!" Thaokae Nia announced to her husband. "It's not in the jewelry box where it belongs. Your 'little cat' has lost it, and she's lying to me besides!"

"I am not lying," Mui Eng announced in her turn. "It must be hidden under something in one of my drawers." She smiled carefully at her father. "I'll have to look again."

At that, Nguan Thong slammed his account book shut and opened his mouth to speak, but before he could Ang Buai ran into the room, momentarily distracting him.

"It's not in your room at all, and you know it!" Thaokae Nia snapped at Mui Eng, "And no thief walked off with it, that's certain."

"Thief?" Ang Buai exclaimed "Nobody ever goes up there but us."

"Ang Buai," her father began, looking steadily at her and speaking calmly, "did you take the bracelet and hide it because you were angry with your sister for behaving selfishly?"

It was a fair guess, but Ang Buai looked as if she had been slapped. "Oh, Father!" she cried with a little sob, "how can you say such a thing to me? No matter what happens in this house, someone ends up accusing me!" Her eyes brimmed over with tears. "And if I had stolen it, would I call attention to it?" She took a key from her blouse pocket and threw it on her father's desk. "Here, take my key! Go through my closet and see whether I am a thief!" Then she covered her face with both hands and ran into the kitchen.

I tried desperately to keep my eyes on my work, though only a deaf man could have looked convincingly busy at that moment.

"You didn't have to talk to the child like that!" Thaokae Nia said sharply. "You know how she is. She probably won't talk to you for a week!"

Since they acted as if I didn't exist, I began to relax a bit at that point and looked up to see how Nguan Thong was reacting. He sighed wearily at his wife's last outburst, poor man, and asked, "Mui Eng, when did you last wear the damned bracelet?"

"On the day of the Moon Festival. Then I put it back into my jewelry box, as I always do." For a second, she looked alarmed. "I mean, either my jewelry box or one of my drawers. I didn't leave it lying around, that I know." And her face became a blank once again. I don't know how she does it.

"All right!" Nguan Thong exclaimed, losing his patience at last. "Maybe she's hidden the thing in her mouth—open up, Mui Eng!" And he chuckled to himself, and reopened his account book.

"So it's sarcasm now, is it?" His wife leaned across his desk, covering the page he was working on with her right hand. "You sound more like a Thai every day!"

"Like a Thai? What the hell does that have to do with anything?"

She didn't answer, but straightened up, grabbed Mui Eng by the arm, and marched her toward the stairs. "Come on! We're having one last search, and if you don't find it, you're in trouble, young lady!"

Mui Eng threw me one fleeting glance of despair as her mother pulled her along. They went up, they came down. They couldn't very well find it when it was hidden among my things . . . A fine fellow, the new clerk—the boss's daughter's jade bracelet is hidden in a box in his traveling bag.

"Mui Eng," Nguan Thong said sternly, "How can you expect to run a household when you can't keep track of one bracelet? Soon you will marry, and then you will have your husband's property under your care. Such carelessness as this is unthinkable in a grown woman."

Mui Eng looked almost contrite. It hadn't worked out at all this way in the novel . . .

"Someone has come to ask for your hand, Mui Eng," he continued, pushing his books to one side and turning his full attention to the scene that had forced its way upon him. "This is as good a time as any to discuss it, since you have already made havoc of my morning."

She stood like a statue before him, pale and expressionless.

"My friend Lim," he continued, "has come to speak to me about you."

"What do you mean?" Thaokae Nia interrupted, frowning. "Their oldest boy is ten years old. Does he expect Mui Eng to wait for him until she's thirty?"

"Wife, I am not an idiot!" Nguan Thong exclaimed through clenched teeth. "He wants her for the nephew, Seng!"

My abacus nearly fell from my hands. It seemed as though everything in the street outside was swaying. I was stunned, dumbfounded. And why? What is there to be startled about? I had guessed at it already myself, but as long as it remained unspoken, there was hope.

What have I to compete with Seng? Money? Position? Seng's father supported Lim in his youth, I have learned, and therefore Seng is in an excellent position today. There are other reasons Nguan Thong feels obligated to Tae Lim, but I have not yet learned what they are. So, from two sides Seng has advantages, while I have none from any. What am I, after all—a halfway relative, a clerk eating the boss's rice. Life is not a novel, and I am neither stupid nor without pride. After a moment's dizziness, therefore, I bowed my head and returned to my work, praying that no one had noticed my astonishment and pain, which I am sure were plain to see had anyone looked.

"That boy who just came from China?" Thaokae Nia asked. "What does he look like?"

"Not a bad looking boy. Good forehead—bit of a temper, according to his uncle, but that might do her some good. Why are you so quiet, Little Cat?"

"I have nothing to say, Father. I have never seen him, and have no opinion." She kept her eyes on the floor as she spoke.

Perhaps she has only been playing a game with me to relieve the boredom of her life, while waiting for Papa to bring home a good catch. Maybe she's been laughing at me all this time. How thankful I am now that I did not meet her impropriety, that I never made eyes at her over that cursed novel.

"I'll bring Seng to the house soon," Nguan Thong said. "Of course, it is customary for the man to see the girl first. He saw our Mui Eng the night of the Moon Festival, and apparently was quiet taken with her. And why not? He smiled affectionately at his Little Cat, forgetting, for the moment, the incident of the bracelet. It was unbearable. "So," he continued, "now it's your turn to have a look at him."

"Yes, Father," she said, almost inaudibly. "There is one thing . . . if I do not like him, please do not force me to marry him."

Nguan Thong's face clouded instantly. "What's not to like?" he asked irritably. "He's my friend's relative, he's a merchant, the right age, Chinese and not ugly. What else do you want?"

"Let—let me meet him, please Father."

Her parents looked at each other for a moment, then smiled. They probably think she wants a chance to fall in love with him on her own, as girls like to pretend once a marriage has been arranged. In any event, I guess that's the end of my "romance." I see now how ridiculous my hopes were. If she doesn't like Seng and can talk them out of the match, they'll find someone else like him.

What a fool your son has been.

LETTER #11   TENTH MONTH, TWENTY-EIGHTH DAY
2 DECEMBER 1945   YEAR OF THE COCK

MY DEAR adopted father Lo Yong Chua is here with us. He arrived yesterday and had many things to tell me. But not as many as I had to tell him.

Nguan Thong gave me the morning off to go shopping with Father, and this afternoon we sat on the pier together, behind the store, watching the boats slide back and forth across Khlong Ong Ang and splashing our feet in the water. It was a wonderful day.

"We stopped in Japan this trip," he said, "and it is terrible there. You should see Nagasaki from the bombing. Dreadful! I wonder if Japan will ever recover. I wouldn't be surprised if those people just gave up, son." He shook his head thoughtfully and gazed off across the *khlong*.

I couldn't discuss this subject with much enthusiasm. Politics and all that sort of thing never interested me, and now I have no time for it anyway. There's so much to learn about the business, and that's all I ever think of besides you and Mui Eng.

Father finally noticed that I wasn't listening to him, and after a few tries to capture my attention with tales of Hong Kong and changes taking place back in China, he gave up and was silent. I don't know how much time had passed when at last he said, "I hear you're the new house teacher." At that I looked up quickly, and he laughed. "Aha! I've found a subject that wakes him up!"

"It's—it's nothing much, sir," I said, feeling my face grow hot.

Am I becoming like a Thai, to smile and say no when I mean yes?

"Nguan Thong tells me someone is asking for the fair Mui Eng's hand," Father continued. "In fact, that's all they've talked about since I arrived. The fellow's name seemed familiar to me—Seng, isn't it?"

"Yes, sir, it's the same one . . . the boy on the ship."

"Hm-m, I thought so . . . the one Kim argued with—" He was silent for another few moments, smiling to himself. Then, "In Thailand only four months and looking for a wife already. Must be a rich one, that uncle. What's the boy like? Any education?"

"Seng? Oh no, sir! He can read and write a little, but his calligraphy is poor. He has a bad memory for details and—and he's conceited for all that." I stopped suddenly, aware that I had said too much.

"Did you know that he hasn't made much of an impression on Mui Eng?"

"But—but I thought her father liked him," I replied lamely, "and she doesn't even know Seng . . . "

"Yes, I know. It's odd. But Ang Buai tells me Little Cat has something up her sleeve . . . When she meets him, she intends to ask him a lot of 'questions.' I don't quite understand—" He paused, then said, "Let me tell you something, Suang U. I've known Mui Eng all her life, and if she doesn't want to marry that boy, Nguan Thong doesn't stand a chance of forcing her. She told her father she wants a man she can 'look up to and learn from.' Discussions, women want nowadays. A lot of nonsense, if you ask me. But she insists she won't marry anyone who's not better educated than she is. Where do you suppose she got such ideas?" He grinned. "Wouldn't be from her teacher, now, would it?"

"Of course not, sir—I mean, I don't think so. In the novel we're reading, a girl gave her suitor a list of questions to answer—it does sound as though—well, as though she had something like that in mind."

Father sighed deeply and shook his head. "These days, who knows what women are thinking? Or what they will do? They belong in the home, and should not be confused about their duties, given all kinds of strange ideas out of books. A girl must be raised as a girl. How can she ever be satisfied with a woman's life if she's raised to think like a man? It isn't fair, you know."

He is quite right. Look at poor Ang Buai, yearning after the duties of a son! Even though I shall probably not be a father for many years, I am resolved to raise my sons as sons and not educate daughters beyond what is necessary.

We chatted of other things for awhile, then I gathered my courage to tell him about the incident of the jade bracelet.

"Father, do you know the story of Tieo Chui Kim? That's where Mui Eng got the idea of questioning Seng, I think. Well, in the book, a rich girl who falls in love with a poor boy—"

"Yes, yes," he interrupted, "I know the story. She throws him her bracelet, right?"

"Right. Well, I've got a bracelet in my room. From Mui Eng. She threw it through the kitchen window."

"Good heavens! I trust you haven't been in her closet acting out the rest of the story!"

"Certainly not!" I replied, shocked that he would even mention that. "I haven't done anything . . . dishonorable." My forehead began to grow damp and my hands to shake, but I told him everything from the first morning I saw her to the confrontation between Nguan Thong and his women over the bracelet the day he announced that Seng's elders had spoken for Mui Eng.

"So," he said when I had finished, "she's quite the little student of literature. What does it all mean? The girl likes you—that's plain. Nguan Thong is right to call her his Little Cat. She's like the cat on our ship, always pretending to sleep in the sun until a gullible mouse dares to run out from under a barrel. Then, pounce! She's on him before he's had time to twitch a whisker."

"You're right about Nguan Thong having his mind set on Seng," he continued, "but that's because of Tae Lim. I'll tell you more about their friendship this evening, after supper. The debts Nguan Thong owes that man cannot be repaid by money. Now, keep your head on

43

straight for a few days and behave yourself. Let's not talk about it anymore today . . . I want to think."

I noticed then how tired he looked. Too much traveling, too many years of toiling between sea and land. I wish he would stay with us, and I think he would like that himself. This man, whom I met by chance, means so much to me. I have never regretted deciding to call him father.

—

AFTER MY last letter, the hours and days dragged by endlessly. Everyone went about the house looking grim, especially Nguan Thong and his eldest daughter.

I have learned that when Bangkok was bombed during the war, Nguan Thong's family was invited to take refuge with Tae Lim across the river in Thonburi. They accepted that invitation, and although Nguan Thong paid for his family's food and lodging, he still feels a debt of gratitude to his old friend.

Mui Eng did not seem to care at all about that, but perhaps it is not unusual for young girls to think of themselves first. I, the outsider who stepped so clumsily into the circle of this family, felt sorry for both father and daughter.

Finally the day arrived when Seng was to formally meet Mui Eng. He ambled into the store, smiling cockily and obviously sure of his welcome, totally ignoring me, of course. Nguan Thong rose rather stiffly, motioned Seng to follow him to the back room, and sent his wife to fetch Mui Eng. I kept my eyes fixed rigidly on my work, unwilling to acknowledge the only face in this world besides Kim's which recalls to me my boyhood and home. A moment after they left, I heard Ang Buai's teasing voice behind me.

"Is my new brother-in-law here?"

"He's here."

"What does he look like? Is he more handsome than our teacher?"

"As a prize-winning ox is handsome beside an old water buffalo."

She covered her mouth with her hand and giggled. "Do you want to know how my sister dressed herself to meet Seng?"

"Not as much as you want to tell me."

"You're nasty!" she said, with what looked suspiciously like an imitation of her sister's dignified frown. "But I'll tell you anyway. She's wearing a pair of hideous bright green pants a red blouse, and spectacles. And she's dragging an enormous book around with her everywhere. Inside it, what do you think she has hidden?"

"I can't wait to find out."

She laughed merrily. "You are nasty, aren't you? Inside the book she has a list of questions for Seng. And if his answers aren't good enough?" She pounded on the desk with her little first. "Then no bridegroom, no brother-in-law!"

I laughed aloud in spite of myself. Whatever would Seng do when he saw the girl he intended to marry dressed like a madwoman, waiting to quiz him as if he were a schoolboy? And what wouldn't I give to see his conceit tested this sorely? Suddenly the door of the back room burst open, and Nguan Thong stalked into the office. The thunderous expression on his face turned me quickly back to my tasks, and Ang Buai jumped away from my desk as if it were on fire. Thaokae Nia scurried into the room behind her husband, twisting her hands nervously, and when her eyes met mine, she glanced quickly away.

"Suang U!" my boss called out. "Give your work to Ang Buai and come with me. We have business to discuss—alone!"

My heart sank. "B-but, sir, my work is not—I mean, I couldn't . . . "

"Leave it to the girl, I said. You and I are taking a boat into Khlong Bang Luang for a few hours. I need to get away from this madhouse."

He paced up and down the room with his hands clasped behind his back, while with fumbling fingers I attempted to pull my papers together. It occurred to me that perhaps he meant to get me out into the middle of the river and push me overboard. At last I pushed the still disorderly papers toward Ang Buai and, avoiding her eyes, stood before Nguan Thong.

He turned to his trembling wife. "Keep an eye on young Seng. He looks ready to burn the place down, and Tae Lim says he has a temper."

As I followed him out to the *khlong*, I felt as though my feet might turn around at any moment and run away with me. He called to a young boy who lay napping in one of the delivery boats that rocked lazily in the waves near shore, and the boy jumped up to pull the boat close to the bank. Nguan Thong hopped in deftly and I clambered down after him, praying that I might be stricken and die right there on the muddy bank, and be spared whatever was to follow.

But as the boy poled our little boat out into the river toward Khlong Bang Luang, I began to feel better in spite of myself, for it was easy to be distracted by the wonders to be seen on the banks of the Chao Phraya. Flourishing trees burst with fruit, temple and *chedi* spires poked up into the clear blue sky above Bangkok, and every manner of river craft jostled for position on the busy, colorful river. But Nguan Thong seemed to notice none of this, and it was a long while before he began to speak.

"I wonder if you will think ill of me, Suang U, if I tell you something about our family. About my Little Cat, in particular . . . "

"I think, sir, perhaps I know something . . ." I began, then lost courage and subsided into a stammer.

"From Ang Buai, no doubt, that irritating child. What has she told you?"

Could it be? My heart began to race with hope. Could it possibly be that he did not know?

"Not very much. Only that Mui Eng is, well, not pleased with Seng."

He nodded slowly. "And that is not all. She insists that she must marry a 'learned man.' Seng? The poor lad can scarcely read a printed page, as we all know after this afternoon's foolishness."

"But," I dared, "she will have to do as you wish. You are her father."

"My dear boy, Mui Eng is a hard child. Even when she was small, we could not force her to do anything against her will. Since she has become old enough to shame me, to tell you the truth I have not dared to be strict with her for fear she would . . . would run off with the first fool who took her fancy. This is a pitiful confession for a father to have to make." He lowered his eyes and I was still, for there could be no reply to his embarrassment. We sat together quietly, watching the warm, brown river water rush against the sides of the boat.

"Yong Chua, your adopted father, has told me that he will soon give up traveling and settle here, near us. You will probably work for him, which is only right, though I don't mind saying I will be sorry to lose you." He cleared his throat and glanced quickly about us, as if someone might be eavesdropping on us in the middle of the Chao Phraya River. "He has also told me that he would like to have Mui Eng for his daughter-in-law."

Father had told him that? I felt afraid to breathe.

"It is not what I wanted," he continued. "You see, Tae Lim is a friend to whom I owe much, and I must consider seriously my responsibilities to both these men, my friend and my cousin. Also, it is essential that Mui Eng agrees to marry a man of my choosing. You understand that, don't you?" I nodded dumbly, and he went on. "Now, she doesn't want Seng—the gods know she has made that clear. Probably because I have encouraged him and she has had time enough to scheme her way out of the match, just to spite me. But she knows nothing of Yong Chua's idea. She would never suspect such a thing." He was silent again for a few minutes, considering his dilemma. I was silent, too, praying. "But surely," he continued, "Tae Lim ought to understand if I tell him that my elder cousin has asked for the girl as wife to his adopted son. As for Mui Eng, you are a learned man, are you not?" I nodded again, with less certainty. "Learned enough for her!" he grumbled. Then, abruptly, he laughed. "Well, boy, have you nothing to say for yourself?"

"N-no, sir, nothing . . . except that I am poor, sir, and—"

"Of course you're poor," he interrupted. "But what of it? Do you think she cares? Money to her is like rice and water, there for the taking. What else has she ever known? She respects brains—odd in a girl, but there it is—and you have brains. I respect work, and you are a good worker, and loyal. That much I know about you already. You are not a boy who will disappoint his elders." He grinned slyly. "You like her, eh? She is pretty enough for you?"

I could only grin and blush foolishly and stare at the floorboards, but he laughed merrily and didn't seem to mind. "Then it is agreed. When Yong Chua returns, we shall set the date. I don't want Little Cat to know anything of this, do you understand? This time there will be no foolishness; I shall have my way for a change." He smiled at the thought.

I could barely keep a straight face. Nguan Thong, the wily old merchant of Sampheng Lane, was roundly beaten by his daughter before the battle had half begun.

"I think it would be a good idea to visit some of my customers this afternoon. We'll give ourselves the rest of the day off. What do you say?"

I grinned broadly. Had I ever known such happiness before? Nothing my eyes beheld that day could displease me, and all the world was full of wonders. I shall never forget it.

Near the riverbank, I saw two men stripped to the waist wading in the shallows, their shoulders caked with sun-dried mud. Each of them carried a wire basket, and I thought they were fishing until I saw that each basket had a large hole in the bottom.

"They're sifting," Nguan Thong said, noticing my interest.

"Sifting for what?"

"Things in the river bottom."

"Is there anything precious down there?"

"No, but people are always accidentally dropping things into the river. These men earn their living by selling what they find. Or at least they earn their drinking money," he added disapprovingly.

"But if they worked at regular jobs, wouldn't they earn more? They must not make a very steady income that way."

"They don't. But there are people who would rather scramble in mud on the chance of finding a diamond ring than work at a regular job which would keep them fed but not much more. It is an important thing to learn about Thai people, that they love to gamble. There was a Chinese named Yi Ko Hong in Bangkok some years ago who became stupendously rich allowing Thais to gamble on their money, to his profit. But most of us don't think like Yi Ko Hong. We look for our fortunes the surest way: buying and selling, and hard work—not so quick a way, but certain and honorable, and it has not failed us."

Toward evening, we returned to the store to find Mui Eng and her mother looking terrified, and Ang Buai burning with curiosity. I dared not look at any of them, and hurried out to walk the streets until they would surely have gone to bed. It was near midnight when I lay down beside the snoring Kim. The last thing I remembered before falling asleep was Nguan Thong's remark about the Thai love of gambling. That is bad for them, but good for us. I shall not forget it.

I close this letter knowing that you will be pleased to gain a daughter-in-law. And before long, I hope, grandchildren to rejoice in.

TODAY I became engaged to Mui Eng. When Father returned from Japan three days ago, he and Nguan Thong went to visit an astrologer in Thonburi to set the date for our wedding. (The astrologer is blind, which is believed here to be one sign of his powers. His reputation for making accurate predictions is well known everywhere in Bangkok.) We are to be married only two weeks from now, for there is not another auspicious day for us before the end of next year. Of course, I am glad that we shall marry soon. I hope that my mother will not be too critical of a son who is, he confesses, joyful beyond what may be proper.

I never realized that becoming engaged was so complicated. Without Father, to begin with, none of this could ever have happened, for even the betrothal gifts for Mui Eng and her family were beyond my wildest expectations. We gave 2,440 baht to Nguan Thong and his wife in money for the raising of a daughter. I have learned that the number must always include four: 2,440 baht, or 6,440 baht or, in poor families, 40 baht. Did you know that the Hakkha do the same thing, only using the number nine? Father told me that it is their symbol of longevity.

When I saw all that money for the first time, I thought I would faint. Father said nothing about it, but I have made up my mind that someday I will repay him. Even if he doesn't want it, I must—an amount like that!

Then there was twelve baht in betrothal money for Mui Eng's jewelry: a necklace, bracelet, and earrings—everything gold. It is too heavy to be pretty, in my opinion (not nearly as beautiful as jade), but gold is what Thais like, and so does Mui Eng.

Father told me that some Thai women wear their family's entire fortune around their neck. He says they would rather have nothing to eat with their rice but mashed peppers and fish sauce than give up the few strands of gold that make them feel respectable before their neighbors.

Besides money and gold, we provided a hundred boxes of almond candy to be sent to the bride's relatives. It is our custom for only the bridegroom's family to attend the betrothal dinner, but since I am a stranger here Father is saved some expense, for which I am grateful. There was a dinner for the near relatives, the men who work in the shop, and a few of Nguan Thong's old friends (excluding one). The food prepared early in the morning as an offering to our ancestors was sufficient to feed the guests who arrived later in the day. Of course, Mui Eng and I did not attend the betrothal dinner, but Father told me about it later and said he strongly suspected Mui Eng and her sister spent the afternoon at the top of the stairs, giggling and peeking down into the room where the men feasted.

He has already quit his job and rented a shop, and where do you think it is? Directly next door to Nguan Thong. I was pleased, as he knew I would be. Mui Eng and I will have the large bedroom upstairs, and he will use the smaller one. Kim will have a room all to himself downstairs, which pleases him mightily. He says he looks forward to my wedding night more than I do.

"Ah, you are the sly one," he said last night as we set up the boards between our familiar barrels and boxes. "I used to be jealous of Seng— Seng! Where is he now, compared to his enemy, eh? You came along and plucked the choicest flower right out from under his nose. Do you realize how angry he is?" he asked, laughing and shaking his head.

Not only angry, I thought to myself. Filled with revenge, and with hate I do not want to return.

"The guys in the shop are jealous of you too. They don't exactly hate you," he added magnanimously, "but they're jealous all right."

"I know, and I don't blame them. I'll get used to it, and so will they."

Of course I understand how they feel. I have thought about it often since that afternoon in Nguan Thong's boat. They look at me and see a man like themselves, and it is natural that they resent my good fortune. My future stretches out invitingly before me, but for them the future will probably be only an extension of the present. Back-breaking work for a few baht a day, day after day, year after year.

It is Father's plan that I shall continue working for Nguan Thong until we have accumulated stock. At first, we will sell only food and everyday necessities, expanding as we see where our successes are. In a few years, when our capital has grown, we hope to realize his dream, manufacturing pastries and Chinese confections. To tell the truth, I hardly know one Chinese confection from another, but he knows a great deal about such things, and I can learn. Anyway, it will be a long time before I have to.

Now that we are engaged. I don't see Mui Eng at all. I would like to return her bracelet, but I know that won't be possible until she is my wife. Nguan Thong will no doubt learn the truth someday, and when he does I hope he will not despise me. I respect him, and I would be sorry to lose the respect I think he has for me.

When next I write to you, I will be a married man. Your son has great happiness. I trust that you rejoice with me.

LETTER #14   MY WEDDING DAY

AT LAST I have been able to steal a bit of time to write to you, on a day when I miss you more than ever before. How I wish you had been here to lead these ceremonies as is your right, receiving the respect of your beautiful new daughter-in-law. You have not been able to accept tea from her hand, according to our custom. I hope that, when Younger Brother has a fine wedding of his own, you will accept one cup from your second daughter-in-law on behalf of Mui Eng. And I also hope that it will not be long before your younger son brings home a wife to attend to your comforts, as a son's wife should.

The money I send you embarrasses me, for I know that you would rather have the affection of a real son than words and money from a paper one. My letters are all I have to give you now, and I trust you can feel the love that is sent with each one.

Today I was alone as never before. I had no relatives to greet at my wedding, no Younger Brother to stand beside me. I thought of his cheerful face all day, of how he would have enjoyed the wedding. But worst of all, Mother, I did not receive a letter from China, not even the four characters.* Can you be that angry with me?

For many people these days, the word "friend" does not seem to

---

*The four auspicious characters seen at wedding ceremonies. These are (in Teo Chiu dialect) Chiang, Meng, Pu, and Kui meaning, respectively, Gain, Honor, Rank, and Praise. Four additional characters are also usually seen; these are Chai, Chu, Buang, and Sung, "A Thousand Children, Ten Thousand Grandchildren."

mean much, but I cannot forget anyone who has once been my friend. Of course, it was unthinkable that Seng would attend my wedding, but I missed even him. I was grateful for Kim's presence; he smirked and guffawed his way through the day and remarked at one point that it was a great day for us both. I might be getting a rich wife, he said, but he was getting a cot to sleep on instead of two boards, and one can't have everything in this world.

Before the wedding feast, the two of us waited in the kitchen, peering out cautiously at the guests assembling in the outer room.

"I saw Seng yesterday," he whispered. "He's telling everyone you're the curse of his life. You even stole his fiancee!"

"Must I go to my bride listening to gossip? Please, spare me Seng's wild tales just for today."

"But he says he's going to get his revenge for this . . ."

"My mother always told me, 'No hand can rise up to strike a hand that will not rise up to meet it.' It's good advice, and I intend to keep on following it."

"Maybe, but Seng is the kind of guy who'd punch you in the face and run, and never understand why your hand didn't rise up!"

We both laughed. Then I saw Father nod to me from the next room (now decorated with flowers and barely recognizable as the office where I spend my days with an abacus and ledger). "Come on, you fool," I said, pushing Kim ahead of me, "it's time for me to get married." He turned, grinned, and punched me hard on the arm, and I was glad he was with me.

It was during the wedding feast that I missed you most, though Father sat beside me looking pleased and proud. Mui Eng showed not the slightest trace of nervousness, but I cannot say the same for myself. At times during the earlier ceremonies, I got so dizzy that Father had to signal me with his eyes to remind me what to do next. He made me feel that I belonged to someone here, that I was not alone before the curious eyes of elders and guests.

And my wife? I am a little afraid of her, though I vow she'll never know it. She must learn that I am her master, in spite of the way things began between us, and I am determined that my household will never be like her father's. I lived in his home long enough to have learned a few lessons. Mui Eng is too beautiful, and too used to having whatever she wants. She always has her feelings under control, even more than is suitable for a woman. Will I ever learn to guess her thoughts?

When it came time to send the bride,* Mui Eng's parents led her solemnly into her new home. Everything was ready, tidy and clean, for Father and I had scrubbed and cleaned the whole house. My new mother-in-law looked about her approvingly.

Mui Eng spoke to me for the first time since becoming my wife when we heard her parents close the door downstairs. "I'm exhausted," she said, crossing the room and leaning across the small table in front of the window to look out.

"I'm tired, too," I said. "Why don't you rest for awhile? My father's house is cool and breezy, isn't it?" She did not answer, but turned away abruptly and began to unpack the basket of clothes her father had carried up this morning.

"Well, I guess I'll go write a letter to my mother," I said, "about the wedding."

"Where is my bracelet?" she asked, with an unmistakable smirk, as she brushed the wrinkles from a length of pink silk. "I want to wear it."

"Mui Eng, what will we say if your father notices it?"

She laughed and said, "You're the learned man . . . you think of something."

I fetched the bracelet from my box of treasures and gave it to her. She turned it over and over slowly, smiling as if secretly amused. "You're a strange man, Suang U."

"I am?"

"You are. You don't even know what you're supposed to do with your bride."

I felt both rage and laughter welling up within me. Mui Eng giggled, pushed me from the room, and slammed the door. For this I had tried not to make my bride feel shy? This, then, is the time I found to write to you, while my bride smiles and sleeps.

Marriage is an important step in a man's life, but I confess I don't understand why we have to spend so much money in celebrating the

---

*"Sending the bride" is the last ceremonial aspect of marriage. In many weddings, especially Thai, there is a "laying of the sheets" ceremony in addition, performed by friends of the bride's parents. *Trans.*

53

perpetuation of our race. Ceremonies are only a show of wealth, at best a gesture of good will toward our friends, and I think perhaps it all goes too far. I wonder if you agree with me.

I pray for your blessing, and close this letter with love and respect from myself and my wife. I think perhaps she has smiled and slept long enough.

—

LETTER #15   NEW YEAR
2 FEBRUARY 1946   YEAR OF THE DOG

IT IS now three days since our marriage, and I believe I have proven to Mui Eng that her husband is not such a fool as she thought. I shall not speak further of this, however, as you are also a woman and have been a bride, and probably understand Mui Eng's feelings at this point in her marriage better than I do.

I shall write instead of my work, and how my life is changing. Sometimes I wonder if you want to hear all of this, but how can I know? (I just realized that I wrote the word "hear" instead of "read." To me, these letters are conversations, and often I am sure I can "hear" what you are thinking as you read them!) This is the last time I shall ever mention your not writing to me; I decided so this morning. From now on, I shall write to you without a word about it, and pray only that you do not write to forbid me. I would rather know nothing than that.

Mui Eng remained in our room for the full three days following our wedding,* until this evening when we visited her parents. Of course, it is hardly the same as in bygone years, when our people had to make a real journey to visit the bride's parents for the traditional greeting of a married daughter. Mui Eng and I simply walked next door on the front path. But her parents acted as pleased as if we had come a thousand miles and set the table as they would for honored guests. This annoyed Ang Buai.

"It's ridiculous to treat them like strangers," she said to her mother, "when you've been shouting at Mui Eng across the yard between your

---

*It was the custom for a bride to remain in her room the first three days after the marriage, and in the house for the first month, except for the visit to her parents' home and special occasions in the company of her husband. *Trans.*

bedroom window and hers ever since the wedding!"

Nguan Thong and Yong Chua laughed at that. "So Ang Buai disapproves of our customs, as usual," her father said. "A long time ago, daughter, we Chinese married strangers, because most of the people who lived near us were of the same *sae*. By the time a bride could visit her parents, perhaps two weeks had passed. And sometimes it was such a distance that the 'bride' arrived with one fat baby clinging to her skirts and another in her arms. But it remains our tradition to honor a married daughter on her first visit home, even when her journey is from the shop next door. And what have you to complain of? You're getting a better dinner than you might have. Now run and fetch us some tea. It is chilly this evening, and strong hot tea will clear our throats."

He watched Ang Buai pour boiling water carefully into the family's best porcelain teapot, then turned to Yong Chua. "Why must this child always have some irritating remark to make? She was born here, and it shows every time she opens her mouth. I tell you, soon it will be impossible to raise a child properly in Bangkok. She even wants us to rest on Sundays like the Thais, who have forsaken their own religious days to imitate the foreigners. Some of them even take off Saturdays! That's like working half-time, building half a future. And then in two days they spend what they have earned the other five."

Yong Chua nodded soberly, "It is so. They will snatch at any chance to escape work. I think it is enough to rest an hour during the day and sleep one's fill at night. We Chinese close our shops twice a year, once at half-year and again at the New Year, and we go visiting on New Year's Day. Surely that is enough 'free time' in this life, and what is 'free,' anyway, about a day when no money comes in?"

I had never thought about free time before. I only learned recently how many days of the year Thai people do nothing but play and visit, and I could hardly believe my ears. No wonder they do not like to be merchants! In business, a man must expend all his effort, not half. Who would want to patronize a store that was only open for business five days of the week?

We work from childhood on, until it becomes second nature to us. I shall raise my children the same way. Nguan Thong was right about Thais working half-time, using only 50 percent of their ability. We

Chinese use 100 percent of everything except money. You might say that if the Thai work 50 percent and spend 110 percent, we Chinese work 100 percent and spend 10 percent.

I still work for Nguan Thong, as we agreed. Our own store is not fully stocked yet, but soon after the holidays we will begin to work in earnest, and I will leave Nguan Thong. Father will buy our stock because he knows the suppliers better than I do. Mui Eng will help with the customers and keep daily records. She has never done so in her father's store, but she is a married woman now, and it is her duty to help her husband earn a living. I am not sure that she is used to the idea yet.

On this last day of the year, we observed the customs I have known from my childhood. Just as you have always done, Mui Eng, Ang Buai, and their mother prepared dishes of pork, fish, and chicken, offerings to our gods. At eleven o'clock we offered food to the spirits of our ancestors. We have plenty of dried fish, squid, and other foods that will not spoil over the three days we may not cook. After paying our respects to gods and ancestors, we visited with each other and relaxed. Then late in the afternoon, we made our offerings to the spirits of those who died without descendants. These offerings were particularly generous, for Father says these spirits will remember our generosity in the months ahead as we strive to establish our business. It is too bad that we may not give any of this food to the monks,* I have always thought, though I realize that it is "left over" (even if by spirits) and therefore may be shared only with our family and friends. Nguan Thong gave all the employees a three-day paid vacation and a New Year's bonus: one month's salary, more for long-time employees, less for the men who, like myself, have worked here less than a year. Father says the foreigners give such a bonus at the end of the year too. Perhaps they believe, as we do, that the little finger and the thumb are both important to the hand.

My bonus from Nguan Thong was a half-month's pay, since I have worked here just half a year. Kim's was the same. When all the employees had left, after receiving good wishes for the holidays and

---

*When Buddhist monks walk through the streets at dawn, each carrying a bowl, they are not "begging for alms," but providing an opportunity for householders to make merit. *Trans.*

envelopes full of money, Nguan Thong called his wife, his daughters and me to his desk.

"Now, my children," he said, obviously pleased with himself, "It's your turn! Mui Eng, you are the eldest. You and your husband first."

"Sir, I've already received mine," I stammered.

"Yes, I know," he said impatiently, "But that was as an employee, not as a son."

As we stepped forward, Ang Buai gasped. "The bracelet!" she cried. "Father, she's wearing the jade bracelet!"

Nguan Thong looked at the bracelet perplexedly for a moment, then shifted his gaze to my burning face. "Ah, yes . . . well, it is enough that the bracelet is found. That will be enough, Ang Buai," he said. "And Mui Eng, take care of your things better in the future. Do you care so little for your father that you misuse his gifts?"

"I—no, Father," she replied meekly.

"It is as I've always said, a daughter is only a daughter until she has her sights on a husband, and where is loyalty to parents then?" He looked directly at the bracelet, extending his hand toward it. "There is loyalty to parents . . . "

"Oh, Father," Ang Buai interrupted, "that is so unfair! There are many parents who must rely on their daughters even when they have plenty of sons. Do you imagine that all sons are perfect?"

Her father's eyes flashed with anger. "Even a worthless son carries on the family name, which is something the most faithful of daughters—supposing there are any left these days—cannot do!"

"Oh, that again!" she retorted. "Who made it so? It is a stupid idea that a child may only bear its father's name. If it is so important to the Chinese to have their name carried on, then why not let a child carry its mother's name if there are no sons in her family? If Suang U's family were here instead of in China, you would never see the children they will have. How would you feel then?"

"Of course I wouldn't like it, but a child belongs to the father's family. That is only natural."

"Father, it is natural because you think it's natural!"

Her mother joined the argument by saying, "A mother's blood flows through her child's body too, husband. And it is the mother who bears the child, after all."

Then Ang Buai laughed. "It is a good thing Father had no son," she said, "because he would probably have raised him like an egg in a bag of stones and ruined him."

"You women! Do you want this money, or would you rather stand here and argue?"

I do not believe that a man should argue with women. It is impossible to reason with them anyway. It is better to control the money. In Thai families, the wife often controls the purse, but we Chinese know better.

"Of course I want my money, Father," Ang Buai replied cheerfully, "and I humbly apologize. New Year's Day is the only time I ever get enough money to buy anything for myself. Are you going to take my money away just because I'm naughty?" She grinned at her father, and he frowned at the envelopes before him, unwilling to meet her gaze and her infectious grin.

"I certainly ought to," he grumbled.

She bowed her head penitently. "Please, Father. I want to buy a jade bracelet like Mui Eng's. It won't even have to be a very good one to serve the purpose." And she giggled, covering her mouth with her hand and glancing mischievously at me.

"What are you saying?" her mother snapped, bustling up to her. "Have you no shame before your brother-in-law?"

"Not particularly," she replied, then snatched up her envelope and flounced from the room.

"Take your money and go, then!" her father shouted after her. "Use it as you wish . . . buy a bracelet, or buy a husband who would have such a wife and—and keep the change!" He sighed, gazing at the doorway from which she had fled, then shook his head resignedly and turned to me with an expression which surprised me by its pleasantness. "It seems that my daughters are not so different after all, except in manner. One is quiet and sneaking, the other never shuts up or shows a particle of respect for her elders. They make it difficult for me to pick a favorite . . . but enough of this. It is an ill omen for the household if harsh words are spoken on this day. And tomorrow there must be absolutely none of this women's spite and foolishness, do you understand?" His wife and eldest daughter nodded quickly. "We must make our hearts calm and speak only of pleasant things on the first day of the new year. And of course, there will be no work or cooking of food in this house." He handed an envelope to me, for both of us, and another to his wife.

After only a month, he had learned the truth. But somehow I felt that he was not angry with me, in fact I was quite sure of it, and this was confirmed when he stopped me as we were preparing to leave and sent Mui Eng ahead with Father who threw me a reassuring glance over his shoulder). We stood alone in the doorway, watching them until they disappeared into the store.

"Don't let this nonsense upset us," he said gently, resting a hand on my shoulder. "I only thank the gods she didn't fall for some scoundrel who might have courted the silly child with an eye to my business. And I'm glad she didn't marry Tae Lim's sullen dullard of a nephew, if I say it myself!" He laughed quietly in the growing darkness. "Girls grow up, they think of nothing but men, and romance. Someday you will probably know for yourself what I have gone through (though for your sake I fervently hope not). Do you remember that day in the boat, when I told you I hesitated to be more strict with her for fear she would run off and shame me?"

I nodded, embarrassed in spite of his kindness.

"Well, today I was reminded of an old Chinese saying. Not quaint, perhaps, but apt. 'Be strict with a daughter and she will run off to your shame; let her fly free as a bird and she will befoul your head.' And there's another one I rather like, quite appropriate to the circumstances, too. 'If the bitch hadn't wagged her tail, what dog would have dared to follow?'"

I burned with shame, but Nguan Thong only roared with laughter and slapped me on the back. "All right, son—go home. May the new year bring us profit." Then he turned and shuffled back into his store, still chuckling at his own jokes.

So passed my first New Year's celebration in Thailand.

—

LETTER #16   FIRST MONTH, THIRTEENTH DAY
14 FEBRUARY 1946   YEAR OF THE DOG

A NEW year, a new era in my life. Many things are happening, some bringing joy and some bringing worry. You taught me that there are three things no man may escape in his lifetime: work, sorrow, and illness. Of these, work and illness concern us most as the year begins. You will be surprised to learn that ever since the holidays I have had to look after my father-in-law's business. He has not been well. Fortunately, our own business, Father's and mine, has not yet attracted so many customers that I am unable to help Nguan Thong. I find it hard to call him father, and still hear myself calling him by his name, or even Thaokae, but if he notices he doesn't seem to mind.

He has a peculiar ailment. There is a lump on his neck which seems to be growing larger at an alarming speed. It doesn't hurt, but it is annoying and unattractive. At first, he tried to cure it by applying healing leaves and herbs, but they didn't help. Then he went to the Chinese doctor for a salve, and that didn't help either. He is also very tired, although I don't see why a lump on a man's neck would make his whole body tired. Perhaps there is something else wrong with him. At any rate, Ang Buai tried to convince him to go to a foreign doctor, but he would have none of that, at least not at her suggestion.

"What, and have foreigners poking their knives into me? Never. One slip, they'd sever a blood vessel, and then what? There would be your old father lying dead, and would the foreigner care? Hah! My neck doesn't hurt, and I wouldn't go running to foreigners if it did."

"But Father, foreign doctors use knives and operate on people only when they have to. They know many things the Chinese doctors don't They might even have a treatment that would cure you without an operation. I'm not promising they will, but you won't know unless you go to the foreign hospital and let them examine you."

"They're not going to examine me," he grumbled. "I've heard all about them. Whatever they can't figure out how to cure, they slice off or cut out."

I know that this lump is not a sudden thing, for I noticed it weeks ago. At first it was tiny, like a mole, and he kept his collar buttoned over it so that no one would notice. I realize now that he should have gone to a doctor then, when it began, but like many people Nguan Thong believes that an illness or affliction which came by itself will go away by itself. I have never seen anything quite like it. The lump seems to have a life of its own, growing and changing shape week by week.

If Ang Buai had no success in getting her father to see a foreign doctor, his old friend Yong Chua was more clever. One afternoon when Nguan Thong was resting in bed, as he does most days now, we went to visit him. I carried a large basket of fruit, Father a book. While I was peeling an orange for Nguan Thong, I glanced at the book and was surprised to see that it was a copy of *Three Kingdoms*. Strange that he should bring that, I thought, for it is a book we Chinese know almost by heart.

They chatted for a long while before Father's purpose became clear. "Well, my old friend," he began, "I see that your youngest daughter is as sassy as ever, carrying on about the foreigners and their 'new' idea of cutting into people to cure sickness. The truth is, we Chinese invented operations thousands of years ago."

On these words, Ang Buai entered the room. "Oh, Uncle, we all know what the Chinese doctors do. They hold your wrist, so—" She grasped her own wrist, frowned at it fiercely, then looked up at Yong Chua with mock solemnity. "Your pulse shows, my dear fellow, that you have an infected liver, a bad heart, and too much blood!" She dropped her hands then, and grinned mischievously. "And if your ailment is external, why, they have any number of filthy poultices to choose from—a few dirty herbs, a dirtier bandage, and then what? Usually you get better because you're healthy anyway, and you go on believing the Chinese doctor is a clever fellow."

Father smiled, amused. "Don't you know that the foreign doctors you so admire use many of the same 'dirty herbs'? They simply clean them up, process them, and package them in pills and potions to impress people like you. Medicine doesn't grow inside a pill, niece. Someone has to put it in there."

"How do you know?" she asked, slightly deflated.

"You forget that I have spent many years at sea and have traveled to every nation in Asia that can be reached by ship. I have seen much illness, and much doctoring. Ang Buai, how well have you read *Three Kingdoms*?"

"Oh, that," she said, glancing at the book on the bedside table and wriggling her nose impatiently. "It's all about wars that happened ages and ages ago. I don't see what it has to do with a growth on Father's neck."

"That's where you're wrong. Have you forgotten Hua To, the surgeon who offered to operate on Cho Cho's hand? Cho Cho wouldn't allow it, and the doctor was killed, though he was the father of surgery."

"Father of surgery, indeed," she repeated scornfully. "That is only fiction."

"Perhaps, but it tells us that surgery was known by the Chinese many, many ages ago. Now it is a science reborn among the foreigners, but you cannot deny that it was a Chinese science long before. What do you think, cousin?" He turned to Nguan Thong.

"I—I really couldn't say," he replied, blinking rapidly. "I never finished *Three Kingdoms* . . . "

"Well, then, this is a fine time to do so. If I know you, you'll never have so much time on your hands again. As soon as you get rid of that nuisance under your chin, you'll be busy day and night making up for lost time."

The next afternoon, Nguan Thong demanded to be taken to the foreigners' hospital to "get this nonsense over with." I visited with him and helped him dress while Ang Buai went to fetch a *samlo*.

"I read that part about the Chinese surgeon," he said gruffly, pulling on the shirt I had taken from the closet for him. "And Yong Chua was quite right. People in those days had operations all the time. It was nothing. Frankly," he said, lowering his voice, "that Cho Cho must have been a bit of a coward. And we did start the whole thing. I only wish we had kept it up so that I could go to one of our own people instead of some jabbering foreigner with red hair. I'll be surprised if he's any better than old Hua To. Hah!"

He paused in the midst of pulling up his slacks, frowned, then jerked them up and fastened his belt. "The store is what worries me most, Suang U. If this foreigner decides to cut off the damned lump, what will happen to the business while I'm in the hospital?"

"Mui Eng and Father can easily take care of our store, and I will be here. You mustn't worry."

"Thank you, son." Glancing toward the door quickly, then, as if fearful of being overheard, he moved closer to me and said, almost in a whisper, "Stay on top of the books, boy. Don't trust the Thais in the shop. And never put off your book work. Do it every day—here, and over there in your own place, too."

Then we left the bedroom, and he descended the stairs leaning on my arm. Why is he so weak? I wondered, and felt a sudden stab of fear at what the foreign doctor might find. Aug Bui was waiting at the curb with the *samlo*. She smiled and held her arm out to her father, and I returned to my store.

I am more worried than I would admit to him. If his illness proves to be serious, what then? I had to make an important decision, one that I felt even Father could not help me make. Already some of Nguan Thong's employees had begun to gossip about my taking over, and though I don't understand all their words, I do understand the Thai word for "inheritance." I cannot jeopardize my pride by walking into Nguan Thong's job the day he leaves for the hospital, except to help Ang Buai take over. And that, I have decided, is the only answer. She is capable, but I am not yet sure his pride will allow a daughter to have the business he meant for a son.

Mainly as the result of an argument I had with Kim late this afternoon, Ang Buai will begin to supervise her father's employees tomorrow morning. He came into the office just after she had stepped out to go upstairs and check on her father, napping after his visit to the hospital.

"Can I talk to you for a minute, alone?"

"What's on your mind, Kim?"

"Well, I just wonder if it's such a good idea for you to spend so much time with your sister-in-law . . . "

"Don't even tell me. I can guess. The guys in the shop are talking about us." Kim nodded quickly, embarrassed. "Look, Kim. The old man is sick, and he may stay sick for a long time. What if he doesn't recover at all? It's a terrible thought, but I have to think about that possibility. Who would run this place then? Whatever your buddies in the shop may think, I don't want it. I'm teaching the business to Ang Buai right under her mother's nose, every day at noon. Is that the best they can do for something to gossip about? In a few weeks, she'll be on her own, and I'll be back next door where I belong."

Unexpectedly, Kim laughed. "You expect those guys to take orders from a girl?"

And then, I am sorry to tell you, I lost my temper. "You're damned right I do—starting tomorrow! How do you like that?"

I could not take back my words. I had been planning to start her at the beginning of next month, if her father agreed, but we may as well get it over with now and see what adjustments will have to be made. As for Nguan Thong, maybe it is better to say nothing to him, for to say anything is to admit that I am afraid for his life, and I suspect he has had such thoughts himself.

The doctor sent him back home after a brief examination. They took blood from his arm but did not tell him what is wrong, or what caused the lump on his neck. He will go back to see the doctor next week, so perhaps I will have better news in my next letter. Father says that many Chinese people have been cured of their illnesses by doctors at the foreign hospital, when Chinese doctors had failed to help them.

I HAVE not written to you in almost a month because we have been very busy and had many problems. The foreign doctor is not going to operate on Nguan Thong, and frankly I don't know what he is doing. I think Ang Buai knows more than she is telling the rest of us, but she is unwilling to talk about it, which is unusual for her.

If that were not enough to worry about, Nguan Thong's employees reacted as badly as Kim had predicted to her taking over operation of the business. At least, one of them did, and he has caused us all trouble.

His name is Saeng, and he is a young Thai laborer, insolent, lazy, and sometimes drunk even before the day begins. I don't know how Nguan Thong ever came to hire him. Kim says he thinks the man's parents came to ask that he be hired because they are very poor, and Nguan Thong felt sorry for them. I can't ask him myself, because I don't want him to know what has happened.

The first morning Ang Buai took charge, I stayed with her in the store to help explain the situation to the employees.

"So, a kid is running the shop now," said Saeng, grinning broadly at Ang Buai. She stiffened with embarrassment but continued to look straight into his eyes.

"My father is ill, and I have to take his place. If you don't want to take orders from a girl, you don't have to. Go work somewhere else."

He dropped the insolent smile. "Yeah, I'll go," he said, looking her up and down in a very ugly way. Then he turned and loped non-chalantly out of the store.

Ang Buai quickly dispatched the other men to their jobs, and in their relief they all but tripped over one another rushing out to begin the day's work.

"Go home, Suang U," she said, "and give me time. That's all I need."

"I know, but . . . call me if you need anything."

"I will, thanks." She smiled, pulled some ledgers from a shelf, and sat down to begin the morning's billing and correspondence. Nguan Thong always began the day by reviewing the previous day's business, but she does things in her own way, which is good. Suddenly she seems more of a woman than a mischievous girl.

The next day I had a headache and, instead of making my usual noon visit next door, I lay down upstairs to take a short nap. Ang Buai was working alone; all the employees were out on jobs. Her mother had gone to market and, unknown to me, Nguan Thong had gone to the foreign hospital with a neighbor who had kindly offered to take him there for his appointment. (He goes every week, but what they do for him, I don't know.)

If only I had known—but it does little good to regret what cannot be changed. Saeng had been looking for just such a chance, hiding across the street in an alley, waiting until everyone had left the store. Next door, I was just falling asleep when I heard her cry out. I leaped out of bed, down the stairs, and ran through the back yards into Nguan Thong's shop, slamming the back door behind me. When Saeng heard the door bang, he turned and bolted, leaving Ang Buai huddled in a corner of the office, shaking with fear and outrage.

I helped her up, weak with relief to find that she was, if disheveled and terrified, unhurt. She rubbed one shoulder absently as she tried to blink back tears. "Please, please don't tell anyone," she said, her voice shaking. "I know I can manage . . . I know it! He won't come back now, and if Father should find out . . . " She shut her eyes tightly and covered her face with her hands. "Oh, please go home," she sobbed. "I don't want you to see me like this."

Her determination is incredible. I vowed that this would never happen again, but to tell the truth I couldn't feel as angry with Saeng as I wanted to. More than angry, I felt embarrassed for a man who could bring himself to bully a young girl. When Kim returned from the dock that afternoon, I told him that he must see to it Ang Buai was never left alone again. Of course, this aroused his suspicions, though he wasn't sure quite what to suspect. As things were to turn out, I should have told him and everyone else exactly what had happened, but that day I could think only of Ang Buai's plea for time to prove herself.

"What's the matter?" Kim asked. "Why are you so worried about her being alone?"

"Why shouldn't I worry about her? Damn it, Kim, do as I ask for a change, would you?"

He looked at me curiously for a moment, then said "All right, boss, whatever you say," and strolled out of the office, whistling softly.

I was annoyed, but not nearly as annoyed as I was by my wife's behavior that evening at supper. The minute I sat down at the kitchen table, I knew something was wrong. When she set down the serving bowl of rice, she could have pounded a nail through the table top with it.

"If you were sick today, why did you have to go running over there?"

"Frankly, I was just dozing off when I heard your sister call for help."

I heaped my plate with rice and passed the bowl to her.

"Well, what was the matter with her?"

"Nothing. She thought she saw a thief running from the alley across the street, that's all." I spooned curried chicken and fish onto my plate and began to eat. Mui Eng chewed her food angrily, the little muscles in her jaw popping up and down. Her eyes weighed me suspiciously as she decided whether or not to believe me. And I didn't care if she believed me or not. I am learning to ignore her outbursts of temper. She will never threaten me with her temper, as she did her father.

The next day at noon, I looked in on Ang Buai. She was busy and in good spirits, and since there was no reason for me to stay, I went upstairs to chat with her father for a few minutes and then left. When I arrived home, I found Mui Eng leaning across the counter on her elbows, her expression stiff and sullen.

"So, you can't leave her alone for even one day, can you? At the stroke of noon, there you are, hanging over her desk!"

66

This was my beloved, the face of the moon? When I recovered from my astonishment, I began to feel disgust. Jealousy is no friend of beauty. I left her fuming there and went about my work, too angry to answer her silly accusation. I decided to haul some rice sacks in from the back yard and, hopefully, work off my anger. But before I had half begun dragging the heavy sacks into the back room and stacking them, I caught a glimpse of Mui Eng dashing across the path to her father's house. Before she even reached the door, she began shouting to Ang Buai in a voice loud enough for all the neighborhood to hear.

"What are you trying to do, whispering and flirting with my husband? It's gone on long enough, do you hear me? What's the matter, Little Sister, can't you find a man of your own?"

I slipped into the back of Nguan Thong's shop and listened, horrified.

"Oh, Sister," Ang Buai replied, "how can you say such a thing? He comes here to work, to help me, to visit Father . . ."

"Indeed. I see you sitting here with your faces together day after day. Do you think I'm stupid?"

"All he does is teach me bookkeeping. Do you think he can do that from across the room? As long as Father is ill, what choice do I have?"

Mui Eng ignored the question. "If he misses a day, you can't stand it, can you? You'll even scream thief to get him out of bed when he's sick . . ."

"Is that what he told you?"

"What do you mean by that?"

"Nothing. You know I've never flirted with a man in my life. I don't know what else I can say . . . please go home."

"He's handsome, isn't he? And you like him . . . admit it. I've seen the way you look at him."

"How dare you? You're the one who knows how to act around a man, Sister. Why don't you keep him locked in a closet, if you think other women are all like you? How dare you call me a flirt when you threw yourself at him the way you did . . . like you threw the jade bracelet!"

"So you did see me, you lying little bitch . . . you made all that fuss just to amuse yourself, and to punish me because he never looked at you! I should have known, and I should have slapped your face then like I'm going to slap it now!"

I heard scuffling noises, but no slap. Ang Buai was more agile than her elder sister. Women arguing . . . one jealous, the other hurt and humiliated, both ugly in their rage. For once Mui Eng's cold reserve had deserted her, and as I stepped into the office, it occurred to me that they looked like a pair of witches in the Chinese opera, squared off at each other across a desk instead of over a steaming cauldron of wicked potions.

I crossed the room and took my wife's arm firmly. "Have you no shame before the neighbors? In a moment you'll have them all out on the sidewalk watching your performance. Is that what you want?"

"I'm not ashamed of anything," she retorted, thrusting her little chin out stubbornly. "Let the neighbors see who has cause to be ashamed!"

I felt the blood rush to my head. "You dared to go around me like this, to run to Ang Buai with this—this nonsense instead of coming to me!"

"Why not?" she asked angrily. "You ignored me. You walked right past me as if I were nothing." Her lower lip began to tremble. "A stupid sack of rice is more important to you than me."

"I will not be the victim of your temper, Mui Eng. If Ang Buai were the elder sister rather than you, I'd make you get down on your knees and apologize to her."

Then I seized her arm and marched her out of the store through the back door. She stumbled along the path next to me, sobbing with rage. "If you ever do a stupid, shameful thing like this again," I said, "I will take another wife, and it won't be your sister. Maybe I'll find a cute little Thai girl in that bar down the street, one who would show some respect for her husband!"

Mui Eng's mouth dropped open and she stared up at me, her eyes wide with disbelief. I had to struggle not to laugh. Could she believe I would do such a thing?

It is time to close this letter. In addition to everything else, Mui Eng is sick. In fact, right now she's throwing up, and furious because I'm writing to you instead of tending to her. She won't go to a doctor—like father, like daughter. But don't worry, I'm sure she'll be well by the next time I write.

IN THIS letter you will find good news. Our first child has been conceived, and before many months pass you will be a grandmother.

Mui Eng is still sick and irritable, dizzy and nauseated all the time, but how happy I was to learn that your grandchild is the cause of it! I've been too happy to speak to her further about the silly incident with her sister, and of course Ang Buai says nothing. She works hard and manages very well, as I knew she would. Now that that drunken brute has gone for good (she was right, we never saw him after that day), she is perfectly capable of assuming responsibility for her father's business.

But I don't want to write about that. I want to write only of my coming child. I am about to become a father, and how shall I ever express my feelings? When Mui Eng first told me, I couldn't believe my ears. We have not been married long, and now we are to be parents, but I was unprepared for my own response to the most natural result of taking a wife.

"I'm pregnant." Such was her blunt reply when I asked her why she wouldn't see a doctor. For a moment I was too shocked to speak.

"I said I'm pregnant. There's nothing the matter with me."

I continued to stare at her, and I seemed to hear my own thoughts shouted at me from far away: "Suang U is going to be a father! Suang U's wife is going to have a baby!"

Mui Eng frowned. "Well, why don't you say something?"

"I can't believe it! A baby! A boy or a girl? Oh, it must be a boy, Mui Eng!—a son, and I shall call him . . . what? I know! I shall call him Weng Khim—Tan Weng Khim. Don't you think that's a fine name?" I seized both her hands, and I was filled with joy.

She closed her eyes for a moment, sighed, and pulled her hands away. "How can I tell you that it will be a boy? I could just as easily be a girl, you know."

"No, I don't want a girl. I want a son . . . Mui Eng, please give me a son, no girl, no stubborn little girl like her mama." I grinned at her, but she would not return it. "I want to raise a family of sons, not daughters to carry other men's names."

"You sound just like my father. It's ridiculous—I can't promise you sons. If it's a boy, fine, but maybe I would like a pretty little girl, Suang U . . . Don't I have that right, to want a girl child?"

"The eldest must be a son," I said firmly. "Let girls come later. Do you think he will look like me?"

She shrugged and turned away. "You're very odd, Suang U," she said, then lifted a hand to her mouth to cover a yawn. "I need a nap, and it's almost time to close the shop anyway. Can you watch the counter for an hour?" Without waiting for a reply, she went upstairs, and in a moment I heard the bedroom door close.

What shallow thinking! "A pretty little girl," and no thought for the future. A son lives with his parents all their lives, and honors them after they die. His wife honors them, and their children. Who in China ever wanted daughters besides the rich, who could afford to dress them up like dolls and show them off? The poor don't want daughters, for they cannot work as hard as sons, and usually they are not even considered worth the wedding gifts poor parents must scrape together or lose face before their son-in-law. And what does his family lose? Nothing, and they gain everything. She accused me of sounding "just like her father." Yes, I suppose I do sound like him, because I understand him. He still thinks like a poor man, as I do. Even a poor woman would understand. Only a rich, spoiled girl would announce that she wanted "a pretty little girl." The phrase continues to annoy me.

My first thought was to share our good news with her parents, and as soon as I had closed the shop I ran next door. Their door was already closed, and I shouted and knocked until someone came to let me in.

"It's you!" Ang Buai said, unlocking the door and peering out at me. "I hardly recognized your voice." She swung the door open and I entered the darkened store.

"Ang Buai, good news! You are going to be an aunt!"

"Well, well. Congratulations."

"I want to tell your parents right away."

"They're up there," she said, nodding toward the stairs. "Go on up."

"Don't you want to go up with me?"

"I think I'll stay downstairs for awhile. I have work to do."

I sprinted up the stairs, two at a time, and as I reached the second floor Nguan Thong stuck his head out the bedroom door. Even in my dazzled state of mind, I couldn't help being struck by the change in his appearance over the past week. He looked gray and thin and old, and the growth on his neck bulged out menacingly over his collar. When he spoke, he seemed to have difficulty getting his breath.

"Whatever is the matter, son? I thought we had burglars when I heard all that racket on the stairs."

Then his wife appeared beside him, smiling broadly. "It's Little Cat, isn't it?" she beamed when she saw my face. I nodded happily. "She didn't tell me, but I thought this illness of hers was suspicious," and she reached up and patted my cheek fondly.

Nguan Thong looked bewildered for a moment, then he began to grin as he realized the truth. "Good for her, boy, and good for you!" he said, gripping my shoulder. "Two months married, and going to be a father. Why, that's better than most of us did in my day—look at that blush, Mother—ha ha ha!"

"Yes, sir. If it's a boy, I'm going to call him Weng Khim."

My mother-in-law raised a hand to her breast nervously. "Suang U, remember that we are not given to choose—"

"Quiet, woman!" her husband snapped, glaring at her. "Mui Eng may not be as inefficient as her mother at producing sons. Why, if I had had any sense I'd have taken another wife long ago and kept on trying. But I've always been too busy," he grumbled, "and now I'm too sick. So it's up to Little Cat to put my blood into sons."

"You have a daughter who runs your business as well as any man's son," she said, undaunted, "and still you carry on with this silly talk. You'd better start considering her feelings!"

"I—of course I consider her feelings, "he muttered irritably. "But it isn't the same. She does the work, yes, but can she leave here alone, or go anywhere at night? And how does it look to my friends—'Nguan Thong and Daughter'— bah!" He turned to me, seeming suddenly tired. "Good luck, Suang U—better luck than mine." He smiled, his face full of kindness. And full of hope; the hope, I am afraid, that he will look into the eyes of his first grandson before his own close forever.

BEFORE GOING on to other matters, I wish to write about the money I have been sending you. You know that I have sent a bit whenever I could, but I want you to know also that none of this money has come from the profits of our business. I have taken it from the salary I allow myself. It would be impossible for me to accept all that Yong Chua has done for me if I did not dedicate every day's work to repaying him. He thinks of me as a true son, of that I have no doubt, but, for my part, I feel that I owe him more than if I were his son by blood.

Whatever work we do in this life, problems attach themselves to us. When I lived at home, our problems were the most basic man can face. Too little rain to nurture our growing crops, too much sun, insects gnawing our precious rice shoots. And, in some years, flood. You taught me that we Chinese never allow misfortune to ravage us. We fight, and when we can fight no longer, we move on and continue the struggle of life elsewhere, hoping that success will at last be ours before the struggle is over. With this philosophy to sustain us, the world is ours to roam, and strange lands do not daunt us. For we know that we shall remain Chinese wherever we find ourselves. We do not choose our occupations; we accept them as they appear. A farmer becomes a businessman when the earth is parched and trade is good. This we can do because of our most essential quality: will. When there is no other work to be had, we work as coolies, laboring at the meanest tasks, and still we do not give in to despair, for nothing in life is permanent unless we allow it to be so, and many a wealthy man once hauled other men's riches on his back.

Here on Sampheng Lane, there is no drought, rainy season flooding in the streets is inconvenient at worst, and the only insects we fight are mosquitoes, ants, and roaches. But I must stretch my wits to conquer . . . my customers.

"The fruit I bought at the orchard last week was half this price," a customer complained yesterday. He leaned across the counter, an old Chinese merchant in a tattered, faded blue shirt tied loosely at the waist with a length of frayed rope. (He is rich, tatter and all.) "How much

72

profit do you expect, young man?" He peeled a rambutan, dropped the peel onto the floor, and ate the fruit slowly, never taking his shrewd old eyes from mine.

"This is not an orchard, sir," I replied, returning his steady gaze. "Of course fruit is cheaper at an orchard. But how much time do you waste going there and coming back? I am sure a man like yourself has more to do with his time than haul baskets of fruit up and down the Chao Phraya River to save a few baht."

"All right, my friend," he said, his eyes twinkling, "I can see you are a suitable addition to your father-in-law's household. I will accept your robbery this time."

But not all our customers are so agreeable as this charming old man, and some of the Thais mutter under their breath about "the greedy *chek*," though they depend on us to extend them credit.

In business, too, there are insects that would devour the tender shoots, in particular the customers who pay on a monthly basis. Most of these are either Nguan Thong's employees or Thai neighbors who work for their government in menial jobs. These people never seem to be able to make ends meet. They charge rice, fruit, noodles, dried shrimps, even peanuts, and my problem with them you can easily guess. At the end of the month, several familiar faces around the neighborhood vanish overnight. Then I have to pay my "visits," which I detest. Last Sunday was one such visiting day.

The customer, a Thai woman of about thirty, sat cross-legged on her rickety front porch peeling bananas, dropping them into a wok of bubbling oil over a charcoal pot, then pushing them slowly in circles with a large, battered spoon.

"Why do you come after us for such a little bit of money?" She did not look up, but spat over the side of the porch onto a pile of rubbish below while continuing to stir the bananas. "Do you think I would cheat you?"

"I only want to know when you'll pay."

"You can wait a few days, at your prices. I wouldn't bother to cheat a *chek* grocer out of ten baht."

"I don't want to argue with you. I just want my money."

"Then go ask my husband for it."

"Where is he?"

73

She poked an arm in the direction of a circle of men squatting in a circle several yards from the house. They were gambling, shouting and laughing, drinking beer. This is their way. Instead of working an extra day to pay off the bills, or even taking a day of true rest, they spend their free time gambling. They say it is another way of making extra money, but gambling is only another stone dragging a poor family down. I saw that in Nguan Thong's shop, where many of his employees gambled their wages away, depriving their wives and children.

"No, lady. You get it from him. You're the one who buys in my store. I don't even know him."

"When he's gambling," she said, continuing to avoid my eyes, "I'm afraid of him. When he gets angry, he beats me." She grinned nervously, and her husband turned to look up at us.

"Hey *chek!*" he shouted drunkenly. "You like getting rich in Thailand?" He turned to his friend. "It ain't enough to charge double what the food is worth—this guy gets interest on a lousy ten baht besides. Ten baht! "Richer, the *chek* gets richer," he sang out, waving his hands in the air. He sucks the money out of people who belong here . . . hey, *chek*! Why don't you go back where you came from? You think you can get interest on ten baht from another *chek*?" He snatched up a half-full bottle of beer. "You know better, don't you? You're gonna stay right here where all the suckers are, right?" He tipped his head back and drained the rest of the beer, then wiped his mouth with the back of his hand and turned his back to me.

What could I do? At least ten of his friends were with him. And if I let him provoke me, if we ever went to court, what Thai judge would take my side against his own countryman? Many Thais feel hatred for us, it is true. There is no mistaking it. I suspect that envy is the main reason. Surely they could do as we do, but it only makes them hate us more because they don't want to. They don't want anything badly enough to "work like a *chek*."

Another problem in the store is that many of our customers are too quick with their hands. While I'm measuring a sack of rice, they're stealing half a dozen eggs. If I had as many eyes as a pineapple I still couldn't catch them at it.

In spite of everything, the business is coming along well, our profits are increasing, and I like the work I do. After all, I never expected to become a rich man overnight anyway. I am strong and young, and before many years have gone by, my son will work beside me.

—

THERE IS nothing in this world on which we may entirely depend, least of all our fellow human beings. Nguan Thong, his wife, and Ang Buai decided, quite suddenly, to move to a newly built row of shops some distance from here. They will sell only over the counter, and the wholesale side of the business will be discontinued.

I was under the impression that they would stay here until the landlord put up new buildings on this site. That is what Father told me long ago, and what influenced me to suspect that Ang Buai is responsible for this unexpected step. I was told nothing until everything was resolved. It is useless to pretend, least of all to you, that I was not hurt and angry to have been told last, and then only by my wife.

"My father is moving the business," Mui Eng began casually, "to a new block. Very fancy, Mother says."

"What are you saying? No one told me anything about this."

She shrugged. "I don't know. I wondered myself. At first I thought you were the one who knew and weren't telling me—it would have been like you. But she said no, they hadn't told you.

"She . . . Ang Buai?"

"Who else? The business will be easier for her over there, she says. No more deliveries, no runners, no coolies. She says Father is too old for it and she doesn't want it. You should hear her brag . . . she wants this, she won't do that . . ."

"That's fine with me. Let her learn a thing or two on her own," I grumbled, knowing that such words were meaningless.

"Maybe we should try to find a husband for her. She'll end up an old maid otherwise, believe me. And, well, it isn't right for her to run everything like that," she added. So she is jealous of Ang Buai in this, too.

In the evening, I went next door, feeling a little sheepish as I faced Ang Buai in the doorway. But she was pleasant enough, inviting me into the kitchen to eat a dish of the dessert she had just finished making.

I sat down, bumping a table leg with my knee and then laughing stupidly.

"Don't ask me, I'll tell you," she said, setting a plate and spoon before me. "We found a shop we like better, that's all. It's new, nicer than this place. You'll see it before long." She dished out a generous helping of bean jelly and coconut cream for both of us.

Gathering my courage, I asked her "What will you sell over there?"

She laughed. "What do you expect? Just about what we sell here, only no deliveries, no wholesale import items."

"That's what Mui Eng said." I blushed furiously, cursing myself for answering my own question.

"We're letting all the men go."

"Yes, Mui Eng mentioned that too. Well, I may as well come right out and ask you—why didn't you discuss it with me?"

"Why should I have done that? My parents agreed with me, and you're busy in your own place."

"Then it was your idea, wasn't it?"

"Why should I depend on you? I won't have any trouble. Maybe we'll hire a couple of girls, that's all I need. No men in the shop . . . I've learned my lesson."

"Ang Buai, all men are not like that crazy Saeng. You can have men in your shop without that kind of trouble."

She looked at me steadily for a few moments, then smiled. "Suang U, what makes you think I meant that? Didn't it occur to you that perhaps I don't want any more green-eyed wives stalking me?"

We finished the dessert in silence.

I climbed the stairs to Nguan Thong's room slowly, taking time to prepare what I wanted to say to him. When I entered his room, he put down a book, hoisted himself up against the pillows painfully, and motioned me to sit next to him.

"You make such a sad face, tch tch! Can it be as serious as all that? Sit, have a cup of tea and talk to me." He leaned over and poured two cups of pale tea from a little table piled with medicine bottles, bills and letters. "You are always so in earnest," he said. "It is not necessary, you know . . . Here, have some nice hot tea."

I took the steaming cup from his hand and sipped it slowly, gathering my courage. "It seems a bit sudden to me. Your being sick and all."

"Sudden that I'm sick?" He frowned slightly.

"I mean, sudden that while you're sick, you would move. That—that seems sudden to me, yes, sir."

"Ah, well that isn't going to matter . . . " He looked out the window just as a chain of rice barges appeared, gliding heavily down our *khlong* on its way to the river, and was silent until the last barge had disappeared from view.

"All that remains is to transfer our residence legally from this district to the new one, and you and the movers can do everything else. I'm not paying any of the employees this month's wages until we're moved in, so I think you can count on their enthusiastic help."

"Must you transfer legally to a new district every time you move?"

"Indeed. The tax authorities take a dim view of unannounced relocation."

"Oh. Who found the new shop for you?"

"Who else? Ang Buai, and I can see by your face that you know it. Suang U, you may be the worst liar I've ever met. She has a friend there, and when she learned that one of the new leases was being cancelled, she was first in line to pick it up. We'll have an extra room, and I'm sure it will be easier for her there than here, where I've always been boss. You were right about her, you know, but I don't want to have to listen to any 'I told you so's' from my wife, so please keep it to yourself."

"I will," I smiled. "What about this shop?"

"Already leased to a new tenant. I have something else to discuss with you tonight, while we're alone. When I leave here, I want to turn over to you all the customers we won't be able to take care of anymore. You know them all, and of course Yong Chua's known most of them for years. It's child's play, really—our credit is good, their credit is good. Most of them are Chinese, and serious about business. They don't play at it like Thais."

"They are . . . in earnest?" I asked, grinning at him.

"Very good. In earnest, yes. Even Ang Buai, a woman—look at her! There's nothing so special or smart about her. She's just a damned hard worker." But Nguan Thong was unable to conceal his great pride in this daughter, and I was glad to see it.

He leaned back against the pillows and closed his eyes, but when I got up to leave a few moments later, he opened them again and motioned me to stay.

"I have lived in this land many tens of years, Suang U, and I have learned much about my own people seeing them struggle and often prosper among people of another race. What makes us so different, and what keeps us that way? I have thought much about it over the past few weeks. Listening to Thais talk about the Chinese, you would think we all came from one village, were born of the same father and mother, and all think and act alike. So many thousand grains of rice thrown into one basket. Still, I can understand why we appear that way to them. We are strangers here, and we know that we must share our strength. Our rich keep an eye on our poor, and we do not look down on our weaker brothers. We all need each other. This I have believed all the tens of years I have lived in Thailand, and I very much hope that you will believe it too. It will serve you well." He closed his eyes again, yawned, and said, "Now you go downstairs and talk to your mother-in-law for awhile. and let me get on with this business of dying." He raised his hand swiftly. "Do not contradict me. I refuse to open my eyes and see the shocked look on your face. Don't be shocked. It is natural to die, the most natural thing a man does in his life, and the most honest. And I will speak of it as much as I like." Then Nguan Thong nestled down into his pillow gently, pulled the blanket up to his ravaged neck, and slept.

Downstairs, I was relieved to find that Ang Buai had gone to her room, and her mother sat alone at the kitchen table, chopping vegetables. Deftly she scraped them off the chopping block onto a plate, and soon the plate was covered with neat mounds of onion, pepper, tomato, and crushed garlic. "There," she said, "that's done, Now we can talk," She pushed her chair back briskly, got up and washed her hands at the sink, then covered the plate of vegetables carefully with a soup dish. "I am going to tell you something, Suang U," she began, wiping her hands on a towel and sitting down beside me. "When women are pregnant, they find life a little more difficult. Things which never bothered them before suddenly become important. They become irritable over nothing, and Mui Eng is no exception! Now, talk to me." She smiled encouragingly.

"It's just that she speaks out before she thinks, sometimes, and . . .

78

and I'm afraid she's been unfair to Ang Buai." I didn't know how far I ought to impose on her encouragement, or how much she already knew.

"Unfair, eh? I'd say she's behaved wretchedly toward Ang Buai!" She laughed heartily then, and I couldn't help but laugh too. "I saw the two of them that day, you know. I was just coming downstairs to stop them when I saw you enter the room, so I hid on the landing and watched . . . ah, but you were impressive!" She chuckled and patted my hand affectionately. "What are you blushing about now? You were a good, strong husband. The two of them were a sight, I must say. Black in the face, screaming at each other like a pair of hags in the market place. Shameful?" She shrugged. "Maybe, but mostly very silly."

"I'm sorry—"

"Don't be! It isn't your fault. Soon we'll be gone, and anyway you mustn't scold your wife for acting pregnant. It is better to forget what happened, don't you think?"

"Do all pregnant women act like that?"

"Some more, some less. But she'll behave better as her tummy grows, believe me. They all do."

"Please tell me, has she been here other times? I mean, here acting like that?"

"Remember that they are sisters," she replied evasively, "They know each other well . . . it will come all right in the end, you'll see. Now!" She clasped her hands together and smiled. "Let's talk about something else. I know that Nguan Thong is going to turn many of his old customers over to you. Let me congratulate you. I know you will do a fine job."

"Well, it isn't settled yet," I said. "It's a big responsibility, and I will have to talk it over with Yong Chua first."

I felt embarrassed. What have I done to earn all the new business that is coming to Yong Chua and me? It seems my fate to have to prove I am worth the good fortune that has come to me ever since I arrived in Thailand. Perhaps I shall have to work harder justifying success than other men do earning it.

That evening, Father and I discussed Nguan Thong's plan.

"I understand your embarrassment at taking over Nguan Thong's customers," Father said, shaking his head slowly. "But you must get over that. You are the one who will have to work twice as hard, and put money out for extra help, too. You must live up to his reputation and build your own at the same time. Not many men would want to meet that challenge. If you succeed in both, and I believe you will, then you will owe no man an apology. And Suang U, the dream of a factory of our own will be realized sooner because of our new customers. Think of it that way when you have doubts."

Truthfully, it is a little hard for me to believe in Father's factory. It is overwhelming to think that I, Suang U, farmer of Po Leng village, will someday be a partner in so grand an enterprise. And I have another fear: what if I am not as capable as Father and Nguan Thong believe me to be? What if I lose the new customers through my own inexperience? I shall work harder than ever before in my life, and strive to put the fear of failure out of my mind, for I know that fear is the enemy of good judgment.

I should be pleased at expanding the business, and I guess I am; I should not have laid all my doubts open to you like this. At least, If I do well, I will be able to pay off my debt to Father sooner than I had hoped. That is another thought I should keep uppermost in my mind.

Mui Eng's stomach is growing larger, and I shall take my mother-in-law's advice. Anyway, an argument might upset my son, and he matters more than a quarrel between women.

Ang Buai has taken care of things. I have a feeling that she will do so all her life, while those about her fumble uncertainly with the complications of life. It is hard to believe that, a few short months ago when I came here, she was a flighty girl. Today she is a capable women, and even I have benefited by her wisdom.

—

LETTER #21   SEVENTH MONTH, THIRD DAY
30 JULY 1946   YEAR OF THE DOG

THE AUTUMNAL Feast Day is almost upon us, and we are busy from before dawn to dark. But it is only little, unimportant matters that concern us these days. I am happy to write that most of the important things in life seem to have straightened out. Mui Eng is well, her stomach heavy. In less than two months your grandchild will be born.

Father and I have taken on Nguan Thong's customers, as he wished, and our profits are great. Our only complaint is that we hardly have enough time for the retail business we began when I married Mui Eng. We are all exhausted, and Kim has even stopped his usual fussing. Either he's too tired to complain, or his greatly increased salary has closed his mouth.

As for my fears about taking on the new business, I simply haven't had time to be afraid! Thinking back, it seems that my worst fear was of what people would say about a son-in-law who profited so greatly by his father-in-law's illness. But no one has said anything, and Nguan Thong's customers have been understanding and good to us. Partly this is because they feel sorry for him (having no son—I have heard them speak of it), but I believe that they are satisfied with our service, too, which of course matters most.

I have now lived one year in Thailand, and therefore I had to go to the police station to pay my alien tax this morning. Mui Eng does not have to pay such a tax, because she was born here; the government considers her "Thai." I don't resent the tax, which is not any great amount, but I do resent the time I had to waste paying it. And the attitude of the officials. They demean themselves by their greed and their disdain for us. For a few baht, their service improves mightily. How small a price they are willing to put on themselves!

I arrived early at the police station, carrying my alien identification card, Father's, and Kim's, so that we wouldn't all have to waste time. The first thing I learned is that officials here don't even begin to work until eight thirty at the earliest. By that time, many other Chinese had arrived to pay their tax.

Finally, a clerk entered the office from a back door and sat down at his desk. I rose and approached him respectfully, but he snapped at me before I had reached his desk.

"Sit down! The *nai thabian* is not in yet."

"Who, sir?"

The clerk regarded me with contempt. "The man who handles such matters. He doesn't rise at dawn like a merchant."

I returned to the bench, and explained to some of the others who did not understand Thai at all.

"He says the official we have to see is still sleeping."

"Ha! Sleeping at eight thirty in the morning . . ." An old man shook his head disapprovingly.

"I believe he lives behind the station," another man said, "so perhaps once he wakes up our wait will not be too long."

After another hour, the *nai thabian* appeared and entered his own, separate office. The clerk hurriedly stuffed a morning newspaper he had been reading into the top drawer of his desk. He smirked at me then, nodded his head toward the *nai thabian*'s office, and began to work on some papers. At last, I thought, I can get this over with and return to the store. I entered the office and put the alien cards on the official's desk, waiting silently for him to notice me.

"What is this?" the *nai thabian* asked in a high querulous voice, glancing at the cards, then at me, and finally pushing the cards back across the desk angrily. "Nothing is in order. Nothing! How old is this picture, eh? No good. New picture before I do anything with this one, you understand? And where are these other people? Who do they think they are? You tell them they must appear. Who do they think they are!?" He immediately pulled some papers from a drawer and began to read them, and I understood that I had been dismissed. I backed out of the office respectfully, furious with myself and with him.

Such a foolish waste of time, If we do not pay the tax on time, we can be arrested, yet they make it almost impossible for us to do so. As I sat brooding over this state of affairs, a well-dressed Chinese man burst into the room, marched up to the clerk's desk, and tossed an envelope at him.

"Get this over with quickly, will you?" he demanded, impressing us all exceedingly. "I have no time to waste in here." He tapped his fingers impatiently on the desk top while the clerk passively fingered through the bills in the envelope. We on the bench craned our necks to see the proceedings, and it was obvious at a glance that the amount in the envelope was far higher than the Chinese alien tax! Without a word, the clerk took a blank receipt from a corner of his desk top, filled it out, and stamped the man's alien card. But for the *nai thabian*'s signature, my dear mother, this completes the transaction.

After a hurried consultation, we enlightened newcomers agreed on the probable amount in the envelope, and I was dispatched to a shop on the corner to buy a dozen plain white envelopes. Before very long, we were filing up to the desk, and will you believe that the clerk's face showed not a particle of shame as he filled a little sack in the bottom drawer of his desk? You may be sure that we received no receipt for our contributions to his efficiency.

When it was almost noon, our benefactor with the drawer full of bribes informed us that our papers would be ready after the *nai thabian* returned from lunch. When we showed signs of waiting, he waved in the direction of the door and scowled, "Go on, get out of here! And don't come back before one o'clock!"

Apparently it is the clerk's understanding that the government pays him to read the newspaper and we pay him to work, little of that as he does. By two o'clock, it had become evident that the *nai thabian* takes more time for lunch than those who wait upon him. At four o'clock, he was in his office but we had not yet been called. I felt I might spring up at any moment and throttle the sneering clerk (who had begun to read the afternoon newspaper). He glanced at me over the paper, seemed to briefly judge my frame of mind, and shoved some papers across the desk, nodding almost imperceptibly to indicate that they were mine.

I returned to the store with a terrible pain behind my eyes. How can that clerk bear to waste his days reading newspapers, collecting bribes, and bullying those who come to him for help? Shall a man rise in the morning, like the *nai thabian*, only to look forward to lunch, dinner, and falling into his bed again at night? I will never understand.

I suppose the incident is of no importance, and I'm making too much of it. But I had to talk to someone about it, and Mui Eng would probably think me mad for getting upset about it. She thinks only of money, food, and taking care of herself. Her father said that Mui Eng cared nothing about money. She has learned to care about it a great deal.

Much work awaits me tomorrow, as a result of today's waste. I may be writing to you less often in the near future, but you know that I shall not think of you less.

LETTER #22   NINTH MONTH, FIFTH DAY
29 SEPTEMBER 1946   YEAR OF THE DOG

I WARNED you that my next letter might be long in coming, and

83

apologize that it has indeed been two months since I last wrote. Even tonight, I must beg your patience, for I am almost too tired to make sense.

Nguan Thong, his wife, and Ang Buai moved a little over a month ago. For two days, Father and I and the employees from both shops packed, hauled, and cleaned. Mui Eng refused to go see the new store, complaining that the birth is too near. I suspected that she was embarrassed over her part in their moving away, and it turned out that she was embarrassed—but not by that.

They were all quite right about the new store. It is wonderful. White plaster over brick, sturdy and handsome and clean. It is far from the *khlongs*, on a main street, and many *samlos*, trucks, and cars pass by all day. I could not help but think how I should love such a place, and Father agreed, although neither of us can envision a way to make that happen soon. Nevertheless, we are content and certainly ought to be.

Since the family moved away, I have not had time to visit them. Mui Eng's mother sometimes comes to see us, but Nguan Thong is not well enough to leave home except for his visits to the foreign hospital. Ang Buai works very hard and has not been back either, but her mother keeps us informed on her progress in the new business. Of course, she is prospering.

At lunch today, I asked Mui Eng if she wasn't curious to see her father's new home.

"Not particularly," she answered coolly. "Anyway, I wouldn't let anyone see me like this. It's embarrassing."

She lifted the cover from a steaming soup tureen and began ladling pork, tripe, and vegetables into our bowls.

"Embarrassing? What are you talking about?"

"This," she said, brushing a hand over her belly. "I'm not going anywhere until it's gone. I hate being pregnant . . . you must have realized that by now. First I was sick, and now I have this ugly thing in front of me."

"You mustn't feel that way. I'm proud of you." I had never thought that a woman could have such thoughts about her own baby.

"No you're not. You're proud of yourself because I'm like this."

"Mui Eng, when you have a husband, you have babies. Why do you think people get married? Why, I want a lot of children—maybe ten!"

"You can't be serious," she said, her eyes narrowing with anger.

84

"What do you think I would look like after ten children?"

Then I too became angry. "If I had ever thought you cared more for your own looks than for raising a family, I wouldn't have wanted to marry you. Anyway, what does it matter? If we are blessed with five children or ten, we will have to raise them as best we can."

"What do you mean, 'if we are blessed'? Can you be that stupid? These days nobody has to have children." She covered the soup tureen and got up to pull a pan of chicken and peppers from the charcoal. She served me rice, then spooned the savory chicken over it as if she had just commented on the weather instead of speaking an abomination.

"Who has spoken to you of such things?" I asked, my voice shaking with rage.

"No one. There is foreign medicine. Everyone knows about it. There's even Chinese medicine, but I wouldn't trust it."

"It's the devil's medicine," I said. "If the spirits of men are denied women's bodies, what bodies shall bear them? Dogs? Or pigs? Mui Eng, if I ever learn that you have used such—such devil's medicine, I will divorce you. Believe that. I swear I will divorce you!"

She continued to stand, holding the pan before her. "What about the people who can't even afford the children they have? Would you have them go on and on having children until they all starve?" Then she set the pan in the sink, sat down again, and began to eat.

"That is a problem we can solve without . . . without filthiness. You know very well how. By controlling ourselves. But I don't understand how a poor man can afford not to have many children. Children are our strength."

"On a farm, maybe. Not here. The Thai say one child equals seven years' poverty."

"And of course you believe that. Sure, if you raise a child the way they do. Treat him like a little god, give him everything he wants. If a child is twenty, and hasn't even begun to work—like some I've seen here—then one child is a lifetime of poverty, not seven years. But my children will be raised to work, and study, and grow up able to look after themselves. That is how I was raised."

"Your children cannot be like you, Suang U. Don't you understand that?"

"No. The best education is one that teaches a person to take care of himself. That is necessary for every man, in every generation. A wise man is one who can keep his own rice bowl filled, not depend on others to do it for him."

Mui Eng picked at her food silently for a few minutes, then pushed her plate away and regarded me sullenly. "You speak of children as if they were machines. Work! Study! What kind of childhood is that?"

"Do you believe that I would use my own child like a—a machine? A child needs love, I know that. But for me, to love a child best is to prepare him for the truth. And the truth is that childhood is a dream that passes swiftly and can hardly be remembered in the light of dawn. It is the long day following the dawn in which a man must work and live. Shall I allow my children to grow up lazy, and then hear them curse me for not having prepared them? My mother taught me everything she knew, and I bless her for it every day of my life. When she had finished with my education, I wanted only to learn more. I have scratched for every bit of learning I could get, Mui Eng. My children will have more education than I ever got, and I'll give it to them gladly—is that using a child like a machine? You tell me—is what I believe so strange, so wrong, that you have to sit there and pout all the while I'm trying to explain myself to you?"

She gave a great sigh, then leaned back in her chair and folded her arms across her belly, "I wanted to marry a learned man. But you?" She shook her head and smiled faintly. "No, I can't even talk to you. You're always right. I'd have been better off with Seng."

My stomach churned, and I felt my palms grow moist. "Don't, Mui Eng, please. Maybe it's too late for us, but . . . that's not exactly what I meant . . . we are married, and now we are going to have a child. The best thing you can do is take care of yourself and the baby. Make it strong and healthy, and when it is born . . . everything will be all right."

"What 'everything' do you mean?"

"Us, and—and the family. You will realize that your sister has too much sense, for one thing, to do the things you accused her of. In your heart, I think you know that already, don't you?"

She was silent, and in her eyes I saw resentment and defeat, though the faint, mocking smile was still on her lips.

As I sat here writing the terrible things we said to each other, I began to feel truly afraid. Perhaps, after the baby is born, everything will be all right, as I told Mui Eng. I only wish I could stop thinking of the way she looked at me when she asked, "What 'everything' do you mean?" My answer was poor, because I had no answer.

You once told me never to sit and dream of yesterday when today is waiting to be met. My today is Thailand, the business, and Mui Eng; my yesterday, the farm and you. If I sometimes sit and dream of yesterday, and the dream seems to lend today a little grace, can it be wrong?

—

LETTER #23   TENTH MONTH, THIRD DAY
27 OCTOBER 1946   YEAR OF THE DOG

BELOVED MOTHER, please forgive my last letter—I am so ashamed of it now. Perhaps all husbands and wives expecting their first child are given to such foolish arguments. Surely everything will be all right now, for my first son is born. My prayers are answered, and young Weng Khim is strong, healthy, and beautiful.

Before he would consent to be born, however, my son caused his poor father's heart to twist with fear. I could scarcely endure the last few weeks, waiting anxiously day and night to see his dear little face. Yet he refused to leave his mother's womb—could he not know how we longed to see him?

Then, one night, it seemed that Weng Khim had decided to tease his parents no longer. I had just closed up the store and was getting ready for bed, trying not to wake Mui Eng. She had come up early complaining that her legs ached from standing behind the counter all day. Suddenly she rolled over and faced me. "It—it hurts," she mumbled sleepily.

"Hurts?" I repeated dumbly, my heart pounding. "I'll send for the midwife!" Then I jumped up and kicked off my pants instead of pulling them up. Oh, no, I thought, is this how I'm going to be?

Kim went to fetch the midwife while I sat and worried. Soon the old woman arrived, dragging a large oilcloth bag, but after a few minutes alone with Mui Eng, she came out into the hallway shaking her head. "She's not going to have that baby yet," she said. "This is only a warning—a little pain here, a pinch there . . . you call me when you need me." And she began to pack up her bag.

"No!" I all but shouted, terrified at being left alone with Mui Eng. "You can't leave! How do you know it won't come later tonight? What will I do if—if it starts to come out? And after that? I don't know anything about babies!"

"If I say it's not time, it's not," she replied firmly. "Five other women could call me and be done with it before that baby of yours arrives."

"But you came here first," I said desperately, determined not to let her escape.

She sighed and rolled her eyes toward the ceiling. "I've delivered babies for fifty years, and I know when a baby is ready to be born. Hurting is hurting—it isn't giving birth. Some of them do that before you could boil rice, and without more pain than if they'd stubbed their toe." She chuckled and patted my shoulder. "But this is a first baby, not a fifteenth, and you'll have plenty of warning."

I didn't understand at all. If the pains had begun, could the birth fail to follow? I was frightened, and the only thing I understood was that Mui Eng might have the baby while she was boiling rice, which she couldn't do very well from the bed I wouldn't let her out of.

At last the midwife agreed to stay overnight, and in the morning she made me pay her for nothing!

When Weng Khim had once made fools of his parents, they were prepared to be more skeptical. Late one morning the week following, when Mui Eng complained that her back hurt and went upstairs to lie down, I didn't worry. Father was spending the week with Nguan Thong, so I had to postpone my errands and work behind the counter myself. But as the afternoon wore on and she remained upstairs, I began to wonder, and by early evening we knew that Weng Khim had forsaken his tricks.

I opened the bedroom door carefully, in case she was asleep. She lay very still, curled up under the blanket with her back to me, but when I touched her shoulder, she turned over awkwardly and looked up at me. "It's bad now," she said in a tight, small voice. "You'd better get the midwife."

"Why didn't you tell me sooner?"

"I was afraid she'd laugh at me again, and the pain kept stopping, then starting again. I thought it would go away but then—now—it's bad."

As she spoke, large drops of sweat appeared on her forehead, and she clenched her teeth. I pitied her, for I knew it must really hurt to make her sweat like that.

Kim went to fetch the midwife, and as I sat beside my wife, I thought of you. When I was born, did you suffer like this? Probably you did. I began to think that perhaps we men are unfair. Do we want so many children because it is not we who must suffer giving birth to them? But the gods have divided our burdens thus, and I still believe that the medicine Mui Eng spoke of is from the devil. If I could, though, I would share her pain, and perhaps I would value the child even more knowing the cost of its birth.

Fathers and mothers have each their own importance to a child. A mother is life, nurture, and love, a father strength and sustenance. A father is a kind of god to his son, certainly my own father was to me. Do you remember the time father shot a ferocious bear that was threatening people in our village? All the neighbors congratulated him, but no one was prouder than I. He taught me to use the soil, care for animals, and grow the rice we ate. You taught me not only to read and write, but to cook, mend my own clothing, and take care of myself in many other practical ways. I love you, I loved my father, am proud to be your son. I shall do everything I can to ensure that my son feels the same way about Mui Eng and me. I pray for the wisdom to raise my son well—not, as some people do, simply give him life and throw him to the mercies of his merit and karma.*

The midwife arrived, and this time she didn't argue over whether the baby was ready to be born. "Out you go, now!" she said cheerfully, shaking her finger at me. "I need one gallon of water that has boiled at least five minutes. Everything else is here." She began unpacking the oilcloth bag. "And don't scald yourself running up here with that water," she added. "There's lots of time."

"Can I stay in there with her?" I called back. "I should say not." "Why not?" "Because it's not decent, that's why."

Instead of going downstairs to boil water, I pulled a chair into the hallway and set it down with a loud bang. But the midwife only laughed and shut the door in my face.

*The consequences of good and evil thoughts and deeds from previous lives.

Kim shook his head. "You can't sit up here in front of the door all night."

"What do you know about it?" I grumbled.

"You forget, I already have a kid."

"And you were a thousand miles away when it was born, not sitting in front of the bedroom door scared to death."

"I wouldn't if I could, you can be sure of that. Why don't you come downstairs? We can boil water together."

"No. I'm staying right here. That old woman can't push me around—anyway, I'm paying her, aren't I?" And then I heard Mui Eng cry out. My heart froze. "What's the matter?" I asked through the door. "Is it born?"

The midwife opened the door. "Is it born, you ask. And you expect me to let you in there, with questions like that. You're making us both nervous—now go on, get out of here. The baby won't be born for many hours, and you can't come around shouting and pounding on the door every time your wife makes a little noise!"

I began to realize that this was going to be a grim night, and glumly followed Kim down to the kitchen. I opened a bottle of whiskey although, as you know, I do not ordinarily drink. In fact, this was my first taste. It made my face feel stiff and my belly hot, but I did feel better. One thing I learned the night Weng Khim was born is that there are some things in this life worth getting drunk over. Every time I heard her cry out, I poured another glassful and drank it down. Kim carried the hot water upstairs because he said I might fall down the stairs and boil myself to death before I ever became a father.

Two hours later, I climbed the stairs again, leaning heavily on the railing and dimly aware that I was not at all myself. I congratulated myself that Father wasn't here to see me make an ass of myself.

"S'born yet?" I called out. Even to myself, I sounded drunk as a pig.

"Not yet!" the old woman shouted back. "Go away!"

"Why can't you do something to make the baby come out?"

"I am a midwife, not a wizard. Nobody can make a child ready to be born."

"Well, I'm payin' you," I bawled, "and all you do is sit there an' listen to 'er yell . . . you're no damned good . . . I wouldn' let you d'liver my dog . . ."

90

I leaned against the door dizzily, and then Mui Eng screamed, a hideous, agonized scream. It seemed to enter my spine, and I shivered violently, and began to cry. "Do somethin' for 'er, you stupid bitch!" I sobbed, feeling suddenly sober against my will. I didn't care if I was drunk as a pig, if only I could block out those awful sounds.

"Behave yourself!" she hissed from the other side of the door. "I *am* doing something! Shame on you."

I stumbled back downstairs and poured another glass of whiskey, drank it, and promptly fell asleep at the kitchen table with my head in my arms. When I awoke, Kim was gone, and so was the rest of the whiskey. The midwife was standing beside me, and when I raised my head groggily, she smiled.

"The child is born, and everyone is fine. The birth would have been easier if he weren't such a chubby little fellow. Your wife is asleep, and I want you to leave her alone, do you understand? You stay downstairs until she wakes up and calls you."

"Born . . . the baby is born," I mumbled, trying to shake the sleep from my throbbing head. "Would have been quicker but . . . a chubby—a chubby little fellow?" I leaped up and grabbed the midwife by the shoulders. "Old woman, did you say chubby little fellow?"

"Yes, yes—a little boy, a fine fat one."

"A son! I have a son! TAN WENG KHIM, DO YOU HEAR ME UP THERE?!"

"Stop this immediately, you foolish man! You will wake the child— ah, listen to that now!" She looked up at the ceiling and frowned, while I, transfixed, felt tears spring to my eyes at the beautiful sound, the wondrous wail of my infant son, answering his father.

The midwife threw me a stormy look, turned, and trudged up the stairs, muttering to herself like an angry old duck.

Mother, your grandson is so cute. His little mouth is red and full, and his round sturdy body begs to be hugged. (I haven't dared to pick him up yet!) I must close my letter now, for Weng Khim is crying, and his mother is asleep. I will run upstairs and see what is troubling him. A mosquito, perhaps, or maybe he is hungry again. He is only ten days old now, but before you know it he will be writing to his grandmother himself.

—

YOUR GRANDSON is healthy and growing fast, but that is the only good news I have for you in this letter. Nguan Thong is dead.

What began as a tiny lump he could hide under his collar ended in an agonizing and dreadful illness that destroyed his endurance and, finally, his life. We did everything we could, took him to every doctor who offered hope, but what I have seen in the past month has tried my confidence in doctors, whether Chinese, Thai, or foreign. They could do nothing but prolong his misery, increase the number of days he lived to suffer. Death would have been preferable to what they called life. We spent a fortune on medicines, but money is a pitiful weapon against death, once death has opened its jaws.

He died five days before the New Year, which caused great confusion in regard to the business. There was end of the year bookkeeping to complete in the midst of funeral ceremonies, in addition to figuring out the salaries and bonuses due the men who worked for him before he moved. Ang Buai's careful records have been a blessing.

Nguan Thong was a successful merchant and a good man, and many friends came to pay their respects and mourn him. Father and I were determined to accord him the honor in death that he earned by his life, but it was Ang Buai who arranged everything when the time came.

The first problem we faced was the one he fretted over all his life— that he had no son. The *kong tek** presented special problems, and in some ways it was pitiable. For Mui Eng, as the oldest child, had to carry the joss sticks, and there was no one save Ang Buai to carry the banner. Even Nguan Thong's daughter's son was too young to participate. I believe every man present pitied him as the procession formed, for who does not fear dying without sons? Their faces said as much.

*A procession requiring, ideally, a son and his son. The eldest male heir walks at the head of the funeral procession carrying joss sticks in a sand-filled vase. A white cloth banner bearing the name of the deceased, the district where he was born, and his age should be carried by the son's son, directly behind the coffin. Other members of the family lead remaining friends, relatives and, often, paid mourners. Buddhist monks usually walk between relatives and friends a few yards behind the coffin.

But you will want to know more about how it all came about. Several weeks before Nguan Thong's death, when Weng Khim was one month old, we took him to visit his grandfather. The first thing he spoke of, after admiring the baby, was his funeral. He worried that there might be no *kong tek* at all.

"Father, you mustn't worry about that," I said. "We will take care of everything, Yong Chua and I."

"At least my crypt is prepared, Suang U," he said, speaking slowly as if to conserve his breath. "It is in the country, near Thonburi. That I saw to long ago. I know it is a bit far from here but that is where I wish to be. Soon, when the road is finished, you will all be able to go there by car. Now it is a short boat trip, but pleasant, I think . . . it should not be too much trouble to carry me there."

I wanted to cry, but I did not. He was very brave, and I kept my tears back.

"Suang U, be sure I don't get put into one of those Thai coffins—I shall want to stretch my legs, in death."* He grinned at me, and I nodded quickly, blinking hard and trying desperately to grin back.

He had prepared everything meticulously. His wife's crypt also stands ready, beside his. We Chinese do not fear death, or consider the preparation for it any kind of "evil omen" as Thai people do. Such preparations are a matter of practicality and convenience, enabling us to meet our inevitable end with cool hearts. And why should death be feared, after all, when it is the natural fate of all living things? Every Chinese who attains old age prepares the place where he wishes to rest. I have seen Thais become angry when death was mentioned in the presence of old people. They say that to speak of death is to invite it. Does that make sense? Nothing invites death but life itself, and old people know they are going to die. Knowing that we are ill or growing old, it is our duty to spare others the trouble of arranging our affairs. A man should take leave of life efficiently. Avoiding this responsibility in the hope that death may be cheated by a few years is the cruelest self-deception.

---

*Nguan Thong is making a joke, referring to the funerary urns into which Thai aristocrats were placed, upright and in a fetal position, before cremation. These urns are still used for members of the royal family and very high-ranking individuals. *Trans.*

Ang Buai sat beside her father, holding his hand. Tears ran down her cheeks, but she was silent.

"At least I die having seen my grandson," Nguan Thong said, "but I fear for my youngest daughter, and my wife. How will they manage, an old woman and a girl alone?"

"Father, you don't have to worry about us," Ang Buai said. "I will take good care of Mother, and you know I can do anything I set my mind to! I love the business as you do, and I promise you that it will continue to prosper when you are gone."

Her father struggled for breath. "I want you to get married—"

Ang Buai looked bewildered. "Married? But why now, when I am able to take care of myself? Don't you have faith in me even now, after I have shown you and everyone else that I can run this business?"

"A woman should depend on a husband—and, in her old age, on her son. Now, while you are young, yes, you will do well. But when your mother is gone, when you are old yourself, what then?"

"Father, please rest now. The future will take care of itself, and what good can come of such talk?"

"Good can come of it, if you will listen to me. Child, Tae Lim came to see me yesterday—"

"Seng! So that's it," she said in a flat, angry voice. "I thought Tae Lim came to see his sick friend, but no, he's still playing his old game. No, Father, I'm sorry. That would be impossible."

He struggled to sit up. "Ang Buai, young Seng has done well. Soon he will open his own shop. You and your mother would be fortunate with such a match. At the least, you would be safe . . ." Then he sank back against the pillows again, and Ang Buai tucked him in as if he were a child.

"Now, Father, we all know that you were relieved to get Suang U for a son-in-law instead of that dolt." Nguan Thong frowned fiercely, but she continued. "Am I such a 'leftover' that even Seng is good enough for me?"

"A—a leftover indeed! What does it matter that he once asked for your sister's hand? Besides," he added obstinately, "I never said Seng was a dolt."

"Perhaps not, but he is and you know it. I'm sorry, Father. I won't change my mind."

"Are you trying to tell me that you want to choose your own husband? Such a thing is not done, not in this family!"

"You are tiring yourself, and here is your grandson come to visit you. Is this how you want him to remember you, a cantankerous old man?"

He smiled sadly. "He will not remember me, but I have seen his face, thank the gods. Bring him to me, Mui Eng."

She lifted the baby from his basket and handed him carefully to her father.

"Weng Khim," he grinned, "you look just like me! That is a comfort." (Actually, Weng Khim is the image of me.) He stroked the baby's fat, smooth cheek reverently with a frail, trembling hand. "Don't you see? He's grandfather's boy, every inch of him!" He looked up happily, and we all smiled and nodded quickly. "Mui Eng, raise him well. To be a businessman, to love learning, to know the importance of thrift. Teach him to love our traditions, and do not let him forget our native land." Then he handed the baby back to Mui Eng and said, "You all go now, and let me sleep."

As I reached the doorway, I turned to look again at my father-in-law, so incredibly changed from the day I had come, with Kim, to work and live in his bountiful household. I remembered him telling us how to bathe in the *khlong* before dawn, and insisting that we eat a big breakfast. And pacing up and down in the little room we used for reading classes while I burned with love for Mui Eng, and Ang Buai chirped and teased and exchanged the cheerful insults with her father that never ended, not even on his deathbed. I remembered him in the little boat, floating down the Chao Phraya River and telling me that "he would have his way," and Mui Eng would be my wife. And handing us the envelope of money last New Year's Eve, knowing that Mui Eng had planned the way for him; and still he treated me like a son, and turned my shame to smiles by joking about the fateful jade bracelet.

He lay very still, pitifully thin and weak, his skin yellow-grey. He might have been dead already but for the great, knobby lump beneath his chin, which seemed the only truly living thing about him. An evil, ugly thing sustaining itself on the body of a man I loved, sucking life from him until, finally, it died with him. The only question now was how many days he had left to give it.

The next day, Father returned from Nguan Thong's store shortly after lunch, despondent.

"I tell you, he will not see the New Year, Suang U. He can barely eat. Today he could not even speak to me. He can take only enough water and rice broth to keep his poor heart beating." He shook his head sorrowfully. "Do not take Weng Khim there again. From now on, only you and Mui Eng may go there. But perhaps your generation does not hold with such notions."*

"No, Father, I would not take that chance."

The next day, we went to visit him without the baby, and I worried that he would realize at once why his grandson had been left home. But when we arrived at the store, Ang Buai was preparing to leave, dressed in black.

"You almost missed me. I was on my way to fetch you." She looked away quickly and fumbled with her handbag.

"Your Father?" I asked, afraid to say more.

"He is dead." She blinked rapidly, then looked up. "Last night, in his sleep. I've closed the shop. I won't open it again until—until everything is over." She was pale with grief and fatigue, but determined to be strong.

Mui Eng received the news of her father's death with the same rigid calm, paling for only a moment before she asked, "How long has he been dead?"

"I told you, he died in his sleep. I went in this morning and found him, then I sent a neighbor to tell the coffin maker."

"Is it here yet?"

"Yes, he's in it."

"How did you handle him?"

"It wasn't difficult. He was so thin—I just lifted him out of bed into the coffin and shut it."

"Has he been bathed and dressed?"

---

*It was believed that a newborn child's astrological endowment was not strong enough to withstand the near presence of death or mortal illness in the last stage. After several months, he was not so likely to be influenced by such things. Also dangerous to the newborn, according to custom, was a house where a woman had recently given birth; maternal mortality was generally accepted as a product of negative karma.

"Of course," she replied quickly, with more than a trace of anger. "Did you think I'd put him in there in his *phakhaoma*? I dressed him in a new white suit. I bought it last week and kept it in my room. He— he would have approved of that, but I—I just couldn't let him see it." Her voice broke into a sob then, and she paused for a few minutes, covering her face with her hands. When she looked up again, she had regained her composure. "I was going to visit you first, and then go to Leng Noei Yi Temple to invite the monks to pray. I thought we would have seven nights of prayers here, then take him to the crypt on the seventh day. We'll have the *kong tek*, of course, as he wanted, and the paper burning.* I've already sent someone to the paper shop with our order."

"What can we do?" I asked.

"It would be a help if Mui Eng would stay with Mother. And you could buy the cloth for the banners and have the proper characters put on them, if you know what they ought to be." I nodded. "And mourning bands," she said. "I didn't want to buy them before."

So Mui Eng stayed, and Ang Buai and I set out in different directions. I was glad she let me share these responsibilities, and I even managed to persuade her that I could visit Nguan Thong's old friends and customers. She would have done everything if we let her, and ended up ill herself.

I returned to my own store first, to tell Father. When I walked in, he took one look at my face and swiftly raised his hand, bidding me not to tell him. Then he began to close up the store, slowly and methodically, and when he had finished he went to his room without saying a word.

All the neighbors were Nguan Thong's friends, and some were kind enough to leave their own work and visit others, saving me a few trips. I told our employees they could go home, but I was pleased that those who had worked for Nguan Thong chose to stay, or to go to his new shop and help Ang Buai.

Besides ceremonies attending the funeral, the New Year was only days away, and its ceremonies may never be neglected. Although many

---

*The deceased is sent to the next world with various material possessions which are prepared of paper, in miniature, and burned ceremoniously. In modern times, tiny paper television sets, automobiles, and even curvaceous paper dolls are not unusual. *Trans.*

days would pass before our store could open its doors again, I was busy day and night, and Weng Khim took it into his little head to cry every night that week, which he has never done before or since.

Every evening, we attended prayers at Nguan Thong's store. Poor Father would just sit and stare, first at the monks, then at the coffin, hour after hour. I know he feels that his cousin should not have died, and might not have, had his illness been treated differently from the beginning. Had Nguan Thong not buttoned his collar over a lump. But what would have been the use of talking about that now? I did not.

As always, on the last morning of the year we honored our ancestors and, in the afternoon, the spirits of those who died without descendants. There was some confusion over the food to be offered this year. Mui Eng wanted to buy all the poultry killed and dressed from the market because we were so busy. I wouldn't have animals killed at the market in my house—who knows what they might sell you? Kim slipped out in the midst of our argument and bought live chickens and ducks from one of his lady friends at the market, and the employees helped him clean them out back, on the bank of the *khlong*. We were still arguing when they trooped in the back door, rather sheepishly, their arms filled with fresh, fat pink birds.

I grabbed a duck from Kim and threw it on the table. "Look at these fine, fresh ducks!" I said to Mui Eng. "The ducks you would have had us buy in the market today looked like this two days ago." What a nice surprise! I was pleased at Kim's thoughtfulness.

The next evening, the first of the new year, instead of resting, we all had to rush about preparing for the evening prayers at Nguan Thong's. When I pinned the mourning band to my sleeve, my heart sank, for this was the day he had insisted, only a year ago, must be spent quietly and happily, that the new year might be prosperous. On the seventh day following his death, we prepared for the *kong tek* and the journey to Thonburi.

The coffin was carried out into the street by four of his former employees. They slid it carefully onto the waiting truck, then piled it with flowers. One of the men handed a large photograph of Nguan Thong up to another man who placed it in a black and white wreath mounted on a tripod ahead of the coffin. I thought Nguan Thong looked rather startled up there, perched on top of a truck surveying the large assembly of his friends and relatives. I suppose it never occurred to him, on a day long ago when a photographer's flashing light caught him by surprise, that his descendants would know him only by this picture, dazzled for eternity.

As the monks began their low, rhythmic chanting, the truck creaked slowly forward. Mui Eng walked before it with her chin raised proudly, carrying the pot of joss sticks. Ang Buai followed stiffly behind, gripping the white banner with all her might. When she turned her head to glance at me, I saw that she was crying. The low, wailing chant of the monks entered all our hearts and brought tears to our eyes, for at this moment we realized that our beloved father and friend was truly lost to us in this life.

That evening, when all the ceremonies had come to an end, Ang Buai collapsed. Father lifted her gently and carried her to her room. I did not help him, for I was afraid to touch her in front of everyone (and Mui Eng), and Father showed by a slight nod that he understood.

On the way home, he spoke to me of his sorrow, and of his own fears.

"Nguan Thong may have had no son," he said, "but I would be pleased with such a funeral myself."

"Many years will pass before that day, Father."

"Perhaps, but one cannot help thinking of one's own death on such a day as this. The last time I thought of it was the day I asked you to be my son. I was so alone, Suang U, you cannot know how alone. No wife or child to mourn me if I should die. In death, I would have been one of the spirits we honor on the last afternoon of the year . . . the pitiful ones, who must cling to the charity of strangers because they have no descendants to honor them."

"Father, when you die, I will be your son truly. You know that."

"Yes, and it is what I have wanted more than anything, not to die and wander forgotten in the spirit world. I want to rest in a fine crypt, a sturdy coffin, and on the days when people honor their own ancestors, I want someone to honor me. Children to remember me, and pray for the cleansing of my sins." He looked at me steadily in the darkness. "Can't you understand that I don't want money from you, Suang U? And don't think I don't realize that you brood about that everyday!" He smiled, then said, "I don't want money. I want to be remembered in my death by a family who loves me."

"You have a son now, and a son's son. I promise you I shall do everything you could want, Father. As for the money . . . well, even if I were your blood son, I would feel this way. It is yours to use, for making merit, or buying the crypt you want to rest in after your death, or whatever. A grown man should not look to his parents for money. I can't help what I believe." He smiled again, and I returned it gratefully, glad to see sorrow lifted from his features for the first time since the death of his cousin and beloved friend.

Another matter that arose soon was Nguan Thong's will. My mother-in-law called us to her home the day after the funeral.

"Nguan Thong has divided everything between you girls," she said softly. Mui Eng and her sister sat quietly, looking down into their laps. They did not look at each other.

She dabbed at her red eyes with a handkerchief and said, "Cash is divided exactly in half, but the store, and what is in it, he has left to Ang Buai and me, so that we can make our living without using capital. I hope you will not think this unfair, Mui Eng." She looked very sad and small, her grey hair pulled back into a wispy bun. Strands of hair framed her face, and, for the first time, she looked old to me.

Mui Eng did not speak. "Mother, we expect nothing," I said quickly. Half the money left by Nguan Thong would not be a trifling sum, I knew. As for Nguan Thong's wife and daughter, surely they deserved to be protected, not that Ang Buai hadn't earned her share on her own merits.

Mui Eng said nothing about the will until we were alone that night, but I had seen her compress her lips angrily when I answered on her behalf, and I knew she would have something to say before long. I was not mistaken.

She jerked off her blouse and threw it onto a chair across the bedroom. "My, but you're the generous one," she said. "What about your son? He left Weng Khim nothing!"

I took a fresh *phakhaoma* out of a drawer and wrapped it about my waist, taking my time and trying to decide how to reason with her. "He gave Weng Khim a thousand baht when he was born," I said, "and what is ours is our son's, isn't it?"

She turned away and pulled on her nightgown. "Don't you realize

100

that my sister got much, much more than I did?" Then she climbed into bed and pulled the blanket up to her chin like a sulking child.

"Yes, Mui Eng, and she earned it. We have no cause to feel bitter. He was very good to us."

"I suppose it would look that way, from your point of view."

"Did you have to say that?"

She stretched and yawned and turned her back to me. "Then take our share of the money, and use it for that factory Yong Chua is always talking about. Maybe it will make us rich. Wouldn't that surprise her?" She giggled, yawned again, and was soon asleep.

Father's dream! Until that moment, it had never crossed my mind that Nguan Thong's money could make the dream come true, and I would never have been able to bring myself to talk to Mui Eng about it. But in her jealousy of Ang Buai, she has determined that the dream shall be realized.

I pray that this money may grow under my hand and that, wherever Nguan Thong is, he may see what we have done with it and be pleased. And I pray also for your blessing on our venture, a dream which will become real long before any of us had hoped.

———

LETTER #25   SECOND MONTH, THIRD DAY
23 FEBRUARY 1947   YEAR OF THE PIG

IN THE future, my letters will not be as frequent as they have been. Please forgive me, but life here becomes busier with each passing month, and my days have ever fewer hours. With this letter, I am sending a little money, for you to use as you see fit. Do not be too sensible!

You will remember that we inherited money from Lo Nguan Thong, but in this letter you will learn of my amazement at the size of the inheritance. I never realized how wealthy a man my father-in-law was— no one did—and now I am aghast that he was willing to have me for a son-in-law, when there must have been many suitable prospects besides Seng for his eldest daughter's hand, men who had fortunes to combine with his, and who were far more learned than I. I came to his house with nothing, no diploma to prove my learning, nothing. Yet he accepted me, no doubt for Yong Chua's sake. Now he has left a sizeable part of his fortune in my care. It is a serious trust.

So, the factory is no longer a dream to entertain over a cup of tea at day's end, and secretly doubt in the dark of night. Father and I needed at least 400 square meters of land, not the kind of narrow row shop we have all lived in and Mui Eng grew up in. But Thai landlords are clever, and the cost of everything has soared since the war's end. Before, a five satang coin would buy a man his dinner—now children play with them as with pebbles.

Eventually, we decided on a large vacant lot only half a mile down Sampheng Lane. We have had to build our own factory, which added greatly to our cost but, I feel certain, was for the best. It is small, but made of brick. We both feel this was a wise investment, for the property is high and breezy, and I am afraid of fire. There have been many fires in Bangkok since I came here, and acres of wooden buildings burned to the ground before the few fire trucks they have could reach the narrow lanes where fires usually start. I am afraid most of them were started by men who had little to lose and everything to gain—from their insurance companies. How bold they are! A fire in an insured building is never regarded as an accident, whether foul play can be proven or not.

Dealing with government authorities over permits to build and operate a new factory was frustrating, as are all such matters for us, and Father went about mumbling and shaking his head all the days it took to grind our way toward success. But such things are only a matter of time and money. I have become more patient since the day I first visited a police station to pay my alien tax. Not proud of the change in my attitude, perhaps, but there is no other way.

How much they have made us spend," Father wailed, "over problems that should not be problems!"

"Never mind, Father. In a little while, we will have earned it all back."

He shook his head slowly. "No, son, do not think like that. I have never believed in selling at the highest price a customer is willing to pay. If we sell our products at the going rate, we will do far better in the end."

He is as goodhearted as ever, still the man who gave medicine to sick boys on the ship and would not take money for it. We are now selling at less than the going price for our products, and, in fact, our customers are learning that bargaining with us is a waste of time. What we call a fair price is the fairest they will find.

"Better than selling high and sending them away feeling they've learned a hard lesson . . . every customer has relatives. To take advantage of anyone is to lose."

"What about the money we're losing by selling so low?"

"That money is our most important investment. Someday, when our competitors are wondering where all their customers went, the money you feel you are 'forfeiting' now will return to you a thousand-fold."

I believe him, for he has never been wrong yet. I may confess to you now that, although our first business was not a failure, we would have done better had I followed all of his advice. You see, Father wanted to sell hardware and dry goods. I insisted that, since all people must eat, food must be the surest product to sell. He let me have my way, and though I wasn't exactly wrong in my thinking, I didn't think far enough. I am too tenderhearted to sell food to poor people.

"Oh, please trust me," the shabbily dressed customer would plead, "I know I can pay you next week, but this week the poor babies have no rice to eat. If it weren't for them, do you think I would have come to you like this?" And then, inevitably, a tear would fall. "One bag of rice, a handful of beans, a few dried shrimps, that's all I need . . ."

Gradually, I grew sick at heart. But later, when I tried to apologize to Father, he only smiled and said that I had taught myself well. "It is easy," he said, "to say no when a customer asks for credit to buy a broom. Come to think of it, have you ever heard of anyone asking for credit to buy a broom?" He shook his head and laughed. "No—hungry children don't care whether the floor is clean."

Some of these people remain in a neighborhood only long enough to exhaust the pity of their creditors. In the beginning, you will recall that I visited our debtors once a week. After awhile, I stopped aggravating myself and learned to expect a return of seven baht on every ten owed. When I asked Nguan Thong's old friends what I ought to do about this problem they only shrugged and said, "That's how it is. No sensible man expects to collect all that is owed him. Don't worry, though—if you do your best, you won't go far wrong."

But many businessmen here do go far wrong. Not because they extend credit unwisely, but because of gambling. What a curse it is in this city. Guessing which card will come up next, how many beans are hidden under a cup, how many dots will appear on a pair of dice. Or they allow themselves to become enslaved to teahouse girls, and throw away their hard-earned money on gold earrings and fine silk. We are always told that the temptations of the world are strong, but such "temptations" as I have seen here are an abomination. I have the same desires as other men, I think, but I know I could never allow passion to cheat me of what is mine and my family's.

After we had rented our land and built the factory, we were still far from ready to open for business. We had to buy machinery, and huge ovens which are heated by gas. They are wonderful ovens, fearfully hot, and their temperature never varies. The machines that mix batter, mold and stamp out cookies are a joy to watch. We are beginning with *chan-ap*,* because it is the most popular; other kinds will be made as soon as we discover which sell best in Bangkok. I have sent Kim to all the small food shops within a few miles of here to ask which confections people like best, and exactly who the buyers are. He will have finished this task in a few weeks.

One evening this past week, I took a *samlo* over to the factory to watch Father tinker with a new batter mixer. He was sprawled beneath it, totally absorbed in the dozens of little wheels and levers which, to me, are still mysterious and incomprehensible.

"Does it work?" I asked. He looked up, startled, then smiled and climbed out from beneath the machine, wiping his hands on the baggy work pants he always wears now.

"Of course it works—I'm only playing. Suang U, I believe I shall never tire of these lovely machines! How is the baby?"

"Fine. What do you think we ought to call the business? We haven't talked about it yet."

"But I've thought about it. The Chinese name is up to you—call it whatever you like. And why don't you let Mui Eng choose a Thai name? I think that would please her."

After much discussion, we agreed on the Thai name "Loet Rot" ("the

---

Chan-ap is a Chinese cookie. There are several varieties, some of which are star-shaped. Ingredients include flour, sugar, shortening, and nuts. *Trans.*

peak of flavor") and, for the Chinese name, "Lo Buan Chai Heng.* We argued a long time over which *sae* to use. Father wanted to use mine, making it "Tan Buan Chai Heng," but I would not hear of it, for all our capital is from the *sae* Lo.

At the time of this writing, our dream has been realized halfway. Now we need to attract regular customers, arrange for better transportation of our products, and hire more workers.

I am continuing the import business Nguan Thong handed down to me, even though the factory demands much of my time. But what of that? I am still young enough to turn my head in many directions. Mui Eng and a couple of girls run our old store, selling those non-edible necessities Father recommended. He is in charge of the factory, of course, and his beloved machinery, and I run between all three of our business ventures, attempting to combine their financial aspects profitably. And I marvel at myself. Do not fear that I have become vain, Mother. What I marvel at is the joy my busy schedule gives me. Any fears I had have disappeared, because there is simply no time to be afraid, only time to do what must be done. It is truly marvelous what a man can do when he loves his work, as well trained for it as I am, thanks to Nguan Thong and Father. I do not forget the great debt I owe them both.

Kim is growing up at last, it seems. He is responsible and hardworking, enthusiastic and uncomplaining, and we depend on him in many ways.

I believe that we shall prosper, all of us, and my heart is full of gratitude.

―

LETTER #26   FOURTH MONTH, TENTH DAY
29 MAY 1947   YEAR OF THE PIG

YOUR SON is almost a big businessman . . . almost. Our products are selling better than I ever expected—all the world seems to love *chan-ap*—but our profits are very modest.

We must put everything back into the business. We have to buy

---

Buan "abundance," *chai* "progress," *heng* "gain," all preceded by the *sae* Lo. *Trans.*

almost all the things we need on a cash basis, but then we must sell our products on credit! You see, most of the ingredients we use are imported, and importers never extend credit. But we sell our products locally, where credit is the mainstay of trade. Patience, patience . . . as Father reminds me every day. One way I am able to economize is by combining deliveries of *chan-ap* with deliveries of imports to the old Nguan Thong customers. They are our natural first market, and they love the *chan-ap* too. (If I never ate another piece of it, I could survive very well, and we've only been making it for two months.)

We hire Chinese workers for the factory whenever possible, for they are much more dependable than the Thai. They tend to stay with their jobs for a long time, whereas the Thai stay only as long as it takes to earn themselves a "holiday." The women, especially, come and go. Fortunately, their jobs are easy to teach and easy to learn, and there are always plenty of them available looking for work. The women's job in the factory is to put the *chan-ap* into boxes, wrap the boxes in paper, and stamp our name on the front of each wrapper.

What we have come to think of as "Mui Eng's store" is doing unexpectedly well. Pots and pans, brooms and brushes, soap for scouring, soap for washing and bathing. Thermos bottles, wash pans, plates and forks and spoons. They all sell, and nobody asks for credit.

We give all the employees one day off every two weeks, on a rotating basis. Once a month, we visit Ang Buai and her mother. Sometimes my mother-in-law stays here for a day or two, but Ang Buai has seldom left her store for more than an hour since the day we opened our factory. On that day, she closed it and shared our celebration.

That was a day we enjoyed to the full, and one you would have rejoiced in too, if only you could have been here. Of course, we are still in mourning, but we thought it reasonable to open with a small party.* It is impossible to believe that old Nguan Thong himself would have disapproved, especially since this is "his" business! I seemed to feel his

*According to the Chinese tradition, sons wear mourning garb for three years, the daughters for one year. In modern times, both sons and daughters usually wear mourning garb for only one year, but in some families the Thai custom is observed instead, and all family members observe only one hundred days of mourning.

presence all during that day, although I am not a superstitious man. Sentiment is enough to make our beloved ghosts draw near, I think— ghosts formed of memories and bidden by love.

In the morning, we gave a feast for several monks from Leng Noei Yi Temple, and when they had left we had our own feast. Later, we demonstrated our machinery for our guests and everyone enjoyed free samples of Father's skill. Weng Khim was an important personage at the party, you may be sure. He spent the day traveling from one pair of arms to another, chuckling happily at every tickle and funny face. He seemed to be wondering, "What are all these people doing in my house?" and deciding, "They are here to amuse me!" Everyone admired his chubby, healthy body and congratulated his mother on the richness or her milk. But, in truth, Weng Khim had too big an appetite, and Mui Eng had to wean him to canned milk a month ago. She also gives him bananas and rice gruel, so it is no surprise that he is a healthy little fellow. But Mui Eng is too thin from feeding him even as long as she did.

While we celebrated, Kim was off in another direction. He had been seeing one of the Thai girls in the neighborhood every day for weeks, and even on the day of our opening, he found important reasons for hurrying to her house first thing in the morning. Mui Eng had agreed to take the girl into her shop, and he couldn't wait to tell her the good news. The girl, whose name is Chaba, is pleasant and an amazingly hard worker for a Thai. Her father is a drunk, but her mother is a good woman, and Chaba is like her both in looks and in character. The old woman raises chickens and ducks, and Chaba has continued to help her since coming into the store. She prepares the day's poultry feed at dawn, hurries to work, hurries back home at noon, then returns to the store and works until dark. With the new job, Chaba has been able to buy herself some new clothes, which she is very proud of. The Thai *chaba* is a red flower with no scent, an apt name for a girl who is attractive and neat but more practical than beautiful. The only unattractive feature about Chaba may be her tongue . . . which is sharp. She and Kim are well suited in that regard, and their constant banter and teasing keep everyone laughing. She has been learning Chinese, and though she works hard at it, her accent is terrible. Nevertheless, she makes sure that she is understood by the customers, and doesn't mind if they laugh at her. She knows they are pleased to see a Thai trying to speak our language.

Kim came to see me late one evening soon after our opening, looking both happy and nervous. "I want to talk to you about my Thai flower," he began, flushing with embarrassment. "If I were to . . . to marry her, Suang U . . . would you blame me? She likes me too, I think."

"I'm sure of it, Kim. No, I wouldn't blame you. If you think you two can live happily together, why should I object? When we first came here, I couldn't believe that this—Thailand—would ever seem like home. But it is home now, and I won't pretend to believe that your wife—your wife in China—will join you soon. Maybe she never will, and maybe you'll never go back. You don't really care, do you?"

"Well, I'd be a liar if I said I did. Honestly, I can't remember her face anymore. The only thing I feel for her now is . . . I feel sorry for her, that's all."

"I understand. Kim. Set the date for this wedding, and I'll be there beside you. I owe you the favor."

"Your wedding—that was quite a day, wasn't it? Mine won't be so fancy, but—what am I talking about? I haven't even asked Chaba yet!"

"Who do you think I am, her father? Go and ask her first," I laughed, "and then we can figure out the details."

So he asked Chaba, and the next afternoon he returned from her house glowing with pride and happiness.

"I did it!" he stated proudly.

"And?"

"Well, she said yes. But she has to ask her mother first."

"Good. She's a good girl."

"Yes, but what if her mother says no? Then what does a 'good girl' do?"

But by evening, when I saw him again, relief was written all over his face. Mama had said yes.

"Well, Kim? Do I have to ask? Or should I just do the rest of my accounts by the light of your face and take it for granted?"

"She didn't ask her father, only her mother. And what do you think her mother said? She said, 'Good for you, daughter! Marry a *chek* and you'll eat pork every day. You won't eat dried fish and chase ducks around a pond all your life like your poor mother!"

"Good. Since I assume that's supposed to be a compliment to you,

I'll accept it as such. What do they want in betrothal money?"

"Chaba doesn't want much. A one-strand belt of *nak*,* two bahts of gold, four trays of wedding cakes, two suits of clothing for her parents, and dinner for nine Thai monks. But even so . . ." He looked down, embarrassed.

"Stop staring at the floor, Kim! We know each other too well for that . . . . you know I'll help you out. She asked for so little, she must love you. Only the traditional things. I approve of that."

I am happy for my friend, and glad to help. I am providing everything except the money for the bride's parents. I believe that wedding traditions, whether Thai or Chinese, should be carefully observed. All traditions are the symbols of a man's race and they remind us, "This is mine, this is what I belong to, this is what I am." So our hearts speak to us as we observe the ways of our ancestors, and continue to discover anew the ancient experience of our people.

―

LETTER #27   SIXTH MONTH, SECOND DAY
19 JULY 1947   YEAR OF THE PIG

GOOD NEWS, Mother! You will have a second grandchild before long! Never did I expect two children so early in my marriage. Why, we will have children old enough to help us before we are of a great age ourselves. What more can parents ask? And if they are all as cute as Weng Khim . . . how I wish you could see your grandchildren. It is the only thing lacking in my life.

I performed the duties of a friend for Kim, who was married to Chaba two weeks ago. Father was more than willing to go to her family on his behalf, as Kim had no elders of his own. The only thing I asked of Kim was that he remember his responsibilities to his wife in China, and I think he understood the importance of this, though our discussion produced an unexpected argument.

"Your first wife suffered with you in poverty," I told him, "and if she should ever find a way to come here, you must accept her and provide for her. I know it is unlikely, but that is our tradition. A first wife is

―――――――

Nak is an alloy of gold and copper, popular in Thailand. *Trans.*

honored before all others, and if she had born a child, the responsibility is even greater."

"I will do it," he replied, somewhat impatiently, "but don't you realize that she can never come here now? Even I know there has been some kind of revolution in China, fighting and everything. You're the one who reads the newspaper!"

"Do not speak of it to me."

"What's the matter with you? Who knows if she still lives in Po Leng village, with what is going on in China? She might have run away, if there was fighting."

I did not want to hear his foolish talk. Whatever has happened, I know you are still on our land, for you would never leave it. Someday when I come walking up the path to our house, you will be there, and Younger Brother too. When whatever has happened there is finally over, I will be there. I write to you so that you can feel I am close to you until then.

Do you read my letters in the evening? With Younger Brother beside you? I have often pictured that. I imagine you telling him my stories . . . the happy ones, and the not so happy. Someday, when you are old, I will read these letters over to you myself, and we will remember together, just as if you had lived it all with me. You will not have to strain your eyes when your sight has grown dim.

But Kim continued to speak of war and trouble in China while my thoughts wandered to you and home. When my mind returned to the present, and his ever more exaggerated tales continued to pour into my unwilling ears, I lost my temper.

"Can't you understand?" I shouted at him. "I do not want to hear tales of Chinese fighting Chinese! Must you believe everything you hear? We don't know what is happening there, and frankly, I don't want to know!" Maybe I am stupid, but I do not understand why men make war. At best, life is short, and no man can realize all his dreams. And it is not like reading of famous battles in *Three Kingdoms*, and then setting aside the book for another day. The knowledge that there is war in my own time, in my own country . . . I cannot accept it. I will set it aside for another day, and think about it when I can bear to.

"You don't want to know or hear anything except what suits you!"

Kim replied angrily, hurt by my outburst. "You, a smart man—how can you talk like that? I tell you, you cannot live your life in a cocoon. Not even if you're rich. It won't work. Even here there was a revolution—Chaba's mother told me about it. Fighting and everything. New leaders grabbing power from old leaders. She says people never learn, so long as there is anything left to grab. She's right, I think. It happened in Thailand, in China—how can you ignore it?"

"I am not interested in who kills who, or why. I just want to be left alone to run my business—"

He laughed. "You talk like a big shot already. 'Let them butcher each other, so long as I make money!' Well, who knows . . . maybe you're right. Look at me, telling you anything. You must know what you're talking about. A big merchant already—and who am I? The big merchant's poor friend from the village."

"You think about that too much. Maybe my luck has been better than yours so far. What of it? In five years you may be ahead of me."

He shook his head, grinning. "Can't happen. Never."

"Why not? You're just beginning, and no man knows his own future. Not every man enjoys his best years when he is young. But we are born to do battle with our fate, Kim. Nobody wants to starve and die, and no one with courage ever gives up—no Chinese, anyway. Think of your wedding now, and the good days that are coming. Before you know it, you'll have a cute little baby of your own. By the way, did you know Mui Eng is pregnant again? Three months."

"Congratulations. You're going to have a houseful, the way you're going. I'd like to have many children too, but—I don't know—we probably won't be able to raise more than one or two."

"Not you too, Kim. Mui Eng said the same thing before Weng Khim was born. It's nonsense. I don't believe there's such a thing as not being able to afford children."

"Sure, you can say that—"

"Believe me, everything will turn out all right for you, especially with a woman like Chaba. And if you don't need too much capital to start a business you and Chaba think would suit you, I'm willing to get you started. All I ask is that you don't start making *chan-ap* and beat me out!"

I smiled to give him strength of heart. Kim is not lazy at all. But he doesn't believe in himself, and he worries too much, If Chaba and I can only get him moving, I know he's got more than a chance at success.

The wedding was quiet and pleasant. Very few guests were invited for, as Kim said, "Her relatives are a bunch of drunks." This pronouncement did not upset Chaba's mother, before whom it was made. She told me privately that all of her relatives live in the countryside anyway, making it politely clear that the bunch of drunks are all on her husband's side.

Later, we learned from Chaba that her father had gone on a rampage when he learned that she was going to marry Kim. He had gone out and got roaring, red-eyed drunk, then returned to the house to berate his wife, who shouted back at him and, being sober, quickly gained the advantage.

"How dare they look down on me?" he had shouted. "Did they ask me for my daughter's hand? Hah! Her mother hands her over to a thieving *chek* behind my back and hasn't the decency to invite my family to the wedding . . . that's the respect a father gets!"

"You got the respect you deserve," her mother had answered. "Yes, she's marrying a *chek*, but not a thieving one—or a drinking one! She'll live like a human being, with food in her house instead of empty whiskey bottles and a stinking lout of a drunk to shame her!"

As Chaba told us about the row, her love and respect for this strong woman were plain to see. As was her own sense of humor—Chaba imitated first her loud, brawling father and then her even-tempered, stern mother to perfection, making us all laugh at a situation which she, better than any of us, knew to be pathetic.

When the wedding day arrived, Chaba's father was not only resigned to the marriage, but delighted with his share of the festivities. A new suit of clothing, a whole tray of wedding cakes for breakfast, a bottle of whiskey, and enough money to keep him out of the house for the rest of the day. Early in the morning, I went to their house intending to help serve the monks, but, to my own disappointment, I felt too uncomfortable with those people to stay. I excused myself after about half an hour, and felt a little ashamed when Kim threw me a grin that showed he understood. He fits in there, as if he were always meant to sit in a Thai house beside a Thai bride, offering food to Thai monks.* Strange, isn't it? I could never have done that.

On my way home, whom should I meet but the father of the bride, already asleep in the gutter, clutching an empty bottle. I felt disgusted, but I reminded myself that all human attachments, however "honorable" or "wicked," bind men to sorrow; whether the attachment is to whiskey, wealth, or our own children. The Lord Buddha taught that we are never impervious to grief while there is anything we would grieve to lose and, thinking of my son, I lost some of my disdain for Chaba's poor father. Which of us is more vulnerable in this life?

I returned to the store and tried to work at my desk, then wandered down to the factory and talked to Father for awhile, and finally went into the house to make a pot of tea and brood in the kitchen.

Kim's wedding day. Who can ever replace him? It is only a matter of time before he and Chaba strike out on their own, and I myself offered them that chance. I will miss him, his cheerfulness and honesty, even his worrying. But it is foolish to feel sorry for myself. I should hire someone now, and start training him against the day I lose Kim. All things are continually in flux . . . again my mind turns to religion. I wonder why. We all resist uncertainty and change as though, somehow, this inescapable fact of life can be bent—just a little, just for us—if we could only learn the "secret." Our religion teaches us that there is no secret, no magical escape, but for most of us I am afraid that simple truth is too hard to bear. I told Kim that we are born to do battle with fate. But why are we made that way? What is the sense of it, when chance and uncertainty are beyond all battles?

When I had puzzled over this mystery for awhile, I decided to dress for the wedding dinner and play with Weng Khim for an hour or so. I am discovering that a baby's chuckles are the best cure for too much thinking.

---

*The religious aspects of a wedding differ somewhat between the Chinese, who practice Mahayana Buddhism, and the Thais, who follow the Theravada Buddhist tradition. Local "secular" marriage customs between Chinese and Thai people in Bangkok would also differ in several respects. *Trans.*

YOU WILL not be very surprised to learn that Kim and Chaba are now working on their own. I am glad that they decided to continue living with us, for I dreaded losing his company more than losing his help. Having prepared myself for their decision, I wasn't too upset when they told us, but Mui Eng was furious. She had more to say over Kim's leaving the business than about anything since she learned the provisions of her father's will.

"Kim isn't leaving with empty hands, is he? Besides everything else, you had to loan him the capital to start a business. Why? Now you have to hire someone to take his place, someone we don't even know, and for that you think Kim deserves a reward!"

"I owe him this much. We're from the same village, and what kind of friend would I be if I didn't help him out? He knows I can do it without hurting us any, and so do you."

"But what right does he have to expect so much? You gave him free room and board all this time, and paid him more than you paid anyone."

"Mui Eng, he earned it! I don't want him to spend the rest of his life working for me. How do you think he would feel after a few years? A man has to be independent, and try himself against other men. Kim's never had a chance to prove that he can. The worst thing I can do now is to continue supporting him like a poor relative, or a child, until he loses all respect for himself and all courage to try."

"So he's going to sell pork in the market. Is that your idea of 'trying himself against other men'?"

"Yes. Why do you look down on it? Pork and poultry, too. They've even talked her father into helping. He's going to slaughter the animals—it's the one thing he likes to do. He'll earn enough out of it to go out and drink for the rest of the day after he's through. Kim doesn't think he'll live another two years, but he'll be out of their way until then and contribute something into the bar gain. I think it's a sad arrangement, but what else can they do with him? At least he won't be stealing to get the stuff."

Mui Eng had no intention of being persuaded, so I dropped the subject and let her stew in her own resentment. She'll get over it once the loan is paid back.

Kim was mistaken when he guessed that his new father-in-law would drink himself to death in two years. Chaba's father fell into a *khlong* on his way home one night only two weeks after the wedding, and his body was found the next morning. What a pitiful way for a man to end his life. The most surprising effect of his death was that his wife cried her heart out for days. I wonder what memories she wept for.

I was curious to learn how a Thai funeral would be conducted, but it turned out to be not only a disappointment but, to my mind, a disgrace. I will not say that it was a typical Thai funeral, and to be fair I am sure that it was not. On the other hand, I do not suppose that it was a rarity. (I can see you frowning and saying, "Suang U! Will you ever stop talking up and down!")

The old man's body was carried to a Thai temple by his friends and family, and many monks chanted. This part was much like our own custom. When most of us left, however, a few relatives remained behind at the temple to guard the body or, as Chaba said, "to be his friends." A few days later, Kim told me what transpired as the night wore on. You will be astonished.

His relatives, all afraid of ghosts, bolstered their courage with liquor, played *mak ruk*,* cheated each other at cards, and brawled until dawn.

"So they're afraid of ghosts," Kim said, a little embarrassed by the shocked look on my face. "Lots of people are."

"But the dead man was their own relative."

"Well, in a temple, you know he's not the only corpse that ever spent the night there."

"Then why didn't they go home?"

"A black cat might have jumped across the body."

"What's supposed to happen then?"

He grinned. "The body would leap out of the coffin, howling and shrieking."

"They actually believe that? When they all get drunk and noisy, I should think it would be enough to scare any cat into leaping over the body, if that was the only way out of the place. Maybe the ghost of the dead man would have sprung up and put an end to their spree—no, I

*Thai chess. *Trans.*

115

forgot—this was the ghost of the biggest lush of them all. He'd probably have joined in . . . I wonder if they'd have noticed? Anyway, I'm thankful you didn't ask any of them to the wedding. Who knows what they'd have done, if they would disgrace even a funeral."

Apparently, drinking is a part of all Thai special occasions. Chaba has more reason to disapprove of it than I. Years ago, she told us, when one of her cousins was being ordained as a monk, her family went to attend the religious and family ceremonies, and the parties, which are always part of such an occasion. As usual, she said, everyone got drunk. One of her uncles pulled out a gun and began firing it into the air, then staggered from the room where the party was going on, out onto the front porch, and began firing at random into the darkness. By the time he ran out of ammunition and staggered back into the party, Chaba's little brother lay dead in the garden below.

Which brings to mind another peculiar Thai trait: this need to show off one's "strength" with a knife or gun. Of course, no one escapes harm in such a contest. We are always reading in the newspaper about tragic crimes that take place at weddings and other celebrations because some of the guests came bearing weapons. There are times when a man must carry a weapon; I cannot say that I disapprove of weapons themselves. But to carry one to a sacred ceremony such as a wedding or an ordination? That I find appalling.

Enough of unpleasantness! I must make up for it by writing of happy things. Your grandson, for instance, who can now say "Papa" and "Mama." He babbles all day long, is very strong, already sleeps on his belly, and crawls around putting everything into his mouth. Mui Eng has to watch him constantly lest he choke.

Father can never get any work done when Weng Khim is near. They love each other—as truly as if they were grandson and grandfather by blood. Weng Khim sits on his lap, grabbing pens and pencils and scribbling on everything he can reach. He will love learning, we are certain!

Mui Eng doesn't let a day go by without reminding me that she wants a daughter. I'm not arguing. I almost wish she'd have one and get it over with, so that I might have peace. I already have my first son, and I feel confident that more will follow.

MY SON walks! Holding onto the edges of tables and chairs, he solemnly gropes his way about the house. He doesn't make much sense yet when he talks, but he understands every word we say to him and likes to try out a few words of his own when he feels inspired (usually by a favorite food out of reach).

Chaba and Kim often take him to the market, and he stays with them all day, until the last pieces of pork and the last chicken have been sold. He never tires of it. "Weng Khim refused to come home!" Chaba will say with a grin. And then Kim will appear in the doorway with the triumphant Weng Khim perched on his shoulders, happy and messy and tired. And starved—a day at the market gives him a tremendous appetite, however many treats he managed to wheedle during the day. Most evenings, Chaba makes Thai food for us. I like some of it, especially *kaeng khilek** and Thai-style dried fish. But there are other dishes I can't bear the sight or smell of. Fermented fish steeped in brine (or anything else fermented in anything), and all the dishes the Thai people call "yam"—salads of meat that is raw, or nearly so! They are dreadful. I won't even try such things, for fear of getting sick, and I can tell you they don't agree so well with Thais, either. They grow old quickly, sicken and die on these raw and rotten foods, while the Chinese, eating prudently of well-cooked and healthful foods (not loaded with peppers and other harmful spices), live to see our grandchildren.

I have never put a piece of ice into my mouth, or taken an iced drink. Cold liquid rushing down into a man's stomach is unnatural, as anyone with common sense must agree, and I have observed that old people who take iced drinks become stiff and move painfully. Thailand is very

---

*A kind of curry made with beef and thrice-boiled leaves and buds of the *khilek* (cassod) tree; these are also used to make medicine. The leaves are extremely bitter and somewhat resemble spinach. *Trans.*

hot, and cold drinks only increase the heat within our bodies. I decided long ago to drink only hot tea, which cools the blood.

Weng Khim likes a nice refreshing glass of *nam kek huai* [chrysanthemum tea]. He loves to eat *kaeng khilek*, shrimps, and rice; wear his red shirt; and listen to the radio. These are Weng Khim's favorite things.

Mui Eng nagged me into buying the radio, but there's nothing to listen to that interests me, just a lot of Thai chatter and Thai music. I wish they would have the Chinese opera on radio, or even Chinese songs, but I haven't heard any yet. Perhaps the radio people will come to realize that most of the people who can afford radios are Chinese. I am aware that products are advertised on the radio. If the advertisers of soap powder who never seem to be off the air over ten minutes at a time ever find out that nine-tenths of their listeners don't know what they're talking about, there may be progress.

If the programs they have now don't interest me, the radio itself does. What a miracle that sounds made in a building I cannot even see find their way to a little box in my house. Talking with my new neighbors the other evening, I learned that pictures may one day be sent through the air in much the same way. That is incredible, but I have seen many incredible things since I left Po Leng. I have forgotten, in every letter so far, to tell you about the "telephone." It is a marvelous invention. If I talk into a certain part of the telephone machine where I am, a man two miles away can hear me by listening to a different part of an identical machine where he is. And he can answer me, too. Who would have thought we would see such miracles on this earth? Of course, they are not real miracles. The red-haired foreigners made these machines. I believe that we Chinese will learn to make them ourselves before many years have passed.

We have electric lights now, and it is one of Weng Khim's favorite jokes to turn the light switch on and off. He laughs merrily at his "power" whenever he manages to pitch his parents into darkness as we work on the books after dinner. And whenever the radio is turned on, he shouts, "Man! Where man?" and toddles about the room in search of the mysterious voice.

There are other new developments in Bangkok that may interest you more. The women here are cutting off their hair and having it curled with electric machines. (That is, they curl the hair that is left, dear Mother, lest you misunderstand and surmise that it is the fashion to keep one's curls in a box!) If such an electric curling machine is used by a person who knows nothing about it (which, I believe, describes almost everyone now using one), the woman having her hair curled may die a fearful death for her vanity. Of course, that does not stop the ladies from following each other like sheep to the "beauty parlor." They come out looking like sheep, too.

A few days ago, when Ang Buai brought her mother to have supper with us, I hardly recognized my own sister-in-law. Her hair was gone, except for a dreadful fuzzy fringe that hangs to just below her ears. Mui Eng exclaimed rapturously over the new "style," though I thought it a thousand times ugly.

"Oh, Ang Buai, you're so different!" she cried, clapping her hands delightedly. "And you're wearing lipstick . . . you look so—so modern! Do you think I would look as well with my hair done like yours?"

All their lives, Mui Eng has been considered the beautiful sister. Now Ang Buai walks in the door, no longer just plain but truly grotesque, painted, cropped, and frizzed, and Mui Eng doubts herself! It is proof that women can never be understood by men.

"Oh no, you won't!" Ang Buai replied, laughing and pointing to me. "Look at your husband's face!"

"Ang Buai, weren't you afraid to have that done?" I asked, finding it difficult even to look at her.

"Afraid? Why?"

"That machine. Haven't you heard that some women curl up before their hair does?"

She laughed heartily, but her mother sighed and leaned toward me anxiously. "Oh, I tried to tell her, Suang U. I begged her not to do it! But do you think children today respect their mother? 'I'm grown up now,' she says, haughty as you please, and goes right out to get that— that hairdo."

"Oh, Mother," Ang Buai cried, flopping into a chair wearily, "I wanted a change. Why not?"

"I read in the paper only yesterday," I said, "about a couple of girls who went to get their hair curled. One of them left to get two bowls of noodle soup, and when she returned her friend was gone. They told her the girl had gone home, which seemed strange, since they had just arrived . . . and where do you think they found her? In the back of the shop, her whole body burned black from the machine. The owner of the shop had noticed her gold belt and done it on purpose!"

Mui Eng's mother gasped and raised a hand to her mouth, but Ang Buai only yawned and said, "What luck! Saved from a grisly death by my cheap belt. Sorry to disappoint you, Suang U, but that machine couldn't burn anyone's whole body black—the head, maybe, but never the whole body."

"You see, everything must be a joke!" her mother cried. "Even if they didn't die, Ang Buai, some women have had all their hair burned off—and it never grows back!"

"Hm-m-m, yes. Ang Buai stroked the top of her head thoughtfully. "That would be serious . . . I think I'd be very ugly bald."

"Look at her! More afraid to be bald than to die!"

"Not really, but I'm ugly enough as it is. If it's a choice between dying and being even uglier, well . . . " She shrugged and smiled.

"Oh, I agree!" Mui Eng said earnestly. "I'd rather be dead, too, than bald for the rest of my life." She raised her hands to the thick coils of hair at the back of her head as if to reassure herself that they were still there.

"It wouldn't be all that bad, Sister. After all, we could always wear wigs."

"Oh, I don't know," Mui Eng said, unaware that she was being teased, "I think I'd better keep my hair the way it is."

"Well, I cut mine off and I'm glad. And I got a permanent and nothing happened." She raised her hands and fluffed up her short hair vigorously. "And I'm not bald or burned up dead."

Her mother leaned toward me. "You see? She does as she pleases. Lipstick, writing on her eyebrows—and she even wears a foreign skirt when she goes shopping with her friends. If her father could see her . . ." She rolled her eyes up to the ceiling and shook her head slowly, as if imploring Nguan Thong to help her in this extremity. "If only she would get married . . . her poor father begged her on his deathbed—"

"Mother, do not mention Seng again!" Ang Buai's eyes flashed angrily, and she jumped up from her chair. "You think happiness for a woman means one thing—marriage, a man! And that isn't so, not for me anyway. I don't need it. Don't you realize that a woman can be married and be unhappy? Look around you, look at all the bad marriages! If I get married, I'll still have to work. And raise children, and spend any free time I'm lucky enough to get trying to please a husband. That's the Chinese way—the woman just gives and gives and the husband takes and takes. Do you think I'd put up with that for a toad like Seng? I want freedom, and I want to wear a foreign skirt when I feel like it, and cut off my hair when I'm bored with it. Is that so terrible?"

"And not worry if your mother disapproves, I'm sure—that's what you want, 'freedom' from your own mother!"

"You're confusing everything, Mother. This is not a contest. So long as I behave myself, which I do, and don't disgrace my family, which I won't, I don't see why I shouldn't make my own decisions. That doesn't mean I win and you lose. I respect you, Mother, but I am a woman now, too, like you."

"A Chinese woman wears pants," her mother retorted irrelevantly, sniffing into her handkerchief.

"What, by law? A Chinese girl in a skirt is still Chinese, just as a Thai girl in Chinese pants is still Thai. Clothes today are not just uniforms we put on to identify ourselves and keep each other straight—'she's Chinese, she's Thai' . . ." She smiled at her mother, then, and said "Don't worry, you won't see me out on 'dates' with men, or going out alone at night. What are you so worried about, then? The world is changing, but all the changes are not bad. Even in your lifetime, you'll see our Chinese ways change. I'm not the only Chinese girl in Bangkok who's stepping out from behind the counter or the kitchen door. I— I may even learn to drive an automobile one of these days," she declared. "I would like that."

Mui Eng's eyes almost popped out. "Oh, Ang Buai, do you mean it?"

"Of course I do. Think of it—I could come over here anytime."

"You could come over here anytime on the bus," I said.

"Oh, you . . . you ought to trade in that wreck of a truck you got from Father and buy a new one, and a decent car besides. You can afford it."

"That is not necessary."

"Suit yourself. But if I had a car, I'd pick up old Weng Khim here and we'd ride all over Bangkok together." She grinned at Weng Khim, who was sitting on his grandmother's lap. "Wouldn't we, Khim? How would you like to ride in Auntie's car?"

"Khim go car," he said eagerly, and reached toward her.

"Not so fast!" his grandmother laughed, hugging him closer to her. "How this boy does love to go. Khim, you'd better stay home with Mama until that baby comes. Soon you won't have Mama all to yourself."

"Baby?" He frowned, confused by the unwelcome turn in a promising conversation, "Khim go car!" he declared finally, decisively abandoning the subject of the baby. "Khim go car market, Khim go car gimme candy!"

"Tch! Greedy Khim!" Mui Eng said, grinning at her son proudly.

"Khim greedy boy," he repeated happily.

"Who's greedy?" his grandmother asked.

He pointed to himself, then stuck his finger into her cheek. "Khim greedy—Grandma greedy too."

"Grandma greedy? Oh no, Khim!" she cried, making a comical face. He squealed with laughter, then shouted "Grandma greedy! Auntie greedy, Papa greedy, Mama greedy—greedy all people!"

We all laughed, then, the tension between us dissolving in the baby's simple joke. I felt tears come to my eyes—what a wonder a little child is, Mother. No entertainment has yet been invented that can give a man as much joy as the innocent speech of his own child. Weng Khim refreshes me when I am tired to death, and gives me a hundred little moments to remember, and smile at, as I go about my daily work.

—

LETTER #30   FIRST MONTH, FOURTEENTH DAY
23 FEBRUARY 1947   YEAR OF THE RAT

WELL, MY wife has got what she wanted. Your second grandchild arrived with little trouble and is a girl. She has large black eyes and fair skin, and everyone says she is the image of Mui Eng as a baby. Mama, Auntie, and Grandmother hover over her all the time as if she were a fairy come to life. They are her slaves. Which is all right, I suppose. I'm not upset about the baby being a girl. One girl isn't worth getting upset over. I've been tolerant of their gushing and even picked her up once, which naturally thrilled them. My mother-in-law gave her a gold necklace, and Ang Buai gave her a heart-shaped gold locket with a tiny ruby in its center. Mui Eng, not to be outdone, bought her a ring, of all things. And I did my duty—I bought her a pair of gold ankle bracelets.

Kim and Chaba's gift was dismaying. I must explain that little Thai girls wear a kind of medallion suspended on a belt to cover their private parts. This thing, called a *chap-ping*, is made of gold or silver woven into a fine, soft mesh. The one they gave the baby is red-gold, and I think it's terrible.

"Well," Kim shrugged, with his usual sly grin, "she seemed to have everything else, and somebody had to buy it."

"Why? Keep it for your own daughter," I said. "I would rather see my daughter wearing pants than one of those things."

Mui Eng looked up suddenly, "A pair of pants? How dreadful!"

"Look, nothing could be as dreadful as that—that thing dangling there."

"If you think that's bad," Chaba said, laughing, "you should have seen the little girls in the countryside, where I grew up. People who had no cloth and were too poor to buy a proper *chap-ping* used a length of twine and a tiny coconut shell instead. But people with money bought silver or gold. You could always tell the family's wealth by looking at the baby daughter's *chap-ping*."

To that, I could only bless the impermanence of folly. I don't think I'll ever look at a small coconut again without thinking of it . . . but we had to accept the gift, of course. I had already been too rude about it. I made it clear to Mui Eng that I never want to see it on the baby.

"All little girls here wear them," she said, genuinely bewildered at my attitude.

"You can sew, can't you? Make her some clothes!"

"If I had a sewing machine, I would."

So the result of Kim's ill chosen gift was my having to buy Mui Eng a sewing machine. She has made some clothes for the baby already, and they look very nice. I am relieved that my daughter will take her first steps properly clothed instead of with a piece of Thai jewelry draped over her private place.

Naming the baby was a more difficult problem. When I suggested

"Chui Kim," the name of the novel heroine who threw her bracelet to her lover, Mui Eng didn't speak to me for two days. Was that so terrible? I thought she wanted romance . . . after that, I left the naming up to her. A girl's name, after all, doesn't mean much—she's just as likely to be known by a nickname all her life.

Weng Khim likes the baby, but when he pinched her cheeks yesterday, his mother descended on him with both arms swinging, and he ran to me.

"Don't you dare run to your father!" she shouted after him. The poor child nestled closer in my arms and peered out at her, wide-eyed with fear. I am sure he meant no harm. He probably wondered whether his sister wasn't just a big doll, and had to satisfy his curiosity. I swung him up onto my shoulders, and together we escaped our women. He knows that Grandpa and I are his friends. Mother makes green, angry eyes at him and pushes him away when he tries to climb into her lap.

"Weng Khim, will you stop that!" I heard her say yesterday, in an exasperated tone of voice. "You're not a baby now—you're a big boy! You can't climb all over Mama when she's trying to work." As he toddled away, I heard him mutter, "Weng Khim big boy . . . no climb Mama lap." Poor little fellow. But in the evening, I was pleased to see that Mui Eng let him fall asleep in her lap and then gently carried him to his cot and kissed him good night.

A few days ago, Ang Buai and her mother arrived at the house in a new, light blue sedan. My mother-in-law was beaming, which surprised me.

"Oh, Suang U, it's wonderful" she exclaimed as I helped her from the car. "It's like—like nothing else! More comfortable than the tram, or the nasty old bus—a thousand times so. And it's there whenever we want to use it. Doesn't make a dreadful racket, either, like that old truck of Nguan Thong's used to make!"

"Still does, Mother," I replied with a smile, "and it's music to me—reminds me that it was free. How was your drive?"

She looked around quickly and leaned closer to me. "Well, she's not perfect yet," she whispered. "But she didn't drive us off the road into a *khlong*, and if I thought she might have, she'd never have gotten me into the car, and that's a fact!" She chuckled merrily and entered the house.

Mui Eng rushed out to see the car. "Oh, oh—it's gorgeous!" she cried. "And guess what! Suang U has bought me a sewing machine!"

It was a very happy moment for all of them. Everyone had something to show off.

Mui Eng rushed her mother and sister upstairs after briefly admiring the new car, and soon I heard the zuz-zuz of the sewing machine and their excited laughter as first Ang Buai, then her mother, learned its mysteries.

Weng Khim sidled out the front door cautiously, throwing quick, guilty glances my way every few seconds to see if Papa was noticing his escape. He was so funny that I pretended to be absorbed in my newspaper. Once safely outside, he called out to our washgirl, imperiously demanding that she leave her work to come outside and open the car door for him. First he leaped joyously from the back seat to the front and back again, then he meticulously pulled apart the lei of jasmine blossoms Ang Buai had hung from the rearview mirror, then he settled down to play at the steering wheel, making important car-driving noises. Finally I called to him, but he ignored me, too enslaved by his wondrous great toy to bother with silly demands. "Leave him alone!" Ang Buai shouted down the stairs. "He can't hurt himself!"

The washgirl smiled and gestured that she would keep an eye on him, so I went upstairs to join the women. They had finished with the sewing machine and were crouched over the baby's crib, arguing over each feature on her face for the hundredth time.

"What is my niece's name?" Ang Buai asked as I entered the room.

"No name yet."

"What do you mean, 'no name'? Khim had a name nine months before he was born—where is justice in this house?"

"How should I know what to name a girl?"

"H-m-m-m . . . how about—Chui Kim! Perfect, isn't it? Tan Chui Kim!"

Mui Eng reached out swiftly and pinched her sister's arm. "Bah! You're all crazy," she said angrily. "I'm not naming any child 'Chui Kim'!"

Ang Buai rubbed her arm and frowned. "Who's crazy? This is the thanks I get for naming your baby—"

"I thought of that name already," I said, "and she didn't talk to me for two days."

"How silly. It's a pretty name." She bent over the crib and smiled at her tiny niece, asleep and blissfully unaware of the quibbling adults around her. "What do you think, baby? How do you like the name?"

Incredibly, the baby opened her eyes, raised one pink fist to her mouth and uttered a little cry. "Er!" she said, earnestly regarding her aunt.

"There, you see? She says she loves it. But you be a new kind of Chui Kim, do you hear? No nonsense with a bracelet, eh?"

"Er!" the baby exclaimed, drawing her little brows together seriously. Even Mui Eng had to laugh, though she turned quickly away, lest we notice.

Then Ang Buai turned from the crib and said, "Time to take my nephew for a ride in the car."

I had to agree to it, but I worry about the children being with her, growing up near her. I am old-fashioned, I suppose, but when I first came to their home, Ang Buai was a decent girl in black Chinese women's pants and a white blouse, with her long black hair in plaits. And now? I don't know what to make of her. Is the same girl alive under all that lipstick and frizzy hair? I don't understand. Driving an automobile, wearing a foreign dress with her legs bare right up to the knee . . . I don't have to wonder what her father would think of it all. If Nguan Thong were alive, he'd die of shame.

Ang Buai climbed into the car with Weng Khim, who squealed like a little pig in his excitement, and off they went, It seemed as though they were gone for hours, and by the time the sleek blue car reappeared on Sampheng Lane, I was sitting on the curb, sick with worry.

"You look as though you're waiting to be carried off!" Ang Buai shouted. Weng Khim's little face was radiant with happiness, and when I pulled him from the car he shouted "Khim go more!" and attempted to squirm from my grasp and climb back up onto the seat. But he soon forgot his anger in his eagerness to show me the treats Auntie had bought him during their adventure. She reached across the car seat and handed me a large, brightly colored cloth fish from which five or six smaller fishes dangled on strings. "That thing is called a 'mobile,'" she said, climbing out the driver's side and slamming the door. "Hold it up high, and all the fishes will swim around—that's right!" Weng Khim laughed delightedly and said, "Fish for baby!" Ang Buai smiled at him, then turned to me. "Babies like bright colors. You're supposed to hang it over her crib so she'll have something to look at."

Weng Khim held a little stuffed water buffalo in one hand and, in the other, a red, sticky concoction that dripped.

"What is that?" I asked.

"Ice pop!" he declared. "Khim eat ice pop!"

"Why did you buy him that thing?"

"It's nothing but ice with red syrup poured over it. Delicious, eh Khim?"

"He'll have an upset stomach that won't be delicious. That's nothing to give a child."

"Well, who else do you suppose eats ice pops?"

"That doesn't interest me. He has never eaten anything but cooked food. We have plenty of wholesome sweets here at home that won't spoil his digestion."

She opened her mouth to speak, then paused as if changing her mind. Weng Khim stared at us thoughtfully while the melting ice pop trickled steadily from his hand to his elbow, then dripped onto the dirt.

"Throw it away, Khim" she said, her voice shaking. "The flavor is all gone—it's just ice now, see?"

Weng Khim gazed regretfully at his sticky treasure.

"Thank you," I said. "Time for a bath, now, son, and dinner—what do you think? We're having *kaeng khilek*!"

At that, he threw the ice pop down and ran into the house to find his mother. Ang Buai and I followed him silently, leaving the little blob of ice and syrup to a swarm of grateful flies.

"The water is warm, hurry and undress!" Mui Eng called from the kitchen. Weng Khim threw his little water buffalo onto a chair and, tugging at his shirt, toddled wearily out of the room. "Oh, what a nasty little boy you are today," we heard her say. "You must have had a fine time!"

"It's stifling today," Ang Buai said. "Why is she putting him into a warm bath?"

"Because cold water is unhealthy on a hot day."

"My, my—we certainly have our differences. Even over the temperature of a bath. Frankly, Teacher, I'm not up to arguing with you in this weather." She turned and trudged slowly up the stairs.

127

Later, we ate a silent supper together, but when Mui Eng carried the sleepy Weng Khim upstairs to bed, Ang Buai leaned across the table and said, in her usual bantering tone, "We agree on one thing at least— Chui Kim! I'll always have one thing I can remember, and say to myself, "My brother-in-law and I agreed on that, and we weren't even trying!"

Her mother smiled gratefully at Ang Buai's gesture, and I felt rather grateful myself, for I was not sure how our latest argument would have resolved itself otherwise. One thing I must credit her for—she knows how to give in without losing.

In this letter, I have brought you no news very sad or serious—only news of babies, relatives, and squabbles concerning both. It is a hopeful sign, I believe, for we are surely on our way to recovering from the grief we all felt at Nguan Thong's death when we can let our emotions run rampant over an ice pop.

—

LETTER #31   FIFTH MONTH, THIRD DAY
9 JUNE 1948   YEAR OF THE RAT

YOUR SON is gaining a good reputation in business, or so Father tells me, but sometimes I wish I were as successful in other ways. The trouble is, I seem to say the wrong things to people I care for most. I hurt their feelings without meaning in the least to do so.

I discovered recently that Kim has been playing the lottery. Not once or twice, but often. When I learned of it, I lost my temper. It is hard to write about what happened . . . I bossed him, I talked to him as if he were a child, I made him angry. I can't blame him—it was my own stupid fault. But I did it because I care about him. Doesn't that count for anything? I felt it was my duty to warn him about gambling, and I still feel that way, but now I wish that I had not spoken so quickly.

Lottery tickets are sold on the city streets. Whoever buys the one with the winning number receives many thousands of baht. I am not sure exactly when Kim began this madness, but by the time I learned of it, he was wasting money on it every week. He was in the store helping me with our monthly inventory one Sunday when Ang Buai came to visit.

"I had the strangest dream last night," she said. "I must be working too hard. Seven airplanes flew over the store and dropped bombs on it!" She laughed. "It may sound funny this morning, but I woke up thinking that maybe I ought to have a basement dug under the store— sometimes dreams seem so real."

"Seven planes," Kim muttered, turning quickly. "How many times did it drop the bombs?"

"Uh, three I think."

"Seven-three . . . oh, what a day! I'll be rich!"

"What are you talking about?" I asked, annoyed.

He looked away, then, and said nothing, but Ang Buai grinned and said, "The lottery, of course. He'll buy a ticket ending in seven and three, and win ten thousand baht—maybe."

"You mean you've done this before?" I asked, unable to believe my ears.

"Uh—well, once or twice."

"Did you win anything?"

"Once, a long time ago, I won a little . . . See, if you play all the time, you never win. You have to have a sign—like Ang Buai's dream."

"How do you know so much about it?" Mui Eng asked as she entered the room with Chui Kim in her arms. "In our father's house, no one would have dared to play. He told us there used to be an alphabet lottery a long time ago, and some of his friends lost a lot of money. Of course, he never spent any money on that one either."

"Perhaps, but that didn't stop the men who worked for him," Ang Buai said. "They all played the lottery. Kim, how long have you been at it?"

"Not—not long."

I pulled him aside, and the others managed to become suddenly busy. "Kim, please tell me the truth," I said. "When did you begin playing at this—this evil?"

"Evil? You know, you are getting really crazy. It's taking a chance on some extra cash at a few satangs a throw, not any kind of evil. The government runs the whole thing. You make it sound like some back alley game run by criminals. This is legal."

"Legal, eh? And what if they legalize the rest of the 'back alley games'? Will you be proud to play them, too?"

"Look, poor people love the lottery—why shouldn't they? If you don't have a rich wife and a big business, what chance do you have in this world? I sell pork and poultry in the market, and I make enough to eat. For a few satangs, I get a chance at thousands of baht in the lottery, and to me it's worth it."

"You aren't hungry, and you have a home with us. When you throw away money on a lottery ticket—even a few satangs—you're selling your future! Remember your wife—your wives, I should say—and your responsibilities to both of them!"

"Why do you think I'd like to win ten thousand baht? A thousand of it would take care of the one in China for good."

"Kim, a thousand of what? This is madness! You go to the ten richest Chinese in Bangkok and see if any of them made their money in this damned lottery."

"Yeah, now tell me again how hard they worked, how they sacrificed to get where they are," he said with something like a sneer. "Haven't you heard any of the jokes Thai people tell about the Chinese?"

"What jokes?"

"Ask Chaba sometimes. There's one about the Chinese family that hung a dried, salted fish over the supper table and looked at it while they ate their rice . . . so the mother said to the little boy, 'Quit staring so hard at the salted fish—you'll be thirsty all night!'"

"So they insult us even for our thrift . . ."

"I don't think it's meant that way, Suang U—those stories are sort of funny. Who would ever have thought of 'Chinese jokes' in Po Leng?"

"You really believe they're 'funny'?"

He shrugged. "I know a better one. The stingiest man in North China journeyed a thousand miles to see his friend, the stingiest man in South China. As a gift, he took along one stale bean cake. Well, when he reached the house, his friend's son met him at the door. He accepted the bean cake, ran into the house, and came back with a watermelon to give in return. Later, when the son told his father about the exchange of gifts, the old man flew into a rage. 'Stupid boy!' he shouted, 'Half a watermelon would have been plenty!'" Then Kim laughed, and I lost my temper.

"You ass! There are no Chinese people who act like that—and you laugh right along with those who would step on your face. You've had every chance any other man has, and my help, and a hard-working wife who has more sense than you have. To respect yourself, you've got to earn your own success! It's never luck, Kim, never. If you had taken every satang you wasted on those tickets and sent the money to China, or saved it here, it could be working for you instead of for some official who's already rich!"

"You are not my father," he said slowly.

"What do you mean by that?"

"I mean that I am sick of your speeches, and sick to death of your smugness."

"Kim, I care about you, don't you realize that? I shall forget what— what you just said—"

"Don't forget," he said evenly, then turned and left the house.

I am disappointed in him, more disappointed in myself. If I have destroyed our friendship, I don't know what I'll do. Without Kim, nothing would be the same.

—

LETTER #32   EIGHTH MONTH, SECOND DAY
4 SEPTEMBER 1948   YEAR OF THE RAT

FOR ALMOST three months, Kim has scarcely turned his face toward mine. What he thinks of me I cannot say. But he has not neglected Weng Khim, who goes to the market with him most afternoons, returning home after dusk. I spoke with Mui Eng about it recently, for I am afraid that it is no good for the boy to become fond of gadding about.

"What? It is good of Kim to take him, and let me get some work done. Chui Kim sleeps all day, but if Weng Khim were home what would I get done, eh? And there's nothing so terrible about the market. It's not even on the *khlong*, as his own house is. How could he be safer?"

"So it is not on the *khlong*—look at the traffic there! I can't help but worry, and he is too young to be thinking of running out of the house all the time."

"Children today are naughtier than they used to be. You think too much! Why can't you be glad there's someone to take him off our hands a few hours a day? And it won't hurt him to see something of the world outside this house. He'll be smarter for it."

"I don't need to have my son 'taken off my hands'—"

"Then what would you have? You don't want a servant looking after him, and I have the store all day. Anyway, if I held him back while Chaba and Kim went out the door, he'd scream the house down. First we let him go, then everything is changed and he must stay home? Hah! You explain that to a two year old."

"Aha! You see? 'He'd scream the house down,' she says. Does that prove nothing to you, Mui Eng? Now is the time to teach him good habits, not cater to his temper. He ought to be in school."

Her mouth twitched with a half-smile. "School . . . what school do you think would accept him?"

"Then—then I'll take him with me to the factory."

"Oh, Suang U, be sensible. He isn't even awake when you leave in the morning."

I must think further about this problem.

Father has been sleeping at the factory since it opened, keeping an eye on the help; a few are sure to be light-fingered. We leave no money there, of course, but the machinery is valuable and there are other things in sight which must tempt those with the tendency.

Having the factory at a distance from where we live is a great nuisance—or was a nuisance I should say, for all that is changed now. At first I considered moving over there myself, but then, I would be worrying about the store instead. The other possibility was to move everything over to Yawarat—dry goods store, import business, and all. Against that idea was the loss of our access to the river, for the Yaowarat property does not back on a *khlong*. That meant giving up our river-based customers, and the problem of who would take them on. You see, the logical person was none other than Tae Seng.

Why should that have mattered so much to me? I do not know, but it did. I have repeated so often that I bear no grudge, that I would not lower myself to return his hatred. Yet I confess that I could not allow him to have what had been mine. Good customers, never a day late on their payments, men who buy much and sell it all. I briefly considered letting Kim handle them under my supervision, but can I trust him anymore? If he had all that money at his disposal, would he be able to resist his gambling weakness? The chance was too great to dare.

I see Seng occasionally at the docks. The old hatred still flickers in his eyes, and he tries to humiliate me in a hundred small ways. Shall a man do good to one who treats him as an inferior?

Thus, a few days ago I found myself entering the offices of a neighbor whose import business is very similar to mine.

"Suang U! What brings you here?" Li San rose with a cheerful smile, motioned for me to sit down, and poured me a cup of tea from the great porcelain teapot that stands on his desk.

"We are moving the business to Yawarat, and I am giving up my customers on Khlong Bang Luang. I wish to ask you, before I begin to make final arrangements, whether you will consider taking over these accounts. You see, there is someone else who would gladly seize them."

The merchant drew his brows together thoughtfully and poured himself a fresh cup of tea. Mine was not a proposition a man would accept eagerly, nor is my feud with Seng a secret. Certainly, Li San knew my meaning.

"You are the only man in our business," I continued, speaking too quickly, "who has never tried to take any of my customers away. I respect that. I believe that you and I have respected each other, Li San." He relaxed his frown but did not make any reply. "You can begin to serve these customers as soon as I settle their accounts with us. It won't take long, I assure you."

He is not a close friend, that I should choose to further his success. It is a fortunate event for him, to be sure, and I never doubted that he would accept the offer (he is honorable but not a fool). Yet, in spite of his polite reserve, he let me know that he disapproved of the circumstances.

He nodded curtly and pushed his teacup across the desk as if setting aside his reservations, then said, "Your boats—I suppose you will want to sell them. I can take one, and I'll sell another for you. I have a friend who's been looking for one."

So we agreed, and though he had seen my boats many times I insisted that he see them again, inspect them carefully before spending his money and his friend's. Both men paid fair prices for good value, and Li San did not mention the commission that is usually due in such matters.

He is a man of about forty years, from Teo Chiu province, taciturn and fair and the father of seven sons, all of which earn him the respect and envy of his colleagues. I believe he is honest enough, he has never been known to steal a customer, and he does not argue or speak rudely to any man. In short, he is just the sort of man one would trust with one's old customers.

We began to make preparations to move our household, the store, and the import inventory, and in the midst of it all incurred a great stroke of fortune. The building beside our new property, the bakery, came onto the market. The father of the family moving out has lost interest in business, lost heart, really, for his only son does not concern himself with it. At an early age, the boy was sent to America to study medicine. (They gave in to this notion because he was the only son. The mother told me they could not bear to disappoint him, he wanted so much to be a doctor.) When finally he returned to them, he spoke both Chinese and Thai poorly. Incredibly, it was only in the *farang* language that he could express himself well. If that were not enough to break a father's heart, he brought with him a *farang* wife. Now all of them have moved to a house in the suburbs, where the parents can grieve away their days while the son works in a government hospital, and the business has been sold.

I saw the *farang* woman. You could not call her ugly, though she is not nearly beautiful. She looks very peculiar, and if she bears her husband children, I expect they will look even more peculiar. Would they have pink skin, blue eyes, and black hair, I wonder? Or brown skin and red hair? The old couple shake their heads and sigh; a pitiful situation, and all because they sent their only son to be raised and educated by foreigners. I cannot imagine entrusting my son's upbringing to foreigners.

I haven't begun to look for someone to take over our lease on Sampheng Lane, for Mui Eng and Chaba haven't yet moved the store. The inventory of stock alone is a time-consuming task. But the babies are already at the new house, and Father is overjoyed to have his little ones with him again.

It all puts Kim in a difficult situation, for of course he will have to move. He and Chaba could move in with her mother, but if the old woman is wise she will make something more of that piece of property than a chicken farm. The value of her land, which is directly on the *khlong* bank, has increased many times. I suggested that she lease it for a row of shops, thereby holding onto it and realizing a steady income. She seems interested in that alternative, for Chaba has two much older brothers who have been fighting over the property's future since their father's death.

Kim has spent his life leaning on others, and I have finally got over the nonsense of blaming myself for his weaknesses. I had only his own good at heart when I confronted him about the lottery tickets, and if he feels he must continue avoiding my glance like a child who has been punished, then that is his business. Kim must learn to rely upon himself at last, if he is to become fully a man.

—

LETTER #33   OUR NEW HOME
5 DECEMBER 1948   YAOWARAT ROAD
                                  ELEVENTH MONTH, FIFTH DAY
                                  YEAR OF THE RAT

MAY I congratulate you on the prospect of a third grandchild! It is due to arrive the middle of next year, and I am so very pleased that some recent unpleasantness has failed to disturb my happy frame of mind.

While we were moving into the new place, who should appear but Tae Seng, ostensibly to look over a piece of property across the road. He greeted me courteously enough, even to performing a curt, bouncing bow.

"So, you too have moved to Yaowarat. It is the place to be these days, I hear." His eyebrows slid upward meaningfully. (Of late, Seng affects a meaningful lifting of eyebrows, usually accompanying a commonplace observation.)

"Yaowarat is the center of trade now, yes . . . you know that as well as I. The road is good, plenty of people. And for me, of course this house is next door to the bakery. It would have been foolish to pass up the opportunity."

"Indeed . . . how fortunate to be able to take advantage of changing times. And you'll be so much closer to your sister-in-law." Again, eyebrows.

"She's still two blocks away, not so close."

"But you wouldn't want the other half of Nguan Thong's estate to elude you, I'm sure—"

I struggled to compose myself, "The last time you spoke filth, Seng, you ended up on your back on the deck of a ship—"

"I recall it very well, Suang U. I was teasing you—no harm meant, of course—and you knocked me down before I could defend myself. A man who would knock his friend down without cause would steal his bride, and that is what you did, out of spite. But I should have known: Suang U wanted a rich wife, and he got her. It didn't matter how, and the fact that she was intended for another? A minor detail—"

"That is so long ago, Seng—even if it were true! Mui Eng was never meant to be your bride, and everyone knows the truth of the matter. You—you make an ass of yourself with this, if you want to know the truth."

Seng's face darkened. He forget his fine speech. "You stole her from me! She was pretty, and I wanted her, but you stole her away. And when I would have taken the sister, humiliating as that was, oh no! The great Suang U had to have her, too!"

"I don't know why you think there is anything between Ang Buai and me, but your ugly thoughts are not dignified by even a grain of truth. We live in separate houses, we seldom see each other." I didn't bother to add that our relations are strained at best, for that would only have added fuel to his suspicions.

"But she refused me!"

"If she did, it's nothing to do with me. Ang Buai is a hard woman. She's tough," I told him truthfully. "But I can tell you what she likes: everything modern and fast—automobiles, fancy foreign clothes, why, she even cut her hair off. If you're not her kind of man, do you think I am?"

Seng's eyes clouded with bewilderment for a moment as he tried to deal with the logic of my words. "You know damned well I have no time for such foolishness!"

"Do I?"

"Shut up! I won't listen to this! You wanted them both, and you have them both, and now you're trying to confuse me. Two blocks away, eh? Nice . . . you know, you ought to use the *sae* Lo, you and your son too, now that you're grabbed all the old man's money. Even the money isn't enough for your kind. Your hands itch for more than money—"

I felt dizzy, and I ached to smash his sneering face with my fist, but it was almost noon, and everyone in the neighborhood was home eating lunch. Bad enough for them to hear Seng shouting that I had stolen his bride, without my turning it into a brawl. There is a Thai saying that Chinese people having a conversation sound like Thai people having an argument. I have determined never to feed that prejudice. I am educated and have learned self-control, and though I do not affect lifted eyebrows and ironical phrases like Seng, neither do I stand before my shop shouting at my enemies for the world to hear. I concentrated on the veins bulging in Seng's neck and counted to a hundred while he ranted on.

The idea that all Chinese are loud and coarse is as false as the notion that Thais are always smiling. If you live among them you know that it is not so. There are sullen pouting Thais, plenty of them! And Thai thugs who hang around bars and coffee shops all day and night hoping for a fight, any excuse to spring at a stranger and kill him without reason or pity. The stranger is the natural target of such bullies for whom violence is the basis of life. When a Thai is full of liquor, he cannot tell an elephant from a pig, much less an enemy from an innocent bystander. Yet people praise Thailand as a land of peace, of endless smiles and yellow-robed Buddhist monks, of people whose culture is deeply ingrained, and who follow the five moral precepts faithfully.

Yet I have seen men kill and torture animals here in ways I had never conceived of before. They raise a kind of fish whose only reason for living is to tear each other to pieces before cheering spectators. The people love cock fights, ox fights, fish fights—any fight! They steal and gamble, and lie with each other's wives. The famous Thai smile is only frosting on the cake. What the cake is like, only those who have tasted it know. Thailand's greatest admirers are those who have spent two days in the country, mostly foreigners who have no idea of what life here really is. They nod wisely and say that the Thai "really know how to live" and "know the value of an easy life." They do not guess to what extreme of laziness and irresponsibility this philosophy is carried, or how great is the disregard for order and civilized behavior.

Thus I meditated while watching the veins in Seng's neck swell and contract, having decided that the neighbors, too, must take Seng as they find him. I had nothing to lose so long as I kept my own temper.

"It is no different from your other actions! You do all things treacherously, Suang U, giving those customers to Li San instead of to me!" (Getting down to essentials at last.) "You know all those shops are in my territory, you know it! I should have had them, and you snatched them out from under my nose!"

"I snatched my customers out from under your nose?"

"Don't try to be funny, Suang U. Li San is a man you hardly know, yet you think of him before you think of an old friend from your village—that is the measure of you as a man."

The last ensured my holding my temper. "Listen, old friend from my village, Li San has done me several favors. Even you should be able to understand returning a favor. I'm not out to 'get you,' Seng. In this or in the matter of Ang Buai. If you want her, go get her, and admit the truth. You know I've never been your competitor, not with her . . ."

He clenched his fists and said, in a now shaking voice, "She already turned me down, damn it!"

"So what? You ought to know a woman's mouth and her mind don't work together. Another few months and she may soften up."

"No, no . . . they aren't the only two girls in Bangkok. Why should I hang around another couple of months?"

"That's the first sensible thing you've said. If you'd be satisfied with someone else, why do you stand here and insult me with all this nonsense about Ang Buai?"

He closed his eyes and shook his head slowly. "Because if it weren't for you, I'd have everything you have now. You're—you're some kind of curse. If only I had known, when we were leaving Po Leng . . . you'd still be pushing a plow! When I think that I brought you here, asked you to come along—it must be a curse, it must—"

"Ah, Seng! That is the refuge of the disappointed, believing that things might have been different than they are. But no man ever made a 'bad' decision. Sometimes good decisions bring bad results. Look, my friend, there is no use in our going on like this. We left Po Leng as friends and arrived in Bangkok as enemies. I came to this house, you went to that house, and—and things happened.

"The years are going by, and this grudge of yours is losing all meaning." I sat down on a packing crate and Seng, rather reluctantly, sat down on another and began tracing designs in the sawdust on the floor with the toe of his shoe. "This can be the day we end the quarrel.

Who wishes us well in this land but our own people? You and I gnash our teeth, we narrow our eyes and curse each other and for what? If we can't understand each other, then we are truly alone, for the Thai sneer at our ways, they gather around and laugh at us when we perform our most sacred duties. Did you know that people in the street laughed while Nguan Thong's body was being carried to his grave? We're superstitious, they say, because our superstitions are different from theirs. They speak as if they were gods, to know that burial is wrong and a funeral pyre the only release of the spirit, that the ashes of a dead man's burning possessions only fall again into the gutter and do not follow him to the other world, as we believe. What, have they seen for themselves how the spirit of man behaves after death? Seng, we were brought up to respect the same way of life. Don't throw that away because you have suffered a disappointment, and that over a woman. There are good-looking Chinese women with big dowries all over Bangkok. A man like you won't have any trouble finding a wife. Come back and see me again when you've thought it over. Now, I have work to do!" I rose and left the shop the back way, to spare his feelings. When I returned a moment later, he was gone.

It is for our children and grandchildren's sake that quarrels among us must not be allowed to grow, for the unity of our people in a strange land is more precious than gold. It is crucial, if our descendants are to live peacefully and prosperously in the world they will inherit.

Had the ten customers been Seng's, would he have given them to me?

—

LETTER #34
1 MARCH 1949

YAOWARAT ROAD
SECOND MONTH, SECOND DAY
YEAR OF THE OX

THE SITUATION in which I find myself these days leads me to wonder whether my stars are up to mischief! Our dry goods store is doing very poorly in the new location and, far more important and worrisome, the import business is slowing down, which has never happened before. Less affected are *chan-ap* sales, for it can be stored indefinitely, and laying in stock there is a kind of asset. When sales are up, we have all we can do to keep orders filled on time.

In my heart, I have never held with "stars," horoscopes, and the like. Only women and old people are enamored of such things (excepting Ang Buai, who laughs at astrology but is hardly a woman anyway). Nevertheless, in this letter you shall learn how Mui Eng entrusted the fate of our business to the supernatural.

Thaokae Nia, visiting for Saturday dinner, nodded sympathetically as she listened to Mui Eng lament our falling profits. Ang Buai contented herself with playing winking games across the table with Chui Kim and Weng Khim.

"Oh, Mother," Mui Eng wailed, "nothing sells now, and look around!" She indicated the room full of unopened crates and boxes with a despairing sweep of her hand. "We have no place to put anything, and Suang U's distributors won't take another crate. They say they can't move the merchandise they already have. And has he told you about the troubles in the bakery? It's not like when Kim and Chaba were here. Now we have to keep an eye on everyone ourselves, or they'd steal everything that can be lifted. I can't even keep a washgirl in the house."

"Now, now, dear—a washgirl, indeed! You can always find people like that."

"Oh, yes, but one I can trust? How do you tell if a girl is honest, or will turn out like that little chit last month?"

The little chit last month was a girl who walked off after her first and only week's work with Mui Eng's new dress in a shopping bag, together with all the money she could find. She didn't get away with it; the police found her, and I remain astonished at the police having done anything for us. Another troublesome lady worked in the bakery for two weeks, winking and mincing around the bakers until they nearly came to blows over her obvious favors. I was afraid someone would surely be killed before that episode ended.

"Maybe it's this place," my mother-in-law said, glancing fearfully around. "Perhaps there's something here. The house is old, you know, and—and then there was that red-haired demon girl in here, don't forget that!" She shook her finger in the air dramatically. "She may even have put a curse on the house."

"No, Mother," I said, shaking my head and trying to hide a grin, the

140

red-haired lady was only a human being like us. Tae Seng says I'm a curse," I laughed. "How do you like that?"

"Go on, then, laugh, but you don't know," she replied, injured. "Perhaps the spirits of this place hated her, and drove all of them away, and are trying to drive us away too! I advise you to see one who knows about such things—Mui Eng understands what I mean."

Father, who had been listening politely to our conversation, spoke up, and wisely he did not make light of her fears.

"The dry goods are not selling well because we are new here. It is another beginning, isn't it? As for the imports—well, prices have gone up frightfully, and people are trying to do without luxuries they used to take for granted. You wait and see; before long, one baht will be worth only a fourth of what it is worth today. And then, after a few months, people will shrug that off too and go back to their luxuries; that is always the way."

I agreed with his explanation, but Mui Eng and her mother scarcely listened, so carried away were they by other, infinitely more exciting possibilities. To pacify everyone, I assured the two women that I would not stop them from exercising their passion for mystery. What could it hurt? It is not surprising that people are more easily comforted with magic than with common sense, for so much that happens in our lives is beyond our comprehension.

Ang Buai agreed with Father too, but she was less polite. "How can you believe such nonsense? It's a waste of time and money to hire magic against bad luck. Prayers, incantations—never in my life have I believed in such things. Our father worked hard and was successful, but sometimes even he had a run of bad luck—and he never tried to explain it away with silly things like ghosts, or curses. I can remember when he sold everything and anything, trying out the market . . . do you remember, Mui Eng? For awhile, he even sold coffee. But he always solved his problems by looking for reasonable causes, not by throwing holy water on his abacus." She laughed heartily, then, and helped herself to another dish of fried pork.

Mui Eng jumped up, white with anger, and leaned across the table at her sister, resting her weight on her hands. "You are trying to make me look stupid! Do you think no one realizes that? There was a foreign woman here, and the house spirits have put a curse on this place.

Nothing will go well for us until the curse is removed. I believe that, and there is nothing you can do to prove me wrong, with all your spite and jealousy."

"We'll invite monks to pray," Thaokae Nia said dreamily, as if nothing had occurred, "and they will sprinkle holy water over—over whatever needs it."

"Nobody's dead," Ang Buai said through a mouthful of pork. "What do you need monks for?"

"When have monks prayed only for the dead? Weddings and house-warmings have need of prayers as well. So there's another benefit. The house is new to Suang U and Mui Eng, isn't it?" The enthusiasm in the old woman's face made me glad I had not forbidden her the fun of exorcising whatever ghosts may stalk my property. Surely Ang Buai ought to have seen that, too.

"Mother, where does the curse go when they take it off?" Mui Eng asked, wrinkling her brow and sitting down to consider a new facet of the problem. "I have heard that people cast curses into the sea, or burn them in paper—will we have to do that?"

"I expect we'll be told what to do," her mother replied uncertainly.

"I cannot believe this," Ang Buai said, shaking her head slowly. "Do whatever makes you happy, Sister. Throw your bad luck or your curses into the sea, or wherever you think they ought to be thrown. But don't expect me to be part of your nonsense. And my car won't be available for the festivities."

Mui Eng regarded the younger woman with intense dislike. "You have time enough to waste on the movies, I notice. And the Chinese opera. Time enough to run around with your silly friends buying clothes. What time do I ever take for myself, Ang Buai? What time for fun? But you have no time for me, have you? Finally the others see into your heart, Younger Sister, and it isn't a pleasant sight!"

Ang Buai stared at her calmly, chewing. "Why should I be ashamed that I'd rather go to the opera than grabble around after a nonexistent ghost? Or sit spellbound before some old fraud who fakes a palsy and rolls his eyes up and pretends he's inhabited by a spirit—hah! The spirit of greed, maybe. If you want to have some fun, why don't you go to the opera with me? There's a new one in from Taiwan."

This left Mui Eng speechless with rage.

I don't know about "seeing into her heart," but I learned something new about Ang Buai from their conversation. She didn't mean to infuriate her elder sister. She does not have the ability, or the willingness, to keep from blurting out her honest feelings. And she would gladly have taken Mui Eng to the opera and never said another word about the exorcism. Ang Buai, I am beginning to understand, is a simple person in her own way, as Mui Eng is in hers.

I accompanied Mui Eng to the spiritualist, at a shrine not far from Yaowarat Road. He told us, first, that our money contribution to the project must be "equal to our purpose," whereupon the purposeful Mui Eng almost caused me to scream aloud by placing a shocking sum of money into the tray of flowers and joss sticks that lay before him.

He smiled serenely and nodded. "If your wishes are satisfied, dear lady, please remember to support our shrine in the future. It needn't be much, just enough to help us keep it in good repair. And at the New Year, of course, we appreciate our patrons' generosity."

And then his contribution to the great event commenced. As he rose to his feet before us, he began slowly to shake and quiver; his eyes rolled back in a horrible fashion. I saw nothing enter the room, but he acted as though, indeed, some sort of spirit had come among us and invaded his body. The "spirit" asked Mui Eng what the trouble was and, when she had finished telling him, he explained that our troubles were not caused by the foreign woman at all, but by other serious problems on our property! After naming a few minor discrepancies in our household religious observances, he came to the main point: in our back yard, there used to grow a *pho* tree.* When it was cut down some years ago, the spirits who had lived in it for countless years were robbed of their rightful home. We must build a little house for these dispossessed spirits, he told us, not the Thai kind but Chinese in style, and light candles there at least twice a year to show that we are mindful of our duty. We were given a vial of holy water to sprinkle on the threshold of the house ourselves, to keep demons and other evil spirits away.

When at last we got out of there, I breathed a sigh of relief. For it is not pleasant to admit one is subject to the persuasion of the invisible

*It is believed that the Buddha achieved enlightenment while sitting beneath a *pho* (or *boh)* tree. *Trans.*

143

and incomprehensible, and the man had made the hair on the back of my neck stand on end with his jabbering and quaking. What I liked even less was the business of the *pho* tree. You see, the day we moved into the house, I noticed a slightly raised area about ten feet in circumference not far from the back door. It is plain to anyone who looks for it. The spiritualist? Could he have known? I do not believe that Mui Eng ever noticed it, and she did not speak of it to that strange man. He could have come prowling around our house, looking for something that would impress us with his "vision" . . . did he? I am trying to think so, and dispel thereby the dark cloud he drew over my cheerful skepticism.

Terrible events are often blamed on angry, evil spirits who were driven from their natural homes, but when many houses are built in one place, causing many trees to be cut down, why do not all the spirits from those trees get together and cause mischief in the whole neighborhood? If a thing is true in particular, must it not be true in general? It makes my head ache; I think I had better forget it. When I was a farmer, I loved every tree on our land for its shade, its fruit, its beauty, but I never dreamed that, should I cut one down, I would be incurring the wrath of evicted ghosts.

All things have been accomplished as the spiritualist dictated, and it wasn't as expensive, in the end, as I had feared. The tree was planted, and the spirit house built, a fine structure filled with candles and flowers, joss sticks and various implements of persuasion. I hope that all concerned spirits will be pleased. Since Mui Eng seems to be, I consider the benefits already sufficient. She will enjoy paying homage to the spirit of the back yard, handing up little dishes of food on feast days and donating money to her shrine occasionally. Since the ceremony, sales have even drifted up a bit. Perhaps I ought not to be so smug! Before long, things will be back to normal, the market and all spirits willing, and Mui Eng will smile that prim, secretive smile of hers and raise her eyebrows, and I won't mind letting her congratulate herself.

Weng Khim is wonderful, Chui Kim grows fatter every day, and soon your third grandchild will be born. My heart is full of love for you this evening. I am in a rare good mood. What must you think of our foolishness? I see you smiling.

YOU HAVE another grandchild, but I am sorry to tell you that it is a girl. This child is not as strong as the first two. We have named her Bak Li. There isn't much else to say about her. I, like other Chinese men, consider five sons and two daughters a perfect family. Now I have presented you with two granddaughters, and only one grandson. Should another daughter be born to us, the disappointment would be very great.

Since my marriage, at the end of the Year of the Cock, until this year, I have become a father three times. So perhaps I should take heart. Who knows? With such a fertile wife, I may see more than five sons, and bring great honor to our family the certain promise of continuation.

Weng Khim is as clever as I could wish. I have already begun to teach him simple sums; his memory is excellent. But he continues to ask after Kim and Chaba, whom he misses terribly. That is a void I cannot seem to fill.

"I want go market, Papa! I don't like this house—I like old house, house with Kim and Chaba . . . and the boats . . . Khim want go boat every day!"

They used to take one of our boats to market, and I know that Weng Khim's favorite days began by crossing the Chao Phraya River. Waves would rock the boat and make him shriek with laughter, and river breezes would ruffle his thick hair, and fan his beaming face.

"I miss Kim, Papa! I want go boat, blow air on my face like before, and eat food from Chaba, Papa. Sai makes the food no good, and Sai not love Khim—she make a angry face on Khim every day."

But Sai is trustworthy, even if she isn't fond of children, or as cheerful and easy going as his old friends.

"You want to help?" she'll say, when he is pestering her to let him chop peppers or peel onions. "Your help is nothing but trouble for me—go outside and play, go on! Where's your mother, eh? Go see your mother."

Once, after much pleading, Sai let him go to the market with her. On their return we could hear her grumbling long before she reached the back door.

"Wretched child! They're lucky you're back in one piece, I can tell you." She opened the screen door with a kick and glared at us. "Wriggled out of my hands like a fish, he did. Run here, run there, touch everything—bah! I almost lost my mind." She dropped her market basket in the middle of the floor and stomped across the room to the sink, where she began to wash her hands furiously. "Never again. One ice pop, two ice pops, a bag of candy—and then he has the nerve to whine for pastries too. And when he's sick tonight, whose fault will that be? Don't look at me, sir!"

Mui Eng threw me a quick grin, which I had to return in spite of myself. Sai is forever lost to Weng Khim as a ticket to the market, but a clever boy will find a way to his sweets. Weng Khim has made friends with a neighbor boy who enjoys the freedom to poison his constitution at will, and ice pops continue to appear via this amiable fellow, who takes a commission of 50 satangs for a run to the street vendor.

"Why do you give him money to buy those unhealthy sweets?" I asked Mui Eng. "Yesterday I saw him trying to feed candy to the baby. Now it isn't enough to ruin his own digestion, oh no! He must convince the baby that sweets are preferable to decent food."

"But it shows he has a good heart, Suang U, sharing a treat with his sister. Would you rather have him selfish?"

"Of course not, but I don't want my children eating sweets that flies have crawled over all day while they turned rancid on a dirty pushcart. Can't anyone around here support me? My word means nothing."

"I seldom give him money. I don't have to—he wheedles it out of his grandfather. Or he begs change from Sai's grocery money and well, maybe sometimes I do give him a baht or two to stop his whining—but not often."

"His character is being spoilt. Let him try that whining on me and he'll soon learn his lesson, I can tell you. I'll have a talk with the seat of his britches that will put a stop to begging for candy money."

Weng Khim's dissatisfaction with life seems to grow by the day. He whines after Kim and Chaba constantly, and I can understand why. They gave in to him in everything, laughed when he pleaded for treats—why shouldn't they be his favorites? To show him that I mean well, I took him to see them two weeks ago Saturday, though they have not been thoughtful enough to contact us in months.

We found Kim in the heart of the market, in one of the cramped, squalid stalls where hundreds of people like my old friend make their living feeding the city of Bangkok. His round face was as greasy as the huge cleaver with which he whacked great slabs of pork into one-kilo pieces, and Chaba sat behind half a dozen baskets of fresh vegetables and two more brimming with gleaming fresh fish that flopped and wriggled and spilled out onto the ground. At her breast was—a baby! I had never even noticed that she was pregnant while they still lived with us; now her child was already laughing, not a newborn. So many months without word, even of this.

"Kim! A—a baby? I don't know what to say. Is it a boy or a girl? Couldn't you even come to tell me of this?"

"Girl," he replied curtly, not looking up. "Not important, one girl child." He whacked another chunk of pork in two. "We work late, you know. By the time we have a few minutes to ourselves, well, it gets late."

"Where do you live?"

"In a row house, on the river. It's about as big as this stall, but at least the floor is dry. Usually."

I felt that Kim had greatly changed. He didn't even sound like his old self.

"How are sales?"

"Enough and no more, and nothing left over."

"Will you be angry if I ask you a question? Do you—still gamble?" (Why do I say such things?)

But Kim only grinned and shook his head slowly, "If I said no, it would be a small lie. Why should I lie? When I can't stand it any longer, I buy one lottery ticket. But not like before."

"Do you ever send money home?" (Worse, worse—I can't help myself!)

He stiffened and dropped his eyes again. "I did, until the baby came. I'm sure you still do."

"Yes, I—I'd like to do something for your girl. I'll bet she'll be as pretty as her mother when she grows up." Chaba made a wry face. "I hope you'll remember my son then—"

"I don't want to talk of such things, Suang U. Remember Seng and Mui Eng. I'm sure you wouldn't want your boy to be disappointed someday."

I felt as though I had been slapped. "I'm trying to do something about that." I said, my mouth beginning to feel dry. "As a matter of fact, I think that Seng will be getting married before long, and that will help more than anything. He's already coming around, though . . . we had a chat recently. Kim, Weng Khim misses you, and Chaba."

He looked down at the boy, and his expression changed. "Leave him with us and go about your business. Pick him up anytime."

So I left Weng Khim scampering about among the fish and vegetables, poking into the fish baskets, enjoying himself enormously. On my way back, after seeing a few customers on the other side of the market, I stopped at a gold shop and bought gold bracelets and anklets for the baby.

Chaba was pleased to receive a gift of such value for her first baby and, as anyone could see, touched that the gift came from me. "But a child in gold is not safe!" she pronounced seriously. "I'll put only the bracelets on her, and save the anklets for when we go visiting. Thank you. It means a lot."

How happy Weng Khim is with this family. It hurts me, but it is true. I know that he would visit them every day if I let him, and I fear that he will run off and try to find them one of these days when we aren't watching him closely enough. School is the only answer, but the present term began almost a month ago, and he is much younger than most of the other children. I wonder if they will accept him. But they ought to, for he can read several characters already and do sums up to ten. Surely he could handle the work. He can practice at home if he is behind the others. I have told him that his grandmother in China wants to see his calligraphy so that she may be proud of her eldest grandson. You see his name below mine today, written in his own young hand. My son and I bow respectfully before you, with love in our hearts.

THE BUSINESS is taking shape once again. Father was quite right when he said that familiarity must precede success. Now the customers know where to find us, and Mui Eng's store is full of people from dawn to dusk. The new *tambon* in which we live is even more populous than the old neighborhood, and more of the people are Chinese. We have fewer credit problems with these people, of course, for which Mui Eng insists on congratulating the little house in the back yard.

The only worry we have now is Weng Khim's schooling. Do not fear that your grandson is a poor student. Far from it! But he learns Thai at the school, and he has begun to use Thai with our employees, our cook, and anyone else who will answer him. Not the good, school Thai, unfortunately, but the speech of the lower classes, which he seems to delight in.

"My son must speak Chinese in our home," I explained to Sai, who stood before me sullenly, her arms crossed defiantly, "and you continue to encourage him to speak Thai! What do you have to say for yourself?"

"All the Chinese children born here speak Thai. Whether I speak it with him or not will not matter." And she left the room with her eyebrows raised majestically, her arms still crossed.

Mui Eng, entering the room, was almost knocked down, for she was carrying a dozen whisk brooms in her arms. Sai, sailing through the doorway with her chin in the air, looked as though she were colliding with a haystack, but she didn't allow this further indignity to stop her. She kept going, leaving Mui Eng and me to pick up the brooms.

"What was that all about?"

"Sai keeps speaking Thai to Weng Khim. He gets more than enough of it at the school. If I didn't put my foot down, he'd forget his own language. He's too much with the Thai children there. Before you know it, he'll think he's one of them."

"What child doesn't want to be like the others? It's natural, and I doubt if you can stop it."

"It's his knowing who he is that I care about, Mui Eng. He must speak Chinese well, and—and know who he is."

"You're repeating yourself."

"Yes, and I'll repeat myself many times more before he grows up! I don't want any make-believe Thais in this family."

I don't mind Thai citizenship, and I don't expect the boy to think of himself as a Chinese citizen, which he is not. But the origin of his family, his *sae*, all the past which produced him and made him who he is, these are the most important facts in his life. I want him to be able to move easily in both worlds, Thai and Chinese, but as a Chinese. I have seen some who shame themselves by standing apart, laughing at their own people, saying *chek* this and *chek* that, every other word. Do they suppose they escape this insulting word themselves, when their backs are turned? Or that a Thai respects a Chinese man who can barely speak a hundred words of Thai, and already seeks to disown the people to whom he belongs? When we conduct ourselves with pride and seek to benefit our adopted country by the honest work of our lives, no man will despise us.

When I explained these things to Weng Khim, what do you suppose he answered?

"*Khrap*, Khun Pho!"

"What is this?" (We both knew he was teasing me, saying "Yes, Father" in polite Thai.)

"Oops, sorry!" He giggled nervously.

"You realize, Weng Khim, that you are Chinese?"

"Yes, Papa, but why does my birth certificate say I'm Thai? I saw it."

"Because you were born in Thailand. That makes you a Thai citizen, like Mama. But you are still Chinese, as Mama is Chinese. Do you understand?"

He nodded abstractedly, and I did not hear him speak Thai again. One day the following week, Mui Eng said, "You must know that Weng Khim is speaking Thai in the factory when he goes out there to help wrap the *chan-ap*. And you should hear him chatter! He knows quite a lot already."

"Well, the kids out there are mostly Thai. It doesn't matter. It's not our home. I think he got my point, that's all I care about."

Weng Khim must help wrap boxes on the days he has off from school. I am teaching him to use his time carefully. On school days, he rises at six to practice calligraphy, at least one new character each day. (Later, of course, I will assign him several.) Then he eats breakfast while

150

I quiz him, and he never makes a mistake (perhaps because I keep a sweet or a few satangs ready as a reward). Then Father takes him to school. Most of the neighboring children walk alone, but I don't trust the traffic. At noon, someone takes him a hot lunch from our kitchen, for although he could buy noodles on the street, he isn't used to such food. At three o'clock, Father or Mui Eng fetches him, and he has a snack. He does his chores, and after dinner I drill him in arithmetic. On his free days, he works in the factory doing simple tasks. On Sunday afternoons, he usually goes for a car ride with Ang Buai, but I allow that only when he has nothing more important to do.

"You are far too rigid," Ang Buai complained last Sunday while he changed clothes for the ride. "Leave him alone some of the time, or he'll turn into a little old man. You give that child only a half-day a week to play, and the rest of the time he's working or studying. It's not right. Even you ought to know that."

"So now I am 'rigid.' I don't know where you get these words. I know what I'm doing, Ang Buai. He will be a disciplined human being, a person who knows how to use time. He is learning that work is noble, not just an irksome necessity."

"He's a baby, much too young to understand. He will simply think that his parents don't want him to have any fun."

"I suppose you think I ought to raise him like a Thai, eh? Let him run through the streets half-naked like those urchins outside? Never! I suppose you'd like to see him dirty and wild, 'enjoying himself' and dependent on his parents until he's a parent himself—no respect, no fear, no sense! He is seeing how we get taught, Ang Buai, what life is all about. How we Chinese work hard and stick together, and take care of our *sae* brothers. It isn't as if I ignore him, you know—he sees that his father has time to teach him the things he must know. Every man has enough time in every twenty-four hours to teach something useful to his son. The love of a father is more than indulgence and sentimentality."

She had nothing to say to that, I can tell you. She just stood there swinging her key chain and blinking at me. I believe that for once I quite defeated her, which pleased me not a little.

So she picks him up every Sunday afternoon and I don't complain, for I have had my say. Weng Khim waits for the arrival of his aunt in a frenzy of anticipation, and when she cannot come for him, I have to make it up to him in some other way. Strange, he is such a good boy all week, but if Ang Buai cannot take him driving on Sunday afternoon he becomes quite sassy, not at all like himself. So I treat him to one of his favorite sweets (which otherwise I do not allow him to have) or let him run about outdoors with the neighborhood children, or he and Chui Kim play with dolls until they both fall asleep.

A surprise, saved for last. It seems that Seng has abandoned his grudge. An invitation to his wedding is proof enough, don't you agree? The bride is, of all things, a friend of Ang Buai's. I assume that he is satisfied with her, for his Uncle Tae Lim did not arrange this match. Seng found her himself. He met her at the Chinese opera with Ang Buai, and after only a couple of weeks' courtship he begged Tae Lim to go to her people on his behalf. Changing times! She is a seamstress, and her family owns a coffee shop. Kim was also invited to the wedding, and on this occasion he ran to our store to share the news.

"Funny that he should invite me, wouldn't you say?" he grinned, holding out the invitation for me to see.

"I'll show you something even funnier," I replied, tossing my invitation to him across the desk.

"His eyes widened in amazement. "Well, I'll—you were right!" Then he frowned slightly and said, "I wonder what's on his mind? I'm not sure I trust this yet—"

"Nothing is 'on his mind.' We're old friends, he's getting married, and he invited us. I told you I talked to him, didn't I? I guess I finally got it across to him, you know, that there's no reason to go on like we were."

Kim still looked suspicious, but pleased. We both are, for if the three of us could begin our friendship anew, it would be a wonderful thing. We are a remarkable people. When one errs, another is always ready to offer good advice; when one is in difficulty, another hurries to help. I believe that Seng took my words to heart. Unity is the basis of our success and prosperity, and we do not cast a countryman aside in a strange land. Always have I believed this; now I see for myself that it is so.

I HAVE purposely waited many months to write this letter. I was busy, and then I said to myself: wait, write to her when the child is born. Well, that has come to pass, and has brought only tragedy and despair.

My great hopes have been shattered, and for the second time in my life I have drunk whiskey. I cursed it once before, and vowed never to debase myself with it again, but I drank more on the occasion of my fourth child's birth than on the occasion of the first.

I so desperately wanted another male child, but it was never meant to be. How kind it is that we do not know our fate. The day Mui Eng was brought to bed, I was so excited that I closed up the shop, the bakery, everything. I sat outside the bedroom door as I had on the day, many years before, when my beloved Weng Khim was born. But this time my excitement was shadowed by fear, for Mui Eng had carried this child only seven months, and had been carried to bed by Father and me after she fell in the bathroom. The floor in there is cement. We have always complained that it is too slippery when it is wet, but we never did anything about it. She was careless, and fell, and we found her unconscious. I sent a factory hand running for the doctor (I realized at once that the midwife would not do). He arrived, examined her quickly, and said that she must go into the hospital at once. There was no indication that the birth was imminent. Mui Eng had regained consciousness, and was crying because she was afraid to go to the hospital, but the doctor insisted. I returned home to work after taking her there, but of course I could do nothing. I had already sent everyone home, and I had the whole place to myself. I sat in the middle of the bakery, beside the great oven, with my head in my hands, staring at the floor, afraid.

The next morning I returned to the hospital, where a cheerful nurse told me the pains had begun in spite of some kind of medicine they had given her. The child would be born this day. Suddenly Thaokae Nia, Ang Buai, and Father appeared beside me, all talking at once. My mother-in-law's face was pale with fear. "Oh, Suang U, what does the doctor say?" she asked, her voice trembling.

"The nurse—she says the pains have begun."

She closed her eyes for a moment, then composed herself and crossed to sit on one of the long benches and wait.

"Well, we mustn't worry so much." Father said gently, sitting beside her and smiling reassuringly. "She didn't have such a hard fall, did she? And here she has the best of care."

The shaking sensation within me only increased.

"I took little Weng Khim to school," he continued. "Of course, he wanted to know where his mother had gone. I told him she was spending a few days at grandmother's house—furious! He was so angry, you know, because he didn't get to go too. So I said, 'Khim, you might have missed school had you gone too' and that stopped his whining. How the boy loves school!"

"Who is watching the babies?" I asked, thinking of them for the first time that morning.

"I told Sai and the washgirl to let the housework go and take care of the babies instead. Once Sai realized she wouldn't have to make dinner today, she stopped pouting; and we can trust her, you know that."

But I couldn't help worrying. Leaving babies with servants—who knows what they would do in an emergency? Ang Buai seemed to read my thoughts.

"I'll go over there myself," she said, "Trust me?" She grinned. "I never took care of a baby before, and maybe I'd mix the milk wrong or something, but old Sai ought to know how to do those things. I'm— well, I'm family . . ." She looked up at me, then away, quickly. I was surprised to see her blush, and grateful for her thoughtfulness.

"You!" her mother cried, drawing her brows together. "I'd better go myself—" She hesitated, uncertain. Ang Buai knew, as I knew, that her mother feared more for Ang Buai than for two healthy babies left home with the servants.

"You stay here," Ang Buai said firmly. "I'm going, and that's that."

"Mother," I said, "you're too upset to contend with Chui Kim today. She's almost as naughty as her big brother, and home all day."

Ang Buai nodded in agreement, gathered up her purse and keys, and rushed off down the hallway before her mother could protest further.

"That girl," Thaokae Nia said in a voice that attempted to be gruff, "always rushing around—she'll probably join the babies in making mischief, and Sai will quit, and then where will you be?" Then she choked back a loud sob, wiped her eyes with her handkerchief, and glanced about her severely as if searching out the person who had made that unseemly noise.

For hours we waited, while my heart grew heavier and heavier. Then a nurse came through the door that led to wherever Mui Eng was. We saw a long corridor behind her, lined with narrow beds on wheels. There were a dozen doors on either side of the corridor, and I wondered which one Mui Eng lay in, and in what condition. In one long glimpse down the corridor, I saw too much, and not enough. I wanted to know everything, or nothing. I could not bear to think of Mui Eng lying on one of those beds on wheels. Suffering, dying perhaps . . .

The nurse's mouth was moving, she was telling us about Mui Eng, but I could only hear some of what she said, for there was a terrible roaring in my ears. Too loud, too loud for me to hear what the nurse was saying. Mui Eng had suffered much, had been injured in the fall, would recover well but must stay in the hospital two months. The baby was a girl. There would be no more children.

I did not want to see the baby. They wanted me to see her, but they couldn't force me to! Why should I see her? She disappointed her father and ruined her mother, and there will be no more sons. Do you understand how I felt, Mother? No more sons! One son and three daughters. I cursed my fate, the baby, Mui Eng, and myself. A doctor appeared, dressed in strange green clothes, wrinkled. He had a tight green cap on his head. It made him look very odd. He began to talk in a cheerful, ordinary way, but I couldn't get over looking at his cap. It was very tight. You couldn't see any of his hair, only a little beside his ears.

"She can't have more children. Her uterus is damaged, do you understand? But then, this is your fourth, isn't it? Sir, is something wrong? Well, then, I'm sure we're all grateful for the way things turned out. Your wife will not suffer any permanent effects from what happened, and the child will be strong in a few weeks. She's tiny, of course, but strong."

You could see a little of his hair in the back, too, when he turned his head, but you couldn't tell if the hair on top of his head was long or short. He looked like a bald man with a green head, like a cabbage! I tried not to laugh when that occurred to me. A cabbage!

155

I said, "I have four children, one son and three daughters. It's a baby girl, that makes three daughters!" I looked away from his cabbage head and straightened my face.

"Well, I'm afraid I must be off . . . is there anything I can do, sir? No? Well—"

"Nurse, take the patient's family to see the baby. No visitors for Mama until tomorrow. I hope you all understand."

I waited until they had seen the baby. Then we left.

Ang Buai stood in the doorway with Bak Li in her arms.

"How is she?" she called out, when she saw us draw up in the *samlo*.

"She's fine," Thaokae Nia replied, climbing out on Father's arm. "They're both all right—the baby lived!"

"Then why does Suang U look like that? He scared me to death just by the look on his face!"

"Will you hush! The baby is normal, but Mui Eng can never have another child."

Father began to pull me toward the stairs. Ang Buai turned to us and regarded me peculiarly.

"Is it a boy or a girl?"

"A girl—now be quiet! Suang U is very disappointed, poor man. Please be kind, child."

"Is that all? Four children in four years, and he's disappointed. I'll bet she's not disappointed. I'm only taking care of two of them, and look at this place. It's a mess! Sai is out in the kitchen snarling into a pot of fish soup. I told her she didn't have to cook and she nearly bit my head off—I'm sure I didn't do anything to make her angry!"

Father left me alone in the bedroom. An unspeakable ache in my chest seemed to pull all the energy from my arms and legs, and I lay down on the bed and pressed my palms hard against my eyes. A houseful of girls. How does a man raise a houseful of girls these days? Look at their aunt! (Or their mother, throwing a bracelet through the kitchen window to her father's penniless clerk.) How much worse will it be in fifteen years?

I decided to send a servant out for a bottle of whiskey. I couldn't think of any reason why I shouldn't get dead, stinking drunk. The bottle arrived and I drank it, all of it. I wanted to drink enough to sleep like the dead, but I wasn't even that lucky. I felt sick and hot and drunk, but sleep only stole further from my grasp.

And though the doctor had assured me that Mui Eng would recover, I worried about her. I know that women die sometimes, after giving birth too early. I heard a story from Thaokae Nia about a man who was asked by the doctor, while his wife labored to give birth, whether he ought to try to save the "boat" or the "oar," for both could not be saved. The husband told him to save the oar, meaning that the child should live, and the wife die. Too late he learned his lesson, for a boat has much more value than an oar, which is easily replaced. The poor man had thought only of his child, the extension of himself and the honor of his family. When he returned home with the baby in his arms and no wife to suckle and raise the child, he realized the bitterness of his choice. Mui Eng and I have not been the happiest of couples, Mother, yet I know I would have shouted, "Save the boat!" (The gods know, the oar has been saved too and I don't even want it.) If Mui Eng had died, I should have hated the child a thousand times more.

Suddenly there came a pounding at my door. Father!

"Open the door, Suang U. I know you're in there, and I know you've been drinking!"

"Go away, please . . ."

"Open the door or I'll kick it down."

This was Father? Never until that day had I seen him truly angry. I shambled across the room and turned the lock.

He looked at me steadily for a long time, then quietly shut the door behind him. "This is—unnecessary. Do you think what has happened is cause for such a display? Lie down. I can't stand to see you stagger around like a common drunk down at the corner."

"I'm low, low Father . . . I want to drunk, to drink, to—you know, drink an' sleep . . . I'm so tired . . . I'm tryin' t' fall asleep, but . . . mus' be late now. Are the babies all right? All those girl babies an' li'l Weng Khim . . ."

"You want to drink and sleep!" he said scornfully. "The wife is in the hospital, the husband lies on his bed in a drunken stupor—what kind of family is this turning into? What kind of man are you?"

"Mui Eng's gonna die . . . l know it."

"Die? Where did you get that idea? The doctor told you she's out of danger."

157

"He can say whatever—he—likes, and how would you know th' difference, eh? What'd you expect him to say, 'We did our best but we don't know whether she's gonna make it'?"

"Do not be insolent with me, my son. You must compose your mind, whether you like it or not. And you're not so drunk as you're pretending to be; you want to be, but you're not."

"Oh, Father, I'm so miserable. There will be no more children! No more sons for me, no more grandsons for you! I never wanted any girls, and now this—"

"She is born, and you will raise her. Suang U, I came near to having no grandson at all. I consider myself a fortunate man! The gods are wiser than we know, for if men could choose, we would have run out of mothers long ago." He chuckled quietly, then rested his hand on my shoulder.

"I—I wanted five sons, Father, and two daughters at the most, for Mui Eng. What do I have now? Oh, I'm afraid . . . if I don't raise them right, I'll lose face, we all will. Girls can—can shame their fathers, it's not like it used to be, raising children."

"Son, no man ever got everything he ever wanted from life. You must stop . . . pitying yourself, and think of all you have. A fine business— who among your friends has done better than you? You should not set your sights so high, then hoard your grief when life is imperfect. I had one child and lost it, but I got over even that, and I found you. Why must you assume that your children will 'shame' you? Why, that poor baby in the hospital is still in an incubator, and you're already imagining her—well, imagining absurd things . . . What nonsense! Rejoice in them all. Assume that they will grow up a credit to you, marry well, honor your name, and be a comfort to you in your old age. Isn't that a better way to look at it all?"

I buried my face in the pillow. Feelings of gratitude and humiliation welled up within me, and I couldn't bear to look at him. He left, then, and within seconds I was fast asleep.

I work even harder since Mui Eng is in the hospital. Perhaps there is some self deception to it, for I know I am trying to bury my disappointment in exhaustion. But there is another reason, too. I can pretend that she is here, in another room, that if I wanted to I could walk into that room and find her there if I weren't so busy.

158

I rise in darkness and open the store. Sai brings breakfast to me at seven . . . I eat out in the store now, for I can't bear to take breakfast with Father and Weng Khim as before, when my dream was still possible and Mui Eng ladled rice gruel into our bowls, leaning over the table carefully, her belly swollen with the promise of a son.

The babies eat separately. I hired another girl, a young Thai, to take care of them. This girl has the ability to sleep through any level of noise, so that some nights I finally get out of bed and go pound on her door to tell her that one of the babies has been crying for two hours. It takes her twenty minutes to wake up to the pounding! Often, Father wakes her and sends me back to bed. He says old people don't need so much sleep, that he may as well be up when he's awake anyway. About half the time, he attends to the babies' needs himself and doesn't waste the twenty minutes pounding on her door. If ever there were a fire, I swear she'd burn to death fast asleep. During the day, she does no work that should make her sleep so soundly all night: eat, sleep, shuffle around the house with a baby on her hip. She will never make anything of herself.

I used to eat rice porridge for breakfast, but I have been eating plain rice lately, left over from the night before. Otherwise, Sai would have to get up even earlier to begin cooking. It isn't worth aggravating her. It fills me up. When I have finished eating, I check over all imported goods due to leave the store during the day, to see that everything is in order. The performance of this task is crucial, our only insurance against error, and I never pass it onto anyone else. Our Thai workers move quickly while I am watching them, but I am not deceived. They know that I know. Such is the game I am expected to play.

What annoys me more is their hypocritical flattery and constant belittling of each other. Their disloyalty to each other is depressing. Any one of them is ready at any moment to assure me that he alone does a fair day's work, though the truth may be quite the opposite. The only solution is close and constant supervision and infinite patience, which keeps the business moving but leaves me weary in body and spirit. Couldn't I hire better people? These are the best that can be had. And when will I learn to accept these people, to stop complaining, to not be disgusted by their lack of responsibility and ambition? I don't know.

When I have attended to these duties, I leave things at the store in Father's hands for an hour or so while I go over the books at the bakery and make my rounds among the bakers, wrappers, and all the other people who turn out *chan-ap*. Here, people do work hard, and it lifts my spirits to watch them. Especially the young man who toils before our great oven. I respect him, and pay him accordingly. When he came here, he knew nothing, but Father patiently trained him until he became a master of his trade. He never says much, this boy who was born in Bangkok of Chinese parents and honors them by his diligence. It has occurred to me to try making a brother-in-law of him. Well, why not? Ang Buai's father furthered his own enterprise by welcoming into his family one who had only gifts of diligence and honest labor to offer. Iu Kieng is a fine young man, yet somehow I cannot picture him sitting beside Ang Buai in her new car. It is even more difficult to picture him doing the driving! It is now my duty to find her a husband. I cannot think of a less enviable position to be in, but this I owe Nguan Thong.

Afternoons, I return home to work at my desk and, usually, I forget to eat lunch. By the time my stomach reminds me, the afternoon has passed. Father, assuming I must have eaten lunch at the bakery, doesn't think to remind me (otherwise he would, you may be sure). Dusk is settling before my tasks are done, then I have dinner, read a couple of newspapers, talk with Weng Khim about his schoolwork, and go to bed. Each day now, he has two new words for me, and his calligraphy is improving wonderfully.

Once a week, I visit Mui Eng, and each time she urges me to see the child. Her appearance is of no importance to me.

"Have you thought of a name for the baby yet?" she asked, grinning nervously.

"I have not thought of the baby," I replied truthfully.

"Ang Buai asked—she comes almost every day. You—you hardly ever come to see me, Suang U." She quickly wiped a tear that was slipping down her cheek, It was embarrassing.

"You know better than anyone how much I have to do. Time is more precious than anything in the store. Oh—Weng Khim asks after you, and Chui Kim."

"I miss them so much," she said, giving way now to unabashed crying. "I wish the hospital would let them come to see me, or let me go home. Mothers and their children shouldn't be kept apart!"

"Don't be foolish. Children have little resistance to disease. Would you have them here, where everyone is sick? Thais break their own rules; that is their concern. We need not imitate them. Oh, I see them sneaking children in and out of the hospital, the fools. But it is none of my business. I don't say anything. I look after my own children. It is enough."

"I suppose you're right, you always are," she sniffed, wiping her eyes. "If you don't mind, I'd like to name the baby 'Meng Chu.'"

"After the novel heroine? 'Meng Chu was clever enough to thread a needle that had no eye . . .' So, do you suppose your Meng Chu will be able to live up to that? Name her whatever you like. It is of no interest to me."

So this letter ends, at last. It is late, I must rest. Good night, my dear Mother, and please forgive me for bringing bad news.

—

LETTER #38   TENTH MONTH, SIXTH DAY
15 NOVEMBER 1950   YEAR OF THE OX

BEFORE ANYTHING, I apologize for my last, sad letter. How I must have worried you! Much time has passed since then, and Mui Eng and the baby have been home for several months. I am happy that my wife is no longer in danger of losing her life, but I cannot yet accept the loss of all my hoped-for children. My heart is still shrouded in disappointment, and I have tried to speak with Mui Eng about it, but my dear wife feels nothing, and has no sympathy for me.

"It is just as well," she said, folding a shirt of Weng Khim's and tossing it onto a stack of freshly ironed clothes. "Look at me—even with the servants, I end up folding clothes when I should be out in the store. Four children make a lot of work, Suang U."

Each time she reached out to flatten a piece of clothing, the flesh on her upper arms quivered. Since the baby's birth, she has begun to grow plump. It is not flattering, I am afraid, though at least she is healthy.

"Mui Eng, you don't understand how it hurts me."

"Hurts you! Having a baby hurts very much if you want to know! What do you understand of what a woman goes through, eh? Nine,

161

ten months of it—the sickness, being tired all the time, climbing in and out of bed like a great, fat fish! And then pain, pain enough to burst your heart. Yes, seven or eight children bring honor to the father, when the mother's body is spent with bearing and birthing. What is she then? An old woman, worn out, important to no one. I've had enough of it, and then you grieve because I'm spared going through it all again." She turned her back on me and began to stuff the clothing into drawers with an annoyed efficiency. The breadth of her bottom continues to startle me.

She sounds more like her sister every day. "Women's rights"—tschah! Women never used to prattle on so. You taught me that it is the duty and privilege of a woman to obey her parents and then her husband. I wonder whether women of our age in China have changed as much. The power of husbands declines steadily as wives grab it from them and teach their daughters to disobey. Shall families continue to be families? Shall "home" mean anything, when no one respects anyone else? With everyone demanding his rights, how can people expect to live together happily?

Father recently chided me on what he calls my "dim view of the world."

"What's the matter, son? You are so pale lately, and so critical of others."

"Nothing's the matter. I'm just a little dizzy from the heat, that's all."

"No, I don't believe it. You work too hard. You are not one of those machines out in the bakery, you know, and even they have to rest, and be cared for."

"I sleep enough."

"Yes, but you need good food, too. And I've noticed that you don't eat well. Half the time you skip lunch, or you eat quickly and then dash off. It isn't good for you."

"I always sit down with a newspaper after dinner, you know that."

"Always, eh? What is that stack of papers there beside your desk? You've got every one for the past two weeks, none of them touched."

I cannot argue with him, but neither can I cut down on work so easily as he imagines. Money is finally flowing into this office, and money is a great responsibility. Mui Eng is busy with her baby and the

162

store, and there is no one else I can trust. Chui Kim is now easily Weng Khim's equal in mischief, and when they get together we are no match for their ingenuity. Bak Li, second daughter, is suddenly fascinated by fire and whatever will produce it. Meng Chu, third daughter, is still only interested in eating and sleeping. If she is to be as clever as her namesake, there is no evidence of that yet.

The bigger children get, the more trouble they are, counter to my expectations of reasonableness increasing with age. They only grow more obstinate! When Weng Khim and Chui Kim were babies, they were like dolls. Wherever we put them, there they stayed, and did not impose upon the good nature of those who cared for them. Now, wherever we want them to be is where they least want to be.

I see to it that servants have little to do with them, for a mother must raise her own children if they are to turn out well. Thai mothers, whenever they can, think nothing of handing their children over to servants. Some of them work outside the home and hardly look at their children from one day to the next. So the children talk like servants, have no love for their parents, and generally do not behave as their parents would like.

A child raised on the milk of cows, in the arms of servants, will have the wit of the one and the manners of the other. He will not even respect the servant, whom he knows to be his inferior.

Ang Buai has been urging me to get more rest too, in her fashion. She and Weng Khim had returned from one of their Sunday afternoon rides, and she was turning a cup of tea in her hands while it cooled.

"Why don't you go to a teahouse sometime and let the pretty girls give you a massage?"

Mui Eng swung around and stared at her younger sister as if she were mad. "Teahouse? I should send him out to a teahouse?" She set a plate of pastries before us but continued to stand, hands on hips, staring at her sister.

"Men relax there."

"Oh yes, I'm sure they do. Why don't you suggest that he take up opium? Or maybe he could smoke marijuana behind the bakery—"

Ang Buai laughed heartily and reached across the table for a pastry. "That's not relaxation, Sister, that's sin. But he could smoke cigarettes, the plain kind."

What do you think? I bought some cigarettes. And on my second try, I rather enjoyed the sensation. The smoke clears my head, and I like the aroma. On the other hand, I disapprove of spending money on such things. One may as well set the money on fire as the cigarettes (and one pack costs as much as a decent meal). If they didn't make my work a trifle lighter, I wouldn't bother, but it is pleasant to add up figures, lean back in my chair from time to time and watch the smoke curl up into the darkness. I have heard that some men smoke two whole packs in one day, but I smoke one pack a week, and sometimes I have a few left over the next week. I am aware that anything one cannot do without is evil, so I have resolved not to become dependent on them and thrash around when my pack is empty like an opium addict.

I have chosen myself a moderate vice! Modern man is presented with novelties at every turn, and I successfully resist most. Of the more important novelties, who would ever have thought that one day men's voices would pass over wires, and speak to every corner of the earth? Shall I someday be blessed to hear your dear voice over a wire? How wonderful that would be. For tonight, let the winds bear my love to you. It will have to do for now.

LETTER #39　　　　　　　　　TWELFTH MONTH, SECOND DAY
9 JANUARY 1951　　　　　　　YEAR OF THE TIGER

I HAVE been to see my first movie in Thailand. It was most enjoyable, although it was an old tale I know well. Or perhaps I should have said, I enjoyed it so much because I knew it so well. Do you remember *Cheng Si Mui*?

The heroine was quite good, wept stupendously and sang as sadly as anyone could wish. (Si Mui I found a bit too "modern.") Unfortunately, the women in the audience cried so loudly that it required concentration to fully appreciate the story, but one great advantage of film over the live opera is the sense of reality that can be conveyed, especially in the military scenes; they were truly splendid. I was fascinated by the character of the soldier assigned to kill Si Mui's first wife and children.

The film was over so soon, yet everything had been told, unlike the opera, where one becomes numb before the story has half begun. The palace was beautiful, just like a real one, and I felt as though I had returned to China for a brief, fabulous visit and had been shown things I had never dreamed of seeing in my poor youth. Gorgeous palanquins, ladies of the court, every detail—everything. One had no need to imagine things from a few scraps of painted canvas on a makeshift stage. The movie was all Ang Buai's idea, and an excellent one. I told her so, too, which I believe pleased her.

The actor who played the part of Pao Kong had his face blackened and a quarter-moon painted in the center of his forehead. He was not afraid, as actors used to be, that an evil spirit might mistake him for the real Pao Kong. No opera player would dare, but perhaps the spirits are fearful of modern machines, movie cameras, and electric lights, and keep their distance.

The movie theater is not far from our store, but I never noticed it before. Ang Buai teased me when I said so, claiming that I am like the ox who sees only the furrow. She and Mui Eng both went with me, but I would not allow them to bring the older children, as they wanted to do. It is too crowded and unhealthy in there, and how long would they be amused? A few minutes, perhaps, and then they would begin to fuss. I saw little children carried in by their parents and pitied them when their impatience earned them angry slaps and pinches.

"How can I enjoy the film with such a troublesome child?" one mother whispered furiously, as she delivered a swift pinch to her little boy's arm under cover of darkness.

Who is "troubled," the mother or the child? Why should a child sit in a great dark room aching with boredom, expected to stare at a picture that is far away and meaningless to him, if indeed he can see it at all over the heads of the adults in front of him?

As we left the theater, I encountered my old nemesis—begging. And so many of them—mothers, babies, youths, old men, "blind" men who stared after us malevolently and caught at our arms and legs when I refused to hand out coins, as Mui Eng was ready to do.

"If we give to one," I told her, "we have to give to all, and I have only three small coins with me. It is simpler to refuse altogether. You know I disapprove of all this, anyway."

We turned off down the street to a noodle shop Ang Buai suggested, and as we were enjoying a late snack a dirty, ragged woman carrying a dirtier baby appeared in the doorway, holding out a tin cup. This time I reached for my wallet, but Ang Buai shook her head quickly.

"Have pity on the poor!" the woman whined. "I have no milk left for the baby because I am starving—I have had no food for three days!"

"If you are hungry," Ang Buai said calmly, "take this!" And she pushed her plate of pork and rice across the table. The woman pulled back as if she had been struck, then threw Ang Buai a look of pure malice and fled into the darkness outside.

"What was that all about?" I asked, completely bewildered.

"She wasn't hungry, and it wasn't her child. It's one style of begging, the worst I think. She rents the baby and begs in places where women are eating, because women will always pity a baby, especially when they're sitting down to eat a good meal."

"Rents the baby?!" Mui Eng and I exclaimed together.

"Oh, yes! I've heard they pay as much as fifty baht a day for the children. There are people who steal babies to rent them out. Sometimes a kindly person will even offer to take the child in and raise it. Then the beggar is in a difficult situation. Usually, he'll ask the person for 'enough money to take the child home for a last goodbye.' By the time the beggar walks out the door, he's usually richer by a hundred baht or so—'a little something for the child's family.' Do you think that child ever appears again? Hah! Not so long as he's the beggar's only capital."

"We ought to be more careful!" Mui Eng said fearfully. "Think of our babies stolen, out in the streets with beggars—"

"They aren't always stolen," Ang Buai continued. "Some Thai parents both work, and a servant cares for the child all day. Sometimes you read in the newspaper about the baby son of a government official who's been out in the streets begging, unbeknown to his parents, earning money for the servant."

"Horrible!" I said to myself, pushing my plate of noodles away half-eaten.

People! Whatever is the matter with them? For a few coins, there are those who would debase themselves that far. Were they brought up with no religious training at all? Do they feel no shame? I never in my life heard of anything so vile as stealing infants to rent them out. How lazy can a man be, to let a baby earn his rice? Even cripples do useful work, those who are determined and have self-respect. I have seen legless men do an honest day's work with their hands.

That poor child we saw tonight, knowing nothing, least of all why adults use him so; hungry and thirsty, brown from being exposed to the hot sun, dragged through the streets day after day. The woman who "rents" him can never feed him enough to fill his little belly, or he would not be able to serve her despicable purpose. And the money, where does it go? To buy fat ducks and chickens to feed his captors, or for lottery tickets, teahouses, prostitutes . . . all manner of vice.

So Suang U treated himself to an evening of fun and relaxation, and then could not work for two days because he had no heart for it, or for anything. Two whole days! I can't believe it myself. But you, who are even more tenderhearted than your son, must understand. When I told Father what I had seen, he only shook his head and said, "I know, I know—it is a terrible thing." I wonder how long it takes a man to accept life as it is, how long it will take me.

⚊

ONCE AGAIN, I have seen things I never thought to see in this life. And wish, as ever, to share them with you, though I fear the telling is likely to give neither of us much pleasure.

Mui Eng talked me into going with her to ceremonies at the shrine we visited to exorcise our bad business some months ago. It is located on the grounds of a large temple where a fair is also underway. Mui Eng is very diligent, by the way, about paying back what she owes, and our business has indeed prospered since the day the spiritualist trembled and shook and told us about the stump of a tree in our back yard. I make no objections. She ordered, for the occasion, a gigantic candle as tall as a man with a design of dragons encircling it. Very beautiful, almost too beautiful to spoil by lighting it. This she presented, together with food: a fat chicken, a monstrous crab boiled scarlet and most appetizing to look at, rice and boiled eggs and dried squid. The man in

charge of the festivities was so impressed with the candle that he immediately set it before the shrine and lit it. Its fine aroma dispersed
throughout the grounds, and everyone who passed by stopped to admire it, making Mui Eng the happiest lady at the fair. When the
evening had come to an end, it still burned brightly and was scarcely
diminished.

Mui Eng divided the food among "the poor," a disheveled mob that
had to be firmly persuaded to stand in line, having no other idea than
to get something before there was nothing.

So I come again to grieve and grumble over the evil of begging. But
then, what temple fair anywhere ever lacked beggars? They sit in rows,
six here, eight there, wherever one turns. Lepers. Fingers and hands
missing, arms and legs missing, swollen legs and grotesque feet, their
faces—how pitiful! And among the worst of them sit whole men who
snatch away the best of whatever the poor wretches have been tossed
by those who averted their faces while they dropped money into the tin
cups that lined their path.

The lepers, too weak, too ravaged by their horrible disease to protect
what is theirs, lie forlornly huddled in the dust, hoping there will be
enough left to sustain them when the day is done.

If one could put the lepers out of mind long enough to enjoy himself,
there was a large traveling Chinese opera company on the grounds,
performing selections from *Three Kingdoms*. Nothing difficult or out
of the ordinary—mostly dancing, fighting, singing, and crying, the
most portable elements. Both Thais and Chinese gathered to watch as
Be Thiao sought revenge on Cho Cho by chasing him furiously about
the stage. This scene was succeeded by a much better effort: The Third
Princess Descending to Hell. The princess was good, and the black-
faced demon who dragged her there, excellent, his voice deep and
resonant. Except for these two, unfortunately, the troop was dreadfully
bad, consisting mainly of beginners and Thai children. Thai children?
Yes, these are contracted to the troop by their parents for a five-year
period. It would not be fair to say they are sold, and they are not at all
mistreated. On the other hand, there are some unscrupulous people
who deceive unprotected children and do indeed sell them to the troop
managers. Fortunately, these children are treated as well as the others.

When opera company children grow up, they cannot return to their homes. The reason for this is that they can barely speak Thai, after growing up in a Chinese opera company. By and large, they grow up to marry other opera players, Thai or Chinese, and spend the rest of their lives with one troop or another. One troop will have sixty or seventy members, including musicians, and they perform anywhere between Bangkok and Malaya, wherever prospects look good.

These people fascinate me (and interest you more than lepers, I am sure). There are many Chinese people in Thailand, and not all of them live in Bangkok between Sampheng Lane and Yaowarat Road. Chinese opera troops thrive everywhere in the country. At noon, I chatted with one of the players, a friendly fellow who happened to be eating his lunch at the table next to us in the improvised fair kitchen. From him I learned that some of the real professionals began practicing their craft in China. They emigrated, often in hopes of a new career, but actors they remained. Perhaps it is true, then, that an actor's destiny is marred by his craft, that assuming another man's life on a stage casts a shadow on one's own. Nor do their children and grandchildren see any other way of life open to them, for they toddle about a stage from the moment they can speak clearly, and grow into the world of theater as other men's sons grow into the world of business. Thus, many of the troops are actually large families, and since actors wish to succeed in life as much as the rest of us (with or without marred destinies!) the family troop is a business enterprise of seemingly tidy organization. Finances are administered by the eldest male, and everyone shares according to his position; in this, they are much like the rest of us. Even the smallest child earns candy money for simple chores, and every member of the family contributes according to his ability. It is not an atmosphere of employer and employees, according to my informant, but a family that looks to grandfather for advice and authority, and rewards justly due. What could be more sensible?

If I had ever wondered how many physical deformities a human being could survive, my curiosity was sated at the fair. Besides the lepers and other usual beggars, this fair abounded with "freaks," whole columns of unfortunates. Dwarfs, the armless and legless, one child with a tiny body and a head as large as a giant green coconut, far too great for his poor neck to support. This child, in particular, I cannot forget. Such poor monsters, unable to do more than open their mouths for food, are dragged to temple fairs in string hammocks or stretchers, and put down under a shady tree to stare witlessly at the people strolling by. Meanwhile, their parents hover over them, whining and beseeching.

"These are the real professionals!"

The voice startled me, and I turned swiftly to see a smiling Thai man.

"You see the same ones at every large fair," he continued. "But you mustn't worry about them, my friend, they do quite well! Those poor wretches, what do they know? It's all the same to them, don't you suppose?"

"You may be interested to know," put in a soft-spoken man beside him, "that most of these people were once poor farmers. When a deformed child is born to such people, should they grieve? Why, some of them are delighted—after the first shock and all, you know—here is their great chance! Don't you see, it is much easier to earn one's living like this." He swept an arm toward the row of beggars, and I tried to picture them toiling in their fields, threshing rice, feeding oxen a hundred miles from the city of Bangkok. "No drought here," the man continued. "No flood to deprive them of their livelihood. After a lifetime of slavery to nature, they have been freed by one of its accidents!"

Another fellow, who had been listening to our conversation and drawing steadily nearer, joined in with a story of his own.

"The Chinese family next door to us—you will excuse me?" (A polite nod in my direction.) "They have a witless child. The father grieves over his son, you know, but he never speaks of his misfortune. One day, a cousin came to visit him from upcountry. (I wasn't there myself, you understand. I heard of it later—) 'Why do you grieve over him so?' the old woman said to him. 'A friend of ours never ate pork in his life until his wife gave birth to a daughter without arms or legs, and now he is a rich man!' 'Indeed,' the old man replied slowly, 'and how could that be? He won the lottery, perhaps?' The old woman cackled to herself and said, 'No, no, my dear fellow—think! From one temple fair, hundreds of baht can be earned, if the affliction is obvious enough.' Well, that old man drew himself up stiff as a board, his ragged little beard twitched with anger! 'There are men who would send their children to beg?' he shouted. 'Such money I would not want! I am able

170

to support my child without forsaking my honor, sending him to grovel in the dirt and beg his keep, or a thousand times worse my own!'" Having told his story, the little man shrugged and raised his hands, palms upward. "For myself, I say give me just one without his legs or wits—I've seen little enough profit on my others!" Then he chuckled slyly, rolled his eyes toward me and added, "My beard wouldn't twitch, I can tell you!"

Odious man.

Trading on the sympathy of men is a less than respectable endeavor, but it is not as despicable as trading on perverse curiosity. I am ashamed to admit that Mui Eng and I paid our good money to see a show performed by cripples. The moment I walked through the dingy curtains that shrouded the entrance, I was covered with shame and despised myself, but Mui Eng refused to leave, and I refused to let her stay there alone.

The first to appear were a man with no arms or legs and another with parts of each. The former lit a match by holding it with his teeth and striking it against his shoulder, the latter actually wove fabric using his mouth and the stumps of his limbs. So far, at least they had displayed aptitudes; that is not an ugly thing. Next, however, came a poor fellow with elephantiasis who was trundled out onto the decrepit stage in a wheelbarrow. Holding out his grotesquely swollen hands, he declared that, in a former life, he had struck both his parents and one monk.

This was followed by "the man with a mouth as small as the eye of a needle" (whose mouth was tiny, but not that tiny). He informed us, by means of a blackboard, that in one of his former lives he had cursed his parents. And so on and on, the sins of a former life were sworn to be the cause of the infirmities suffered in this one.

Can a man who would run such a show have any good motive at heart, besides the obvious "good" of profit which accrues from enticing people through dirty curtains to ogle at those less fortunate than themselves, and enjoy a little thrill of fear? If any man truly wished to advise his fellows against the sin of abusing parents and elders, he would ask no money for the advice, nor would he use cripples to emphasize this teaching. It is a livelihood and no more. Men who earn their rice in such a way are beggars too, but less respectable than their diseased and misshapen charges. I have never seen a "freak" show before and I assume that you have never even heard of such a thing. It is a well-known fact that men, when they find themselves in a crowd, are easily persuaded to indulge their curiosity about the strange, unusual, and lewd. I have heard that naked dancing shows are performed at some of these fairs; thus are challenged the pure impulses of those who have come to earn merit, and on the very grounds of the temple! For such depravity there can be no excuse. Less disgusting, if not admirable, there was an outdoor dancing stage at the fair Mui Eng and I attended. Pretty girls sat in a row, showing off their shapes in the hope that some male passerby would stop, buy a ticket, and dance a turn with them. Where do you suppose this leads? I have read in the newspaper of fights that broke out over dancing girls. Sometimes death has resulted—on temple grounds! But what do the owners of these "concessions" care? Seemliness is not their concern.

Ah, I know I take too much of the world onto my shoulders. Whenever I try to have a good time, something evil or depressing strikes my eye and blinds me to what there is to enjoy. Why can't I accept what is? I am afraid that a person like me can never have a very good time, but I am as I am, and I cannot change. Can anyone? I'm afraid to speak of such things to Father or Mui Eng; he would worry about me, she would shrug her shoulders and laugh. Do you know, I believe Mui Eng has never had a serious thought in her life. Everything about her is superficial, which she proved once again by giggling all through the freak show and pleading with me to stay and watch it all over again. The only way I escaped that was by insisting that she must not tire herself unduly.

She loves Chinese opera, especially the heroines, so she agreed to leave the freaks and use our remaining time there. The best part of the evening show was a five-year-old girl. She sang very well, considering that she could barely pronounce the words. Very impressive, about as high as her father's belt at the top of her head. I should mention that most of the opera players here are women! Men are used only for the roles of warrior or hero, wherever a woman couldn't do the part believably. So different from home, where the players are men, and female roles are played by boys. One gets used to that difference easily enough. (As for the movies, women are women and so on.)

I see by the clock that I must bring this letter to a close, though there is much more I want to tell you. Of course, I cannot really tell you anything . . . but writing isn't so bad, is it? I feel good writing, whatever else during the day has made me feel bad. The moment I take my pen in hand is always a moment of peace, though my news may be sad or disappointing or even, as when our dear Nguan Thong died, tragic. It is my dearest hope that your day is brightened when a letter arrives from your son. It is a kind of sharing.

—

LETTER #41   SIXTH MONTH, FIRST DAY
4 JULY 1951   YEAR OF THE HARE

I CAN read Thai, and even write a bit! You will be amazed, after I have written that I have no time for anything but work, or even to read the newspaper after dinner. Well, that remains so, but this I must do. Dealing with the government, especially, we depend too much on their dubious largesse even with some knowledge of their language.

To be more than averagely successful here, a Chinese must read Thai, write reasonably well, and speak with a decent accent. There are a few Thai sounds which trip on Chinese tongues. Even though Mui Eng was born here, I am aware that her Thai sounds different from that spoken by a real Thai.

I can practice speaking anytime with our employees, but I take care to do so only when Weng Khim is at school and Chui Kim napping. To learn reading and writing, I went out and bought the books myself and pulled one of our more literate bakery workers off his job for an hour a day to help me get started. The major difference between written Chinese and Thai is that Thai is written with an alphabet: sixty-four symbols, each with its own sound. When you put them together, they make words; there are no characters. That makes it rather easier than Chinese, for in Thai, if you know how a word ought to sound, you can read it when you see it. Writing is not so easy, for the letters must be combined in a particular manner, and for some sounds there are several possible letters. I do not know why that is so. Still, a man can study on his own, with the book as teacher. I know enough of the language to learn in this way because I have been listening to it for years. To learn this way when I first came here would not have been possible. Before long, I shall be able to read and write fluently. If only the Thai wouldn't write their words all run together in a string! That is what they do—there are no spaces between the words. But I shall get used to that in time; what is far more irritating is my handwriting. Why, when my calligraphy is graceful and controlled, is my Thai handwriting so awkward, I do not understand. It has occurred to me lately that the concept of calligraphy will certainly change because of the new pens we use. For the thickness and shape of a line made with an automatic pen depends entirely on the pen, not on the skill of the calligrapher, and our life is too busy to spend hours contemplating style as men used to do. The world I live in has far more respect for speed than for style and subtlety. Another sign of the times: the costumes of opera players, which used to be gorgeous. Now, they are put together with any inferior stuff which can be had cheaply and studded with tarnished sequins, acceptable under electric lights.

Now I can read contracts and newspapers (I read the financial page every day). No longer shall I fear being duped with paper and pen because I am Chinese. The newspapers often carry stories of illiterate Thai farmers (even their own, they cheat) who are tricked into signing away their land on the assumption that they are signing a loan agreement.

And I can read street signs. The first time I recognized, with pride, the name of our street, I thought of Ang Buai's plea, so many years ago, that she be allowed to study Thai. (She has taken care of that, by the way, long since.) How nice, not to have to embarrass myself asking strangers for directions. In short, I no longer need to borrow another man's nose in order to breathe. Before, whenever we received a letter written in Thai, we had to call on one of our Thai workers, most of whom would read with ponderous inaccuracy, guessing half the words—a dangerous nuisance at worst and boring at best, and I would always end by losing my temper and demanding to know why they didn't practice reading at home, to which the answer was always that they "didn't need to read in order to make a living." One fellow remarked sullenly that "books don't fill an empty belly." What a fool. Work, get paid, run out and spend everything—that is the extent of their imagination.

When I had mastered the newspapers, I began to look around for something more satisfying. The newspapers, after all, are mainly concerned with lurid murders and other unwholesome events; beyond the financial page, they do not interest me. I want to learn something of Thai literature, but I don't know where to go. I do not believe that the opinions of my cookie stampers represent the summit of Thai thought. Surely, the Thai must have their own good literature.

I picked up a few of Weng Khim's schoolbooks the other day. They're for children, of course, but I found admirable the tales encouraging kindness to animals (and it is gratifying to be able to read anything, when one is beginning). But I am a grown man, and talking animals could not keep me amused for very long. Yesterday, I bought a novel in the small bookshop down the street. He loves her, the parents disapprove, and after several hundred pages the parents see that they were wrong after all, especially when it turns out that he is the long lost son of a rich prince. These are called "ten satang tales," describing both price and literary value.

Chinese novels are expensive and difficult to come by, so this morning I picked up the newspaper again, resulting in my learning more disturbing facts about my homeland. So China is divided now; this news saddens me. History repeats itself, and if there is yet another division, we may see *Three Kingdoms* return in our own lifetime. Why? With wits and skill in abundance, why do we allow our greed and stubbornness to drag us down to civil war? And still China remains behind the rest of the world, so poor that its sons must desert it in order to survive.

I tend to my business and do not encumber my mind with politics. If only all men could put aside this obsession with power, and work sincerely toward their nation's progress. What do these people imagine politics can do for them? Thailand is no better. No one has gone so far as to divide the nation. But unity? No, it would be easier to find a needle in the ocean, as the Thai say. I wonder if it is much different in the countries of the red-haired ones, the *farang*. My reason tells me that it is not, except for differences in local customs, the details of treachery. (Do they kill the losers? Exile them? What fine-sounding name do they give to victory over the weak?) Power and money blind men to the things that matter most in life. More than enough is more than I want.

As for family news, I am resolved to send Chui Kim, first daughter, to the school too. Nowadays, boys and girls go to school together. Ang Buai says it is "a matter of equal rights." A lot of good that will do them, when they go out to take men's jobs and gain only the right to come home at night dead tired. It is nothing more than another case of grabbing power toward a dubious goal. I cannot be pleased with this business of sending boys and girls to school together, but I must go along with the times, for I am given no choice. You will be shocked, no doubt, for when I was a boy no girl saw a man's face outside her own family. Here they see everyone, anyone, even sit next to each other in the school from their earliest years. But I have been thinking, dear Mother, that such familiarity may not give them any ideas about the differences between the sexes. They may never notice any.

<hr>

LETTER #42   TENTH MONTH, THIRD DAY
1 NOVEMBER 1951   YEAR OF THE HARE

I HAVE taken Chui Kim to school, the "nursery class" where children do little but play and sing rhymes. Oh, they learn a word here, a simple number problem there, nothing worthwhile. It doesn't matter for her, of course, but if I were the father of a boy in that class, I would not be pleased.

I do everything possible to supplement Weng Khim's schooling, for the teachers are terribly lax. He cannot even read a newspaper yet! The only books he knows well are those I have taught him in the early mornings. Why should the school do less? They waste time on all kinds of foolishness and encourage the natural laziness of the pupils. I am more concerned about his Chinese studies than the nonsense they expose him to, but what do you think? He cares less for Chinese than for anything!

"It's so hard, Papa! So hard to remember all those—those lines and things, how to draw the characters just so."

"But you have been drawing characters for a long time, Weng Khim."

"Yes, but now that I have learned so many, they—they all seem to

176

jumble together in my head!"

"It is simply a matter of discipline. That is why we write our characters every day, son. Why do you not whine like this about your Thai studies? Or mathematics? Why must it only be Chinese that is so 'hard'?"

"Thai is easier," he said, averting his eyes and drawing a little man in the corner of his practice paper. "You know that is true, Papa. And the stories in the Thai books are funny. Our Chinese master yells all the time, and it's impossible to please him. One line too short or too long changes the whole meaning of the character, Papa, and who can remember every line all the time?"

He is quite right, but shall I let him think his own language is too difficult to be mastered? He will learn that millions of other Chinese boys have learned to write their characters properly and accurately.

He is so good with figures, such a quick mind. Why shouldn't he be as quick at Chinese? When he's working in the store with Mui Eng, what a joy it is to watch him. He will scoop up a kilo of dried shrimps, toss it onto the scale, and the arrow leaps precisely to the mark. By the time a customer has finished ordering, Weng Khim already has the total in his head. It is a fine sight, yes, but he doesn't seem to enjoy it, and I want him to love work, not endure it! Do you know, I love this business more than I used to love the soil. The bakery, hot, steaming and bustling all day; the dry goods shop, full of chattering people and the good smells of spices and tea, dried shrimp and squid; the import business, which challenges me in some new way every day. These are my "trees," bringing forth fruit in due season in return for faithful tending.

What of the day when Weng Khim must take my place? Will he follow in my footsteps, do things as I do them? I wonder . . . all that time he spends with Ang Buai, all the things he is learning in school, and the ideas he gets from other boys. Of these, the last worries me most. Last night, he dared to criticize the Chinese master to my face!

"He makes his face look—like this, see? A tiger! And he is always angry, Papa. When anyone makes a mistake, he strikes the boy with his ruler, or throws a blackboard eraser at him!"

I disapprove of this lack of respect, as any father would, though this teacher sounds unfit to instruct small children. What if he should cause a real injury? Nevertheless, I cannot allow Weng Khim to see my doubts about the man.

"Sometimes he pinches us, Papa . . . oh, it's not at all like Thai class. The Thai teacher smiles and uses polite words with the children, and she never yells. Sometimes she wears a blue dress the color of the sky . . . she's beautiful."

"A woman teacher? A Thai woman?"

"Oh, no! Her parents are Chinese people born in Thailand. She's even prettier than Mama. She has short hair and short skirts and red lips. Who wouldn't love to learn Thai, with her as teacher!" He laughed at his own joke, as he often does.

Mui Eng's eyes flashed dangerously. "So! We like Thai because the teacher is pretty!"

Jealous! That is how Mui Eng shows interest in her son's education. But she is absorbed in her precious Meng Chu, who grows only more unattractive. She is not a likeable child. She is plain, puny, and fussy. But she is Mui Eng's favorite, and Bak Lee has been handed over to a servant so that her mother can devote all of her attention to her youngest.

"The Chinese master should be fired!" Weng Khim continued, looking immediately terrified at his own daring. "That—that's what we think, my friends and me . . ."

"Enough! You must at least show respect for the man. If a teacher is strict, it is only because he wants his students to succeed."

His earnest little face puckered into a righteous scowl. "Our parents pay him, and they aren't getting their money's worth!"

"What nonsense this is! Who is putting these thoughts into your head?"

He wilted visibly, swallowed, then persevered, "Well, he's hired by the school to teach us, that's what my friend Lim says. That makes him an employee, not some kind of god, to pinch and hit us whenever he feels like it."

Ah, so it is young Lim who has brought my gullible son to doubt and defy his elders. The boy's father is a wealthy gold merchant, and the mother indulges him ridiculously. He takes expensive imported toys to school to impress his schoolmates and according to Weng Khim, "Lim has a motor car that runs like a real one, Papa!"

"The Chinese master is not to be thought of as an 'employee,' Weng Khim. Of course he must eat like other men, but the money we pay him is given out of respect and gratitude. He teaches because it is the work he likes best. Don't you realize that he could earn far more in another job? He cares about you boys, and how do you think you would learn Chinese without him?"

"You could teach me!"

"I could not. I haven't enough time, and many of the other fathers cannot even read Chinese. They want their sons to be better educated than they were. You should be glad of the opportunity, all of you."

"Nothing can make me like him, Papa. I don't like our mathematics teacher either, but at least I like the subject, and I don't get hit because I never make a mistake. Lim doesn't even like the Thai teacher, and she's the nicest one!"

"This is the boy you choose to call your friend."

"His desk is beside mine. I can't not talk to him, can I?"

"You sit in the rear of the classroom, don't you? Well, then, tell the Thai teacher that you can't see from back there—you seem to have her wrapped around your finger."

"What if the boy who sits in that desk doesn't want to trade places?"

"Well, what if he doesn't?" I was beginning to lose my temper. "You seem to care more for the opinion of a lot of ill-mannered boys than for the opinion of your father!"

He promised to try, but before many days had passed there was an unexpected and, for the boy, disastrous development. The young Chinese woman who taught Thai left to be married and will not return. Since then, he has moped about the house, inconsolable, and his school work grows worse with each passing day. But children forget their little sorrows easily, and I am sure he will soon attach his affections to another teacher. He has been avoiding me, no doubt because he is afraid I will quiz him about his lessons. Well, no matter. I am trying to raise him as you raised me, and I haven't turned out so badly, do you think? Your son's dearest wish is that you will feel pride in his achievements.

179

THE NEWSPAPERS continue to bring bad news from China. I do not trust news that comes indirectly, and from afar at that. Do you remember the old tale about a woman who, it was rumored, had given birth to a baby elephant? As it turned out, the baby's nose had been a bit long, and each time the tale was told, the nose had grown a bit longer. I have been thinking of this old tale as I listen to reports of the situation at home in China. Can things be as bad as we hear?

How are you, Mother? Are you well, as I remember you? I am enclosing money, and I pray that if there is trouble of any kind in Po Leng, you may be better able to keep it from your door. I don't know myself what I mean, but there is nothing else I can do.

I visited Kim and Chaba one evening last week in their little home on the riverbank, and he held forth on the state of affairs in China (as interpreted by various sages in the market).

"From what I hear, it is really bad," he said, shaking his head solemnly. "They say that anyone who disagrees with the new government this week is a bag of fertilizer next week!"

Chaba drew her eyebrows together warningly, but I only laughed. "Don't worry, Chaba—when I listen to Kim talk about it, I feel better."

"Laugh! Go on and laugh! I tell you, these stories are word of mouth, not just the stuff they give the newspapers. It is a fearful situation. And now Korea is at war, too . . . I wonder why Thailand is so peaceful."

"Peaceful? Only because the fighting goes on above your head. The people do not involve themselves; they are content to let the government govern. So, when there is a 'revolution' in Thailand, who learns of it last? The people! As for us, old Kim, we have our living to earn and enough to keep our minds occupied without worrying about politics. Perhaps I shouldn't have said, 'as for us,' though; that is one thing we have in common with Thais. They never think about politics until it hits them on the head. Then it is too late."

"Don't ordinary people ever fight? I mean, they can't agree with every change, can they?"

"I don't know . . . Long ago, the Thai people looked up only to the man they called king. Later, whoever assumed power received respect, and when he was knocked down by a rival, the people were always willing to shrug it off. They don't seem to care much, since the king's power was challenged. One leader is very much like another, and their love still belongs to their king. Or so it seems to me, Kim."

"Chaba's mother says Thailand has tried to make its government like those of the *farang*, but it hasn't worked so well."

"I don't know much about that. Yong Chua knows far more about such things than I, because of his travels. He once told me that in America, ordinary people decide who their rulers should be, and they have never had a king. Whoever is most popular becomes ruler—people have to vote for him, you see—and after a few years he has to give up his power to someone else. That's what Thailand tried to do, but—its leaders are less willing to abandon power once they have tasted it."

"I don't understand about America. Before they started that kind of government—people choosing their own leaders—how was the country governed?"

"I have read that in ancient times, only the forest men lived in America, savages. Then Europeans arrived, and soon they took over the country. The people who are Americans now, at least most of them, were once Frenchmen, or Englishmen, men of many nations."

"I would think the leaders of America must favor their own kind. I mean, an American from France would naturally favor all the other Frenchmen, wouldn't he?"

"I do not know. I regret the way our people have tried to imitate foreign ways. And they have, you know. That is part of the trouble now in China. Choosing what is best, considering carefully what the *farang* do that could work for us—I have no argument with such thinking. But look at what is happening in China today! And it is the result of aping other nations' ways! What 'careful choosing' was there? What 'consideration' brought the changes that plague our people now, that cause them to butcher each other? Well, enough of this kind of talk. What are you going to name your baby?"

Kim blinked several times, then threw his head back and laughed. "Oh, you are a strange one, Suang U! The baby is like Chaba, no? She looks like a Thai." His eyes followed Chaba as she walked out to the tiny kitchen with the baby on her hip.

"We're giving her two names, Chinese and Thai. The Chinese name

I've chosen ought to get a laugh out of you—" He grinned mischievously and lowered his voice as he said, "Kha Hieng! I'm calling her Kha Hieng, get it? For old times' sake . . . She calls the baby Rose, and that's the name she'll use. I remember those blossoms on every hedge in Po Leng. They looked just like roses, but everybody thought of them as weeds, you know?"

"They are of the same family, I suppose. I've seen the same blossoms on the hedges here, too. But what they call roses are a little fancier, raised for sale. In some country, probably, even the blossom we call stinkflower is highly prized!"

Kim laughed and said, "It just so happens I've seen a stinkflower in a vase on my next door neighbor's table—only it was red, and it didn't stink. Not while I was there, anyway."

"Oh, those! They're called 'cow's face' and they're a little different—to the nose, mainly. The *farang* pay a lot of money for those, too—almost as much as for orchids, which used to be wild jungle weeds nobody looked at. I guess they still are, in jungles! One of the men in our bakery told me that Thais from the North come down to Bangkok and can't believe the 'weeds' that are selling as 'flowers' here. And they're not even from another country! The world is changing every day, my friend. What is good now in time becomes worthless, and today's weed is tomorrow's orchid."

"Then there's hope for us all! I wonder why all the rich people in the world don't get together and agree on what's valuable."

"Hm-m, let me think . . . we'd either all be at peace, or have killed each other off long ago . . . or we'd all have perished of boredom."

"I believe you're right. If everyone agreed on everything, men would lose their will to achieve. Eat, sleep, and die, like—"

"Animals! But we are men, and so we argue and fight and make wars. When peace comes, it comes only because we are too tired to fight anymore, not because we longed for peace. Nonetheless, without that peace, however we come by it, we could not go on."

I know what life is, you see; I have no illusions. I simply avoid thinking about these things most of the time, for if my own flesh and blood must suffer . . . no, it is an unbearable thought. I pray that you are well, and that no danger befalls you in these terrible days.

MORE NEWS of your grandson, for his problems dominate our life these days. As for the business, it gives me no problems, other than those with which I have become comfortable.

I am not a very good letter writer, I fear, for I have not even the decency to spare you bad news! But you know me better than anyone, and can see from what I write that I am myself, and as happy as any man may expect to be. Mui Eng is rude about my letters to you, for reasons I do not understand. Yesterday, I was telling the older children some tale from my childhood when she interrupted, "You and your family! Your mother may not even live in that—that Po Leng place anymore. No mother could be so hard-hearted that she wouldn't write even one letter, after all those long letters you've written to her."

I felt humiliated before the children. How dare she! "You do not know my mother at all, or you would not speak so foolishly. Especially in front of her grandchildren. She reads every letter, you may be sure, but—but she is not the sort of person who does what—what most other people do. It is not at all peculiar of her not to write. If you knew her, you would not shame yourself by speaking this way!"

"It is possible that the government there isn't even delivering your letters. Who knows what they do now?"

"Mui Eng, what kind of government would stop a letter from a son to his mother? Now, do not speak foolishly in front of the children again!"

She stalked out of the room with exaggerated disregard for my words, a familiar action of hers which has become more flamboyant with the increase in girth, and considerably less dignified.

I have moved Weng Khim to a new school. At the end of this past year, I am ashamed to report, he failed in his examinations. I was shocked and dismayed, for he is a clever boy. Most of the things I have taught him at home lately were of no use in the examinations. I realize that now. To buy and sell, to understand customers, to smile and behave correctly, and always to leave personal troubles in the back of the shop. Weng Khim can weigh and measure, add figures in his head quickly, and think on his feet. Do you suppose they value such things in the school?

Reading and writing are essential. That is what I expect the school to teach him, in addition to Chinese and arithmetic. But I was disgusted with the other subjects they include in their curriculum. "What is a peninsula? A chasm? An island? How does one get milk from a cow?" These are from "social studies"! Most of the children have never seen an island, but can they fail to recognize one if ever they do? Most of them have never seen a cow, either, but I should hope they will figure out where the milk comes from when they do see one. "Which animals are warm-blooded?" Who cares? Perhaps I am a stupid man, but I cannot see why my boy has to study such things to succeed in this life. I asked the head teacher why so much time was devoted to such things and was told, peremptorily at that, "For the sake of learning itself . . . and, you know, the *farang* are still far ahead of us . . ."

Now, I believe that a boy should study that which will profit him as a man. A farmer's son should study farming, so that he will one day reap more from his land than could his fathers before him. Practical skills benefit a man until the day he dies.

Thai people always encourage their children to choose careers unlike their own, something "better." And, too often, they are rushed into occupations without sound training. Such notions give rise to a generalized incompetence.

To change careers out of necessity is another circumstance altogether. I did not desert the land so much as it abandoned me, and there was nothing else for me to do, unless I was content to survive instead of live. And how fortunate I was to be taken in by kindly people who wished me well. Because of them, and my own hard work, Weng Khim need never strike out alone, neither to improve himself nor to escape hardship. Everything awaits him. He has been well trained from birth for the position that awaits him.

Shall I pretend not to be disappointed in the boy? It is a bitter thing to admit, but if the school does not suit him, I must find another that will—one where the Chinese master is not so hard that the boy's regard for our language is destroyed. This is the sad duty of the man with only one son. If the son cannot be made to fit the world, then the world must be altered to enhance the son.

The new school is rather far, so they take their lunch with them in a sack. (Chui Kim goes there too, for convenience sake. Also, she can keep an eye on her brother. Oddly enough, it seems that she looks out for him. She will grow up to be a good mother.) The first few days, Father took them to school and fetched them, but we have found a cautious *samlo* driver who can be trusted with them. He lives in a dilapidated row of houses behind the bakery, and his daughter works for us as a wrapper. She is only eight years old, but her work is good and we don't have to pay her much. According to Thai law, all children must finish four years of school, completing Prathom Four, but the poor here, as everywhere I suppose, cannot afford such laws. Their children attend the first day, and occasionally thereafter—often enough to keep the authorities away. But the schools are crowded anyway, teachers are scarce, and more children are being born every day, so that I suspect it is a boon to the school system to have a certain percentage of children who can be counted on to be truant! Of those who do manage to complete Prathom Four, many still cannot read well, and most cannot write. I could hardly blame the Thai mother I overheard scolding her daughter: "Just when you get old enough to be any help around here, they want you in school! And if you ever finish, much good it will have done me, nah? You'll be old enough by then to run off with some no-good . . . well, then you'll find out . . . you'll know what I put up with!"

Weng Khim must finish Prathom Four, of course, then continue his studies where they will do the most good here, with me. No more warm-blooded animals, no more peninsulas or chasms or cows. He will learn bookkeeping, the abacus, pastry-making (every step, with his grandfather beside him—that is the only way he will earn the respect of our employees). He will learn everything I know, and do every job that is done here. In the evenings, I want him to go to Chinese classes, and gain the deep love for our language that only a good teacher can give him.

And, for Chui Kim, dressmaking school. Someday when she is the wife of a businessman, she will be an asset to her husband and a credit to her father. Do you find the developing plan of our lives agreeable, Mother? I hope so. Do not worry unduly about Weng Khim. At least he became literate in Thai, and the rest of what the school offers will neither help nor hinder him in the business of life.

SOMETHING TERRIBLE has occurred, something unthinkable, and all because of your son's thoughtlessness . . . Oh, dear Mother, I feel so ashamed! No man can blame me more than I blame myself for the death of Lo Yong Chua! I have attached a sin to my soul that will gnaw at me all the days of my life.

I have not slept all night, nor shall I rest during the day now dawning, for my weary eyes close only to see his beloved face, kindly even in death, and I am overwhelmed by grief and guilt.

Once, when I was a little boy and had done wrong, you hit me. Then, even before the tears had sprung from my eyes, you pulled me close and hugged me, cradled me in your arms. How I wish I could be a child again, to be punished and then quickly held, and comforted, driving away both punishment and bad deed. That day I had killed a little bird. Pulled out all his feathers to see whether he would still fly. His poor body, plucked bare, was raw, pink and quivering. Do you remember? Strange that I should think of it at this dreadful dawn . . . You've probably forgotten. (Wonderful it would be, if you wrote to me now, even to scold me—but no! I mustn't say it.) You hit me with a switch, and when I opened my mouth to begin bawling, you threw the switch into the corner and buried your face in my little heaving chest. Every life, you said, even the tiniest bird's—every life is precious! The bird had suffered greatly before he died, poor Mister Bird. Had I snapped his fragile neck swiftly, he would not have suffered. But feather by feather he died, a hundred agonies. I remember your words as if it were yesterday, dear Mother, and if I had remembered them in time, Father might be alive today.

Last month, Father was ill with a bad cold. The change of seasons never did agree with him, but he took his medicine and got well without seeing a doctor, and I scarcely thought about the illness when I saw that he was back at the dinner table, back to work. I thought very little about anything at the time, for the bakery was in danger of failing behind on orders, and for the first time our import stock came dangerously near bottom a full two weeks before the next expected delivery of goods from Swatow. What time had I to wonder if he was completely recovered? Mui Eng's shop, too, has been full of customers. The income from it alone has been double that from the bakery, though I never spoke of that to Father. He encouraged me to attend to the business and let him look after himself ("A bit of a cough hanging on—that's nothing!") and I was selfish enough to be grateful! Never did I think his life would be tragically shortened because I preferred to deceive myself.

Then Weng Khim became ill, frighteningly so (as well as Meng Chu, third daughter). Mui Eng lay beside her youngest for many days, and I worried over Weng Khim so that my work did begin to suffer. His fever was so high. He even became delirious, slipped out of the house when we weren't watching and ran about in the rain, laughing and shouting. I was out in the bakery talking to a repairman who had come to adjust the great oven. When I heard shouts coming from the yard, I went outside, holding a newspaper over my head, and peered through the rain across the muddy, flooded yard to see which neighborhood urchin had dared to come celebrate the storm at my back door. When I saw that it was Weng Khim, I dropped the newspaper, ran to him on shaking legs, and caught him up in my arms. Drenched with rain and burning with fever, he shouted with laughter, babbled, out of his head. I knew for the first time in my life what true terror is.

The Isan* servant who opened the back door for us took one look at Weng Khim and began screaming that a spirit had entered his body, which Mui Eng showed every sign of believing as she rushed into the kitchen with Meng Chu whining under her arm. But I knew that fever can cause delirium, and the answer was stronger medicine from a better doctor. I sat up with him all that night, and the next day I fell asleep at my desk.

"Son, let me stay with him during the night. I don't sleep much at night anyway, you know that, but you—you must work, and you are used to a night's sleep."

*"Isan," which means "northeast," refers to the northeastern region of Thailand, bordering Laos. Isan is a relatively poor region. A seasonal migration of farmers, looking for work in Bangkok, has long been a fact of Thai life. In recent decades, great numbers of Isan farmers have settled in the slums of Bangkok, and very few have returned to their rural homes. *Trans.*

"Don't, Father, really you mustn't—"

"Enough! You must not abandon your responsibilities, and I am strong. Or are you telling me I'm an old man, now? Go to sleep in your own bed tonight and don't tell me what to do. Isn't Weng Khim my grandson? Well then, I have every right to share in worrying about him. And I might have stopped him from running out into the rain, Suang U. I should have been with him then . . . that I cannot forget."

That night I slept soundly, for the first time in three days. But Father did not sleep at all. It was noon of the following day before he rested, and then not peacefully, for days are noisy in a house so full of customers and children, workers and visitors and relatives. He returned to Weng Khim's room late in the afternoon and dozed fitfully in his chair with one hand on the boy's pillow, touching his feverish cheek.

The modern doctor said he had pneumonia, gave him an injection, and sent us home with a large bottle of pills. The next day we returned for another injection, and that night Weng Khim slept soundly, his brow was cool, and he did not cry out with nightmares as before. "The doctor is an angel," Mui Eng whispered, stroking her son's forehead gently while he sighed peaceful in his sleep. "He looked like a child himself, so young to be a doctor. I couldn't believe he knew what to do, but after this I would never call anyone else. It is a miracle!" Weng Khim mumbled something unintelligible and smiled, and I felt a great lump begin to grow in my throat.

So happy we were to see Weng Khim become himself again; to see, hour by hour, the color return to his complexion, hear him ask for food! No one thought of Father, myself least of all. But the cruel nights of Weng Khim's delirium and his own fear, of no sleep and no thought for himself, began to tell, and the coughing became worse. He never complained. On the third night he took to his bed, and he did not rise from it again.

In the morning, I stopped in to see why he had not come down to breakfast, and when I saw his ashen face, his eyes sunken deep above two deep red spots on his cheeks, when I touched his arm and it seemed to burn through my hand, I turned and ran. From his bedside to the doctor's door, I never stopped running. My hand still burned with the fever when the doctor opened his door and regarded me with mild surprise. What a sight I must have been—out of breath, my hair disheveled, my eyes red with unshed tears.

I led him up the stairs to Father's room. A feeble, gagging cough greeted us. The doctor frowned and bent over him as if searching for something he had lost.

"Why didn't you call me sooner? His fever is very high, and his lungs are filling. Do you understand what that means? The old man's body is in generally poor condition, too. He put his stethoscope to Father's thin chest, listened carefully, and shook his head. "Surely he must have felt ill for several days?" It was not really a question, and he did not wait for an answer.

I began to tremble, visibly I was sure. "He—he sat up with our son several nights," I stammered, "when he was ill . . ." While I slept soundly! "Never mind the money!" I blurted out suddenly, too loud, "just do whatever you must to make my father well!"

He regarded me curiously for a moment, then turned away and spoke abruptly. "I will try, certainly. But I cannot guarantee anything. I—I am not sure, do you understand?"

He gave Father an injection and left several kinds of medicine, pills and liquids both, with instructions to give each kind exactly on time, keep him in bed, and give him as much nourishing food as he would take.

"And none of your 'sick man's diet,' do you hear? I want you to give him proper food—pork, duck, beef! And if he can't get down the solid food, then give him strong beef broth. No dry fish and rice, that won't do him any good at all."

I nodded dumbly, frantic with fear. Our people have always eaten dry fish and rice when they were ill, for we believe that rich foods weaken a sick body, but I would not have dared to disobey the doctor in anything. Everything was prepared in accordance with his orders, but it was a feast come to a man already starved in body and spirit, and I felt like a man trying to shelter a candle against a strong wind. He would eat a few spoonfuls of food, then push the dish away, turn aside, and begin again the tight, dry, agonized coughing that convulsed his frail and steadily weakening body.

I never left his side, day or night, but I would always fall asleep in the evening before he did, then wake with a jerk hours later to see him staring at me with his kindly eyes, as if to say, "Don't take it so hard, son . . ."

189

I have kept myself apart from the others, for I feel justly critical eyes upon me wherever I look. Here he is—the man who loved his son better than the man to whom he owed that son! Lo Yong Chua was a father and friend beyond compare, and without him I would have been nothing. I would be lucky to have a stall next to Kim's in the market-place, and toil day and night for a few coins . . . and I let him die! How can I ever know happiness again, after what I have done? I have kept the children away from me, too, for I do not deserve to look into their once trusting faces, especially Weng Khim's. Do they look at their father with despising eyes, or do I imagine it? Does it matter?

The fine funeral I shall give him cannot erase my sin. Do not fear that I imagine it can. It is nothing but a farce! With his own generosity I mock him, making a show of wealth over his wasted body, he who gave everything to an adopted son under whose roof he sickened and died.

It is customary to mourn one's father three years, but I shall remain in mourning for ten. A black armband does not always signify a grieving heart, I know, but for me it shall be a reminder that Father is with me in all I do, in death as in life. What other men may think does not matter.

It is late, dark and cold. Though the electric lights still burn, awaiting the dawn, I feel darkness, in the room, in my heart. The cold penetrates my chest, creeps out into my limbs. It remains within me, for my spirit has no warmth to chase it out. Now in my mind I try desperately to see, instead of his face, yours. You and me, treading the dikes of our field, leading our oxen home in the shadow of the mountain. That is my favorite picture, you know. Of the people who cared for me, another is lost forever. My turn has come to be eldest, and who have I to turn to now, but you? Your son is a lonely man, and in pain. Please, I beg you, do not forsake him.

P.S. The child Meng Chu improves.

LETTER #46　　　　　　　　SECOND MONTH, TENTH DAY
24 MARCH 1953　　　　　　YEAR OF THE SNAKE

190

FATHER'S FUNERAL was very beautiful. I did the best I could, arranging everything as he would have wished. It was this, his funeral, that worried him most, because his only son had died young, and would not walk in his funeral procession, and honor him after his death. So, rest with a peaceful spirit, Father . . .

After some deliberation, I decided to have Buddhist ceremonies as well, and monks prayed for seven nights before the *kong tek* procession. My friends all said the crypt we bought is sure to bring good luck to his descendants. Truly, I spent a good bit on it. We will invite monks to pray again on the twenty-first, fiftieth, and hundredth day. May this merit reach the hand of dear Lo Yong Chua. In his death I have been a faithful son.

I have been ill since the funeral, and the doctor doesn't seem to know what is wrong. My face is flushed, and I get dizzy spells all the time. Then, though I am exhausted at night, I can't sleep, which is most annoying. After a week in bed, I went back to work. He would have had me lie there like a cripple until my business ran into the ground. What is it to him? And Mui Eng continues to nag me about it. Every time she opens her mouth, I feel worse.

"I can tell you why you don't sleep at night," she said accusingly, standing before my desk with her arms crossed. "You work too hard, you've always worked too hard. Then when you go to bed, you're overtired. The doctor knows it, I know it, but you won't listen to anyone!"

"A man has to work. I don't hear any complaints when you're out spending the money."

"A man has to work, yes, but you do more than any one man should. There are plenty of people working here now who could take some of these tasks off your hands. Why must you take it all on yourself, as if no one else had a brain in his head?"

"What do you mean, 'take some of these tasks off my hands'? If I didn't keep an eye on everyone in the place they'd all be running around town three hours a day."

"You're impossible!" She leaned against the desk and was silent for a few blessed moments. "When you don't sleep at night, when you lie there staring at the wall . . . what are you thinking about?"

I put my pen down and looked up at her. "Thinking about? Why, I couldn't say . . . about—Father, and about my mother, too. You know I worry about my mother, with everything that's going on there."

"Your mother! Well, I'm not going into that again . . . Ang Buai says you should show more faith in the employees. She says they aren't happy here, working under suspicion all the time."

"Ang Buai says! Ang Buai says! She says too much! Does she think my employees give a damn whether I'm happy? And since when do I need her advice to run my business? I'll never be that sick."

"You could at least get an assistant to help with the book work. That's what takes up most of your time."

"At least . . . at least help with the books? Have you lost your mind, Mui Eng? They see a little cash, these people, and before you know it, your money is going to buy lottery tickets, whiskey, bad women! Nobody but me touches these books—not you, nobody, do you understand?"

She's fed up with me, I know. I don't care, because I'm fed up with her, too! Fancy food, fancy clothes, that's all she thinks about. She lets the servants get fat on our food, hands it out like water, but none of them can match her bulge for bulge.

She sits before her mirror for an hour every morning, and for what? I wrote before that she was getting "plump"—but now! Her eyes look like little black worms perching above her fat cheeks. Not long after Meng Chu was born, she went out and got one of those damned "permanent waves." Every time I look at her and see those short frizzy curls around her flabby face, the white scalp showing through all over her head, the back of her pale round neck bulging out over her collar, I want to throw up. How could such a beautiful girl turn into such an unattractive woman?

After breakfast, she drags a chair to the front of the store and plants herself there with Meng Chu on her lap. When a customer comes in, she lets the clerks do all the running. When the customer leaves, one of the clerks gives her the money and she drops it into a bag she keeps beside her. And there she sits, all day long.

Not only is she aging swiftly and turning herself into a mountain of fat, but Meng Chu is becoming impossibly spoiled. Mui Eng says she's afraid the child will cry and disturb the customers, so she picks her up every time she whimpers. She knows full well how aggravated I feel when I look out and see the two of them sitting there. I am certain it gives her pleasure.

Before, I had Father to talk to; now nobody cares to listen to me. I miss him so! I hope it isn't bothersome for you to read these things, for your sympathy is more important to me than anything these depressing days.

My illness aggravates all these annoyances, and the dizziness is driving me crazy. Naturally, no respect is shown me, in spite of Mui Eng's nagging insistence that I "get more rest." She listens to the opera on the radio, turned up as far as it will go to drown out the noise of the children's quarrels. All day it drones on, relentlessly. Sometimes I feel like running out of the office and shouting, "I'm the master of this house! Everybody here can do as I say from now on, or GET OUT!"

And sometimes, in the afternoon, I doze off in spite of it all. Then I have a nightmare. It is always the same. Mui Eng and the children are dead! I never find out what happened to them, but they are definitely dead. She's sitting in her chair in front of the store with Meng Chu on her lap, both dead of course, and I go into the house (where have I been? I don't know—) and find the rest of them lying on the floor dead—children, servants, everybody. And I feel—how can I explain the feeling—the way you feel when everyone around you is serious and, suddenly, your mouth begins to twitch with a silly grin for no reason at all. The more you try to control your face, the sillier the grin. Perhaps you are too sensible a person to have had such a feeling, but that is the feeling I have when I realize that everyone in my house is dead.

Always, at that point in the dream, I begin to wake up. I hear the children yelling and the opera whining away on the radio, and even though I hear them, I feel that I must go and see if everyone is really alive! That is crazier than the dream, even I realize that.

Kim came to see me while I was still in bed. He opened the door with a sheepish smile and held up a huge basket of beautiful ripe mangoes. I felt embarrassed to have him see me sick, in bed.

"Thanks, Kim. How did you know?"

"A customer in the restaurant told Chaba. 'What!' says I, 'My old friend the cookie tycoon of Bangkok laid low? I must leave my hot stove and see what the trouble is!' So, here I am. How are you, Suang U? You look rotten."

"I'm all right," I replied gruffly. "I'll be on my feet and out of here by the end of the week. Sorry I haven't been around lately—how's the restaurant business?"

"Hey, how did you know? It was supposed to be a big surprise. Well, fine . . . just a little hole in the wall, you know. Food, whiskey, cigarettes. But we do all right." He grinned proudly. "Everyone in Bangkok but you eats lunch out. By noon, we're packed—I think we'll make it."

"I'm glad for you. How about pork—you give up selling pork?"

"Nah—Chaba and her mother get up early and sell before we open up.

"And you sleep late."

"Yeah, I lie around like a bum until six o'clock."

"You said you sell liquor. Better watch out."

"Have no fear! Never touch it. Only on Chinese New Year, and then everybody else had better watch out. Come on in when you're on your feet again so I can show off. You can have noodles—on the house, of course—and a nice plate of Thai curry. I'm not a bad cook!"

"You're a good liar, anyway," I laughed. "You cook Thai food?"

"Well, I can chop peppers as well as anyone. Shred coconut, throw it all into a pot with some fish sauce. Chaba's mother tells me how to do it. But the Chinese food, I make myself, no interference allowed. Cook a little, eat a little . . ."

"Looks more like cook a little, eat a lot. You've put on what, five inches around your waist since the last time I saw you? How's Chaba, by the way—as fat as my wife?"

"Yeah, I noticed . . . Chaba will never get fat, not with all those hot Thai peppers she eats all day." He frowned. "They're bad for her."

"Is anything wrong?"

"Just hemorrhoids, she says. She bleeds all the time. I don't know, it doesn't seem right to me, but she won't go to a doctor."

"Thai food isn't healthy, I've always said it. Why don't you make her eat Chinese food?"

"Oh, she eats Chinese food, all right—with hot peppers sprinkled on top of everything. You're right, though—there's nothing like Chinese food. The whole world likes it, fortunately for me."

"Too bad it's so greasy." I remarked, unable to resist teasing him a little.

"Greasy!" he exploded. "What do you mean, greasy? You have to drink lots of tea, that's all, hot strong tea to make the stomach light. Drink a pot of tea and you can eat a whole chicken!"

It was good to see the old fool again.

"As soon as you're up and around, Suang U, we expect to see you." He rose to leave, cocked his head at me critically and said, "You look like you could use the food. What's wrong with that wife of yours? She's plump as a pot and you look like a dried shrimp."

"You know I've never been a big eater. And Mui Eng—well, she seems to be healthy. She'll live a long life."

If she would only dress suitably, it wouldn't be so bad, but she insists on wearing those *farang* "stretch pants" that Ang Buai wears. My sister-in-law weighs about ninety pounds. Mui Eng's got fifty pounds in the rear end alone, and her front side looks like it's tied into five-pound bundles. The pants cling to every lump and ripple.

There I was, nineteen years old, hurrying in from my bath at the *khlong* . . . a kitchen shutter opened, and a girl appeared, a girl with a face like the moon. It's been nine years since that morning, and the red glow on the *khlong* at sunrise. What was it I wrote to you that day? "I'm surely not going to starve in this beautiful land"—something like that. Well, Mui Eng surely has not starved in it.

LETTER #47   FIFTH MONTH, FIRST DAY
11 JUNE 1953   YEAR OF THE SNAKE

BUSINESS HAS been a little slow since my illness, but I'm feeling better all the time and have even put on a little weight. More important, I have more strength to argue with Mui Eng lately. That must mean something.

"We ought to buy a car!" she announced a week ago, at the breakfast table.

"Ooh, Mama!" chimed in Weng Khim. "Then I could go to school in it and all the boys would see me. What wouldn't I give to see their faces then . . . They all think we haven't any money because I take my lunch." He scowled, "I'm the only one."

"Food from home is clean," I said. "What do you care what a lot of

195

silly boys think? We live in our own house and don't owe money."

"Oh, Father, the boys don't care about things like that. What they notice is well cars, things like that."

"I see."

"Well, I'm tired of taking the bus," Mui Eng added plaintively. "In this heat, to be packed in with every sort of person . . . and you don't dare take *samlos* any more. Why, almost every day I see one forced up onto the sidewalk by a bus! If we have money for delivery trucks, we must have money enough for one car."

"One car. That's considerate of you, Mui Eng, only one . . . We need the trucks for business, and we do not need a car for anything. Where do we go, anyway? We're either in the house or at the factory."

"Speak for yourself! I like to go to the *ngiu* sometimes, at night. Or to the movies. If we hired a driver, we wouldn't have to worry about coming home late, and in the morning he could take the children to school. You wouldn't even have to learn to drive."

"Your consideration knows no bounds. Do you know how much your sister spends on that car of hers? And she doesn't even pay a driver."

"Mama says we have more money than Auntie," Chui Kim said, "and she has a car. If we can afford one, I don't see why you won't buy it."

Breakfast is our customary time to argue, since we are all working or at school during the day, and I am too tired for it by dinner. If I don't fall asleep early, I like to read Thai for an hour or so in the evening, or write to you. Breakfast is our only convenient time for arguing.

I'm reading a pretty good book now, about a war the Thais fought in a long time ago. It isn't as good as *Three Kingdoms*, of course, but I'm enjoying it. The Thai have even translated some Chinese novels, but my feelings about them are mixed. A bad translation encourages disdain or, at the least, misunderstanding. For instance, there is a Thai saying to the effect that it is foolish to make offerings at the temple like a Thai, when you could make offerings like the Chinese and then eat the food at the next meal. Well, they just don't understand the first thing about it. That sort of bungling is what I refer to.

Three days after bringing up the subject of a car, Mui Eng dropped her bombshell. Another breakfast hour: "I'm going to buy a car out

196

of—out of the money my father left me!" She set her jaw stubbornly and glared down at her plate.

"Ah ha! So now it's 'your' money and 'mine'?"

"Well, you don't want a car, and I do. And you—you boss me too much! It's my right to have the things I want, and I should be able to use my money as I please. You do."

"Oh, yes, you have every right. After all, he was your father, it was his money . . . we mustn't forget that, must we?"

Her words were like hot needles driving into my brain. Oh, she is so right! What am I? Only the husband . . . only the clerk. That is what lies behind all this. "How dare he tell me how to use my money?" And I'm sure Ang Buai is egging her on all the way. To think that I once dreamed that I might be "destined" to marry Mui Eng! Youth cannot tell destiny from doom.

No man who has any pride can know peace of mind married to a rich woman, and the boss's daughter besides! How could I have thought we would be any different? Maybe I did use "her" money in some ways when we began, but I've worked myself almost to death to build up her inheritance. Does that touch her at all? Hah!

If Younger Brother isn't married yet, plead with him to find a poor girl.

The car was delivered this morning. Mui Eng seemed happy, riding around the neighborhood beside one of our truck drivers. Weng Khim and Chui Kim were beside themselves, poking their grinning faces out the windows and shouting at everyone they knew. The younger girls curled up between them and went promptly to sleep. So my children grow up, dreaming of unearned luxuries in their padded pleasure craft. Hear my vow: unless I am bleeding to death and can't get a bus that passes the hospital, I shall never set foot in that car.

It is Italian, quite handsome really, a light blue color with a gray top. I asked around to see if there were any cars made nearer Thailand, but there aren't. I spent a whole day looking at different models, trying to save a little of poor Nguan Thong's money. The import tax is scandalous.

I've heard Chinese businessmen talk about setting up an automobile assembly plant right here. No Thai will ever do it, that's certain. They'd rather build nightclubs with their money, sell liquor, hire girls to dance *farang* style with the customers, hugging them in public. They think it will be someone else's son who comes home drunk at midnight, someone else's grandson or wife or sister who is poisoned by the existence of such places. It's true that some nightclub owners are Chinese, or at least part Chinese, but most of us prefer businesses that depend on wholesome necessities.

Now that I have been forced to give in to Mui Eng, what will she do? Run out and buy every trinket and bauble that strikes her fancy? If ever I was head of this household, that is all over now. Such a marriage is bearable only for a man so "modern" that he is willing to live off his wife and let her run everything. "Modern," hah! We used to have other words for it.

I always thought my marriage would be like yours . . . I remember the two of you sitting before the stove, chatting quietly, in the years before Father died. The time has come to quit pretending that Mui Eng and I are anything but miserable together. After Meng Chu was born, I feared so for her life that I almost convinced myself there was something left . . . love? Grief and guilt and pride imitate it cannily. A fog has descended around us, a thick gray fog of frustration and misunderstanding and defeat. It is terrible to realize, but true: as we are now, we shall remain for the rest of our lives.

—

LETTER #48   SECOND MONTH, FIRST DAY
5 MARCH 1954   YEAR OF THE HORSE

SOMEONE ONCE told me that the purpose of life is the pursuit of happiness. You know better than anyone how hard I have tried to teach Weng Khim the folly of such a view of life. Yet Mui Eng sets the boy against my ways at every turn.

"He is mine, too!" she cried vehemently. "You know he wants to go on in school, to become a teacher—a good one, like the Thai teacher he was so fond of. With the right encouragement, he would do well in school, I know it!"

"Teacher? He will be a merchant. Do you think I have done all this, built this business, so that he can toss it aside and become a miserable teacher? His duty lies here, in the business—"

"Do you think that will make him like it?" she all but sneered. "Ability is not the same as love for the work, Suang U, and love for it he will never have. Don't force him, or you will break his heart and—and your own."

"Tch tch. Wonderfully dramatic, Mui Eng, but unrealistic. He is a child, and he thinks like one. As you still do. What does it matter if he hates what I make him do now? When he is a man, he will thank the gods he had a father who chose prosperity for him instead of letting him drag out his days with a lot of brats in a classroom. So, you turn your head, eh? You won't look at me—you scorn my 'greed' . . . see whether he will scorn it when he is thirty-five!"

"As you wish, then. You will ruin him, but he is yours—"

"Yes, mine! Can you not stay out of this matter? He is the only son you gave me. Do what you will with your daughters."

"Then you are willing to let me raise my daughters exactly as I wish?"

"Of course. Especially your youngest."

"Is Meng Chu to grow up feeling that she is not your child?"

"Don't make yourself ridiculous. But—yes, you may raise her exactly as you wish. After what you have already done with her, do you think I want credit for the results?"

"Promise me that her future is in my hands alone, and you shall never hear another word about Weng Khim."

I almost laughed in her face. "What is it to me? It's hardly worth— oh, all right, I promise. I am sending Weng Khim to study Chinese at night. And when he finally passes his Prathom Four examinations, I'm taking him out of that school. It has nothing for him. Days, he can work beside me."

"Oh! He is too young! Too young to work all day, Suang U. He should be in school at his age, getting to know other boys and—and playing, yes! Do you honestly believe a boy of Weng Khim's age should be at work all day?"

"You think I am some kind of monster, don't you? But I have no intention of overworking the child, spoiling his health. You give me no credit for heart, simply because I do not give in to his every whine and whim—your notion of love."

Thus we divided our responsibilities regarding the children. The idea that I would interfere with her precious Meng Chu still makes me smile. If I never saw her face again, I could bear it. Let her mother chart her future. To be fair, I do not think that the child faces a bleak future. Mui Eng does want her children to do well. She simple fails, like so many mothers, to provide the discipline that would produce such an outcome.

There are Thai brides who cannot boil rice, wash or iron their clothes. When it is time to eat, they wonder why food does not magically appear before them, for Mama has been feeding them all their lives! I have observed that Thai children are always "too young," in their parents' eyes, for anything besides school (and such schools!). The saddest part of it is that the child's life is spoiled into the bargain, and all with the kindest of intentions.

Our little Chui Kim can already make good rice, sweep the floors and collect soiled clothes from the bedrooms for the washgirl, and she can be trusted with the younger girls. As for Weng Khim, you know that he is already at home in the store, and it is never necessary to supervise him. Some people would say that I am too strict, but most Chinese raise their children as I do—even Kim! Though he is no slave to work himself, he would not raise a lazy child.

"Should they sit and play while we work? Hah! That's what children are for, to lighten our burdens, right?" He set an appetizing bowl of noodle soup before me, wiped his hands on his apron, and surveyed his shop with pride. "We raise oxen to make use of them, chickens and ducks to fill our bellies. So? We raise children to carry on our family name—and work. How's the soup? Good. Let them take care of us in our old age, I say. It is our way. And I don't intend to work until I'm a doddering old crank, I can tell you!" He glanced quickly about the room, then threw a grin and a nod to young Rose, who toddles about between tables earnestly collecting spoons.

Kim sounds selfish, but perhaps he is only less subtle than other men. Who is not selfish about his children. Who does not hope he can rely on them in his old age? I have heard people say they expect their children to "leave the nest" some day. But even if they have much wealth, Mother, don't they hope in their hearts that their children will take care of them in other ways? Bring a favorite food to the house once in awhile unexpectedly; stop in for a chat, a polite plea for advice on a matter of business—what could be sweeter?

Whenever Weng Khim or Chui Kim ask my advice, I am proud. I

never tell them not to bother me at such a time, or to come back later. To know they have faith in their father, believe in me and need me—there is nothing more warming to the heart. Nowadays, many children and parents lead separate lives. The old closeness is going and often, when children ask questions, they are rebuffed. They learn not to ask again.

The worst result of our battle over the damned car is the division of our children, for I believe we would not have come to such separate corners otherwise. In the future, shall every small disagreement become momentous and widen the breech that is already evident? I must not think of it, lest I will it so by my own fear.

One other thing I cannot keep from you. The child Meng Chu resembles—you! She will be the most beautiful of the three girls. Thus am I mocked in everything. Though I want to hate her for what her birth denied me, I cannot deny what is true. When that little face catches me unaware, my heart turns over.

—

LETTER #49   SIXTH MONTH, TENTH DAY
9 JULY 1954   YEAR OF THE HORSE

HOW QUICKLY the months fly by! Weng Khim is now enrolled in the Chinese school at night, helping in the store during the day. He will not attend the Thai school anymore, which ought to cure the "teacher" nonsense.

There are only seven children in his Chinese class, so the teacher is able to work individually with each one. Weng Khim brings work home for us to see every week, and although he says nothing about the class he seems to be doing well. The teacher arrived in Thailand only recently. He was in the revolution with Sun Yat Sen and taught in Shanghai before that. We are pleased and honored that such a person is available to give our children a proper education.

We had an unfortunate incident this week. Weng Khim got into a terrible argument with one of the Thai children in the bakery. She is a girl, ten years old, whose family lives near us. The father pedals a *samlo*, the mother stays home with most of their sixteen children (each of whom is tossed out as soon as he can fend for himself), and they all but begged me to take the girl on. I gave her a job in the packing department, pasting labels. The oldest son of the family, who is seventeen, works at the docks. There are seven other sons.

Eight sons, the man has! Why should people like that, who can't afford the children, who don't even want half of them, have eight male children, while I have only one? The gods have been too generous with some people, may I be forgiven for saying it.

The girl dropped a box of candy on the floor, and Weng Khim scolded her. I heard it all from the office.

"You clumsy girl!" he said sharply. "You got the candy all dirty. Do you know what it's worth?"

"Don't you talk to me like that!" she spat out.

"Why, I can talk to you any way I like. You're just a common worker, and my father is the boss of everybody here. I'll—I'll make him fire you for this!"

"So he's the boss, eh? How come he had to get out of his own country, you stupid *chek*? This is my country, not yours. You come in and rent a piece of it and think you're something special—*chek*!"

"You can't call me that!" Weng Khim cried hysterically. "And if you don't like working for a *chek*, you can get out! Go on, GET OUT!!"

"Go back to China," the girl said in a hard, bitter voice, "and eat cowshit like you used to!"

I looked down and saw that my hands were trembling. Terrible words, but somehow I couldn't bring myself to be angry with the poor child. I leaned back in my chair, closed my eyes, and heard the voice of a Chinese girl, the daughter of the water carrier.

"Weng Khim, go tell your father she called you a *chek*! He'll kick her out for sure for insulting you like that."

"Who's insulting whom?" an older, Thai woman put in. "You insult us in every breath you take!"

It was time for me to stop it, calm or not, trembling or not.

"Enough! Don't any of you have sense enough to handle these children?" When they saw me standing in the doorway, some looked startled; others looked at their laps, in shame. "How can you let them carry on a shameful argument and not have the decency to quiet them—or at least come to me?"

"Father," Weng Khim blubbered unattractively, "she says we have no country!"

"Well, he always says that Thai people are clumsy and lazy!" she retorted, unabashed even by my presence.

"Shut up, both of you. Weng Khim, do not come out here again. I don't want any more trouble, any of this kind of trouble."

I led him to my office, sobbing and rubbing his eyes, and shut the door behind us.

"I never thought you'd take her side!" he wailed, then gulped and wiped his face with my handkerchief, glaring at me as if I had betrayed him.

"Don't take it so hard, son. By payday, believe me, that girl will have forgotten all about it. She's only a child. What would it gain us to fire her? Remember how poor the family is."

"But Yai Daeng, that old woman who took her side," he said, his lower lip still quivering violently, "she's practically as old as Mother!"

"That old, eh? This month, how would you like to pay all the women in the wrapping department, young and old? You won't have to argue while you're handing out money. If you're really the boss, that's all the discussion you need, Weng Khim. An envelope with money inside."

"You mean, a good boss should—should let people insult him?"

"No, of course not. But he doesn't argue, either. He never lowers himself that far."

"Papa, what did she mean about our renting pieces of their country?"

"That's nonsense, son. I pay out more money in taxes in a year than she'll ever see in her whole life."

The boy doesn't understand yet, but he is pleased at the prospect of handing out pay envelopes. I try not to think about the incident, but I cannot rid my mind of the girl's ugly words. Her big, black eyes are already old, and tired. I pity her! She is jealous of the easy life my children have, the pretty dresses our girls wear, the good food they eat. She has one poor suit of clothing and hardly enough to eat from day to day. If she has heard something from her parents that makes her suspect her tragic life is our fault, why shouldn't she be filled with rage? She spends her childhood pasting labels on boxes of candy she never gets to eat.

If only more poor Thais had such rage! But most of them live a day at a time, without ambition, not interested in more than enough to eat and a place to sleep. Is this want it means to be a "peaceful people"? Buddhism may teach that a man should be content with what he has, but on the other hand it doesn't forbid his trying to get a little extra.

Every man has the right to work and the right to save. The Thais complain about their lot, but they never avail themselves of these rights. And I notice that after a Thai has made a display of his temper, he feels a lot better and is willing to forget whatever was bothering him—until the next time. Righteous anger ought not to be squandered . . .

Do you know what the Thai remind me of, Mother? A butterfly, who lights for a moment on a lovely flower, then soars up into the sky to show off his gorgeous wings. He never thinks of food when he isn't hungry. The Chinese are like a bee, a plain little fellow busy at his tasks. When a bear comes and steals his honey, the little bee is frantic. "Aha, my diligent friend," thinks the graceful butterfly as he glides past, "see now how foolish your efforts were!"

But what choice does the poor fellow have? Once a bee, always a bee.

***

Chui Kim has been pestering for a dog ever since she visited a friend who has one. Her mother has taken her side, of course.

"A big dog," I said, "is not a suitable pet for a little girl. And I don't want a puppy here. Puppies often die, and if it died you would feel very disappointed."

"Then why don't we get a full-grown, little kind?" Chui Kim asked.

"If I get one for you, everybody else will want one. Can't you see anything at a friend's house and not beg for it? You can't have everything you lay eyes on, Chui Kim, you may as well know that now."

"The people next door to Ang Buai are selling some Pekingese dogs," Mui Eng said cautiously, "and they're just darling. Only three hundred baht each."

"So, it's Mama who wants the dog, eh? 'Just darling,' she says. 'Only three hundred baht each,' she says. Three hundred baht for a dog, Mui Eng? Are you mad? Can you seriously consider spending three hundred baht for a dog?"

"Yes!" Her mouth snapped open and shut. Oddly enough, Mui Eng has come to resemble a Pekingese herself. "Chui Kim wanted a big dog, but I said no. Pekingese are good pets. Anyway, I already paid for a pair of them, and tomorrow I'm picking them up. The woman said that one would have been lonely."

I could feel the blood rising to my head. "But why only two? Why not five? No—pardon me! That would leave one odd dog out, a lonely one! Why not six? We must have eighteen hundred baht lying around here and nothing better to spend it on—what better investment than six Pekingese dogs?"

I never should have given in about the car.

The dogs are here. When I saw the car pull up before the store with two Pekingese dogs drooling out the window, I felt despair. However, I have to admit they're cute! They look like fat kittens with lion's faces. You told me once that such dogs were the favorite pets of royalty. I never thought then that someday I would own two of them myself. They are good with the children, and content to play with anyone. Even me.

I've had a fence built behind the house to keep them out of the bakery, and as I go back and forth they watch me hopefully, posted at the bars of their little prison, waiting for someone to come and set them free. It occurs to me that the dogs and I have a good deal in common.

ODD, THAT a girl should turn out to be a better student than her brother, but so it is. Chui Kim is again at the top of her class, even in Chinese. I am well satisfied with her progress, but—why couldn't she have been born male?

At the breakfast table, she helped herself to a second bowl of rice gruel and lavished spicy dried pork over it.

"I am going to be very clever when I grow up, that's what my teacher says. She says I could be a teacher, if I want, or even a doctor." Thus she brags, understanding nothing of a woman's duties in life.

Mui Eng asked, "But what would you like to be, Chui Kim?"

She cocked her head to one side, considering the question. "One of those ladies on the radio, the ones who act in stories. Their voices are so wonderful, I always think they must be beau-ti-ful."

I cringed. "Such work is suitable for some women, not for all. The real responsibility of a woman is to run an organized household and raise children."

"Like Mama?"

"Yes, like Mama . . . We Chinese say, 'A good woman boils rice that doesn't stick and sews a straight seam, fattens up the children and sweeps the floors clean!'"

"Ugh, who wants to stand in front of a stove all day, or scrub floors? I don't mind the sewing part, though. I could sew while I'm on the radio—"

"Such work is unsuitable for you, daughter."

"Why?" Weng Khim asked. "Why shouldn't Younger Sister be a different kind of woman, if she can?"

"There, you see!" Chui Kim exclaimed, pleased that her brother would champion her cause. "I'm the one who came in first in the examinations, Papa, not Weng Khim, and you expect him to do all kinds of things."

"That is quite beside the point. I don't know what 'a different kind of woman' is supposed to mean, but I expect to see my girls marry and present me with lots of grandchildren." I smiled. No one smiled back. Sounds of further dissent issued from the other end of the table.

"Aunt Ang Buai isn't married. She hasn't any children, and she's a grownup lady." This from the full mouth of Bak Li, second daughter. She is now seven, as round as a rain barrel, and only occasionally stops stuffing herself long enough to join our conversations.

"Don't talk with your mouth full, Bak Li. You're quite right, Ang Buai is not yet married, but—she is still a young lady, and she will marry someday."

"My friend Cheng lives with her aunt," Chui Kim added, "and her aunt is old already and never got married."

"Women like that aren't normal, Chui Kim, believe your father. And there are very few of them. Most women marry and have children, like your Mama."

"I still want to be on the radio—"

"And I want to be a teacher!" Weng Khim dared, inspired by his sister's courage.

"I want to be—beautiful!" Bak Li pronounced through a mouthful of toast.

Mui Eng giggled, wrinkling up her tiny nose between the ripe apples of her cheeks. "Like the beauty contest winners in this morning's newspaper?"

Bak Li nodded and giggled back. I felt faint. Our times! Girls dressing in clothes that look like underwear and barely preserve their modesty, parading in front of men, abandoning their natural feelings of shame. However much flesh they own, everybody knows, as they compete for the fine honor of being praised, flattered, and photographed in every noodle shop and nightclub in the city. Until the next year, when another "beauty queen" is crowned.

And what does the "queen" look like ten years later? Ha ha ha! Mui Eng was a beauty once. Heads don't turn anymore.

As a normal man, I too like to look at well-dressed, pretty girls. But as the head of a household, responsible for the character of my children, I do not like to see my family admire such things. What if that girl in the newspaper photograph, with her simpering smile, her short skirt and well-rounded thighs—what if that were my Bak Li? I would die of shame.

"Meng Chu, tell Mama what you would like to be when you grow up!" Mui Eng was enjoying herself immensely.

A five-year-old child, to be thinking of such things! Meng Chu's pretty eyelashes fluttered, she turned her dazzling smile on me.

"I want to be like Papa—stay home and think about money all day!"

"Why, child?"

"Because you are so rich, Papa. You have a lot of money."

"You are a monkey!" Mui Eng exclaimed, fondly ruffling her daughter's hair. "What do you want with a lot of money?"

"Keep it, to buy things—"

"She wants to flatter Papa, so he'll like her!" Weng Khim announced, narrowing his eyes at Meng Chu.

Mui Eng's glance slid over the children and rested on me, as if to say, "You see?"

"She will change her mind soon enough," I said. "Having money, buying things—wonderful, yes! But what of work? The more money one has, Meng Chu, the more work, and the confusion multiplies."

Mui Eng laughed then, and Weng Khim, neither of them sure why.

"Be a good girl, Meng Chu," her mother said deftly wiping the child's face with a damp cloth, "and Weng Khim is right—Papa will love you."

I let that go, rising from the table with my mind fixed comfortably

207

on the day ahead. As I passed through the kitchen on my way to the bakery, I felt something tugging at my shirt.

"Papa? When will I go to school?"

"Why, Meng Chu! Next year, I suppose. But I thought you were going to stay home and help Papa make lots of money . . ."

"Oh, I will—but what help can I be if I haven't been to school?"

"Er, you're quite right—five or six more months until the next term begins, isn't it? You can go then."

"You'll see, Papa. I'll be the best! Better even than Chui Kim—"

Not better than Weng Khim, no! "Better even than Chui Kim" . . . But Weng Khim has not shown the character I had hoped for, and Meng Chu is so eager, so—bright. Is it possible that Meng Chu will be the most capable of my children? Chui Kim does well in school, but would Meng Chu ever say she wanted to be a radio actress? I think not. She is already such an earnest child. ("You are too much in earnest, Suang U," Father had said, so many years ago.)

I don't know. A few years ago I would have refused to think such thoughts. But now? Who knows?

LETTER #51   SECOND MONTH, SIXTH DAY
27 FEBRUARY 1955   YEAR OF THE GOAT

WENG KHIM passed his Prathom Four examinations at last, but when he learned that his days at the Thai school were over, he burst into tears.

"But you are no student!" I said, bewildered by his reaction to news I had thought he would welcome. "Why should you be unhappy to leave school and come into the business? You should be proud of yourself, not sulking about the house as if the world had fallen apart!"

"For me it has! I wanted to be a teacher, Papa, I want to learn more . . ." His voice trailed off into gulping sobs, his nose began to run, and he wiped his tear-stained face shamelessly on one sleeve.

"Learn more—hah! Study and fail, that's all you've done, boy. Anyway, it's about time you did something worthwhile with your own language. Thai books will always be available. You will never forget the Thai you've learned. But it is time now for you to study the most important things, here with me."

He shook his head helplessly, buried his face in his hands, and ran up to his room. What is a father to do?

Mui Eng behaved worse than the boy, weeping with him and tossing angry glances at me over his head whenever I passed through the shop. Most of the day he sat behind the counter with her, sobbing into her lap like a baby deprived of a sweet.

That evening, she pleaded with me to change my mind.

"Just one or two more years, Suang U. How could it hurt the child?"

"No! I have seen what results from allowing the people in this house to follow their whims. If I give in this time, I am finished, my presence in this house will have no meaning at all. You gave your word not to interfere, or have you forgotten?"

"No, I won't interfere, but it hurts me to hear him crying his little heart out. What mother can hold her tongue when she sees her own child suffering?"

"Suffering, indeed . . ."

Weng Khim continued to make a fool of himself for four or five days, and then it was over. For that is the way of children—if you ignore their tempers, they settle down readily enough. I was pleased to see that Mui Eng kept her word and said no more about the school he supposedly loved, in spite of his consistently mediocre grades. If the boy were at the top of his class, like Chui Kim, I could almost understand his attitude, but what kind of child is willing to stay on without even that satisfaction?

It is hardly my wish to extract cheap labor from my own child. The time has come for Weng Khim to teach himself, train himself for life under my tutelage. Then, if ever a less prosperous day comes, he will survive. But how can I explain such a thing to my wife? I could as easily describe the desert to a fish.

Ang Buai learned of the latest family crisis from Mui Eng, and came to call.

"Is this how you show your great respect for education?"

"He will continue to get an education after work. There is nothing more for him at the Thai school."

"And what did you expect him to have learned there by the age of ten?"

"'The age of ten'! You speak as if he were three years old. I have ten-year-old children in the bakery who have been with us two or three years. Is it a crime, then, to put an abacus into Weng Khim's hands? He's luckier than most."

"They are the children of the poor, Suang U, but think what you could do for your own. They could study anywhere, be anything! Why must you compare them to the children of laborers, when you've worked so hard to put all that behind you?"

"This is a school, too, Ang Buai, and I am a teacher! Why can't you ever let me do things my way, without criticizing and sneering?"

"I won't argue with you further, but Mui Eng says you will send him to a Chinese master at night, to study literature. I think that would be wrong."

"Why? The class is held three blocks from here, and Weng Khim is a big boy."

"There are other reasons—"

"Look, why don't you get married and dump all your worries on a few kids of your own for a change!"

For a moment I thought she would burst into tears, but she only narrowed her eyes and said coldly, "In the future, Suang U, I'll not annoy you on their behalf," then turned and left my office without another word, and in over a month she has not returned.

Weng Khim and Chui Kim sneak off to see her now and then, and I pretend not to know about it. Mui Eng, of course knows why her sister is angry with me, if not the details of our meeting.

"All right, so I asked her to speak to you! But Suang U, why must you always hurt her so? I know her—it wouldn't be anger keeping her away this long. You must have said some terrible thing!"

"And I suppose you've always been kind and loving toward her? I told her she ought to get married and worry over children of her own, that's all," I said irritably. "I don't know why that's so terrible. I—I was only joking."

"Joking! And what woman would laugh at such a joke?"

"So, let the children go over there if they want to see her so badly. They should visit their grandmother anyway. Didn't you tell me she's sick? Take your car, go. All of you."

"You have no time for your family, have you? Even my poor mother, who may be on her deathbed!"

Mui Eng's accusation was quite fair. You know how infrequent my letters have become, and writing them is my greatest pleasure. Let her judge from that how much time I have to ride around town visiting her relatives.

AS I recall, in my last letter I did nothing but grumble. You will be relieved to know that, as I lift my pen today, I have nothing to grumble about; things are much improved in our household. Weng Khim goes to the Chinese school every evening and says not a word about it, and even little Meng Chu attends Prathom One, so that all your grandchildren are students in one way or another. It would be easy for me to take this simple fact for granted, but I shall never take it for granted. That a man has four children all in school, it is a great thing, a matter for rejoicing.

Little Meng Chu amuses herself by counting every chopstick and teacup in the house, and if we allowed it I think she would try to count every grain of rice. It is obvious that she is the cleverest of the children, and now I regret having promised Mui Eng that I would not interfere where the girls are concerned. Still, there is no reason why I cannot encourage the child's natural affection for me, or her interest in the business, an amazing thing in one so young.

I am sending money with this letter, and it is time that I told you something of the economic situation here. The baht is worth only a fraction of what it was when I arrived in Bangkok nine years ago. Every morning I give the girls two baht and Weng Khim three, an unheard-of sum a few years ago. (He receives more, as the eldest, and never has a satang left at the end of the week. Meng Chu, by contrast, has saved thirty baht in the past month alone.)

Two days ago I visited Kim and found him guffawing over a beer with Seng.

"Over here, Suang U!" Kim cried, waving his arm. "Did you know Seng's a papa now? A girl!"

"How should he know?" Seng shouted jovially, and in his expression there was no hint of the old resentment. "Suang U is a rich man now, too busy for peasants like us! I see your wife and children in that car—and what a car! Riding around town with stiff necks, your boy staring down his nose like a venerable one already. And that youngest girl of yours—what a beauty! Even Mui Eng wasn't prettier as a girl."

"Ah, now there's something to meditate on," Kim sighed, "Mui Eng as a girl . . . you and your wife must have been eating different food all these years, or is it hard work that makes your bones stick out?"

"Nah—intelligence!"

Seng slapped Kim on the back and bellowed at my small joke as if it were an example of precious wit.

They meet like this often, and I doubt whether either of them realizes that the rare occasions on which I join them are my only "vacations" from business.

Mui Eng's mouth dropped open with astonishment one evening last week when I offered to take her and the children shopping. She had been talking for weeks about going to Phahurat Road to buy material for school uniforms, so I thought, why not all of us? Never before had all of us gone out together of an evening.

We could not take the car, for I had sent the driver off on an errand. (Mui Eng realized then that my suggestion had not been entirely spontaneous, but wisely made no comment. She sent a clerk outside to wave down two pedicabs without so much as a glance in my direction.)

They are rather pitiful, these men who drive the pedicabs. Their legs are all bone and knotted muscle, with scarred, rough skin scantily covered by tattered mud-colored shorts. When Mui Eng hoisted her bulk onto the plastic-covered bench of the first cab, then hauled Chui Kim in after her, I had to look away. But what could I do, except to pay the fee agreed upon? At least I did not drive a hard bargain, as is the usual custom.

But I decided not to take pedicabs anymore. It is too painful to watch a hungry man struggle so. Everyone should stop using them—then motor vehicles would have to replace them all, and this picture of human degradation would disappear from our streets. I know the pedicab drivers would suffer while looking for other work, but eventually they would find something, and no job I have seen in Bangkok is capable of so deforming the body, or of causing those starved knots of muscle.

At last we arrived at Phahurat, and after the pedicab drivers took my money they hailed an old Chinese grandfather selling glasses of *nam kek huai*. It pleased me to know that they would have this drink on me.

Most of the Phahurat cloth merchants are Indians in turbans, and though it is said that if a shopkeeper in Bangkok isn't Chinese he must be an Indian, that isn't really so, for the Indian merchants are only interested in textiles and sewing supplies.

Of course, not all the Indians in Bangkok are so prosperous. The poor ones raise cows on the outskirts of the city and peddle milk on the streets, while middle-class Indians work nights as watchmen at warehouses and stores. It has long been customary in Bangkok to employ Indians as guards. They have a reputation for honesty (an Indian wouldn't steal anything small, goes the joke), and Thais have always thought of them as big and strong. I suppose that in the old days they did look big and strong, but nowadays many of the guards are shrunken, tiny old men of seventy-five or so, hardly a match for the generation of hulking Thai youths one sees today.

There is no one who greets you with the fervor of an Indian merchant, bowing and smiling like a fancy-dress puppet. When, as usual, Mui Eng dawdled and dallied and poked at the fabrics, the turbaned clerks hovered about her within human patience, and when everyone had agreed on a fair price for the fabrics she had chosen at last, they wrapped up her purchases and smiled and bowed us out the door—boss, clerks, and all.

Then we went into a Thai shop. The lone clerk was dressed beautifully, but what an expression on her face! She looked as though she had been dragged into the shop and chained to the cash register against her will. A pretty girl who frowns at the customers—what kind of clerk is that? And when we began to discuss the price of her goods, she became, I am sorry to say, rude.

"You expect something for nothing? Ah, you're all alike!" she snapped.

Mui Eng reached for a piece of silk on a high shelf.

"That's expensive!" cried the clerk, bustling over to her. And, grabbing the silk out of Mui Eng's hands, she tossed it on to a still higher shelf. "And keep your kids away from those bolts of cotton near the door—they'll get finger prints all over them. Remember—you get it dirty, it's yours!"

As the children trooped outside to wait for us, their faces burning with shame, the clerk walked up to a young Thai man who had just entered the shop and turned a radiant smile on him. At this point, Mui Eng and I joined our children.

Further on, a middle-aged, plump Thai woman sat behind a make-shift stand draped with handbags. We stopped to listen to the customers haggling over prices, and after a few minutes Mui Eng, engrossed in the bargaining, shouted, "Forty baht!"

The woman turned a look of scorn on her.

"Forty baht? You heard me say a hundred, didn't you?"

"Well, I'm offering you forty," Mui Eng repeated simply, pulling a bag off its hook and examining it carefully.

"Look at it good, lady—what do you think that is, Hong Kong plastic?"

Mui Eng replaced the bag and stalked off, and the rest of us trailed after her, but the handbag seller wasn't satisfied. "Who'd call forty when the price starts at a hundred?" she shouted. "Stupid old tub!"

The children were upset and bored by then, and so was I. At the next corner I stopped at a candy seller's wagon and asked the price of a Thai sweet they all like, having decided that we deserved a treat.

"A baht apiece," the woman said, actually smiling. I felt encouraged.

"What do you mean?" Mui Eng gripped my arm as I reached for my wallet. "I buy those for half a baht every day!"

The smile vanished. "Where?"

Mui Eng mentioned the name of a market near us.

And it was the truth, I knew, but the old woman drew her head back and tucked in her chin like a snake surveying a nest of mice.

"If *chek* can find them at half a baht, you can buy a bag for me and I'll give you three salung for each—ha ha! That's twenty-five satangs of profit for you, *chek*!" Mui Eng looked away quickly, her face dark with anger and embarrassment. "Not interested, eh?"

"At least I've never had to earn my living hawking candy on a street corner," she muttered as I pulled her along.

"That's enough!" I said, disgusted with the whole outing. "Let's go home, the children are tired . . . we'll have a nice bowl of noodles on the way."

Because this would be a rare treat, the children perked up instantly.

But I had had more than enough of this "night out," which had proven true many things I had long suspected. They have no patience, these people, no endurance, and understand neither the world nor the people whose good opinion is everything to a merchant. Without such understanding, a man simply cannot do business, but Thais continue to search for an easy way to achieve the success we have struggled for so long, and for which we have made many sacrifices. When Weng Khim is my age, and takes his family shopping of an evening, will he see what I have described to you? Or will the natives of this abundant land have learned that imitation of the people they most resent may be more productive of the things they crave than rudeness and slipshod habits?

I wonder.

—

LETTER #53   NINTH MONTH, SECOND DAY
17 OCTOBER 1955   YEAR OF THE GOAT

ANG BUAI has done with her grudge. That is my first piece of good news, and for that Mui Eng deserves the credit. She sent her sister a Pekingese dog—as a gift from me! I learned of the deception when Weng Khim came into my office carrying a reciprocal gift from Ang Buai.

"Auntie sent this to you, Papa. I don't know what it is."

"So you have been seeing her, eh?"

"In the mornings, before school . . . are you going to yell at me, Papa?"

"I am not." I opened the package and found a note inside. "Thanks much for the sweet puppy—I enclose two pictures for your amusement. A. B."

One picture was of a harassed, forlorn-looking fellow sitting with his head in his hands, staring forlornly at an abacus that lay across his knees. A caption at the bottom read, "CREDIT." The other picture was of a prosperous, smiling tycoon sorting piles of money on his desk, the caption on this one, "CASH!" My name was scribbled across the top of each. I stared at them in bewilderment—*what* "sweet puppy"?

Weng Khim picked up the note, scanned it briefly and said, "The day I took that dog over there for Mama, that must be what she means.

215

There was a note, too, but I didn't read it. I wonder why Auntie thinks the dog came from you."

In the evening when I asked Mui Eng to explain, she only laughed and asked, "Do you begrudge the money?"

"Well, no . . ."

I may not care much for my sister-in-law, but she is intelligent, someone I can talk to, and although we disagree, always and about everything, she is family after all, and that too is a consideration.

"Do you mean it, Suang U? Stingy as you are, you don't care about the money?"

"Won't you ever understand? I am only 'stingy' where extravagance is involved. Family matters are beyond price, like friendship."

"How much money do you spend on that 'society' you joined?" Mui Eng asked suspiciously. (How like Mui Eng to slip that remark in so deftly.)

"About twenty baht a year. Does that twenty baht deprive you of some necessity, Mui Eng? It is not only frivolity, you know. The society has serious programs, all kinds of things. Why, they even have shows from Taiwan now, and modern Mandarin plays. I don't say I understand all that, but it's a good thing, it keeps us up with the times."

"Have you joined your *sae* society yet?"

"That doesn't interest me as much, somehow. A fellow came to see me the other day about starting an ancestral shrine for the *sae* Lo here in Bangkok. I told him to see some of the others first."

"Now that is something I would enjoy, Suang U . . . On Cheng Meng Day I'd see lots of my old friends and have a good time."

"I think it is too public! Why should anyone's ancestors want their pictures hanging alongside a thousand others? Our dead deserve some peace too, and I don't need to make a spectacle out of honoring them on someone else's timetable."

There is one good thing about the *sae* societies, however. They make men accountable for their behavior. Recently at Kim's, his friend Tan Chiu told an interesting story.

"This fellow was beating his mother almost every day," Chiu began, sipping a glass of cold tea gratefully after one of Kim's hot curries. "An old woman, too, poor thing. Can't do a thing for herself—pitiful! Well, some of us who live near him paid him a call, told him he was

216

disgracing not only himself but the *sae*, you see, and if he didn't change his ways, we'd give him far worse than he gave the old woman!"

"Did he believe you?"

"Of course. But he whined that the old woman had lived too long, he didn't know what he had done to deserve such a fate—imagine! Other people's mothers had died much younger, he told me himself, glaring at her hatefully as she crouched in a corner, ashamed."

"Such ingratitude is beyond belief!" I said, horrified.

"The story gets worse, my friend!" Chiu said with a bitter laugh.

"He buys a liter of rice a day, and what do you suppose? He gives her the water he pours off the top, and eats all the rice himself! When he can afford meat, he eats that too, and if there is any left over, he invites his friends—but not one scrap will he give to his mother. Well, my friend, what can we do, stand guard in the kitchen every day? Some of the neighbors have agreed to feed her when he is away, and that is how she stays alive."

"What does this man do for a living?" I asked, feeling that I should like to strangle the fellow.

"Sells ice cream—when he feels like it, that is. No wife yet, and who would have him? Would any decent father marry his daughter off to such a scoundrel? If he won't support the mother who raised him, you know he wouldn't support a wife. Oh—and he spends whatever extra money he has on whores at the massage parlor. Well, that's the whole tale. How do you like it?"

I am ashamed that this monster is of my own *sae*; on the other hand, it is impossible that there is even one more like him. I am all the more saddened by this terrible story because my dearest wish is to have my own beloved mother at my side, to serve and to cherish. That a man is fortunate enough to have his mother with him, in his own home, and chooses to commit this dreadful sin, defiling the most precious of all loves and depriving himself willingly of honor and respectability, that is something I cannot understand.

You will notice that I have gone back to using an old-fashioned brush pen. I feel that it completes the tranquil mood of my letter writing, and I think it must be easier for your aging eyes to read the heavier and more varied lines it makes than the thin and even characters which are the only kind new pens know how to draw.

The world does not give anyone much of what he wants, it seems. One man waits in vain for his mother to die; another longs for one sight of his mother's face with a heart so full of anguish, regret, and love that no achievement can ease the pain of distance. And the distance grows, in more ways than one. How I loathe what men call politics!

—

YEARS PASS, and your grandchildren grow. So recently, it seems, they were chubby babies who pounded their little fists on the dinner table and laughed as Mui Eng spooned rice gruel into their eager mouths . . .

"I don't know why we have to eat with these little rice bowls," Weng Khim said, scowling as he stabbed at a piece of beef on a platter. "No one else uses them anymore, just this family. We can't even invite our friends over here, because it's so embarrassing. All my friends' families use forks and spoons, and plates. But not us. We have to eat with rice bowls and chopsticks, the wooden kind. We can't even have good ones, made of ivory or something."

"'Or something' is right," I said. "I want to see the day you find a pair of real ivory ones in Bangkok. They're all plastic, good for nothing. They don't even get a good grip on the food."

"But Father," Chui Kim said, "the food falls off the wooden kind too," purposefully allowing a slice of onion to slip through her chopsticks and fall onto the tablecloth beside her bowl.

"Not if you practice," I said, ignoring the offending onion slice. "If you tried at all, you could use the despised wooden chopsticks gracefully."

"But why bother?" asked Weng Khim.

"That is exactly the point, Weng Khim. We are Chinese, and Chinese people do bother. Thais were still eating rice with their fingers fifty years ago, and now they use whatever the foreigners use. We have used chopsticks since ancient times. They worked better for the purpose intended than fingers did then, and better than forks and spoons do now."

218

"What's so bad about borrowing ideas from other people? My teacher at night school says the Chinese borrowed progressive factory building techniques from white foreigners."

"Perhaps. But I fail to see anything progressive about a fork."

"I agree with Weng Khim," Bak Li ventured. "You can eat faster with a fork."

"Bah! Chopsticks are faster than anything, and if you don't believe me, bring one of your smart friends home armed with his fork and we'll have a contest. When we're down to the last shred of cabbage in the bottom of the bowl, I want to see what he does with his fork. He'll still be stabbing away when my bowl is cleaner inside than out. The use of chopsticks is a lesser tradition worth preserving, and I don't wish to hear any more about it. Meng Chu, please pass the beef and peppers."

But Weng Khim continued to scowl. "We were born in Thailand, so why does everything always have to be Chinese around here?"

"Because it is in the observance of our customs that we show our confidence in ourselves, and in the fact that we are Chinese. Remember that you are responsible to your ancestors, not just to yourself. Our ancestors are not honored by compromise; they are honored by responsible behavior and hard work."

Chui Kim threw him the practiced look that said, "Why don't you realize the old man is hopeless?" then turned to me and said, "You're always talking about hard work, Papa, but I'll bet even you get tired of it sometimes."

"Are you suggesting that work is tiresome? What a novel suggestion! We are no different from the other creatures on this earth, Chui Kim. All animals must struggle in order to survive."

Mui Eng's dogs, by the way, seem to be exceptions to that law of nature. They do nothing whatever while challenging everyone else to keep them alive. They get eye infections, ear infections, liver trouble, stubbed toes, and colds, and for all these maladies they are taken to a doctor who does nothing but treat animals. Here is an occupation that speaks for our times, for this is not a doctor who treats cows or horses, or any other animal on which a man might depend for his living. He treats only the pampered pets of rich women, and the ladies who own these animals are not nearly as fond of them as they are of showing their neighbors that they can afford to spend more money on a dog's

219

earache than a poor man spends to feed his family in a month. The one contribution Mui Eng's dogs make to this household is their ability to consume leftovers. It does relieve my mind to see that good food is no longer being thrown out as garbage.

Is my memory growing unreliable, or did the people of Po Leng have a sense of proportion about life? It seems to me that the fitness of things was an important consideration in the life of our village. Mui Eng, of course, does not understand what is meant by "fitness." It is true, that saying about an old board being tough to saw. If only you were here to supervise the children's upbringing, which is a paternal grandmother's right and privilege, my children might grow up understanding that "enough" can mean more than an irksome limitation of their pleasures. How can they be expected to understand that "moderation" is a positive idea?

Ang Buai came to the house the other day wearing a new kind of *sarong* that is belted at the waist and flares out at the bottom like a bamboo duck basket.

"How many yards of material did you waste making that thing?" I asked, smiling in spite of myself at the sight of her.

"Always a compliment! Six yards, and it's called a hoop skirt, and everyone's wearing them, but then I suppose you hadn't noticed."

"Oh, I've seen them around. But I never expected to see one on my own sister-in-law."

"You ought to know better than that by now!"

I wondered how many yards Mui Eng would need for such a skirt.

"They look especially cute on little girls."

"Not on my little girls," I said quickly, sensing the direction of the conversation. "Not only is it a wasteful fashion, but the three of them wouldn't fit around the table dressed like that. And what happens when you try to do any kind of work in such a skirt? There, where it's folded in the front, it would fall apart if you so much as—well, you must have to walk like a statue not to disgrace yourself."

"Nobody wears them for work, they're for going out around town, and I don't understand why your girls should be dowdy. Let them wear what everyone else is wearing, and give me the pleasure of picking up the tab—what do you say?"

"I say no. Why they should wear what 'everybody' wears is more than I can understand—I don't care what the Thais or the *farang*s are wearing, and I never did. Is it 'dowdy' to be sensible?"

"Exactly! And this idea of yours that one fashion or another is improper for Chinese girls is ridiculous."

"I suppose I am often ridiculous, but I see that most Thai girls still wear old-fashioned straight *sarong*s, and nobody laughs at them. Or at Chinese girls who still wear Chinese pants. I certainly don't like the looks of those 'stretch pants' you wear, or the silly skirt you have on now that looks as though it might fall open at any moment. I have a right to my opinion."

"So have I," Ang Buai retorted, "and I enjoy wearing the latest thing, whether you approve or not. I've worked hard for my money, and what else is there to do with it? It's one of the great joys of life, spending money, and if anybody doesn't like it—to hell with him."

"Meaning me?"

"No," she smiled, "at least, not you in particular."

"Ang Buai, don't misunderstand me. You are old enough to do as you please, but I don't want the children getting this idea that 'spending money is one of the great joys of life.' They have no idea how hard you work, do you understand? They only think about the other part, the spending. I'm trying to raise them to meet whatever life has in store for them, in spite of your sister and her frivolous ways. I am a businessman, and who knows whether all our years will be as successful as the past few have been? What if we have a few bad years? It happens, you know, and I don't want the children so dependent on luxuries that they cannot bear up under hard times."

She agreed with me, grudgingly. After all, she has to give in once in awhile, though since she made the discovery that she can get the best of me in at least two arguments out of three, she's been more amiable in general.

The children continue to use their inefficient, old-fashioned chopsticks they despise, and to eat from rice bowls. Outside the home, I cannot control them, but how much fun can it be to eat lunch with a fork? Not much, unless your father has forbidden it. I am not so stupid as they suppose.

I HAVE been thinking today about our Sae Yit ceremony, which honors a man who has reached his sixtieth birthday, and about the Ceremony of Leaving the Garden, in which the fifteen-year-old acknowledges childhood's end and recognizes that he may no longer be dependent upon his parents. Thai customs in regard to age are different, especially in this modern day, and you may be surprised to learn that the custom now is to celebrate each "birthday" from the first year of life until the last.

Weng Khim asked my permission to attend such a party at the house of a friend from the Chinese night school, and at his replies to my questions regarding the purpose of this party, I could only wonder . . .

"Why, it's his birthday, Papa! It is going to be a fine party with lots of food and games, beginning at noon and lasting until evening."

"Who is this child?"

"Huang? He's thirteen, a year older than me, and he has a birthday party every year, only he never invited me before. Oh, and we must buy him a present."

"You can take a box of candy from the bakery. Why didn't this boy invite you to his parties before?"

"Well . . . Huang only goes around with the rich kids. I mean, before, he thought we didn't have much, but after he saw our car he let me be in his group. Huang says people look down on you if they see you riding the bus."

"I see."

"His father told him that. They're Chinese, too, but his father doesn't—well, make a big thing out of it. When Huang said he wanted to have birthday parties like the Thai children, his father said he didn't care . . ."

"The gods have surely smiled on young Huang. Weng Khim, we do not measure wealth by automobiles. There are plenty of rich, thrifty men riding the bus, and Huang's excellent father surely knows it."

I try to reason with the children, but what is the use? They live in an age of luxury and waste without reason, and there is no place in it for old heads like mine.

"Father, can I have a birthday party?"

"There is no reason for such a party. Wait until you are fifteen, and then you will have the Flower Garden Ceremony. If you wish, we can invite Buddhist monks to pray at the house, too, and you can make an offering to the poor. That is the way Chinese people celebrate, not by inviting a lot of children to the house to run around and stuff themselves with sweets—"

"It's the money, isn't it?" he cried, his eyes filling with tears. "I can never do anything I want if it means spending money! Well, I don't want any stupid Flower Garden Ceremony, I want a party with a birthday cake and games!"

"Someday when you are grown," I said, struggling to control my anger, "you will remember this day and be grateful for your father's good sense."

Weng Khim went to the party, returning in the evening untidy and flushed with excitement.

"It was wonderful! I took the candy, and Huang opened it and passed it around. All the other children gave him toys."

As I listened to Weng Khim impart the details of this glorious event to his eager sisters, I tried to picture it in my mind. Huang is, obviously, a boy whose parents give him his own way in everything. They are Chinese, yes, but they defer to a boy of thirteen as if he were the grandfather of the family. There can be no strength in such a house.

They bought a cake (*farang,* not Chinese), stuck as many candles in the top of it as the age of the boy, then lighted the candles, let the boy Huang blow them out, and everyone sang songs. What is there to envy in such candle-lighting and singing? It reminds me of the chopstick and rice bowl affair, a fuss over nothing. I believe that it is shameful to waste money enough to feed a normal family for a week so that eight or ten over-fed boys might gorge themselves with candy and *farang* cake. Weng Khim says that such parties are becoming common, and soon everybody will be having them. He is mistaken. Huang's younger brothers and sisters all have such annual parties, too. Therefore, if I allow such a thing for Weng Khim, I am four times foolish.

Meng Chu is nine years old, and as different from the others as I suspected she would be. When she wanted new clothes recently, she went through Mui Eng's closet and decided that several of her mother's old dresses could be made over for her.

Chui Kim laughed at her. "Don't be silly, Meng Chu, you can buy new ones. You don't have to wear these old rags!"

"But there's nothing wrong with them," Meng Chu replied evenly. "They're not rags at all."

I know the other children tease her, calling her a "flatterer," largely because she has the audacity to show a little respect for her parents. On every holiday, Meng Chu has a present for both of us, and for the other children as well. Recently she gave me a new account book, wrapped beautifully. Her thoughtfulness is unique in this household. The other children leave cookies half-eaten all over the house. Meng Chu collects them, puts them into a paper bag, and takes them outside for the poor children.

This is the child whose birth deprived me of other sons, and whom I tried to hate. Now, when a day goes by without a moment free to chat with Meng Chu, without time to laugh at one of her stories or share a cup of tea, or when I do not find one of her mischievous notes in my desk—that day is without warmth for Papa.

I hope that my brother is well and has given you grandchildren, and that one of them gives you even half the pleasure my Meng Chu gives me.

—

LETTER #56   TENTH MONTH, FOURTEENTH DAY
16 NOVEMBER 1956   YEAR OF THE MONKEY

THERE IS something new in the world, a wooden box with a gray glass affixed to its front, inside of which a great many tubes and wires work to make moving pictures appear on the gray glass. The pictures do not come from inside the box but from a building far away. It is difficult to explain in our language, but here they call it "television."

To the astonishment of everyone in this house, I have bought a television set. It cost a lot of money, more than five thousand baht, but I looked at some that were selling for less and decided that they were not good. If I am going to buy something frivolous, it may as well be of good quality.

The television expert in the family is—who else?—Ang Buai, who saw the first television sets advertised in the newspapers and hurried out to buy one the same day.

There are no programs during the day, but every evening when they begin, a crowd gathers in the doorway of her store to share the new invention with her. I suppose she attracts a good many customers in this way, but what a mess they leave, and when the programs end and everyone goes home she must sweep up bags of peanut shells and sugar cane stalk from her sidewalk.

"You get stingier and grouchier every day," she grinned over a cup of tea last week, in response to a remark of mine about her beloved television. "I think it's the best thing I ever bought!"

"Yes," Mui Eng sighed, handing out sweet buns to the children, "I'd love to have one! I haven't even seen a television set, except for pictures in the newspaper."

"I never go to the movies anymore, you know. No need to dress up or fight traffic—I just stay home, put my feet up, and watch movies on television."

"You seem to forget," I said, "that three years ago you both needed cars so that you could go to the movies at night. Now you need television so that you won't have to fight the traffic—there are your modern conveniences, stacked on top of each other. And television costs a lot more than the movies or the opera, even if you went every night for five years."

"Stingy! You only have to buy one television set, and you can use it for years. They have news programs and lots of other things, you know, not only movies."

"I receive several newspapers every day, thank you, and I disapprove of the television schedule. All the programs are on at night. I wouldn't want my children up until all hours and then too tired in the morning to pay attention at school. Anyway, the television shows too many *farang* movies. In a *farang* movie we saw last month up at the Odeon, a boy laid his hand on his father's head while the man was sitting in a chair, then the boy sat on the arm of the chair so that his head was even with his father's. It was quite disgusting. The fellow should have given his son a smack he wouldn't soon forget."

"My dear brother-in-law, is that your argument against television?

That children might see a *farang* boy touch his father's head? That means nothing to the *farang!* If the children want to watch television at my place, I'll be glad to interpret any barbarian customs that come up."

"Oh, no!" Mui Eng said quickly. "I wouldn't trust our driver to take them over there at night."

"Too much bother altogether," I said, "and if they stay overnight, which they would no doubt beg to do, it would be more bother . . . Anyway, it is not impossible that I may buy a set myself."

(Let my nasty sister-in-law "interpret the barbarian customs" to her scatterers of peanut shells . . .)

The noises of traffic on Yaowarat Road seemed suddenly to invade our kitchen. Had everyone lost his tongue?

"However, before I bought a television set, I would want a few things understood. For the girls, there would be no television past 8:30. That is when Weng Khim returns from Chinese class, and I would allow him to watch until 9:30, providing he had no homework. If anyone broke these rules, the television set would be sold immediately. Am I understood?"

They nodded in unison, like a row of puppets—all except for Meng Chu, who seemed not even to be listening.

"And if I bought a television set, school work would not suffer, grades would not go down. If even one of you went down one grade in one subject, it would be over. Is that also understood?"

They nodded mechanically again, but this time Chui Kim grinned, for her grades are always good. Plump little Bak Li looked worried, for she has enough trouble getting passing grades without television.

Meng Chu alone appeared uninterested. While the rest of them had sat gawking at me, she had continued helping herself to shrimp sausages.

Shrimps are her favorite food, sour Thai shrimp soup, fried shrimps, scrambled eggs with minced shrimps, shrimp sausage. Pork she won't touch—"too greasy," she says. And Weng Khim is still fondest of Chaba's old specialty, *kaeng khilek*. I don't mind it, but pork is better than anything. I wonder whether you still raise pigs on the farm . . . that was the best pork I ever ate, especially on New Year's Day when we slaughtered the fattest one.

"When are you going to buy it?" asked the excited Weng Khim, interrupting my reverie about Po Leng pork on New Year's Day. "Oh, I can't wait, Papa!" Then, turning to Meng Chu with a reproachful look, he said, "you don't even care about it, stuffing yourself with shrimp sausages. Do you know what the Thais say? 'The cow sees only the grass!' Ha ha ha!"

Weng Khim's laugh has become odd, and unpleasant.

Meng Chu surveyed him coolly, in no hurry to avenge herself. "Is that what the Thais say, Elder Brother? What clever saying do they have about those who would rather play than eat—or work?"

"You—you better watch out," he glowered, unable to come up with a suitable retort.

"You asked for it," she said, and returned to her sausages.

The children finished their dinner and went to the sink for glasses of water, as they always do. I do not allow them to drink water with their food, for it is not our custom. Because Thai people have a pitcher of cold water on the table that is what they want, too, but if they must wait for a glass of water until they have finished eating, they learn to eat quickly and not dawdle for an hour chatting and playing with their food. The last child to finish must help Mui Eng and the servant clear the table, and of course no one wants that job.

After dinner Ang Buai, Mui Eng, and I took our chairs out onto the sidewalk to enjoy the cool night air. Meng Chu and Bak Li sat at our feet sewing doll clothes from scraps of fabric while Weng Khim and Chui Kim did homework on their laps in the light of the doorway. Their eyes wandered to the bustling crowd of evening shoppers on Yawarat Road, silhouetted against the lights of open shops as they paused to inspect the merchandise and chat with friends. Pedicabs and taxicabs, bicycles and carts clogged the narrow street, inching forward at intervals between traffic lights, roaring and blaring their horns at each other. I suppose it is a dreadfully noisy place, but I am so used to it that I scarcely notice.

Shopkeepers hauling baskets of trash to the curb shouted for their children to quit playing and come in to bed, for it was nearly time to pull the clanking gates that front their stores halfway closed, a sign to shoppers that the time for looking and haggling was almost over.

"Mother is sick again," Ang Buai said, slapping at a mosquito that whined about her bare knees. "She is getting so weak, she even faints sometimes, and she vomits all her food. I feel almost sick myself for worrying about her."

"I suppose I should see her more often," Mui Eng sighed, "but there is so much to do here, and I have the children . . ."

I almost laughed aloud in the gathering darkness.

"Mother is afraid of injections," Ang Buai went on, as if Mui Eng had not spoken, "and the Chinese doctor told her she doesn't have enough blood, for heaven's sake. What's worse is that she believes him, and the medicine he gave her made her vomit all the time instead of only after eating. It burned the inside of her mouth too. I'd give good money to know what was in that stuff." She frowned and said, "The government shouldn't allow those crooks to inflict their poisons on people."

"That doctor who treated me after Father's death is pretty good," I said. "He's a Thai who studied foreign medicine—young, but he seems to know what he's doing. Take her to him."

"You are recommending a Thai?" Her face relaxed into its familiar, mischievous grin. "This is the first time I've ever heard you say anything good about a Thai."

"I praise the good and blame the bad! All men are a combination of both, even Thais."

"Perhaps," she said, "but what is considered good in some of us is considered bad in others." Then, after staring off across the street absently for a moment, she added, "And the goods of one age can become the evils of another, don't you think, Suang U?"

What a peculiar thing for a woman to say, even a woman such as Ang Buai.

"Well, I suppose you're right," I replied. "Look at foot binding."

"Foot binding?"

"All those poor women hobbling around on little crooked feet. In its time, it was considered fashionable, but now when we see an old woman whose feet were bound as a girl, we say, 'how terrible for the poor thing.' I don't know who invented the custom, but in ancient times it was not done."

Ang Buai smiled again. "Well, well, you've praised a Thai and criticized a Chinese in one day. Thailand will soften you up yet! Our mother told us a story about foot binding when we were little girls—

228

do you remember, Mui Eng? The story about Tiger Fish Spirit, who changed herself into a beautiful maiden and married a king?"

All the children looked up at her eagerly, for they love to hear their aunt tell stories.

"Ah, look at those faces! Now I suppose I shall have to tell it. Well . . . the only parts of her body that Tiger Fish Spirit could not change were her tiny cat feet. The king, who had never seen a woman's bare feet before, asked her why they were so tiny and odd and she told him that binding the feet of a woman from childhood ensures that she will be beautiful, and since she seemed the proof of her tale, the king ordered all the gentlewomen of the kingdom to bind their daughters' feet, believing that they would all grow up to be beautiful. And that, or so our mother told us, was the beginning of the custom. Only the peasant women were allowed to keep large, useful feet—somebody had to do the work!" She laughed heartily and said, "You can't go to market on cat's paws. Unless, of course, you are a cat!"

"I suppose there must be a hundred stories about the custom," I said, "But my own mother told us quite a different tale. She said that there was once a king with many wives who made the discovery that some of them were climbing over the garden wall of his palace to—er—to meet lovers." I swallowed several times before continuing, wondering whether, after all, this was quite the story to tell before young girls. "He, that is, he couldn't keep them all, uh, under control at once, you see, and, uh . . ."

Ang Buai snorted critically in the darkness. She, with her king who had never seen a woman's bare feet!

"He decided," I continued, "to have their feet tied up so tightly that they couldn't easily escape. If they tried to climb over the wall, you see, they would fall to the ground on the other side."

"And?"

"And that's all. They would just have to lie there and yell until the guards came."

"My, what an enchanting tale," she exclaimed with a wry smile. "Well, I'm afraid it's time Auntie was getting home. "She rose and took her keys from her purse. "Our people still believe many of the old stories, don't they? I suppose most farmers in China still think Tiger Fish Spirit really lived . . . and perhaps she did."

229

"I agree, Ang Buai. Magic inflames men's imaginations to this day. In my village, I am certain people still believe my mother's version of the old foot-binding tale."

"And I myself am afraid of ghosts. On a dark, murky night, I don't like to go out of the house. Especially since I heard the old woman next door tell the story of Kuan U's birth—"

"Oh, please, Auntie!" the children pleaded, their eyes shining with the fearful, delicious anticipation of being frightened to death just before bedtime.

"All right, you little ghouls," she replied, dropping her keys back into her purse and sitting down again. "Kuan U fell to earth in a monstrous egg, landing before the door of an old temple. A voice from heaven told the startled monk who found it that on no account must the egg be cracked before one hundred days had passed . . ." Here Ang Buai leaned forward, wagging her finger at the children menacingly. "But by the ninety-ninth day, the old monk had become mad with anticipation . . . he crept out of the temple, trembling with fear, gripping a heavy club with both hands . . . slo-o-wly he approached the enormous egg, and then, with a mighty blow, he swung the club at its gleaming side! He fell back, staggering, shielding his eyes from the glare of a hideous red eye that shone out from the ragged hole his club had made . . ."

The two older girls clung to each other, wide-eyed and scarcely breathing.

"I think we have had enough of this!" I said firmly.

"All right!" Ang Buai laughed. "The night after I heard that tale, I went to bed and dreamed that an enormous egg had fallen on the sidewalk before my shop and was blocking the door, and people out in the street were shouting, 'Kick it, Ang Buai! Kick it!' And I was shouting back, 'I can't! I have to wait a hundred days!' Ah, we are all a little silly about such things. We have made even the habits of poor house lizards into good and bad omens. A tiny pale *chingchok* falls from the ceiling onto my head and I think, Ah, it will be a lucky day! But if an ugly old tree lizard gets into the house and runs across my path, instead of being frightened of the bad luck that is supposed to follow, I tell myself that it is just a foolish superstition."

"What is more serious," I said, "is man's tendency to tamper with history to satisfy his need for stories, his determination to make life more exciting by imposing fantasy where fact is a trifle dull. In the Chinese opera, Cho Cho is a villain, but in the history books it is quite the other way around. It is a foolish business, insisting on heroes who are perfect and villains who lack in every virtue, and it distorts our view of the past."

"Sister, don't go yet," Mui Eng said. "I want to tell a story I had completely forgotten until tonight, about the precious gift of Tae Uang."*

"Oh, tell it! Tell the story!" the children cried, delighted at their mother's rare contribution to an evening's storytelling.

"Tae Uang's aged uncle came from China to visit him. When it was time for the old man to return, what do you think he was presented with, as a gift from his highly placed nephew? Two dozen jars of pickled cabbage! Furious at what he considered a terrible insult, Tae Uang's uncle threw the jars into the sea as soon as the ship had left port; but then he grieved, for he felt that he must have offended the young king somehow, and he had always been fond of him. He returned to China and lived to be a very old man indeed, and he never learned the truth about the gift. You see, inside each pickled cabbage leaf in the jars he had thrown into the sea, gold and silver had been carefully concealed. Tae Uang had feared that the Thai court would find their young king too extravagant if they knew the true value of his gift."

"The poor man," said Bak Li, shaking her little head sympathetically.

"No." Mui Eng shook her head. "If Tae Uang's uncle had been a wise man, he would not have acted so rashly. The point of the story is that an imprudent man does not deserve a treasure."

Ang Buai was finally ready to leave, and went back into the house to look for her sweater. Mui Eng and I followed her, only to find Meng Chu standing at the bottom of the stairs dressed in her best clothes, with a little bag beside her.

---

*King Taksin, who ruled Thailand briefly before the present Chakri dynasty. The Chinese in Thailand believe that King Taksin's father (who was Chinese) was of the Tae *sae*. To this day, some members of that *sae* pay homage to him once a year. *Trans.*

"Auntie, can I stay with you tonight, please?" She looked up at Ang Buai beseechingly, her eyes enormous, then turned her gaze up to me. "Please, Papa? Can I spend the night with Auntie? I have everything I need for school tomorrow in this bag."

"Meng Chu, you are a little fox!" Aung Bui said, laughing.

Meng Chu stared guiltily at her shoes. "I'm worried about Grandmother . . ."

Mui Eng laughed delightedly. "She is a fox! But, after all, why shouldn't she go? But quickly now, or the others will make a terrible fuss!"

Meng Chu threw me one more quick glance, frightened and yet— fond, somehow, as if she were ashamed of her subterfuge, but not ashamed enough to give up her victory. Or perhaps she only pities me for losing so consistently.

So Meng Chu was the first of our family to see television, the only one who showed no interest whatever in the conversation at the dinner table, who calmly ate shrimp sausages while Weng Khim squirmed with anticipation. When did she make up her mind to pack a bag? It was no sudden decision, of that I was sure, for Meng Chu has never done anything sudden in her young life. From her mother, she has learned patience, and silence; from her aunt, cleverness and enthusiasm. What can she not accomplish?

—

LETTER #57   THIRD MONTH, TENTH DAY
9 APRIL 1957   YEAR OF THE COCK

THIS IS the year 2500, according to our Buddhist calendar, and in Thailand there will be great celebrations to welcome the year. It has been said that our religion shall endure five thousand years, and half of that is excuse enough for Thais to make merry. It doesn't interest me much, but the children eagerly anticipate the proposed festivities.

When I was a boy, I too loved celebrations. One in particular, I remember, was a parade led by a great furry, ferocious lion that scurried through town on the bare feet of a dozen men, and wound its way all through the district town, which seemed enormous then.

And holidays then had another important aspect, for when else could the young of both sexes survey each other with cautious impunity, and young ladies look into the faces of other girls' brothers? How different now, with a marketful of girls on view. Every store, street corner, and noodle shop is brimming over with girls, smiling, flirting, chatting, and giggling; and the boys, strutting and smirking, survey the feast with bold and critical eyes.

Girls of a less respectable sort crowd every bar, as alike as glasses of beer. They sit with the customers and dance with them, for a price. Thai-style dancing is at least graceful and not embarrassing to observe, but in bars they dance like the *farang*. You will be thinking, How does my son know of such things?

It was Seng who urged me to join Kim and himself for such an evening. Mui Eng and Chui Kim had taken the car and gone off to the opera. I finished work, saw Weng Khim and the younger girls off to bed, and felt lonely. So I went to Seng's shop.

"We ought to get out of here tonight and go dancing," he announced as I entered the place, even before I had closed the door.

"I can't—that is, I don't dance."

"So what? You think I do? You get to walk around holding a pretty girl, and the lights are too dim for anyone to notice whether you can dance or not."

"But surely the girl would notice."

"Aw, come on . . . the girl is the last one to remind you you're no good, and you can drink a little weak *farang* booze to get in the mood, eh? Let's pick up Kim and go!" He laughed and slapped me on the shoulder encouragingly.

"You must go often, to know everything—"

"Not often enough. The mother tiger doesn't like it—you know how it is. Once a month is all I can manage. Anyway, she's pregnant again—and mean! Let's get out of here before she comes downstairs."

"What number child will this be?" I asked, as he pushed me out the door.

"Four," he replied proudly. "I guess Mui Eng can't have any more, after that last one. Well, Kim says Chaba refuses to have another one. Too expensive and all that."

"They do all right now, that's no excuse."

"Maybe Chaba just isn't crazy about kids."

"Weng Khim always loved her, and she's good with children, anyone can see that."

"But the restaurant is a busy place, Suang U. How would you like her job? She's up to her nose in work all day, even little Rose has to work hard. They've got three other people in there now besides the family, and still they're running all the time. But the food is still good, really good."

"Kim is doing what he's suited to do, that's the only secret to making a good living, Seng."

"You see his watch? Cost him a fortune, and Chaba wears a gold necklace as thick as her little finger. They've got it in the bank, too, if I know Chaba."

"Hey Kim, how about the opera tonight?" Seng asked as he sauntered into Kim's place with a casual air.

Chaba turned as she heard his voice and lifted one eyebrow, amused. "Guess you won't need me along, eh Seng?" She laughed and brushed by him carrying a steaming bowl of soup. "Just don't be late!" she shouted, already ten steps beyond us.

Kim, amazed at his unexpected freedom, grabbed his wallet from the cash drawer and hurried after us. Chaba whizzed by again and called out, to me this time, "Don't let him make a fool of himself, Suang U. You're the only one with sense!"

We hailed a taxi and Seng gave directions, so competently that I wondered how often his wife was successful in keeping him at home. Outside the nightclub, which was not far away, a great neon-lighted glass case filled with photographs of smiling girls in scanty costumes all but turned me away in confusion (What was I doing going into such a place? How could I have let Seng talk me into this?) Inside, it was so dark that for a moment I could see nothing but the garishly lit bandstand, where five or six musicians played ear-shattering modern music, and a row of female singers sat in a row like so many naughty girls next to the teacher's desk. We groped our way to a table and soon were part of the noisy crowd.

The girls were pretty, both singers and "partners," and their necklines were so low that I hardly knew where to look. The singers wore more makeup than opera players, and most of the songs they sang were foreign. One sang Chinese songs, but they were in Mandarin dialect, and there were hardly any Thai songs, which seemed peculiar to me.

Most of the customers were old men except for a table of youths next to us, and none of these were over twenty. They banged on the table and continually shouted for more liquor and girls. The money they threw onto the table had come from their papas, I was positive, for the look of a youth who has never done a day's work is unmistakable. They wore their hair long, their clothes stylish in the modern way.

Kim and I sat in the darkness sipping beer, not even trying to converse over the discordant, yowling music. Seng was already out on the dance floor. After awhile, Kim leaned across the table and shouted in my ear, "Why should we sit here like two old tomcats staring at a goldfish bowl?" Then he waved to a chubby little Thai girl in a purple dress who giggled, bounced over to our table, and pulled a chair close to his.

"I don't know how to dance, not a step!" he announced proudly. "How about a lesson?"

"Sure, Sweetie!" She winked and smiled broadly, displaying many teeth. Old already, Kim, making money at last, and still a fool!

"What about Sia over here?" She turned to me and bestowed another wink. (*"Sia"* means millionaire. No doubt, that is her hope.) "You can't sit here, all by yourself."

"I shall drink and watch the others. I don't want a girl yet."

She shrugged, bounced to her feet, and pulled Kim after her. He shuffled along, grinning at me over his shoulder, drunk on one beer. Before long, Seng returned to the table, flushed and beaming.

"What's the matter?"

"Why should anything be the matter?"

"Hey, listen—this evening may not cost us a cent. See that fellow over there?" He nodded slightly in the direction of a fat, torpid looking fellow sitting at a table beside the bandstand. "When he gets drunk, he pays for everybody. He's a real *sia*, one of the richest in town, and generous after ten beers."

"He can't do better with his money than that?"

"You just watch. Any minute now, you can count on it."

And at that moment, the fat man lurched to his feet and staggered up to the microphone.

"Lissen, everybody!" he bawled. "Shut up! This club's closed t'yer money, hear?" He reeled up and down the stand clutching the microphone and waving his other hand to silence the crowd. "Anybody tries t'use his money, I shove it down's throat, hear? Money's no good t'night—I made sev'n'y thousand baht today—let's drink it—haw haw haw!" he bawled, relinquishing the microphone to a singer who smiled up at him as if he were a handsome prince in cloth of gold instead of a fat drunk in a wrinkled suit.

A roar of approval rocked the club, and the table of youths rose in a body to toast their benefactor.

"What about the girls?" one of them shouted. "Don't go halfway, sir! That's where the money goes, as you know yourself, sir!" His fellows bleated their approval of these sentiments, and the millionaire nodded and waved his glass in the air, guffawing with pleasure, appreciated.

One of the youths leaned over toward us, his face pink and round like a baby's, his mouth slack with drink. "The stupid old cock!" he whispered fiercely. "He'll spend all the cash he has and have to write a check—but what's that to us, eh? His wife is a bitch, a real bitch." So saying, he turned his back on us and ignored us for the rest of the evening.

"Do you know who that boy was?" Seng asked under his breath, in a tone of respect. "His parents are dead, he inherited a fortune. They say he can never run out of money, so what's the use of saving any? If anyone crosses him, lookout! His temper is famous."

I could only shake my head at this sad spectacle, which Seng somehow found impressive. How did the man who first struggled to make that fortune envision its use? There are so many ways a man may show his wealth and benefit his fellow man at the same time: endow a hospital, a school, a temple. Why, the world abounds with good works to be done. That boy's name could appear on plaques that would proclaim his goodness for a hundred years. Instead he chooses to leave it on bar checks.

The table of drunken boys made me fear for my own son. Our age is one of grave temptations for the young. My child, your grandchild . . . I close my eyes and see Weng Khim sitting where that dissolute young man sat, and . . . I must be depressed tonight. It is better not to frequent such places, for evil places give rise to evil thoughts.

YESTERDAY I went to see Kim, and what a great sprawling place it is now, having swallowed up a shop on either side. A crowd streams in steadily, jostling the crowd of people already seated. Kim is the lord of the manor, still chief cook, expertly flipping and stirring, frying and steaming his famous specialties.

A genial grin split his shining, sweaty face when he saw me.

"Hello, Kim! Your fame is spreading. So let's see what you can do about some lunch for an old friend."

"So far, you're the only rich guy who comes in here. Our place is too noisy, too dirty, some people say. I guess they think we dish out cholera along with the chicken soup, no extra charge."

As for the noise, I agree, Most of Kim's customers are coolies, laborers, ordinary people. And the coffee shop next door to him takes orders for his curries, so that the commotion extends even further.

"It's a fine arrangement," Kim explained, with a nod toward the coffee shop. "I don't want his coffee drinkers filling my tables anyway."

Before I ate, I toured the row of bubbling pots from which Kim's hungry dozens are fed. His mother-in-law stays in the back kitchen while Chaba and Rose wait on tables, figure up the totals, and make change. The little girl is sharp, quick. Kim noticed me watching her and smiled proudly.

"Cute, isn't she? And a hard worker. We're lucky. All of yours in school now?"

"Every one. It is a wonderful thing, to see all one's children get an education."

"You are right." He turned to ladle out four bowls of fish curry. "What are you eating today?"

"I don't know yet."

So much food, so many kinds, a man hardly knows what he wants. Chicken curry, also fish and beef. Tripe with pickled vegetables, pork leg boiled or fried with sugar and salt. Dried fish, fermented fish, Chinese omelets filled with vegetables. Bean thread fried with tiny shrimps, pork stew with *tamlueng* leaves. Weng Khim's old favorite, *kaeng khilek* . . . my head began to swim.

"One dish of boiled pork," I said finally, not knowing which of the fancier dishes I might like. At home, I eat whatever is put on the table, excluding the hot, spicy dishes my Thai-born family dotes on.

Kim sent Rose for a bottle of orange pop from the enormous ice bucket at the rear of the store, an extravagance I accepted politely, though it quenches no real thirst. Why does soda pop sell so well here? Certainly not because Thais have money to waste. Perhaps they are ashamed to be seen drinking plain water or a cup of tea.

The girl also brought me a newspaper, and I read it until most of the noon customers had gone away, for I wanted a chance to chat with Kim privately. At two o'clock, he pulled off his apron with a flourish and motioned for me to follow him upstairs.

"Kim, don't you take a warm shower, after sweating all morning?"

I myself couldn't rest after hard work without bathing first, and I even had a shower room installed at the bakery. The tap water supply is undependable, but we manage to keep a rain barrel in there filled by keeping the tap open, and it almost never spills over the top, wasting its precious contents.

He shook his head. "Not enough water—is it any better at your house? So, I wash at night. Water from a tap is a great invention, eh? If only it worked . . ."

We sat on a tiny porch that hangs precariously off the second story of Kim's restaurant, allowing its occupants to look straight into the eyes of passengers on the double-decker buses that rumble by. Yet, there is a curious sense of privacy up there.

He eased himself onto the floor of the porch, leaned back against the wall of the house, and stretched his legs out before him slowly, sighing deeply. "At least we have a fan in our bedroom now—that helps some in this damned climate . . ."

"Your business is thriving, Kim, anyone can see that. You could use another room."

"We could, but the rents?" He shook his head. "We aren't rich yet, my friend."

"You're no stranger at the bank, either. By the way, Rose is growing up."

238

"Rose . . ." He smiled. "She doesn't favor my family, does she? That's lucky. Picture a girl with my face."

"You're not ugly, and if you didn't eat pork at every meal—"

"Ha ha—that would bore even me. I like the tame curries, and most of the other things we have. Especially chicken, fried things—just about anything, really."

He likes to talk about food.

"Do you send any money to China, now that you're doing better?"

"A little. But don't tell Chaba."

"So Chaba is like that? I wouldn't have thought it."

"Every wife is like that. I know I don't have to tell you. Ever since we've started making money, Chaba's mother goes to the market covered in jewelry. Necklaces, earrings, five bracelets, a gold watch, and she'd put all that stuff on Rose, too, if I let her. Who's going to stop some guy from hitting her over the head to get that jewelry? That's what I told her, and so did Chaba."

"Good for you. I don't let my girls wear gold on the street either, only the kind of silver jewelry no one bothers to steal."

Rose appeared then, with a tray bearing two bottles of cold beer and two iced glasses.

"My treat," Kim said, raising his glass to me.

"I am not accustomed to beer in the middle of the day."

"Aw, beer isn't liquor, and what's the harm in a glass or two? I like it, especially when I watch television."

"I didn't know you had bought a television set."

"Haven't had it long. Five thousand five, a big one. Chaba wouldn't have a cheap model. Chaba, her mother, the kid, the servants—they all stare at the damned thing every night. It's hard getting them out of there so that I can go to bed."

"Doesn't Rose go to school?"

"Why should she? She's happy here, and Chaba has taught her to read."

"I still mean it, Kim. You know—what I said the first time I saw her."

"How do you know they're suited to each other?"

"Why not?"

"Well, maybe they won't like each other at all, when they're grown up—would you want to cross your only son that far, Suang U?"

"What do you mean, 'cross him'? You sound like Mui Eng! It is my responsibility to make the best arrangement for him, and the more I see of Rose the more I am convinced that she will make him an excellent wife."

"What is it you expect of the boy?" he asked in a quiet, thoughtful voice.

"I want him to be . . . big, a businessman with foreign connections, the best ones . . . a cautious hand in the important affairs of his nation. That is my dream—but, at the very least, he must not be less than I am. That is what I expect."

We were silent for a long time then, drinking our beer.

—

LETTER #59   TWELFTH MONTH, TENTH DAY
29 JANUARY 1958   YEAR OF THE COCK

I DO not understand why so many sad things happen in this family. Or do I only imagine that I have known more sorrow than other men?

First, and I humbly apologize for breaking my word: I must mention your refusal to write to me. It is a wound that never heals. Nguan Thong's death was a release from the evils of life, from pain and illness, and must be counted a blessing. Still, I grieved. But when Nguan Thong died, he left me with the certain knowledge that my selfishness hastened his early death. Death and sadness, grief and guilt . . . as I read back over my words, it is clear to me that I have not known more sorrow than my brothers on this earth. It is only that each man must stand alone with these things, for even sharing grief does not dull its pain.

Mui Eng and Ang Buai have lost their beloved mother. The doctor says she died of a "heart attack"; I do not understand what that means, I only know that she fainted in Ang Buai's arms one day last month, as she had many times before, but this time she did not wake. Ang Buai says that her mother's illness has been called the "disease of our age," but that does not make much more sense to me.

Children, especially girls, are apt to have stronger ties to their mother than to their father. Mui Eng and Ang Buai sought their mother's advice and gentle consolation often, and she tried to teach them self control and graceful ways. If her example was seldom taken, surely she was not to blame. Ang Buai grieves most, for they were alone together in the years after Nguan Thong's death, and though they were as different as two women could be, a mother and her child are bound by ties more binding than any other, even in this peculiar age.

My children show strangely little feeling. They are sorry, perhaps, to lose one who gave them a few satangs for candy now and then and was tolerant of their antics, but she did not live with us, and that is all the difference.

The funeral arrangements were odd, to my way of thinking, for no one could decide which customs to follow, Thai or Chinese, and in the end I cannot say whether the old woman went to her grave more honored in the ways of her own people or those of her adopted country. Each funeral in this family has been a bit different from the last, and it is clear that with each succeeding year our customs are becoming more cumbrous to our people; that is inevitable, I suppose. When we thought we would return to China one day, there was more reason for adhering to the old ways.

The children had just removed the mourning bands honoring Father from their left sleeves; now they were required to wear them on their right sleeves, in mourning for their maternal grandmother. For them, it is confusing. No piece of clothing they put on, it seems, is correct, and they invariably have to leave the breakfast table to make some minor change in their apparel. We Chinese used to wear white, as did the Thai; now it is black for the period immediately following the funeral, black and white after several months. I wonder when the custom changed? Perhaps black is simply more practical for people who must do a day's work, and for children who must go to school and play soccer on a muddy field. Actually, my children do not have so hard a time, for I allow them to wear almost any dark color, except red of course. I have seen Thai children dressed in black for months on end, and it is distressing, I think. What can they feel for an old relative they have not know well or loved, for a grandparent who blessed them every New Year's Day and handed them a little money in an envelope?

Funerals themselves are becoming showplaces for hypocrisy of every sort. I have seen women in low-cut black dresses, showing their bare arms to inflame the men, flashing diamonds and gold necklaces, and their husbands laugh and shout to each other as if they were attending a wedding. It can hardly matter what they wear, or what color, when respect for the dead is so lacking.

I read in a magazine the other day that Hindu Indians do not mourn their dead. Instead they rejoice, believing that the loved one has gone to a better place. I cannot imagine that, myself, for how can the heart not ache with the sorrow of that terrible finality? Do these people have no feelings? I miss you, being only earthly miles apart; how much worse the longing, then, when all hope dissolves in death. I still have you, and your hands that hold the paper on which I write my letters, and the certain knowledge of your love and sympathy, but Mui Eng's mother is lost to her forever.

"Auntie doesn't sleep at all, Papa," Meng Chu said, shaking her head sadly after spending a night with Ang Buai. "At first it was Grandmother's bed—every time she looked at it, she would start to cry again, so the servants took it out, but when night came she was afraid of the dark, even of the space where the bed had stood! That isn't like her, Papa—she even muttered something about the servants turning against her, stealing things, and you know they all love her. But they understand, I can see they do, and nobody takes her accusations seriously."

That evening, Mui Eng and I went to visit her.

"No sleep for nights on end! Don't you know that's dangerous?" Mui Eng shouted at her angrily, for she did not know what else to do, but when Ang Buai did not even answer, she took her hand and said, "Sister, you must get a sedative from the doctor—"

"Sedative! Medicine!" Ang Buai retorted bitterly. "You know I hate medicines! Just—go away, leave me alone. I'm lonely and miserable, and I'll get used to it in my own way . . ."

"And before that day comes you'll be in the hospital!"

"That is my concern, Mui Eng," she said, then wearily climbed the stairs and slammed her bedroom door.

She controls herself, but Ang Buai is by nature a temperamental and outspoken person with little reserve. This imitation of reserve is disturbing to see. Who is there to comfort her? It is not the time to mention it to her, perhaps, but a husband and children would make all the difference. Mui Eng undoubtedly grieves too, but she is never alone,

242

and there is no time to cry when Chui Kim is arguing with Bak Li, who turns on Meng Chu and slaps her for no reason, or when Weng Khim has disappeared with his friends on one errand of mischief or another.

Meng Chu asked my permission to stay a whole week with her aunt, and though I was not happy about sending her into that unwholesome atmosphere, she had her usual logical arguments well prepared.

"Auntie is lonely. I will sleep in her room and be sensible when she acts . . . peculiar. She needs a friend who isn't afraid of ghosts."

"And you are not?"

"Oh, Papa . . ."

"As if anyone could comfort the poor thing now," Mui Eng said, shaking her head. "You don't understand, child. You are too young."

But I could see that Meng Chu did understand, far better than her mother.

"Why don't we ask her to stay here for awhile, Papa? She can sleep with me!"

"Ah, she would never do that, Meng Chu. She has the store to look after and a nice home of her own. And your auntie likes her privacy."

The child cocked her head to one side, considering that. "Chui Kim is my sister, and we live in the same house. Why do Mama and her sister live in different houses?"

"Well, they lived in the same house when they were girls, but when Mama got married it was different. Some day you girls will marry and live in separate houses too. Ang Buai stayed with her mama because she wasn't married, but she will marry too, someday."

"Why did she stay with her mother for so long after she grew up? Mama got married years ago."

I laughed and ruffled her thick hair. "Now, how should I know? Maybe she isn't anxious to run after a lot of monkeys like yourselves, eh? Ask her sometime. I'm sure she'll give you lots of good reasons."

Watching television has made the children more aware of such things. I believe they understand that marriage would mean greater distance from their aunt in certain ways. Which I for one would welcome, though I suppose it is an unworthy thought. I cannot say anymore that I dislike her, and in fact I have come to enjoy our long chats. We are more relaxed with each other than we used to be, but I am uneasy around her somehow, and I wish she lived too faraway to

243

come to our house so often. It isn't her curly hair and lipstick, or her car and her carefree ways, or even her influence on the children that bother me nowadays. I cannot say why her presence disturbs me, only that it does.

—

YOU WILL recall my writing about the cessation of diplomatic and trade relations between Thailand and our country. It means that we Chinese businessmen have had to turn to Taiwan and Japan, but there have been, I must admit, few problems. Smaller profits, perhaps, but we are not seriously hurt in that way. What are now called "Red" Chinese goods are still cheaper than anything else we could import, but it is illegal to have anything to do with them.

"How would you like to increase your profits, my friend?"

The man who had shown himself into my office smiled ingratiatingly as he rocked back and forth on his heels, his hands stuck into the pockets of his baggy pants. Not a prepossessing appearance for a man who came offering mysterious riches.

I shrugged and replied, "What merchant would not want greater profits?"

"Indeed. May I sit down? Thank you. Suppose I show you a way . . . we are friends, brothers in the *sae*, no?"

To my *sae* then, I owed this unsolicited visit.

"We must look to each other's welfare," he continued. "That has always been our way. I came to talk to you about import duties . . . there are none, you know, on goods that do not," and here he lowered his voice, "exist. It can be very simple, Suang U."

"So can going to jail. Look, you have come to the wrong man."

"No, no! There is nothing to worry about!" he cried, waving his hand in my face. "The way we operate, no one suspects anything, and our profits are greater even than before on the same merchandise we have always handled. A man with bakery trucks, all those boxes of *chan-ap* going all over the city—why, who would think to look twice at them? Or under them, eh?"

My head began to swim. "Wh-what you speak of is impossible! You would never get away with it."

"We have ways," he said, slowly and rather pompously. "Bureaucrats are poorly paid, and surely you have given them a helping hand in the past?"

"Who has not? That is different, quite different!"

"You would be stupid to refuse."

"Then let me be stupid. I have enough, and my children's future is secure."

"Enough—what is that? There are many things a man can do with money. Another wife, for instance . . . (he has two, I have since learned, sisters who have born him six children, four sons among them). "Or land. You could buy land for your grandchildren."

"I cannot buy land, you must know that."

"Mui Eng can. Unless you have a Thai wedding license."

I shook my head. We Chinese seldom bother with that nonsense, for everyone knows who is married to whom. I like money as well as the next man, but I could not smuggle merchandise from China, not even the same products I had sold for years.

"You are a great respecter of the Thai law," he said with a sneer. "You probably even support the government's stand . . . well, I gave you your chance."

"I do not support the government's stand, and I thank you for your offer. I am simply not interested."

He leaned across the desk then, his eyes bewildered. "Don't you understand, Suang U? The Japanese buy mainland Chinese goods. They build cars with our raw materials and sell the cars here at a huge profit, and still we must pay high taxes to the Thai government on every one—it is wrong!"

"Yes, it is wrong, but it is not against the law. And no Japanese will go to jail in my place if I get caught doing illegally exactly what he does legally."

"Why did that man come here?" Mui Eng asked suspiciously, entering the office moments after the man's scowling departure.

I answered her sharply, without looking up from my work. "He wanted me to handle Chinese merchandise. Hide it under the *chan-ap* boxes in the trucks, store it in our bakery. Some men will get rich that way, some will go to jail. Either way, I am not interested!"

She stood quietly for a moment, digesting my words. "So you will continue to make the Japanese rich."

"The Japanese! One story of their origin is that a thousand Chinese criminals were set adrift in a boat, and landed on that island, and populated it. Crooks then, crooks now! I am busy, Mui Eng. Leave me alone."

"And so you said you won't do it, I suppose."

"Of course I won't! I am taking no chances, not for ten times what he offered. Look at the newspapers, Mui Eng—do you wish to see your husband's face on the front page, furtive and ashamed, handcuffed to a Thai policeman? There is no profit in the world worth risking that kind of shame. And I am not even a Thai. They would deport me, and where would I go then?"

"Many other men will take the risk gladly."

"The hell with them!" I shouted, rising from my chair. "We are busy enough without becoming criminals, and we have enough!"

Some days later, Kim informed me that Seng had eagerly accepted the man's offer, and he was selling Chinese pens and wrist watches himself.

"Suang U, my old buddy, I never made money so easily!" He fairly strutted over to my table in his restaurant, relaxed and beaming after a busy lunch hour. "This stuff is so cheap compared to what's available downtown. Why, anyone would be a fool to pass them by."

"Do you know the penalty?"

His brows drew together in a frown. "What—for buying Chinese pens?"

"For selling them. The Thai government will deport you if they catch you selling these things. Don't you ever read a newspaper, Kim? What a fool you are! The schoolboy who buys a pen from you may be the son of a government official. Suppose the man asks his boy where the pen came from, eh? Wife and child, money and home and restaurant . . . you lose everything!"

Kim turned deathly pale. "B-but, they couldn't send me home to Po Leng, could they?"

"No."

"Then where would I go?"

"They wouldn't care."

He stumbled over his own feet getting to the boxes of pens and watches that stood brazenly open on a table near the soup counter, grabbed them up in his arms and disappeared into the back room.

Before the next day dawned, Kim was clean.

I haven't been able to reach Seng, and I wonder if it would do any good to talk to him anyway. Unlike Kim, he reads the newspapers. If he is handling smuggled goods, it is with full knowledge of the consequences, and he will have already turned these things over in his mind carefully.

Seng has more uses for money than Kim or I. Our pleasures are simple. Seng likes the teahouses, where pretty girls massage him, dance halls and bars and all the rest of it. When there is anything new to be tried, it is Seng who must be first . . . must spend money like the millionaire he hopes to become. His business brings in a good profit with or without Chinese goods, for he has become a big rice trader, and he deals also in hemp and wax. Who expected this much of him? Certainly not I, and even now I cannot see how he does it, for he is not the brightest fellow, but his temper has mellowed and his cunning no longer stands out like a foreigner's nose. He has learned to be subtle, at least in business, and Tae Lim's sons have never surpassed him, though they inherited most of the old man's fortune.

As for your son, he plods along like an ox before the plow, and who is to say which of us is the wiser? Seng will end up either as a New Year's goose or as a boiled chicken. A man who wants riches that badly is willing to risk all.

—

LETTER #61   NINTH MONTH, THIRD DAY
15 OCTOBER 1958   YEAR OF THE DOG

TO MY great astonishment, I have been offered a directorship in the Society of Chinese Merchants, and shall sit among the most influential businessmen of the city, men who have taken Thai citizenship and are known by Thai surnames. According to Thai law, every name that appears on the membership roll of an organization must be Thai. Of course, among ourselves we Chinese use our own names, and observe our own customs. I cannot quite get used to hearing a man of the *sae* Kho called Mr. Khophanich, or Khosakun, or Khotrakun! What is the sense of such a halfway measure? One may as well choose a pleasing Thai name and have done with it, but those who have applied to the government for new names have been given peculiar, long names which purvey the same message: Chinese . . . *chek*. Apparently, it is important to the government to keep the distinction clear.

It is common for the Chinese to petition for Thai citizenship these days, even though it is expensive. Everyone says it is worth the money in terms of future business dealings, and for the sake of one's children, especially should they wish to attend the university. Frankly, I do not believe that a young man will encounter any difficulty in school because his name is Kho Heng Chai and not Chai-anan Khosakun; unless he wishes to become a military officer or a policeman, and what Chinese father encourages such notions? The army and the police don't trust our sons with their secrets, though they are willing enough to fill the lowest ranks with those who are Thai-born, if not Thai.

For the life your son leads here, "Tan Suang U" does nicely, and I try to encourage the children to feel as I do, but I am not sure that I am successful in that.

I do not know why we are on this earth, but I do know that too many of us spend our few years upon it full of anxiety because we want more than is good for us. When I was young, I wanted—what? I scarcely knew what I wanted, but I was full of ambition. "Wanting" can become a way of life, ambition without real purpose. But I believe that I have gone beyond that.

A man ought to do the work that lies before him and find satisfaction in it, and I am grateful to have learned that before I am old.

There is no sense in casting about restlessly to find one's life's work; a man's sons ought to follow in his footsteps. Yet Weng Khim has made remarks to the effect that I left my father's way of life, as if to say that he should also have that right. But it was the poverty of our land that forced me to do as I did. He has no excuse to reject the way of life I offer him as my son.

You know that Kim and I have made an arrangement for our children, and I try to give them opportunities to see each other. In this, too, the boy defies me.

"Grandma Rose, that's what we boys call Kim's daughter. She screeches like a parrot and she's as ugly as a brown toad!"

"Brown?"' Mui Eng looked up sharply from her sewing machine, which of late occupies a corner of the large room downstairs. "Why, Rose isn't dark skinned at all. She has—healthy skin, like your aunt's. Your papa thinks Rose is a very sweet girl, Khim."

"But why is everyone always shoving me at her? I have to take things over there practically every day, and then bring some mess of food or other back here. I'm sick of being an errand boy, Mama."

"You used to be so fond of them when you were a little boy. Why, when we moved here, you cried for months because you missed them."

Weng Khim slouched into a chair and stared off into space thoughtfully for a moment, then said, "*Kaeng khilek*, at the market with Auntie Chaba . . . it's all blurred, I can hardly remember. But I remember the fish baskets . . . playing with the fish . . ." He shook his head as if to clear out the old memories. "But Rose is like her grandmother, not like Auntie Chaba. Every time she opens her mouth my stomach turns over. No kidding, she sounds just like a parrot, and her beady little eyes dart all around Uncle Kim's restaurants as if she expects all the customers to sneak out with the soup spoons in their pockets."

Mui Eng laughed and glanced over her shoulder to catch my eye. The old woman has always been sharp, and Chaba's own quick tongue was the first thing I noticed about her. I was there one day when Chaba's mother had just slipped and fallen on a wet spot in the kitchen. She was sitting on the floor cursing everyone in sight, and Kim laughed and said, "Show me the spot you slipped on and we'll keep it out of your way!" She cursed him then, too, but I knew that in their house, curses could sometimes pass for affection.

"Oh, Mother, you never see the real Rose," Weng Khim continued. "Whenever she comes over here she's all smiles, and she keeps her mouth shut."

"She will change, Weng Khim. You admit that she knows how to behave nicely when it's expected of her, and your own manners are far from perfect."

"But she's not—not nice, like the rest of her family! If I talk about anything I like, television or anything, Rose makes a face and says it is stupid, or childish. She's the kind of person who makes you feel like a

249

fool and then laughs when you get mad."

"Rose's papa and yours are very dear, old friends. The least you can do is try to get along with her."

The boys expression grew suddenly suspicious, then remote, and I felt an alarming sense of dread that Kim's prediction might come true.

"What's the matter, son?"

"Nothing. I—I just don't like Rose, Papa, and I'm sick of girls. This house is full of them, and then you want me to be friends with Rose, who's the worst girl I ever saw. Couldn't I have had at least one brother?"

Only the week before, Kim had laughed when I said nearly the same words to him: "If only Weng Khim had had a brother . . ."

"Get another wife!" he had laughed. "You could have a dozen sons if you put your mind to something besides work for a change."

"Oh, no . . . one wife is all I can stand. If I had more, it would be this one wanting that, that one wanting the other—and more children, probably as troublesome as the four I already have. I don't know, when I see my daughters dressing for school, rushing through breakfast, arguing over clothes, spending money all over town on Saturdays . . . I think to myself, what is it all for? They'll marry and I'll see them every New Year's Day. When thoughts like that come to my mind, then I feel that one son is not enough. But there is no easy answer."

"I wouldn't be so sure about seeing them once a year, old man! Nowadays, young couples are as likely to live with the bride's family, like Thais do. But as soon as they can save a little money, they want to be on their own altogether, instead of living with any of the parents. Not like the old days, when being a proper daughter-in-law was an honorable thing. Now, they get a couple of hundred baht saved, and the old people can look after themselves."

A shiver ran down my spine. What is the world coming to, when children shamelessly cast their parents into a lonely old age? That dreadful possibility makes it even more important. Weng Khim must marry Kim's daughter, someone we know, someone who knows us.

I remember my adopted father's loneliness when we first met, and his pathetic fear of old age and death alone. I put his illness and suffering out of my mind and death took him from me. Shall this be my just fate, then, to be abandoned by my own children, to never see my house filled with laughing grandchildren? If I believe my religion, then I believe that I deserve to end my days in silence, a silence as deep as the one he endured in the darkness of Weng Khim's room the nights he took the place that should have been mine.

I have become acquainted with some of the bigger men in the society, and what I see in their homes makes me feel better about my own home life.

One has two wives in the same house. They used to argue constantly, a situation he escaped by taking a third wife and installing her in a separate house. The first two ladies promptly ended their feud and went off to attack the third, and so he came to take yet another wife, pretty and young—and greedy.

Another man has more wives than he can count, and can hardly sleep at night for worrying how he will support them all, and their children. Honesty has become a luxury beyond his means; swindling and bribery keep his head just above water. He is a big contractor, though, and drives an impressive automobile with an air conditioner inside. The windows are never rolled down, the heat and fumes of Bangkok traffic do not touch him.

Another society member aroused my envy when we were introduced, for he has five sons. But even he has many troubles, for the sons are married and squabble over his will as if he were already dead. He and his wife finally went to live by themselves to gain some measure of peace, but it is a sad and lonely peace.

This business of satisfying one's sons and daughters-in-law (who are by all accounts far worse, hating each other and vying for every necklace and teapot) is obviously a great headache. I am glad none of our children have yet reached the age of marrying. There is still time for me to think about this problem and how I can prevent it. I have the beginning of an idea, but I shall not write of it yet.

I am sorry that Weng Khim is so obstinate about Rose, but he is still young, and it is natural that he prefers the company of other boys. Rose is too young to think of a boy as anything but a nuisance, a creature to be tortured for her amusement. Give them both a few years, and they will see each other in quite a different light.

YOU WILL observe from the letterhead that your son is far from home. Other years, we have celebrated the New Year holiday by going to a film or the opera, and taking a few days' rest at home, but his year they all clamored for a "real vacation." Meng Chu convinced Ang Buai to join us, and here we all are in a rented bungalow on the beach at Hua Hin, with a dozen boxes of food and clothing to sustain us. I have enjoyed some pleasurable hours here and look forward to a good year's business after this indulgence. We return to Bangkok today.

This vacation has provided me with many new things to tell you about life in Thailand. I have seen much that makes me wonder whether this old earth is not spinning into the future too fast for a poor farm boy like myself . . . and I dare not tell anyone else the thoughts that are in my mind. "What a fool you are, Suang U!" my dear wife would say, then shrug her plump shoulders and toss here curly head, and turn from me to more important things. So I tell you instead.

Actually, it was I who chose the seaside as our vacation spot. None of them knows why, though they were too stunned at their good fortune to say anything. When I left Po Leng, I went to the seashore. From the sea I first saw this land, and I wanted to stand on the shore and think of all that has passed since then, to wade in the surf and send my heart's message to you with the winds that blow from here to there. Could I tell them that? Meng Chu would be certain to point out that the winds blow the other direction, or some such scientific thing . . .

Sitting quietly, or swinging myself to sleep in a hammock, I relax while Ang Buai and the children hike in the hills behind us and buy fruit and sweets in the town nearby. In the late afternoons, I stroll down to the sea for a leisurely swim, and it was yesterday afternoon that I encountered the first of three unexpected events.

A group of girls had come down to the beach together. They walked single file, clad from their chests to the tops of their legs only in "bathing suits," leaving everything else uncovered, some of them showing even their bare backs. They appeared to feel no shame in displaying their bodies so, though their bathing suits were no better than second skins, causing me great confusion and embarrassment when they passed by. However, I did not turn away, for I am a man, and they were a feast for the eyes of any man not too old to notice (though I could not help but pity their fathers, for I myself would die of shame were Chui Kim to appear in such nakedness). Then three more girls joined them, wearing two-piece bathing suits—which is to say, two little garments, one on top and one below, baring their bellies and, believe it or not, their navels.

A vision one could scarcely turn away from, yet the longer they remained in sight, the more uneasy I grew. For if this is "fashion" today, what will it have come to by the time my own daughters are grown? Perhaps they will beg to buy bathing shorts like their brothers, and abandon tops altogether. In another twenty years they may abandon these too, and run about like hairless monkeys . . . a disgusting thought! But is it impossible? I don't know whether any excess is unthinkable, if a man lives long enough in this modern world.

From resting too much yesterday, I found it difficult to sleep at night. At about eleven o'clock, I rose and went outside to enjoy the moon-light. I understand that when it is night for us, it may not be so in Po Leng, yet I entrusted the moon with prayers for your happiness. I hope that my prayers found you, sitting on your porch in the darkness as I remember you, waiting for fatigue to steal up and gentle the worries of the day, so that you could sleep.

When I was a little boy, whenever I woke at night and discovered that you were not in the bedroom, I would tiptoe outside and sigh with relief to find you there, still and thoughtful, composing your mind before sleep. Often, then, we would stroll through the garden hand in hand, and I would pick flowers for you if the moon was bright, and put them in a little glass. In the morning I would come to the breakfast table to find them opening their petals, greeting the dawn with us. But then I grew older, and I slept the greedy sleep of a hard-working farmer, and whether you sat on our porch alone at night I did not know.

It is not a peaceful moon that shines above Hua Hin. At home, stately trees framed the moon's silent splendor, and the night air was fresh and sweet. A moonlit night here is dominated by the salt-heaviness of sea air, by the muffled sounds of waves rushing to shore, leaving foamy crescents on the smooth wet sand, tepid suds on a shore that has never known a chilling wind.

A thousand little holes popped open about my feet each time the water sank back, the homes of sand crabs that scuttle furtively across the beach as they have for a million years, before half-naked Bangkok girls pranced and giggled above their heads.

As I sat alone, the monotonous sea sounds were suddenly pierced by the good-natured shouts of young men and women. I picked up my flashlight and, out of curiosity, made my way carefully through the darkness until I found them, wading in the surf. I followed them at a considerable distance, and from their boisterous shouts I discovered that they were gathering crabs for a party farther down the beach where other young people were building a bonfire and calling to the crabbers to hurry with their task.

These youths were familiar to me, for I had seen them in the small, crowded eating place where we had had our dinner the night before. They had danced with each other to the music from a phonograph record machine, and this "dancing" determined me not to expose the children to their example again. Recalling my anger and embarrassment on that occasion, I stumbled along with my flashlight focused on the sand before me, paying too little attention to the direction I was headed. (These young people are staying together in one house, by the way, or so the restaurant owner informed me, with no adult supervision! Where are their parents?) I should not have been surprised, given those circumstances, to discover the lewdness which suddenly confronted me.

"Wh-what the hell!" came a muffled, breathless male voice from the tangle of arms and legs that thrashed about in the beam of my light. I felt paralyzed, and fumbled to turn off the flashlight, not realizing that I would be worse off in the darkness!

"It's only the old guy from the noodle shop!" came a distant voice. "Hey, you've had your fun, fella—go on home to Big Mama now, will you?"

I felt enormous shame for them . . . out on the sand like animals, lacking every scrap of decency. Even if there were no one to stumble upon them accidentally as I did, have they no shame before each other?

Not only were they without shame, they thought nothing of cursing the one who discovered them. How could they appear so . . . comfortable, in a moment which would have filled any man of my generation with humiliation beyond measure?

Stumbling on, my face hot with mortification, I approached their bonfire. They had turned on a portable radio and were swaying to the music, clinging to each other, their bodies locked together, suggesting that other lewd episodes were not only possible but inevitable.

I turned and plodded back down the beach with a sick feeling in the pit of my stomach. What is this society coming to? It is a fearful prospect for a father—my poor children! I could not sleep at all that night, for each time I closed my eyes I saw the shameless young couple thrashing about. In the morning everyone commented that I looked exhausted.

After breakfast, I went off alone in the direction of the king's seaside residence, more a lovely big house than a palace. Its whitewashed bulk stands gracefully on a bluff some hundred meters from the shore, surveying the coast with silent dignity, closed up now in the royal family's absence. It is pleasant to wander past it at one's leisure. Imagine, a king's residence on a beach, which anyone may stop to gaze at without hindrance! I felt strangely moved by that. The great house looked as lonely as I felt, and I continued down the beach in the direction least favored by early bathers. But within a few minutes I was presented with yet another shocking display, a sight so startling that I had to rub my eyes, half convinced that the sun had played a trick on me. Some twenty yards before me a woman lay on her back, naked but for a newspaper carelessly draped over her chest; next to her was another woman, one with yellow hair and pale skin. She lay on her stomach with not even a newspaper to shield her body from the sun, or from the gaze of passersby such as myself. I had read of "naked sun-bathing" in novels, but never did I think I should see such a thing with my own eyes. Real women, naked on a beach in this country, women utterly devoid of natural modesty.

The first girl was Thai. I saw her face clearly before I gathered my wits enough to turn around (why must the blameless turn away, while the shameless never do?). I had no doubt that their embarrassment, should they discover my nearness, would not half equal my own, yet if anyone saw me standing there, would I not be suspected of spying on them? I fled, praying that no one else would appear on the lonely stretch of beach before I was out of sight.

This Hua Hin is no place for people like us. I told everyone to begin packing the moment I returned, and they were disappointed but knew better than to argue. What if Weng Khim had accompanied me on this morning's walk?

We will take the early evening train.

I DON'T believe I ever mentioned before that your two eldest grand-daughters no longer attend school. We allowed them to finish together, which gave Chui Kim an extra year of Thai language classes. She was too small after completing Prathom Four last spring to be of much help to Mui Eng in the store, and even for sewing instruction her little arms were not strong enough. Bak Li and Meng Chu are big girls, more like their brother in build, and he has suddenly shot up to an astonishing height, taller than anyone in the family.

Meng Chu has become all arms and legs, and hardly ever says a word—to us, that is. Only with her aunt does she seem to be her old, lively self. She grows more stubborn and unpredictable every day. She never appears to cross me, yet she manages to do exactly as she pleases. Like Ang Buai, she keeps her own counsel and plans ahead.

It is time to think of the two older girls' future. Chui Kim is now learning to sew from a friend of Mui Eng's, and Bak Li is content to help her mother. She eats, sleeps, and works, dresses neatly and is a good girl; she will make a fine wife. Perhaps they are too young for me to be considering such things, but I do not believe there is any harm in thoughtful planning.

I am afraid I have some disturbing news, but let me hasten to say first that we in the family are all well. It is of the many fires which occur in the city of Bangkok that I wish to write. They destroy property worth a great deal of money, as much as what the Thais call "millions." One million is equal to one hundred ten thousands. The worst fire caused ten million baht worth of damage, and hundreds of homes wore lost. It is said that most of these fires do not result from accidental causes. But why, you may ask, would anyone want to cause such destruction? There are several reasons; to evict tenants without argument or recourse to the law is one. The very poor in Bangkok cannot easily find new homes when the value of the land beneath them tempts their landlords to use it in more profitable ways. But according to Thai law, a landlord must have more respectable reasons than that for evicting his tenants.

Soon after fire has ravaged a slum, new construction begins, not of new homes but of commercial buildings, parking lots, or movie theaters. Who will speak for people who have no money? Even if they could find someone to represent them in a court of law, the immediate need to find a new home overrides everything else, and by the time they have found another place to live, what point is there in fighting the injustice of the situation?

Another motive for these dreadful fires is the collection of insurance money, which I must also explain. There are men whose business it is to "insure" against disaster: fire, theft, automobile accidents, even death. We pay them so much each month, and in the event that some disaster befalls us, we are recompensed according to the terms of our contract with the insuring company. Some of these contracts provide very large sums of money indeed, and a man may be tempted to salvage a failing business through "accidental" fire . . . if he is not caught, he becomes rich; otherwise he finds himself in jail. So are modern man's values further warped, by an invention meant to protect him from the vagaries of life.

There are those who say that the arsonists are mostly Chinese. I strongly disagree, for few Chinese are landowners, though this obvious flaw in their theory does not impress the bigots who are determined to perpetrate it.

"But it is the Chinese who use money deceitfully," they say. "The merchants and the building contractors reap all the benefits of arson, and when are there the most fires? Before Chinese New Year!"

To this, I must admit there is some truth, but why should I hasten to join those who stab our backs? When the increase in crimes of arson first began, punishment was not severe. Then, not long ago, we read in the newspapers that penalties for certain crimes would be made "considerably more drastic," especially arson and the selling of opium and what used to be called red medicine and is now called heroin. Death before a firing squad turned out to be the meaning of that vague phrase, death for the destroyers of property, life, and the public well-being. Well, I thought to myself, innocent women and children died in those fires; for sound sleepers, more was at stake than the loss of a poor hovel containing a few cheap possessions. Perhaps the new law was not too cruel.

Soon thereafter, I read in a Thai morning newspaper that a man alleged to have set several fires within the past month had been arrested and would be publicly executed. My heart sank, though I had not changed my mind about the seriousness of this crime. What if they had arrested the wrong man? Something in the article made me skeptical, though I could not point to any paragraph and say, "There—that is the weak point in the case."

I was astonished, reading further on, to learn that the most recent fire had occurred not far from Seng's house, and I determined to see him directly after lunch.

I ran into Kim half a block from the store and the two of us arrived together to find Seng's household in a state of pandemonium.

The night before, he told us, the sky had been a sea of fire. While he spoke, he lay stretched out on a pile of bedding that had been carried down from his bedroom when it was feared the fire might reach them. The smoke, he said, had made one's lungs ache even though the fire was two blocks away, and the sound of it was like the roaring of devils in hell. He and his family had watched, terrified, as the flames leaped playfully from one wooden house to the next like a puppy in a roomful of toys, destroying indiscriminately and with relish.

Seng and his wife had spent the whole night rushing about the store frantically, upstairs and down, unable to decide what to save and what to leave to the flames. In the end, of course, they were spared that grim choice.

"But if it had reached us, oh, my friends, what a terrible fate for us! You should have seen the things we dragged out into the street before the fire was stopped. Rain barrels that weighed fifty kilos each and cost less than fifty baht, old wash pans, even chopping blocks from the kitchen! But my immigration papers? Or money? No one thought of

258

such things at all. Suang U, it is terrible to learn how a crazy man feels, believe me. You look so smug," he laughed, "because you are sure you would be wiser. But don't think you know what your family would do in such a situation. My eldest daughter would take only her kitten; she stood in the middle of the street clutching it and sucking her thumb, staring at the sky as if she were hypnotized. My clever son took his soccer ball. As for my wife, she was only interested in her damned clothes and the iron! By dawn she had every piece of clothing she owns piled in the gutter, with the iron perched on top. She kept bawling and screaming that for all I cared she could end up in a wrinkled skirt with no home to return to! But the poor people, the truly poor people, they lost everything." He shook his head sadly. "They lost everything, friend, absolutely everything. Many of them crowded into our street, wailing and crying, and they wandered around the neighborhood all the next morning. The children didn't go to school—how could they? No clothes, no books . . . their poor parents!"

Terrible, isn't it? I prayed that this fate might never be ours. I am very afraid of fire, you know. Even hearing Seng's story cost me a night's sleep.

The story about the execution of an arsonist dominated the papers for many days. They shot the follow on the grounds of a temple, before an enormous crowd of spectators. You may be sure that your son was not among them, for I have no desire to see a man die a violent death, though it be at the hands of the law. It is not that I pity the man; I pity mankind, that thousands will gather to witness such an event.

I have read the opinion that public executions serve to warn the potential criminal and are therefore justifiable. Why do we not admit the embarrassing truth? The least worthy part of a man's nature is thrilled by the drama of execution. The criminal blindfolded and trembling; the executioners, straight and businesslike in immaculate uniforms; the ceremony of adjusting the stake, the ropes; the solemn shouts of the officer in charge; rifles ready, aimed, poised for one fearful moment, and then crack! The puppet-like convulsions of the dying man draw a swoon from the crowd, then silence . . . homage to the obscenely slumped, shattered body which has given its one performance to a full house.

How long before men turn from such scenes? Forgive my pessimism,

Mother, and accept once more my apologies for writing of distressing events. My love and prayers are with you as ever, and I feel profound gratitude for the example of your gentleness and wisdom, which sustains me in a world of indifference and cruelty.

—

SALES FROM the bakery are poor, the effects of what our newspapers call "the recession," But I am afraid we have other business problems which I cannot blame on any vague phrase coined by government. The truth is that neither Thai nor Chinese customers are as interested in our products as they were five or ten years ago.

At the time Mui Eng and I were married, before every Chinese wedding there were traditional sweets prepared in honor of the occasion: little cookies wrapped in fancy paper, cut to resemble a bridegroom and bride, special kinds of *chan-ap,* and many other confections. I always thought it a nice custom and enjoyed seeing the pretty boxes stacked on our counters prior to a wedding. But people do not want such things anymore. Instead they buy tasteless foreign concoctions in tins, imported and expensive, and therefore fashionable.

I do not mean to imply that our business has come upon hard times. Yet, I am concerned. Last year, I was the first to sell bean cake slices that were sold for a baht apiece in shops near the schools, and children did buy many of them—for awhile. But children are the most fickle of customers, and within a few months the bean cake slices were growing stale on shopkeepers' shelves. So we turned to tiny squares of *chan-ap,* at half a baht each; these were popular for two months. I turned back to our old products, but in new shapes; almond cookies in the shapes of airplanes and cars, and these too the children liked, bought, and grew tired of.

Ang Buai was responsible for some of these ideas, and if none of them was successful for long, I can hardly blame her.

It is becoming quite irksome, this stubbornness of hers about marrying. Suitors do appear occasionally, men eager to marry her, but she will have nothing to do with any of them. I wouldn't be at all surprised if she picked the worst of the lot in the end. As an old Thai saying goes, she who has one chance to walk the length of the garden in search of the perfect rose may have to pick in haste from the last bush.

I would like to turn on the radio of an evening and listen to the Chinese songs which, for awhile, were becoming popular. But they have suddenly vanished for reasons I do not understand. One Chinese entrepreneur leases a radio attachment that permits reception of a private station which plays Chinese music, but I have heard that all its broadcasts are in Mandarin. It is a strange language we have when we cannot speak with each other except by way of pen and paper. It is fortunate that at least our written language is identical everywhere in China, but that is no help with a radio. No one else would listen to it besides me, that I know, for Mui Eng listens to radio dramas during the day, they all watch television in the evenings, and occasionally Ang Buai and Mui Eng go to the opera, But the children have no interest in Chinese entertainment of any kind. The only dramatic characters whose names they recognize are Americans. I suppose that my temper would improve if I could learn to close my eyes and ears more than I do . . . they cannot, after all, will themselves to care for the things I find pleasurable.

I have written before that people in Bangkok follow the *farang* in many ways. In all fairness, I must tell you that the influence of Japan is growing almost as rapidly, if not as obviously. In the sale of fabrics and gadgets, especially those which use electricity, they have conquered the market. We seldom see the Japanese themselves, however, while we see the *farang* everywhere, especially around the temples, their red and yellow heads bobbing above the crowds of smaller Thai and Chinese people. Sometimes when I am weary of home and work, I walk down to the Temple of the Emerald Buddha, from there to the old palace (where the king no longer resides), and then across the road to the great outdoor weekend market, which is called Sanam Luang, "the royal garden," a marvelous place. But it too is full of *farang*. They like to buy old things, especially small images of the Lord Buddha, which they use as house decorations and even, according to Seng, as lamp bases!

The part of Bangkok where we live is considered "Chinatown"—not officially, of course, for there is no restriction on where we may live, but our temples and businesses and relatives are here, and most of us would not be comfortable away from these things.

On my way home from the weekend market, I pass many buildings that are seven, eight, even ten stories high. In the *farang* countries, there are buildings with as many as a hundred stories—imagine! I wonder if there are such buildings in China. We do not see any pictures of China, and I am very curious about changes there, but perhaps I shall see for myself some day. I shall not give up hope.

In the newer parts of the city, there are many large, imposing, and fearfully expensive stores. In their windows, I have seen a suit of ladies' underwear which cost more than a hundred baht, and a man's shirt for three hundred baht! One Saturday afternoon when Weng Khim and I went shopping to buy him new shoes, we stopped by one such place. Not only were the prices outrageous, but the clerks would not even bargain. They looked at us as if we were peasants, too ignorant to deserve the honor of patronizing their establishment, but whenever a *farang* walked in the door they would break into smiles so wide that their eyes disappeared. The *farang* come to buy, they think, while Thais and Chinese come only to let their mouths water and pretend they are rich.

Once the whole family went to a foreign food restaurant. Their advertising in the newspaper had whetted my curiosity, and I took a good deal of money with me, considering that I was buying knowledge as well as food. But the face of the "hostess" almost sent me home before we had reached our table. Her eyes said clearly, "Who is this Chinaman? He'll be lucky if he can pay the bill!" And, just as in the clothing shop, when a tall, pale fellow sauntered up to her, followed by a skinny red-haired woman and two little boys—oh, ho! Sweet smiles and a gracious manner. All the girls who worked in the *farang* restaurant were dressed expensively and wore too much makeup, and there was no healthy glow to their complexions because the place was cooled by air conditioning machines. And that, curiously, made me think of Po Leng, for it was the first dinner I had eaten since leaving home with an appetite stimulated by shivering. If only the food had been Chinese instead of the bland, coarse stuff they served us. I also worried a little that Mui Eng might take it into her head to have an air conditioning machine installed in our house. There I would make my stand, I decided, for such a machine costs many thousands of baht. Her automobile continues to be a fearful burden, what with the constant expenditures for gasoline, repairs, and "parts"—things that were never mentioned by the automobile salesman.

I am grateful for one thing at least, that we seldom shout at each other, as some couples always do. Mui Eng perfers stony silence broken by sarcastic remarks, and I also restrain myself for the sake of the children. I worry about the children of husbands and wives who do not spare the little ones' feelings, but that is common here. You and my father never argued, to my memory, except for an occasional teasing word, followed by laughter. Such is the entertainment of the rural poor—word games, teasing, the gentle, familiar ways of people who love each other and have no other companionship. We need not depend on each other for entertainment in this enlightened age; radio, television and movies, teahouses and nightly opera, massage parlors and dance halls have relieved us of that burden. If anyone is bored or depressed, he can turn a switch or press a button or leave the house altogether and find his pleasures elsewhere.

In fact, it is seldom necessary for the members of a family to speak to each other at all in 1959. I do not mean to be sarcastic; I simply have no answers to the unhappy questions in my mind. Our life together has so little meaning, and I do not see that there is anything I can do to change that sad state of affairs.

—

LETTER #65   THIRD MONTH, FIFTH DAY
31 MARCH 1960   YEAR OF THE RAT

I HAVE no news of special importance today, only tales of your grandchildren.

Meng Chu has refused to leave school. Neither of her elder sisters made any fuss over it, but this snippet of a girl is different. I called her into my office, and while I spoke to her sternly of a daughter's duties, her eyes darted about the room nervously, then settled on the papers strewn over my desk.

"I will think about it Papa, and I am sorry I made you angry," she said in a small voice, then scurried from the room like a busy mouse.

An hour later I glanced out the window to see her trudging off down the street with her little suitcase under one arm and a stack of books under the other. Had she mentioned going to her aunt's for the night? I could not recall, but I did not consider for a moment that the child was leaving home . . . Two days later, when she still had not returned, Ang Buai stalked into my office, wearing her business face.

"You look like you're out for blood," I said casually. "Mine, per-haps?"

"Let's not waste time," she replied sharply, brushing aside my remark with one neat sweep. "Do you know that Meng Chu refuses to come back here? She's been crying her eyes out in my house for two days."

"M-m . . . so it is the business of leaving school. That's an old tale around here, Ang Buai. Weng Khim fussed about it too, and if I didn't give in to him, I'm certainly not giving in to her."

"But she is different from the others. Weng Khim is a nice, average boy and the older girls think of nothing but clothes and boys. Chui Kim had more going for her, but my dear sister gift-wrapped the girl's brain. I won't let that happen to Meng Chu, not that I think it's likely . . . the tragedy will be if you don't give her her chance, and she grows up bitter. I—I can't let that happen, Suang U!"

"How dare you come in here and say you 'can't' let this or that happen!" I shouted, rising from my chair. (Weng Khim a nice, average boy? And what she said of the older girls—shame!)

"You let me finish!" Ang Buai retorted, undaunted by my rage. "She realizes the injustice of the situation, The others have all had to quit school, and she—she is a sensitive child. But if she were to live with me, if I took over from here on with her, it wouldn't be quite the same as if she stayed at home and got what all the others were denied. And don't bring up money. Even if she should want to go to the university later, that would be my own dream realized."

"But Meng Chu is my daughter! Parents must be responsible for their own children's upbringing. If they are too poor, it is another matter, but I am hardly too destitute to raise my children. This is a matter of—point of view, I should say, and by that I mean my point of view, not Meng Chu's or yours or anyone else's."

"Are you willing to see her crushed, then? That is what will happen, I promise you. I agreed years ago to keep out of your children's lives, but this child . . . oh, please . . . you made no secret of the fact that you

264

resented her very birth. Why not let me take her now, and make of her whatever there is to be made?"

"You are telling me that I hate my own child, and it is untrue. I love them all equally—"

"How can you stand there and lie to me like that?" she cried, her face pale with anger. "I was there, I saw your eyes the day you came home from the hospital and knew that Mui Eng's body had stopped manufacturing babies for you!"

"Shame, shame on you!" I shouted, not caring who heard us. "An unmarried woman, to speak such filth!" Her words pierced me to the marrow, yet I began to realize that Ang Buai had all the advantages on her side. She would easily be able to convince Mui Eng to go along with her, and the child's love of school is greater than her respect for me.

"Enough of this," I said wearily, "I will go with you and talk to the girl myself."

Meng Chu was reading a newspaper at her aunt's kitchen table. (Why is it that the Chinese, even when they can afford to build a house with a proper living room, remain in the kitchen?) When she saw us, she gave no sign of surprise but got up, folded the paper neatly, and began to prepare tea. She knows that her papa drinks only hot tea on a hot day.

"So you think you're staying here, eh?"

"If you let me, yes."

"And what if I don't?"

"Then I will stay here school days and go home on the weekends."

"I say you will live in my house every day."

"No, Papa," she said, her lips trembling, "not unless you let me stay in school."

Impertinence! My head began to swim.

"I don't want to grow up stupid, Papa. I told you when I was a little girl that someday I would help you—"(Little girl? Now she is all of ten years old.) "I don't want to be just a clerk in Mama's store, and you would never let me go to night school like Weng Khim because I am a girl, so if I don't stay in the regular school, it is all over now for me . . . I would study on my own if I could, but there are subjects I could never master that way. You know that is true."

"Who taught you this little speech, eh? Your wonderful auntie?"

"No one has to tell her what to say!" Ang Buai snapped, her eyes wide with fear and pride. There is no doubt about it—she loves the girl.

"All right, Ang Buai, calm yourself," I said quietly, raising my hand to quell any further outburst. "I will talk to the other children, and to her mother."

"You won't have to do that, Papa," said Meng Chu. "They agree with me, and—well, it was Weng Khim's idea for me to stay here until you came, so that we could talk alone. Chui Kim and Bak Li don't care if I stay in school, if—if they get to do what they really want to do." The child took a deep breath, glanced up at her aunt for reassurance, and plunged on. "Chui Kim wants to go to a real sewing school instead of learning from Mama's friend, and Bak Li wants to go to hair dressing school instead of helping in the store." And, on the next breath, "I promise to help in the store and with the housework every single minute from the time I get home until I go to bed if—if you let me go to the fifth grade . . ." Having completed this recitation, she gave a great gulping sob and blinked frantically, staring straight into my eyes.

"And if I agree to all this, to the Master Plan of Meng Chu and her auntie, when do I get my daughter back?"

Meng Chu's voice failed her completely, then, and with a tearful squeak she replied, "In three days, Papa!"

I heard more sniffling behind me and turned to see Ang Buai, her lips trembling daugerously, gripping the back of a chair with rigid hands. She shook her head slowly as she said, "Oh, Suang U! I was going to keep her here no matter what—I was going to make you send the police after her before I'd give her up!" She giggled tearfully, then pulled a handkerchief from her pocket and wiped her eyes. "Meng Chu, you wretched child—I was scared to death for both of us!" She began to laugh again, and cry too.

I was curiously moved. "Ang Buai, you don't have to be afraid of me, not ever—" I stopped, stunned by my words and the emotion in my voice. Then I felt Meng Chu's little hand steal into mine. She reached toward Ang Buai with the other and looked from one of us to the other with a satisfied, faintly mysterious smile.

"I'll take care of Auntie," she said. "You go home now, Papa . . ."

I LEFT you fifteen years ago, and not a day has passed since then without the hope that I shall see you again, kneel before you in gratitude and joy, see your smile, hear your gentle voice. But that dream grows more hopeless with each year, and it only increases my frustration to realize that I have long since earned the money I was once sure would fulfill that dream.

A troop of musicians who dared to visit China not long ago were arrested upon their return to Thailand. It made me think: What if I took my family to China with no intention of returning here? I am Chinese, it is my homeland, but what would I do there? I would not want to be a farmer again. Anyway, Po Leng must have changed greatly, and I have no idea what those changes would mean to us. How would our children, who were born in Thailand, fare in China? Even Mui Eng was born here, so that for their sake I dare not indulge my longing. I must be patient and hope for the day politicians see fit to allow mothers and sons to reunite.

But there is another and more painful aspect to my dream of seeing you again. Without a letter from you, your son will not know whether he is welcome. It is midnight, as I write. Curious that a man never has such thoughts at noon. Only in the hours before dawn do such illogical and frightening thoughts intrude.

The business is still not thriving, to tell you the truth. Our imports, which used to bring in a fine profit, are in trouble because of new government regulations, and I have told you of the bakery's problems in a previous letter. Under the new law, a firm must petition for exclusive national control of particular products, and we are not large enough to become the exclusive agents for anything we have customarily handled. Put simply, I cannot compete at this level. If the children were grown, if I had not only my son but sons-in-law . . . then, there might be ways.

I should be satisfied. After all, when I rejected the offer to handle contraband goods I told my *sae* brother that we have "enough," and so we do. Our bank account is far from small, and we need not fear the future. All the same, I have tendered my resignation as a director of the

Chinese Merchants Society and requested regular membership.

Of course, they refused at first, when I said my health was only fair and my responsibilities already too numerous, but they knew the truth and were relieved at my resignation, though they begged me to stay on. What else could they have said? By the next day, a new director was already installed. I felt a little irritated when I learned how quickly I had been replaced, but I sent him a friendly note of congratulations.

More irritating was the loss of five thousand baht last month. It is difficult to explain to you just how I lost it. Not in gambling, exactly (of which I disapprove no less than yourself), but in a kind of investment plan which is popular here, called *len huai* or *len share*. ("Share" is a *farang* word; I assume it means the same thing.) In any event, the *huai* master made off with nearly a hundred thousand baht all told, and my loss was nothing compared to that of others. I invested five hundred baht ten times. Subtracting the interest, I lost nearly five thousand—and nearly my mind! Had I lost it in a business transaction, even if I had spent it on something I could see and touch—but this! Cheated by my own avarice—I, Suang U! It is bitter to reflect upon, dear Mother.

At first I was not interested in investing money in *len huai,* for money in the bank is at least safe. But Kim continued to pinch at me about it, and to be sure he lost more than I. (Of his cure in the matter of *len huai* there is no doubt.) We have friends in the neighborhood who have made fortunes in it, by the way. I wish now that I had never heard of them!

There are other ways of making money with money in Bangkok. Some people withdraw large sums of their money from the bank to lend it at exorbitant rates, but I know that only the most hard-hearted are successful at this kind of money-lending, for one must be willing to put the money's return above every consideration. If the bank's interest rate is low, at least I am not taking rice from the mouth of a debtor's child.

Another money-earning scheme, one especially favored by Indians, is "selling on time." A man may buy a television set from an Indian merchant for a small amount of money "down." That is, he makes further payment each month until the full amount (plus interest up to a hundred percent) is paid. I have warned Mui Eng and the children that under no circumstances are they to purchase anything in this manner. Credit should remain a function of trade, not a tool with which to gouge retail customers, who are seldom clever enough to see how they are being used. I shall never forget my own earliest business experience, selling groceries on credit. To buy anything for private use on credit is to incur an unwise debt.

For the last few days I have been annoyed with your grandson. He still goes to the night school, and though he does not always come straight home, I do not believe he is out beyond a reasonable hour. (Chui Kim opens the door for him—surely she would tell me if anything were wrong.) What has made me so angry is the discovery that he has been smoking cigarettes! Tobacco is an addictive drug, and no growing boy should waste his health or money on it. Additionally, the cheap brand he smoked emitted a foul stench that clung to his hair and clothing.

One morning at breakfast, I noticed deep yellow stains on the fingers of his right hand. I recognized what they were at once, but when I asked the foolish boy whether indeed his fingers were stained from cigarettes, he stammered that he "didn't know"!

"I don't know what you're so excited about," Mui Eng said with a shrug when Weng Khim had finally been sent off on an errand, sulking mightily. "He is young, but he works like a man, and you smoke yourself. How was I to know you would carry on so? He cannot have all the virtues of a grown man and none of the vices!" She cleared the last plate from the table and set it in the sink with the rest, for the girl to do.

"A boy of his age, addicted to tobacco? You are flippant—virtues, vices—bah! What will he do when he is twenty, Mui Eng—use opium, perhaps?"

"Must you carry everything to such an extreme?" She scrubbed at the table with a soapy rag. "It is no wonder he is afraid of you. But he is a good boy, I don't believe his character is flawed, and I wish you would try not to make him feel like a criminal for every little thing he does that you don't like!"

Tossing the rag into the sink with the dishes, she took a comb from her pocket, ran it through her frizzled hair, and went out front to her shop, sighing and muttering to herself like an old woman.

I cut his monthly allowance, which he took with little grace.

"But Papa, only two hundred baht a month—it's hardly enough for anything!"

"I came to your grandfather's house to work for twelve baht a month."

"Twelve baht was a normal wage then, Papa, but today it wouldn't buy a good dinner."

"That is true, but I had none of what you call 'spending money.' You know you can come to me if there is anything you need to buy that is beyond the limits of your allowance. I have never expected you to buy necessities with your money, and it isn't the money I care about, Weng Khim, it's your health. You are not yet a grown man."

"I am a grown man for other purposes," he retorted insolently. "I work like a man and still you give me no freedom."

"Freedom! I give you freedom to do anything which does not harm you!"

"You smoke."

"Less than a pack a week. There are no stains on my fingers."

"You let Meng Chu do anything she wants, and Chui Kim and Bak Li too! They always get their own way, but I never do. You think I don't understand, but I do—you let them do as they please because you know they will marry, and it won't matter, but the son, the one great hope of a son, he has to toe the line day and night!"

"In your rude way, you have spoken the truth, but do you believe that I would purposely make my only son unhappy? I want you to be a good man, able to take care of yourself. Khim, if I didn't love you, would I care whether or not you smoke cigarettes?"

"I—I don't know . . . but I never—" A sob choked him, and he shook his head angrily and turned away.

"You are so concerned about this business of 'not getting your own way' . . . What does that mean, being allowed to do what is wrong? Would I be a better father if I did not concern myself with your welfare?" Suddenly, I remembered something . . .

"Weng Khim, I think perhaps it is time you had a watch of your own, and of your own choosing. However, if you think I am giving it to you as a bribe, you are wrong. Another bit of bad conduct won't win you another prize!"

The boy grinned sheepishly. He has wanted a watch desperately, but

I feared he was too young to be responsible for a good one. Now it seems worth the risk, for both our sakes. It is an opportunity to show him that I do not forget or disdain all of his desires.

"You see, Weng Khim, I am not so unreasonable," I said, putting an arm across his shoulders.

"Thank you, Papa," he murmured, then deftly shrugged off my arm and hurried away to share his good news with the others. He will tell Meng Chu first, on that I would bet a thousand baht. It occurred to me later, that, had she been in his place, she would have refused the watch and continued to smoke cigarettes. Perhaps it is as well, after all, that she was not a son.

LETTER #67
26 FEBRUARY 1961

FIRST MONTH, TWELFTH DAY
YEAR OF THE OX

I OFTEN wonder what women look like in China these days, and whether the fashion epidemic has swept even our own land.

I have written earlier that in Thailand girls and women dress immodestly. In the old days, they kept themselves covered so as not to inflame men, which had the result of stimulating the imagination. Nowadays they seem to think the men need reminding, and skirts have become so short this year that woman can hardly get up the steps of a bus without shaming themselves.

Almost every female in Bangkok wears her hair in the hideous little curls Mui Eng and Ang Buai are so proud of, while those who have kept their long hair pile it up into a great snarly bush, as if trying to cover some strange growth. As far as I can see, no woman today has long, straight, shining hair.

Makeup, which became widely used soon after I arrived here, has become a national curse. Even the daughters of respectable men paste little pieces of hair over their eyelashes to make more eyelashes, and then smear crayon above that to tint their eyelids green or blue or even purple. They pull out their own eyebrows and paint on new ones, and for a finishing touch they draw a black line all the way around each eye. The first time I saw a girl made up in this fashion, I thought the poor thing had tuberculosis.

271

Under their black eyes they paint their cheeks pink, like those of plastic Japanese dolls and when they perspire in the heat of mid-day, the black eye paint and the pink cheek paint race each other down their faces. Who says this is beauty? Surely no man.

I have to laugh, for not long ago we were talking about foot-binding, and how "barbaric" it was. The shoes they're wearing today must have nearly the same effect, for the toe of the shoe is long and pointy, and the heel is three, four, or even five inches high. The champions of this fashion totter around with their behinds stuck out, barely able to walk in a straight line.

Who would be the first woman of my acquaintance to wear high heeled shoes?

Ang Buai opened the door of her car, placed two pointy, shining black high-heeled shoes on the sidewalk, and stepped out into them. Mui Eng learned on the counter just inside her shop and grinned at her sister.

"How you doing up there?" she called, laughing.

"Fine! These aren't very high, only about three inches . . . they're sort of a learner's model. I don't want to fall on my face, you know."

"Do they pinch your feet?" I asked, walking out to escort her, lest she break an ankle before getting inside the shop.

"Of course they pinch. So what? I can stand it, at least for going out."

Once inside the shop, she kicked them off and headed for the kitchen.

"Let's have some tea and give my feet a rest!" She handed me a square white bakery box she had been carrying under one arm and said, "Here—I brought some goodies."

Meng Chu retrieved the shoes and tried them on, holding onto the table with both hands and clumping around it.

"For beauty's sake you're willing to endure anything," I said, shaking my head in perplexity. "You're lucky the fashion isn't to wear a clothespin on your nose to stretch it out like a *farang*'s."

"You're only fifty years behind the times, as usual," she retorted cheerfully, accepting a glass of hot tea from Mui Eng. "Nowadays people go to a surgeon, and he doesn't use clothespins . . . he just opens up your nose, puts in a piece of plastic, and sews it up again. People get their eyes changed, too," she announced, reaching for a cake.

"Who would want to change their eyes?" Mui Eng asked doubtfully.

272

"Chinese girls who don't have a double eyefold, to make their eyes look bigger and rounder."

The other children had ranged themselves about the table happily to share the cakes their aunt had brought.

"Our eyes aren't bad," said Bak Li. "Not like some. One of the Chinese girls in our shop has eyes like two bent pins. Maybe she'll have that operation."

"Not if she has a father," I said.

"Well, they do wonderful things," Ang Buai continued. "For instance, if a woman thinks her breasts are too small—"

"Ang Buai!" Mui Eng cried, blushing furiously, "what kind of thing is that to bring up in front of the children?"

"Oh, that's nothing," Meng Chu said scornfully, kicking off her aunt's shoes and seating herself beside Ang Buai. "You know we can read, Mama, and those operations are in the newspapers all the time. They put dimples on girls' faces, and make their lips thinner, and fix millions of noses and—and fronts, If you've got a lot of wrinkles, they can stretch your skin to your ears and cut off the extra and sew it up so you don't look old anymore."

Mui Eng eyed her daughters severely. "Well, maybe you do know about such things, but I think it's all—sickening!"

Weng Khim tried to stifle a giggle and choked loudly on a swallow of tea, which brought a snort from Bak Li.

"Asking for trouble," I said, "to go against nature."

"I read in the newspaper," Mui Eng said, nodding in agreement, "about a woman who was strangled by a blob of that—whatever they put in your—bosom—it slid upward slowly, month after month, and finally choked her to death!"

"Asking for trouble," I repeated, noticing from the corner of my eye Meng Chu's subtle imitation of the event just described by her mother. The other children looked about to explode, not to mention Ang Buai, who was biting her lip ferociously. Mui Eng did not notice.

"Well at least women confine their follies to themselves," Ang Buai said when she had recovered her composure after Meng Chu's startling performance. "Women don't go out drinking and carousing, bringing home their hangovers and their diseases, so which of the sexes is more guilty of 'asking for trouble'?"

273

There is nothing of which she is ashamed to speak, apparently. The children struggled to look nonplussed while hanging on her every word, afraid their mother would make them leave the room.

"Ang Buai," I said, "you may be right about some men, but I myself have never—'asked for trouble,' as you so neatly put it." I had to laugh, then, in spite of myself. "You think that all men are as alike as grains of rice, but heaven help the man who says, 'just like a woman'! Wait until you're married, then you'll know something of men."

Until then, she had been obviously enjoying our mutual taunts, but suddenly she looked angry—or hurt, I wasn't sure which. "I don't have to marry to know something of husbands and children," she said. "And I wish you'd stop that nonsense about 'children to take care of me in my old age.' What makes you think children today take care of their aging parents? They leave home to make their own lives—yes, even Chinese children! Some of them only show up when they're out of work and hope they can shake a little money out of the old people."

"Surely not many children are so callous!"

"Plenty are, my friend. Anyway," she shrugged, "all the married couples I know fight. He brings home another woman, or there isn't enough money in the house, or maybe he drinks . . . who needs that? My life is simple, but it's mine, and you can keep the joys of family life. In my old age I'll have servants and money in the bank to look after me."

"Mind your tongue!" Mui Eng said reproachfully. "It is wrong for a woman to be alone. Several men have spoken to us about you, and I think it's time you chose one of them." Then she turned to me with a smug look and said, "They are all acceptable to this family, wouldn't you say?"

Ang Buai's lips curled in a sneer I could hardly resent. "So they're all 'acceptable to this family,' eh? I know your prospects for my hand! Chai the widower, with his three hulking juvenile delinquents? Thank you very much! And how about that thirty-year-old mewling Mama's boy across the street? I know Mama has come by a few times to see if I want to play house with her little boy, but I'd rather have a man for my husband . . . and what makes you think Mama intends to step aside when she gets a playmate for Baby?"

274

She glared at Mui Eng like a cat who has just been stroked from tail to head.

"I don't know how you can be so cruel," Mui Eng whined, changing her smug expression for one of self-pity, her fine intentions having been ruthlessly rejected. "Have you forgotten about that other man, the nice widower with the fish sauce factory? He likes you, Ang Buai, and there's plenty of money in the business."

Ang Buai stopped her sister's recital with a wild burst of laughter.

"That one! Just because he made his millions out of rotten fish, does he have to smell like one?"

The children giggled and poked each other under the table. They know him, and I can't say I disagree with Ang Buai myself.

"Every time he comes into my shop," she continued, "you'd think someone had sneaked up and dumped a thousand dead fish on my doorstep! Oh, no, I'm not going to spend the rest of my life with a perfumed handkerchief over my nose, not even for his millions."

"I suppose you expect to find a perfect man."

"No. But then you forget—I'm not looking for any man. But, as a matter of fact," she said thoughtfully, "there is one man I sort of like."

"So what's the matter with him? Is he already married?" Mui Eng almost leaped across the table in her eagerness.

"No, but . . . there are reasons it can't come to anything."

"What reasons?" Chui Kim piped up, whereupon her mother slapped her hand smartly for interfering.

"He's shorter than me, that's all. His head comes up to my shoulder."

"And is that so terrible? She is already thirty—and the man is too short! You'll be an old maid yet!"

"I don't care if I'm an old maid, and I refuse to marry a man who's four feet ten inches tall even if he's brilliant, devoted to me, and filthy rich, so why don't you stop nagging me about marriage?"

"Ang Buai," I said, "if you truly loved a man, you wouldn't care if he smelled like rotten fish or if he were only three feet tall."

She gave me a long, hard look then, a look I could not comprehend, and said, "Forget it. I made him up—there is no short rich man. Meng Chu, hand me those damned high-heeled shoes. It's time Auntie was getting home."

275

"You don't have to use that kind of language before the children!" Mui Eng said huffily.

"Oh, please—" She waved her hand in the air wearily." Get off my back."

"That is vulgar."

"M-m . . . I am rather vulgar. Not, at heart, the sort of person any of your friends would want to marry, so why don't you quit trying! Let them go on thinking I'm wonderful." She winked at Meng Chu, who grinned at her adoringly.

I wonder if she was telling the truth about inventing the short suitor, because I seem to recall a short fellow with an office across the street from her shop. It should not be difficult to find out.

———

LETTER #68   FOURTH MONTH, TENTH DAY
24 MAY 1961   YEAR OF THE OX

YOU WILL be relieved to learn that Ang Buai's tale of the short suitor was no more than a tale. Why do I say "relieved"? I suppose that it is I who am relieved. After all, I have felt responsible for her future since her father's death. The short man I had noticed on her street turned out to be several inches above four feet ten, and also to have a wife and fourteen children.

Weng Khim has stopped smoking cigarettes and is proud of his beautiful new watch. It is exactly the kind he has wanted for so long. Whether he will disappoint me in other ways I cannot tell, but he is apparently doing well at his Chinese night class, and his work at home is acceptable.

Chui Kim and Bak Li are growing to young womanhood with alarming speed, and somewhat alarming behavior. Nothing serious, of course—our young ladies went out and had their hair cut one afternoon without asking Mui Eng's permission or, needless to say, mine. Even their mother was irritated, for they had told her they were going "shopping," and Mui Eng is no fool. She knew the moment she saw their cropped heads that they had planned in detail how to get round both of us.

"Oh, Mother, so what if we got our hair cut? You were both busy, and—well, it's such an unimportant thing. You should see the way the girls do their hair where Bak Li works, all kinds of crazy styles! We don't live in this world all by ourselves, you know! We have a responsibility to—to look like other people," she finished lamely.

"Spare me the dramatics," Mui Eng said to her daughter, "and let me refresh you on your responsibilities. Your parents come first, well before the girls in Bak Li's shop!" She gave a sigh of resignation and said, "Well, the hair is gone now. Go and wash up, then come and set the table for supper."

The girls exchanged hasty glances and hurried off, Mui Eng began to prepare our evening meal, and I turned on the radio and began to read the afternoon paper. What is the use of letting myself get furious over every thoughtless thing the children do? I must save my anger for more important things than haircuts.

Listening to the radio, I exchanged my irritation with the girls for annoyance at the advertisers who support the radio stations. You cannot imagine how dreadful it is, listening to a fool with an affected voice harangue you to buy a medicine that will cure not only your headache but, he solemnly promises, your stomachache, sore throat, and aching bones too. No one could be so stupid as to believe such claims, yet someone must buy the stuff or the advertisements would cease.

Restaurants are advertised, too, even pepper sauce; and soap powder manufacturers compete with embarrassing passion on behalf of products which are as like each other and almost as numerous as drops of rain. One company, which produces an infant's tonic and thinks it is more clever than its competitors, has a screechy female voice inform us (by way of a very bad song) that she ignores all advertising for tonics because "Kuman Thong has made my children healthy and fat. No other tonic does all that!"

Have these people no shame?

Other advertisers use familiar tunes, altering the original words. When you feel a headache coming on, they theorize, the old song adapted to suit Bamrung powders will spring into your mind and send you off to buy a packet. To tell the truth, I do think of Bamrung powders every time I get a headache, but nothing could induce me to buy them, on that very account! Soda pop advertising is the worst, because they advertise a product of no positive use to anyone. We have a refrigerator in our kitchen now, and there is always a large jug of cool water on the top shelf for anyone in need of refreshment. I have heard that some brands of soda pop contain acids which destroy the lining of the stomach, yet the soda pop business earns profits in the millions.

Another of today's necessities is flavored paste for brushing the teeth, If we believe the advertisements, anyone who does not use "toothpaste" is backward and has a bad-smelling mouth. Strangely enough, it is only in recent years that I have noticed small children with decaying, blackened teeth, six-year-olds who must go to the dentist to have bad teeth pulled because of infection! Why, I recall old people in our village who chewed sugar cane with strong white teeth, and for a child to lose his teeth because of infection and decay was unheard of. Your grandchildren all use toothpaste, and we sell it in the store, but I see no evidence that it does any good. In a society where soda pop, chocolate candy, and frozen sugar water on sticks are necessities of childhood, I suppose that toothpaste is a logical product.

Before long, Chui Kim and Bak Li will undoubtedly be the fashion leaders of the neighborhood. They have already bought high-heeled shoes like Ang Buai's, and powder their faces. (One box of powder costs as much as two days' food; I shall never get over measuring luxuries that way.) Oil for their hair, creams and lipsticks, and a dozen other cosmetic concoctions fill the bathroom and the top of their bureau. So few years ago, Chui Kim was a tiny girl playing with her Chinese opera dolls; now she has begun to look like a woman, especially with all the enhancements she feels she needs, as if youth itself were not enough. When I am home, she wears little of this "makeup" knowing that I observe her more closely than before. This should not be a father's duty, of course, but attending to the development of her daughters' character is not one of Mui Eng's priorities. If she shows any reaction to a new purchase from the cosmetic store, it is to borrow it.

I am a little reluctant to tell you of another, more disturbing development in our family. The children no longer like their names. It is true—do not fear that you have misunderstood my words. They recently asked to legally change them, and did so. I could not prevent this, but do not fear that I will follow their example, even should I remain in this land to my death.

Together the four of them set off for the *nai amphoe*'s office nearest us to sign the papers and pay the few satangs that would diminish their "differentness," for to be "different" is the worst sin of their generation.

For a surname, they now have "Thaiyuenyong." Why the government authorities put the word "Thai" into the name I could not understand, unless it was done in spite. I was too annoyed by the whole business to pursue that. As for first names, they all chose very elegant ones with meanings similar to the proper Chinese names we gave them. The government does not interfere to the extent of first names. So, I am now the father of "Witthaya," "Dueanphen," "Maliwan," and "Phloi-charat"—quite dreadful names, I think.

Their friends have begun calling them by these absurd names, and I can never remember which name is whose. They retain their own names in my household, you may be sure, and that rule is inflexible.

Who knows what folly they will think of next? I only know that I am their father, and in spite of everything I am possessed of great love and hope for them all. They think that I am a fussy old man, out of date and a crank at thirty-five—that is the word they use when they think I am not listening. Will they ever make the astonishing discovery that this crank would do anything for them? Meng Chu, perhaps, has already guessed the truth.

LETTER #69
11 OCTOBER 1961

NINTH MONTH, SECOND DAY
YEAR OF THE OX

YOU KNOW from past letters that girls and boys in Bangkok are permitted to speak openly with each other. These "couples" go everywhere together—for a stroll down Yaowarat Road, through stores and down the side lanes into the marketplace; or they sit together in a coffee shop booth with their faces almost touching. Some of them wear their school uniforms, which only heightens the impropriety of such behavior.

I mention this subject again because I am greatly distressed at having seen our own Chui Kim standing on a street corner nearby talking to a strange boy about her own age, a fellow with long hair, tight trousers, and a wrinkled shirt. His manners seemed to me overly familiar, his features coarse.

She would not expect her father, of all people, to be wandering around the neighborhood in mid-afternoon, but even I change my habits occasionally, and on that particular day I had gone out to collect an old debt. I could have sent someone else, but it was hot in the store, I was feeling groggy and, to tell the truth, I was bored. Boredom at work is new for me, but I have decided that it may be healthy to grow bored sometimes and get out of doors for an hour or two, and I always find that I am able to work in the evening if I have been out during the day.

Each of my children has his or her particular way of entering my office on those occasions when trouble is feared. Chui Kim's is to knock feebly and then suddenly pop through the door with a silly grin. She has always done so. I wonder whether she is aware of it.

"Chui Kim, I shall come straight to the point: this afternoon I saw you talking to a boy out on the street, a boy I have never seen before."

"N-no, Papa!" she cried, obviously shocked at having been discovered.

"With my own eyes I saw you! Do you dare to deny it? I am not blind, Chui Kim, nor have I lost my wits. Who was the boy—who are his parents?"

"I don't know who he is, Papa. He just—started talking to me, so I talked to him . . . is that bad?"

"Ah, so it begins already, at your age! I tell you, you will not leave this house again, if meeting the boys is what comes of going to sewing school. You begged to study at a 'proper shop' instead of in your parents' home, and this is how you repay me!"

"But he followed me, Papa," she said, her eyes filling with tears. "He seemed like a nice boy—"

"That is a nice boy? A long-haired lout, with his trousers like banana skins on his legs?"

"I'm sorry, but I don't see anything wrong with—"

"Shut up! I'll tell you what's wrong and what isn't. You are Tan Chui Kim, my daughter, not 'Dueanphen' or whatever foolish name you call yourself, to go flirting in the streets with boys! If I ever learn that you have behaved in this way again, you will not see beyond the door of your mother's shop until the day you marry, is that clear?"

She nodded miserably, and I felt that perhaps I had been too hard on her, but at least it is certain that the incident will not be repeated. Until the day you marry, I had said to her . . . no, it is not too early to think of Chui Kim's marriage.

Less than a week later, Bak Li returned from the hairdressing parlor wide-eyed and filled with excitement. Chui Kim had come home early to help Mui Eng, for it was a Monday, our busiest day in the shop.

"Oh, Papa! Has Chui Kim told you yet? Oh, Mama, it's so wonderful—"

Chui Kim looked stricken and implored her sister with her eyes to stop whatever she was going to say, but the younger girl did not notice.

"The owner of the shop where Chui Kim works wants to sponsor her for the Vachiravudh Beauty Contest! She says Chui Kim is certain to be at least a finalist. Oh, just think of it!"

"Can you possibly imagine," I said, determined to control my voice, "that I would permit such a thing?"

"Oh, I know you don't like beauty contests, Papa, but whoever thought someone from our own family would be practically begged to enter one of the most famous of all? The winner will get tens of thousands of baht, and her picture will be in all the newspapers!"

Chui Kim's face was by now scarlet and she turned on the younger girl furiously. "Oh, forget about it, Bak Li—it's just a lot of silly talk."

"It is of no importance in any case," I said, "for as long as Chui Kim is a daughter of this family, there will be no beauty contests, you may be sure."

Then, to my surprise, Chui Kim said, "I am not ashamed about it, Papa. Aren't you even a little proud, that people say I am pretty?"

"Proud? Shall I be proud to see my daughter flaunt her body before men? No Chinese father would allow his daughter to parade around in a bathing suit. You should strive to be a real woman, soft and quiet, the kind of a woman a man looks for to be the mother of his children."

Bak Li said, "I've seen pictures of Chinese girls wearing skirts slit up to the thigh on either side. Why don't their fathers forbid that?"

"That is Hong Kong, Bak Li, an island owned by the *farang*. Real Chinese women of good family don't get themselves up like that, not even in Hong Kong. Ugliness of that sort leads to evil behavior. If you are too young to understand that, then I shall have to protect you from your own gullibility. It is my responsibility more than yours."

"But we live now, Papa," said Chui Kim, "not fifty years ago in some Chinese village—"

"Enough! Do you really believe that one age is so different from another? In 'some Chinese village,' Chui Kim, a pretty girl would seldom be seen in public, but if she had both beauty and womanly qualities, the fathers of sons would all vie for her. Plain girls were not so fortunate, it is true, but I don't see that the basic elements of the situation have changed a whit in fifty years. No girl in my village would have dreamed of putting herself on display for money, marching around a ring with other girls like a lot of cattle at a fair!"

They exchanged their "Here comes Po Leng again" look, but I did not care.

"You know, I have listened for years to you girls complain that you should have the same freedom as men, because you also must work. Very well! But when you have that freedom, what do you, do with it? Set out to prove that you are the equals of men? Oh, no—you prance around a hairdressing parlor or a sewing shop gossiping away the day and plucking each other's eyebrows and talking of beauty contests! Tell me, who is stopping you from competing with the boys who sat beside you in school? The day Meng Chu cried all over her aunt's kitchen table and begged me to let you make your own decisions, I was frankly surprised that you longed for such mediocre professions. And now you practice them in a mediocre manner. Why, if your Aunt Ang Buai had gone into a sewing shop at fifteen she'd have owned the damned place before her seventeenth birthday. Look at her if you want to see a woman who does what you only whine about. She's been responsible for a sizeable business since she was your age, and she works, my dear daughters. Besides which, she is a damned fine-looking woman."

"She's old," Chui Kim said disparagingly, "an old maid who lives with her work."

"Old? Ang Buai is only thirty-one years old . . . In any event, you are not entering a beauty contest, this year or any other. And what makes you think you would win, with your face, eh? I do not disparage your beauty, my dear, but I question whether the judges will be looking for a beautiful face that is Chinese, not Thai."

After that unquestionably tactless remark, the girls went off to console each other and I returned to my desk to console myself. Though I criticized the girls in my anger, it is clear that the boys nowadays are little better. No man's son or daughter today is driven to work or study by the ambitions that drove my generation. Girls are obsessed with appearance, boys with carousing around town in packs like stray dogs.

A new assault on whatever virtue remains in the society is the "Turkish Bath." It began as an amusement for the American soldiers who have become numerous in Thailand, but Thais and Chinese men proved eager to patronize them. My first reaction was to wonder why a man needs help to take a bath, but on second thought the logical answer became clear.

(It occurs to me that you may wonder what American soldiers are doing in this country. They are here on leave from a war in Vietnam, for the Vietnamese are having a civil war; the Americans are fighting on the side of the South, a confusing business in which I am not much interested.)

If my family is causing me sleepless nights, at least the business is improving, but how strenuous competition is today! A good product is no guarantee of success whatever, and a businessman must spend terrific sums on advertising, even to offering free gifts if he would gain the customers' attention.

Besides giving free gifts, some companies sponsor contests. If you buy the product, you are entitled to participate in some sort of contest quiz; and in some instances, simply writing your name on a box top and mailing it to the company gives you a chance at prizes or money. It is a kind of gambling, I suppose, and one most representative of our age. There are people whose houses are stuffed with boxes of opened and untouched cereals bought only for the precious box tops. Our next door neighbors, for example, found the ten boxes of cereal he bought inedible but keeps hoping to win a prize which will rescue him from debt forever. If gambling were legal, I sometimes wonder whether anyone in Thailand would ever go to work. Upstairs in this neighbor's house, by the way, gambling goes on every night, and for the privilege of freedom from police scrutiny, he pays a modest weekly fee.

How I do skip from one thing to another! Please indulge my fatigue.

283

Scattered thoughts rise to the surface of my weary mind like bubbles rising to the surface of a pond. It would be pleasant, I think, to be a pampered goldfish in a rich man's garden pond . . . But no, I suppose I would soon die of boredom, with nothing to worry about and nothing to accomplish but the making of bubbles.

My prayers go with this letter as always, and the constant hope that you are well and content.

LETTER #70   FIRST MONTH, TENTH DAY
14 FEBRUARY 1962   YEAR OF THE TIGER

TODAY YOUR son brings only good news and joy to share, for Chui Kim, eldest daughter, will soon be married.

I have chosen for her a young man who is the son of a business colleague, a rice merchant who is comfortably well off. I never expected the child to accede quite so gladly to my wishes in the matter, but apparently the fellow appeals to her, which makes her betrothal the happy event it ought to he. And, may I say, it solves decisively certain problems related in previous letters. She is young, it is true, but not so young that anyone will raise eyebrows. She is sixteen and noticing the opposite sex, and that is old enough.

I feel no little pride in having a daughter so lovely that her hand was sought well before her twentieth birthday, for the daughters of many houses we are acquainted with have had more birthdays with no evidence of interest from houses with sons. Chui Kim's future father-in-law is an old acquaintance of ours, if not a close friend, and it was due to Kim's efforts as go-between that everything has come to pass so much to the satisfaction of all concerned.

"Suang U, one of your merchant friends is looking for a daughter-in-law," he said, seating himself on a crate in the bakery while I tinkered with a balky thermostat on our largest oven. "They want a girl from a prosperous house, and thought of you at once. It would be an excellent match for Chui Kim."

When he told me the man's name, I became interested.

"I see . . . well, what about the boy? How old, what education, and does he drink? Hand me that screwdriver, would you?"

"Hold on!" he laughed, tossing it to me. "Let's see, he's twenty-one, recently avoided the draft successfully (thanks to the old man's money), seems pretty well educated, and he's a big handsome kid, strong as an ox."

"How much did his father have to put up against the draft?"

"Four thousand . . . you'll have to deal with that soon yourself."

"M-m, we need our sons more than the army does."

"Next year the donation will be five thousand, they say. By the time Weng Khim is twenty-one, six or seven thousand wouldn't surprise me."

"That is the amount I had guessed at myself—so, go on about the boy."

"Name is Seng Huat. Finished Mathayom Three, went on in Chinese afterwards at night, like Weng Khim, and he's a first-rate bookkeeper. It probably won't be long before he makes it on his own, because he has a reputation already for—shall we say, 'thrift'? But that won't worry you, I'm sure. Two sisters already married, a seventeen-year-old brother, and the mother died a few years ago. The old man wants to see the son married—you know how it is. He wants to see a few grandchildren around the house before he dies."

"I can't say much, Kim, when I've never met the boy. For all we know, he already has his heart set on some girl his father knows nothing about. Before I went far with this, I'd want all the details."

Kim smiled broadly. "You don't have to worry about another girl in the picture, because the old man told me himself he's pointed out twenty or thirty girls to the boy, and none of them suits his fancy. Besides being stingy—thrifty—he seems to have a critical eye where the ladies are concerned. But Chui Kim is smashing, everyone says so. You should have heard the old man grumbling, you would have laughed yourself sick . . . That one has pointy ears, Papa . . . oh, not that one, with the fat legs, please, Papa . . ."

"Kim, how can you imagine my Chui Kim will measure up to this fellow's idea of the perfect girl? Anyway, he must be a fool if he is after nothing but good looks. Girls nowadays think only of dressing up and painting their faces, but look at them five years after they're married. Fat and sulky, and the ones who don't get fat spend all their time shopping for clothes to show off their figures."

285

"Your Chui Kim won't go to either extreme. She works hard, and she's the best looking Chinese girl in Bangkok. She reminds me of Mui Eng as a girl, with something of you about the eyes. Meng Chu is the one who looks most like Mui Eng, though—I mean, the way she looked when I used to hide behind old Nguan Thong's kitchen door in Sampheng Lane."

"Meng Chu is like my mother, can't you see that? Every time I look at the child, I am reminded of her."

He shrugged and said, "I don't know, I see your mother more in Bak Li."

"Bak Li? No, no—she looks like Ang Buai, if anyone."

"Aw, come on . . . your Bak Li is a dumpling, and Ang Buai at her age was a dried noodle!" He noticed the irritation written on my face then and quickly added, "But who can say? Every child has a little of each ancestor, and a good thing it is, too. Well, are you interested in Seng Huat or not? I guarantee his character and after all, I wouldn't bring you a bad son-in-law, would I?"

"How did you get to know so much about these people?"

"To tell you the truth, one of the girls his father wanted Seng Huat to look over was our Rose. I told him the girl was promised, of course, but it wouldn't have mattered, because the boy took one look at her dark complexion and gave his father the 'never' look over a bowl of hot and sour soup. And you should have heard what Rose had to say about him when she found out—but maybe I'd better not tell you. It might spoil all your wonderful ideas about her."

"I don't know what to say, Kim. Character is so difficult to judge, unless you have known a man all his life. It is not like our village, where we knew that old Li's son had a cheerful smile for everyone but beat his dogs half to death every time he lost his temper. Do you remember? No decent man would marry his daughter to such a boy."

"I understand. Old Li's son . . ." He shook his head. "I'd forgotten all about him until this moment. Look, why don't you let the kids meet, look the boy over yourself, and between you and Chui Kim you ought to pick up any suspicious signs, right? All I can tell you is that he works hard, he seems like a nice, serious boy, and I think it might be a perfect match—she's pretty, he's tight with his money, and they're both hard workers."

"I will give you an answer in two or three days."

It would take about that long, I knew, to conduct my own investigation of Mr. Seng Huat. *Sae* brothers of mine in his neighborhood gave me essentially the same information about the young man: diligent, well-mannered and perhaps a bit too "thrifty."

Given the boy's predilection for criticizing his father's choices, I did not wish to conduct the affair exactly according to our custom, whereby the young man sees the girl first, knowing that her family is willing, and may end the negotiations then and there. Instead, I decided to be sure of his interest in Chui Kim before allowing him to think her available.

Chui Kim, one of our drivers and I pulled up to the curb before their rice warehouse on the Monday following. I sent her in to place an order for two sacks of rice per week and, after fifteen minutes of a precisely timed errand nearby, we returned to fetch her. (If you wonder at my using the automobile, there are valid exceptions to any vow, dear Mother. I considered taking the pickup truck at length before deciding that Seng Huat was to be given no opportunity to insult either my daughter's appearance or her family's situation.)

Chui Kim stood outside the shop, waiting for us patiently with a cheerful smile on her pretty face. I got out of the car and strode into the shop, motioning the driver to park the car and wait. A hulking young fellow rose from a chair behind the counter as I entered, bowed respectfully, and extended his hand.

"Welcome, sir!"

"Everything all right, young man?'

"Yes, sir!" (Not bad looking, pale skin, bright eyes, an intelligent expression.) "We guarantee delivery on time, absolutely! And if you run out, we can send another bag within half an hour. You just phone us, sir, and don't worry—we guarantee good service!"

Well, well . . . perhaps Kim had hit upon something after all.

After this outburst of salesmanship, Seng Huat's eyes strayed carefully to Chui Kim, who stood shyly in the doorway, and rested on her with something like awe . . . and she did look charming in her carefully pressed black slacks and a long, straight, red and black blouse, wearing only as much makeup as she believed I wouldn't notice.

I called her to join us, and she reached my side just as Seng Huat's father emerged from the back room, a small, pleasant-looking man of about fifty with stiff gray hair and several gold teeth.

"I thought I knew that voice!" he declared, shaking his finger at me. "Suang U, what brings you into our shop? I haven't seen you at the society in—why, it must be months! Too busy making money, eh? Ha ha ha!"

"I am here supporting your business, sir!"

"Wonderful . . ." He turned his gaze on Chui Kim, then, and raised his eyebrows comically. "Can this be your daughter? Incredible!" He winked at Chui Kim, then glanced at his son with such meaning that I almost laughed aloud.

"This is my son, Seng Huat. But you must remember him from the society, eh? He often goes in my place."

"No, I'm afraid not. Well, it was nice meeting you, young man."

Once home and in the presence of her sisters, the shy blossom opened its petals and was revealed as a dragonflower. Had Seng Huat's father heard the conversation between my daughters that afternoon, he'd have locked his son in the shop for as long as it took him to make other plans . . .

"Believe me, Bak Li, he was devastated . . ." Throaty, American movie star laughter as she threw herself down on the couch and reached languidly for a spiced plum from the bowl Bak Li had set on the floor between them.

Bak Li sat cross-legged on a small rug, her eyes shining with excitement. "Ooh . . . it must have been thrilling!"

"M-m-m. When I walked into the shop, his eyes bulged out like this—"

Bak Li's mouth dropped open with astonishment as her elder sister imitated someone suffering from goiter.

"If Papa had let me enter the Vachiravudh Pageant, I just know I'd have won at least second place!"

"Yah, yah!" Meng Chu interrupted rudely, passing through the room with a plateful of cakes to sustain her through an hour's study upstairs. "Whoever saw the lovely princess was blinded by her face and form . . . like crumbs of stale cake, she brushed them from her fingers!"

"You're crazy," Chui Kim said, narrowing her eyes dangerously at

288

the younger girl. "Why don't you go watch cartoons on TV or something, child?"

"No time. It so happens I have to improve my mind with algebra, but I'd rather watch cartoons than listen to you two any time."

"What does he look like?" Bak Li asked eagerly, stuffing her mouth with another plum.

"Like a cretin!" Meng Chu shouted from halfway up the stairs, "if Chui Kim's imitation is any good!"

They ignored her.

"Handsome, I would say. Papa, do you think he's handsome?"

I had just entered the room from my office, unable to stand a moment more of this conversation that crept through the wall and destroyed concentration entirely. "Where is your mother, Bak Li?"

"At the dentist's."

"Ah . . . Chui Kim, I do not consider that a man's appearance is of any importance. However, aside from his appearance, what did you think of him?"

"I only spent ten minutes with him, Papa."

"Quite, but do you think he looks like—that is, is he the kind of boy you would think of as—suitable?"

"Papa!" she scarcely breathed, dramatically raising her hand to her throat. "I thought you said I was too young to think of—men!"

"Too young to begin thinking of men, yes! But not too young to be thinking of marriage."

"Oh, it's too thrilling!" Bak Li cried, clasping her hands together ecstatically.

"Bak Li, be quiet! When I listen to these—these improper conversations between the two of you, I know for a certainty that sixteen is not an unreasonable age for betrothal. As a matter of fact, the sooner it can be accomplished, the better for all concerned!"

"But Papa," Chui Kim said, confused, "you hardly know him yourself."

"Chui Kim, how often does Papa take you anywhere in Mama's car?" Bak Li said with a shrewd glance in my direction.

"Oh . . . I mean, I never thought—"

"Never mind that," I snapped. "Do you like him well enough for me to pursue arrangements?"

Chui Kim studied the half-chewed plum in her hand for a moment, then, with a coy, dreadful simper, said, "I can hardly say I'll marry a man I hardly know. I mean, at this point—"

"This is the only point! You'll never see him again unless the answer is yes."

"That sounds like a line from the Chinese opera," she tittered, and Bak Li stuffed two more plums into her mouth with the excitement of it all.

Five days after that Kim stalked into my office, beaming and rubbing his hands together.

"Ho ho, my friend, we did it! Seng Huat is in love, watering at the mouth and begging the old man to settle the deal this week. The kid found out where Chui Kim's dressmaking shop is, and he hides in a friend's place across the street every night to watch her leave. Now I ask you, is that love? Ha ha ha!"

Should I have received this startling news more gratefully?

"The old man is willing to set Chui Kim up with her own shop," he continued. "Seng Huat will continue to work with him for awhile, but of course he'll sleep at her shop. That means they'll be on their own, and she'll like that. You know, plenty of girls would give anything for that kind of future."

"No doubt. And what do you gain from all this, Kim?"

"You think I'm doing this for money? Shame on you, old friend! Out of gratitude, they insist on giving me, perhaps, a few hundred baht . . . but it's your daughter's happiness that makes it worthwhile to me. After all, we're almost relatives."

"It is up to Chui Kim. If she changes her mind, I won't force her, that's never any good. If a girl runs off with another man later, then what? Shame on the whole family. But she seems pleased with him, thank the gods."

And so the financial aspects of the match proceeded.

"Chui Kim's shop has been leased," Kim announced proudly two weeks later. "A beauty, too. The best sewing machines, clothes racks and new cabinets, huge mirrors all over the place, everything the girl could want. Seng Huat has found himself the wife he dreamed of, the old man is beside himself with joy and willing to give her anything, and Chui Kim has made a match you can all be proud of."

290

"They must be spending thousands."

"Thousands? Tens of thousands! It's a three-story building, Suang U: family on the top floor, work rooms on the second and customers below in fancy fitting rooms. And wait until you hear this . . . in two months, the second son is going to work with the old man, and Seng Huat will run a big fabric business in the same building with Chui Kim! Your daughter will be a rich woman before ten years have passed, believe me."

"Are the dates set?" I asked calmly, unwilling to show the great emotion I felt. A splendid future for one's child is the dream of every father.

"Betrothal third month, day of the full moon, wedding tenth month. That's why I stopped by, to tell you—oh, and the wedding cakes. I forgot to ask what you want."

"Kim, for heaven's sake don't ask them for cakes when I own a bakery! It would be foolish.

"Why? A few cakes are nothing to them."

"Household furniture must come from the bride's family," I said, cutting off further discussion of cakes. "I have to start thinking about that pretty soon. What do you think she would like?"

"Just ask her!" he laughed. "I'll bet she's already got it planned down to the last salt shaker."

Kim was right. From a great stack of foreign magazines, she, Bak Li and Mui Eng decorated the new household. They ordered a great double bed with a foreign-style mattress a foot thick, a thousand-baht bedspread, a dressing table, wardrobe closet, bedside tables with fancy lamps, curtains and chairs and pillows and an endless number of other "necessities." For three days after the smiling furniture maker delivered his estimate, I was too sick to my stomach to eat.

Even Meng Chu was drafted to embroider pillow slip edges and curtain hems, but all the actual sewing for the new household Chui Kim did herself, beautifully. Weng Khim, following my example and staying out of their way entirely, seems shocked at the notion that anyone would want to marry one of his irksome sisters, but he looks forward to the wedding festivities.

And in the matter of clothing, dear Mother, is our daughter buying clothes for a lifetime? Anyone would think they were moving to a desert island instead of into a shop where people do nothing but make clothes all day. Whenever I ask Mui Eng about the bills, she freezes me with an icy stare and goes off muttering that I would probably prefer to see my daughter leave her father's house in rags.

But I am pleased, I must confess. My first-born daughter is being married in style, under the approving eyes of merchants whose good opinion I respect. Seng Huat's familly is spending tens of thousands of baht on her future and giving a wedding dinner for twenty-five tables of our colleagues at a fine restaurant. I consider Chui Kim's marriage one of the sweetest fruits of my labor.

I shall allow the two young people to go about together on certain occasions once the betrothal has been announced (provided that Mui Eng is free to accompany them, of course). Seng Huat has already asked if Chui Kim may go with him to buy the bride's jewelry. She has asked for a ring, earrings and a necklace. When I expressed surprise that she had not asked for a precious metal belt, all the females in my house rolled their eyes upward and shook their heads pityingly, for Chui Kim does not even own the outdated garment that requires such a belt. Thus a custom long observed disappears, by order of fashion.

I hope that you are pleased, Mother. I shall close this letter now and go for a walk in the moonlight to contemplate one chapter in the life of this family which appears to be without flaw. My daughter shall marry the man I have chosen, in a wedding that brings honor to us all.

LETTER #71

5 MAY 1962

FOURTH MONTH, SECOND DAY

YEAR OF THE TIGER

SENG HUAT'S family sent Kim to our house bearing gifts wrapped in red paper—the ring, earrings, and necklace she helped choose, together with six thousand baht in betrothal money and a few cakes they insisted on buying at another bakery. So the day of Chui Kim's betrothal passed. According to our custom, no one from the groom's family entered our home, and Chui Kim had to stay inside, hidden even from Kim's view. I solemnly handed him an envelope containing one hundred and twenty baht. What Seng Huat's people gave him I did not ask.

After he had driven off, Bak Li complained, "Some betrothal! He didn't even put the ring on her finger."

"Why should Kim put the ring on her finger?"

"Not Kim, Papa—Seng Huat! I thought he would put the ring on her finger, and all the parents and everybody would watch

"What is that, some Thai custom?"

"Thai custom, indeed!" Mui Eng snorted. "It is the *farang* way! Thai betrothals are like ours, and before the last few years nobody gave rings. Why, twenty years ago Thai young people never saw each other at all until the day of their wedding."

"Oh, Mother, you see pictures in the newspaper every day of society girls getting diamond rings from their fiances."

"That is no business of mine," her mother returned, "and your sister's betrothal was as it should be. I, for one, see no purpose to this ring nonsense."

Chui Kim said nothing but opened the packages carefully, obviously content with her choices. She tried on all the jewelry and smiled at herself approvingly in a small hand mirror.

"Put it all away now," Mui Eng said when everyone had sufficiently admired the bride-to-be and the tokens of her young man's intentions; and slowly she removed the earrings and necklace and placed them in their lovely boxes.

"And the ring!"

"But no one will know I'm betrothed if I don't wear it!"

"It's valuable, child, not a toy. Everyone who matters to us knows you are betrothed, but a thief in the street won't care whether you are or not when he snatches it off your finger, and what do we tell Seng Huat's papa then?"

"But all the girls in the shop are waiting to see it," she wailed. "They think I've had a real engagement, not—not Uncle Kim driving up with three red packages and six thousand baht, while I hide in the kitchen. Some of the girls have even brought snapshots of their engagement parties, Mama. I'd just die if they knew what happened here today!"

"Now, now . . . I suppose . . . well, one day might be all right." She patted the girl's shoulder sympathetically and wiped away a few tears of her own. "You've nothing to be ashamed of, but if it will make you feel better, I'll send you over in the car tomorrow, and the driver will pick you up again in the afternoon. But you mustn't let him see your ring, either, do you understand?"

"Don't you trust anybody?" asked Chui Kim, dabbing at her eyes with a tea towel.

"Of course not! And I am not unreasonable—it isn't a two-hundred-baht bauble. When you show it to your friends, keep it on your hand."

"Oh, I won't ever take it off, Mama. An engagement ring should never be taken off!"

"What do you mean? You should take a good ring off every time you put your hands into soap and water, or the stones will grow dull. Wear a dress with a big pocket when you take it to show at work, and put the ring in your pocket every time you wash your hands."

"I will, Mama. It's the most important thing I've ever owned."

"M-m . . . and one day is enough to play *farang*, too. Tomorrow night you put it back in the box, and if anyone in the shop asks you about it the next day you simply say your mother won't allow you to wear it, and anyone who raises an eyebrow at that is a fool. Playing *farang* is a cheap way to behave, Chui Kim. You are less of a person when you despise what you are. Why, when I was a girl, the government even made laws requiring people to do it, and they tired of it soon enough."

"Do what, play *farang?*" I asked, interested.

Mui Eng took a blouse from her sewing basket, draped it neatly over her wide lap, and smiled. "Hats! There was a time—long before you came to my father's house—when the government decreed that we all had to wear European style hats, and skirts too. I shall never forget the Chinese girls who carry water buckets on poles across their shoulders; they went trundling down the street with skirts pulled over their ordinary pants. They looked like so many rag piles!" She chuckled and began to ply her needle through an intricate pattern of embroidery on one sleeve of the blouse with plump, deft fingers. "And if a woman went out in the evening, she had to wear gloves—that was worse than the hats! Betel nut chewing was declared illegal—it was dirty, they said. And I suppose it is, but old ladies were dropping over in the street from being deprived of it. Worst of all, husbands and wives were encouraged to kiss each other good-bye in public places if one of them was going away somewhere. That, they said, was what the *farang* did to show

294

how much they would miss each other—imagine!"

An uninvited fantasy of myself kissing Mui Eng in the Hua Lamphong railway station floated into my mind and raised the hair on the back of my neck, and I thanked any number of gods that such madness had passed before I arrived in Thailand.

"What was the purpose of these laws?"

"Before the war Thai leaders told us that in the powerful Western nations people wore hats and gloves and kissed each other, and no one chewed betel nut. If we behaved in such ways, we would grow more like them, you see, and the Thai nation might grow to be a great power too."

As if one could dress up a chicken and convince the world it was a peacock! And what is even more to the point, chickens have been of far more use to this world than peacocks.

The next afternoon, Mui Eng, the children, and I carried great boxes of betrothal gifts round the bakery to all our employees.

Was the bridegroom handsome? all the women wanted to know, covering their mouths with their hands and giggling. Chui Kim, without the least hesitation, joined in their game.

"One day I will pull him in here and let you see for yourselves!" she laughed gaily.

My face burned with shame for her, but the conceited girl was not paying any attention to me.

"Are you going to bring him in on the end of a rope, then?" an old Thai crone shouted gleefully as she rolled out a huge square of pale dough.

"No need for that, old one! He's already tamed!"

Everyone in the bakery shouted with laughter as I turned away, clenching my teeth in anger.

I knocked on the door of Chui Kim's room.

"Come in! Oh, it's you, Papa . . . I'm just going over this pattern to be sure it's the right size before I cut the material." She put the pile of cloth and paper aside and looked up expectantly, her hands neatly folded in her lap.

"Where is Bak Li?"

"Over at Auntie's, with Mama. Her dog is sick."

"Ah . . . Chui Kim, your behavior this afternoon was disgraceful."

"What do you mean, Papa?" she asked in a small, frightened voice.

"You showed contempt for your betrothed before our employees. You behaved like a fool, an idiot! Seng Huat is the man who will be your husband, the master of your future, yet you have the gall to speak of him in fun, laugh at him—you, a woman! Do you think it became you to show disrespect for the man you will serve for the rest of your life? I expect no more than that of laborers in a bakery, but you . . . is this all I am to expect of my own daughter?"

The girl stared miserably at the hands she held clenched in her lap. Slowly, great tears began to fall on them, which she did not brush away.

"How could you not realize they were enjoying the fact that you made fun of Seng Huat, that they were spitting in his face?"

"Oh, no . . . surely they realized—"

"Surely they realized—nothing! So you are the great beauty, eh? A stupid, vain, ungrateful girl who allows a lot of common laborers to insult her betrothed! Pray that he will never hear of this, Chui Kim . . . You were born a female, but you should have learned by now how to behave like a lady. With modesty, and respect for others, especially for your father and your husband. You are the daughter of a respectable merchant and there is no excuse for talking like a slut in the marketplace!"

She covered her face with both hands and began to sob, but I was not yet finished. "A truly beautiful woman must be beautiful within, Chui Kim, for the years will pass, and wrinkles and flesh will mock the memory of that beauty contest you once thought so important. You will bear children and grow old, die and rot in the ground just like the plainest girl who ever walked down this street. Look to your soul, Chui Kim, not your pretty face . . . You think over what I have said this evening, and remember that if your Papa did not love you very much, his words would not have been so harsh."

The thick, dark hair encircling her bowed head gleamed in the light of her little bedside lamp, and I felt great tenderness for her. When at last she raised her eyes to mine, I was astonished at the change in her expression, for the smug complacency which had been growing since the day she met Seng Huat had been lifted from her features, and the mischief and self-importance of childhood had begun its retreat.

I feel certain now that she understands what is expected of her. It is too bad that her mother did not train her better, but Mui Eng has worked hard, we have all worked hard. If only you had been here, Chui Kim would be going to her husband more of a woman, and no less a beauty.

NOW I have only three children living in my home, for Chui Kim is a married woman with a home of her own. Bak Li gives less attention to her tasks at home than before and Meng Chu is at school all day, so that we are in a state of some confusion. I am not discontent. Chinese people like us do not hope for more than to see our children well married, producing families of their own. Life has its proper seasons, and daughters must leave their parents when they reach the age of marriage, though having only one son means a rather lonely old age, I am afraid. Most of my grandchildren shall play on other old men's knees.

I have learned that the wedding ceremony in our age is sadly lacking in dignity. Chui Kim's face fell when she was informed of my determination to observe our custom and stay at home. The bride's parents do not attend the wedding.

"But why can't you be there, Papa? All the girls' parents attend their weddings now. Do you mean to say that neither of my parents is going to sit at my wedding dinner?"

"It is not so terrible, child. They have given you a table for ten, and if you take Weng Khim and your sisters, you may still invite seven friends. But your parents will not attend, and that is final. Seng Huat's father would be shocked if we were to appear at the dinner, believe me."

The auspicious time for the bride to be sent to her new home on the wedding day was set at 3:45 in the morning, in the darkness before dawn. During the preceding evening, all the household was in a state of terrible confusion, and we rushed from one room to another loaded down with clothing, pots and pans, blankets and tablecloths, bags of shoes, and boxes of kitchen utensils, all the accumulated "necessities" gleaned over the past weeks.

Mui Eng would have sent almost everything over the week before, had I allowed it, but only the furniture went ahead, and Mui Eng sent a girl to clean the rooms. To do more than that would not have been proper. Or perhaps I am simply more superstitious than I like to think I am.

Kim was with us that evening, supervising every detail in his capacity of matchmaker, and a driver and car were sent from Seng Huat's house. With all this activity, though, there was a queer silence in our house, as if some mysterious plot were being carried out instead of the preparations for a joyous wedding. For three days we would not see our daughter, and she would return to us as the mistress of another house. Our pretty baby, Weng Khim's little sister . . . I had not reckoned with this aspect of marrying off one's daughters, and it was not pleasant.

Chui Kim dressed meticulously and made up her face more vividly than ever before. I said nothing, for a bride always powders her face pink to mask her pallor, according to our own custom. No doubt, however, she did not know that and thought it was her new status which influenced my acceptance of her bright cheeks and dark-rimmed eyes.

When I learned that Ang Buai would attend the wedding dinner, I was pleased. It was well, I thought, to have an adult accompany the children, and she could bring them home herself, which put my mind greatly at ease, for a driver cannot be trusted in the event of an emergency.

Weng Khim has been begging to drive the car, but I haven't allowed myself to be dragged into an argument about it. Now, however, I have decided to let him learn, for soon he will be old enough for a license and able to drive his sisters about, which will save me money and worry. I shall enjoy the look of stupefaction which is sure to cover his face when he learns the unexpected good news.

When the hour drew near, Mui Eng and I presented Chui Kim with our personal gifts—a ring and a gold watch, a jeweled necklace and a matching bracelet. These I bought with the betrothal money from Seng Huat's family, lest they wonder whether I sought money for myself in return for the raising of a daughter. The old man will understand at once when he sees these gifts, which were not spoken of before. She leaves our house with many trunks full of fine clothing, and enters a house we have furnished without stinting.

I began this letter by noting that weddings today lack dignity. Bak Li and Meng Chu returned late the next evening with their brother and aunt, all of them excited and full of stories about the great events of the day, and I heard quite enough to congratulate myself on remaining at home.

Friends of the groom have played their tricks in all generations. I should not be surprised that, in an era which celebrates bad taste, this harmless custom should be twisted into something ugly.

I remember finding a bridegroom asleep beside a stack of rice chaff on our farm one evening when I was about nine years old. The poor fellow woke with a start, looked about wildly, then sighed with relief when he recognized me, little Suang U, leading his ducks home. He had borrowed this uncomfortable sleeping place, he explained with a wry laugh, because his friends had claimed his nuptial bed. His bride had been spirited away by his sisters to the safety of their own room.

Now, none of these boisterous fellows would have dreamed of involving the girl. Her new sisters-in-law were warned well in advance of the joke, and she never saw the pranksters, who sang, shouted, and kept the household awake all night. Now, I do not cite that incident as an example of "dignity," to be sure, but weddings here, today, combine the worst elements of Thai, Chinese, and *farang* customs in regard to teasing the newly married couple. Any piece of foolishness that occurs to anyone can be excused by blaming it on another nation's "custom," though I doubt that the worst of such behavior can be fairly laid at any nation's door. Why is it, in this nation, that the best examples of foreign behavior are of little interest to anyone, while excesses of all sorts are fashionable so long as they are imported?

"It was fun!" Bak Li announced, searching through the refrigerator for a snack two hours after the wedding feast. "Chui Kim had to pin flowers on all the guests, and some of Seng Huat's friends stood on chairs so that we would have to lift her in the air to reach their lapels! She got sort of mad after awhile."

"Ugh!" This from Meng Chu, who was carefully unwrapping the pieces of cake she had brought for her mother and me. "It was ugly. She didn't even know those people, and she was tired. It would have been enough to give presents, it seems to me, without the bride hopping up and down pinning things on people. I would have refused."

"Oh, you . . . you don't have any sense of humor, Meng Chu. Anyway, Chui Kim didn't do that for long. After about ten of them, she pinned a flower on one fellow's pants cuff and sat down at our table with her backs to the rest of them.

Mui Eng looked disturbed. "How can a bride allow herself to be made fun of like that? I don't think it's right."

"Oh, she's been to other weddings and seen the same thing. Chui Kim knew what would happen."

"Bak Li, didn't you look at the old people?" Meng Chu asked. "They were all frowning at each other, and when Elder Sister pinned the flower to that boy's cuff and turned away with her nose in the air, they all laughed. They were glad to see that she had a mind of her own."

"That part wasn't as bad as when they tried to get the bride and groom to kiss," Bak Li giggled, "right in front of everyone!"

"Indeed!" I heard myself splutter indignantly, and everyone laughed.

"Seng Huat was willing enough," Meng Chu said, "but don't worry, Papa—Chui Kim refused even to look at him when they started shouting 'Kiss the bride!'"

"I didn't see anything so terrible about it," Bak Li said. "After all, they are married."

Mui Eng shook her finger at Bak Li and said, "You all see too many *farang* movies! Chinese people don't show themselves in public that way, nor Thais either . . . m-m the cake is delicious." She pressed the tines of her fork to the last crumbs on her plate and delicately licked them off.

Bak Li has left the flower garden. She is fifteen. I expect we will have little trouble with her now that Chui Kim is gone, for certainly Meng Chu will not encourage the giggling, gossiping, and obsession with matters of appearance that she and Chui Kim shared so enthusiastically.

———

LETTER #73   FIRST MONTH, TENTH DAY
3 FEBRUARY 1963   YEAR OF THE HARE

AVOIDING SERVICE in the army has always been a problem for the Chinese people in Thailand. These days the matter is largely one of money, but according to Mui Eng it was not always so.

Years ago, she told me recently, when relations between Thailand and China were convenient, we were free to pass back and forth between the two nations. Not even passports were required. Many a Chinese boy born in Thailand journeyed to visit his grandparents shortly before his twentieth birthday—only to return as an "immigrant," and bearing a new name, for first-generation Chinese, as I have written before, are not desired by the Thai army. This technique cost only the passage to and from China and the yearly payment of alien taxes, which for some reason have never been very high.

Another technique still favored by some (mainly Thais) is "poor health." After the young man has taken strong purgatives and water but no food for the seven days before his physical examination, the army doctor who examines him on the eighth day is sure to shake his head sympathetically and send the pitiful invalid home to live out his last few weeks or months among his loved ones. This method too often has a most undesirable sequel, for a boy with a weak constitution may justify the doctor's sympathy by dropping dead in earnest.

For awhile, there was a condition known as "crooked fingers," an affliction which caused the hands of young men to stiffen into a permanently rigid, claw-like position despite the medical examiners' attempts to straighten them out. The wily army doctors, however, were not long fooled by this sudden epidemic of crippled hands, and before long they perfected a technique for its cure. Cheerfully they would assure the victim of "crooked fingers" that he was useless to the army and free to pursue his life as best he could with his sad affliction. Then they would watch the hand that reached for the doorknob . . .

It is clear to me that our Weng Khim will not escape the draft by any such lunatic scheme, and though some time remains before we must face the problem, I am concerned. For we want to see him married to Rose by the age of twenty, starting a family of his own, not marching around the countryside eating brown rice.

Early this week, I informed him that beginning next month I shall pay him a much higher salary than he has been getting.

"Of course, you are very young, and while a stranger might pay you eight hundred baht a month—which is what I intend to pay you, and what I believe you to be worth—very probably he would not, because of your age. But I am your father, I know your worth."

301

Weng Khim ducked his head and grinned, pleased at the rare compliment.

"Most of the money you must save, son, toward the draft . . . this should be your own responsibility now, for you are nearly a man. With eight hundred baht a month you should have enough for your own expenses and, say two hundred baht a month to put away against the day the government tries to turn you into a private in the Thai army! You might give it to your mother to keep for you, or to me, but I shall leave that decision up to you."

"In the bank would be better!" he said quickly. "I mean, it would earn interest and—and I would have the feeling, you know, that it was really in my own hands. I would like that very much, Papa—"

"Very well. At the end of this month, then, you will become a man with capital. But from now on, you must dedicate yourself to your work with a new sense of purpose. As the son of the house, you are more accountable for what you do than any of the other employees. I shall put you in charge of bookkeeping for the bakery and your mother's shop. After all, they will be yours someday. At the end of every week, I shall check your work and before long you'll know the business better than I do myself."

Weng Khim's face shone with pride, and—something else, some other indefinable emotion. Always before, he has had to come to me for everything. Now, he is the master of his own purse. Perhaps I am overly optimistic, but even if he squanders a little of the money, it seems to me that he cannot help but save six thousand baht in the three years ahead.

"There is one more thing I wish to speak to you about, Weng Khim."

He frowned slightly, unable to think of any other serious business I might have with him.

"We would like you to marry at twenty."

His eyes widened with surprise for just a moment, then suspicion clouded his features. "I—explain what you mean, please—"

"Rose."

"Rose?"

"Damn it, why must you say her name with that sneer in your voice? She's a fine-looking girl and she will make you a strong, sensible wife."

"But—I can't stand that girl!" he cried out desperately, fighting back tears. "Rose is just a common working girl! She has no manners at all!"

"Because of that 'common working girl,' you will prosper, believe me—and who are we, Weng Khim, millionaires in a palace?"

"You don't understand, Papa," he replied, shaking his head miserably. "It isn't as if Rose were—well, like the girls in our family, wearing pretty clothes, acting educated. Rose acts like any fish peddler in the Yaowarat Market. She screeches and scolds, and she doesn't care about her clothes, or fixing her hair, or anything like that. I would be ashamed to have such a wife . . . oh please, Papa, don't make me marry Rose . . ."

It is irritating, I cannot deny it. But who knows how either of them may change in three years? It is not an easy thing to plan the futures of one's children today. I am gratified by my success in the matter of Chui Kim's marriage, but I know that it would be unreasonable to expect them all to go so well.

Though Bak Li works away from home, she has been helping her mother more lately, usually until ten in the morning. She works into the evening at the beauty parlor, which her employer actually prefers. Meng Chu continues to rise from one class to another with no sign of leaving school, but she has carried out her promise to help us every spare moment she has.

"I'm sure now that I want to study bookkeeping when I graduate," she announced yesterday with her usual aplomb. "And Chinese, and more English, but I'm not bothering with the abacus. Why don't you buy an adding machine, Papa? You could get a good one for only about five thousand baht."

"M-m . . . I never cease to be impressed at the way you people can dash off these 'only's.' A man earns that much in a year and considers himself fortunate, and anyway, it's a poor mind that needs a machine to do its thinking."

I have bought a typewriter, which Meng Chu uses for our Thai correspondence, and which I myself consider a good purchase. It is satisfying to see her make her careful way around the elaborate, intimidating keyboard, with its sixty-four letter keys and numerous other numbers, signs, and symbols, and then to see the finished product: a neat, respectable letter with all the words and figures in clean, orderly rows. Even though she studies hard, she finds time to help me whenever I call on her, even watches a television program now and then, and still she stays at the top of her class. When it came time to leave the lower school, she made all the arrangements herself and went to Mui Eng for tuition money to enter the upper school. It is not expensive, because it is supported by the government and available therefore to all children—all, that is, whose parents can afford to postpone the wages they might earn if they left school. The only added expense she has had since changing schools is lunch money; for the first time Meng Chu refuses to take food with her.

"I am too old now to take my lunch, Mama. Everyone would stare at me as if I were crazy."

And Mama never refuses her anything, but I do not complain, for even now Meng Chu takes her mother's and sisters' old clothes and makes them over for herself, just as she did when she was a small girl. In the upper school, she is associating for the first time with children from other backgrounds than her own, and it is not a painless experience.

"There are a lot of rich Thai children there with long names like poems, and they laugh at me because my Thai surname is Thai-yuenyong . . . well, so what . . . I ignore them, because they have something bad to say about everybody except themselves."

"The hell with them!" I said, "We live our life, they live theirs."

"I won't be first in my class in this school, Papa. Some of the kids' parents have had government posts abroad, and they know a lot of things that girls like me never heard of. Some of them speak better English than the teacher, and even French, and they have tutors at home for science and mathematics. How can I compete with that?"

"Do your best, Meng Chu, and if you aren't first in the class you will have nothing to be ashamed of. If it makes you feel any better, your Papa is very proud of you . . ."

She works like none of the other children. For two months before an examination, she never looks at the television set, and even during school vacations she is at the books every day. No man can hope for more from his children than that they do their best, and this child knows no other way.

I end this letter with the cautious hope that our family is approaching greater harmony than it has known in the last few years, and pray as ever that you are well and happy.

I WAS a fool, to tempt the scorn of the gods by suggesting that our family was "approaching greater harmony". . .

What now, you will be thinking, when Chui Kim is well married and Suang U, for once in his life, should be content. Your grandson, it grieves me to write, has brought unhappiness upon us, and my head feels as though it must burst with the confusion and humiliation which he has called down upon our household. Never did I dream that my love for this only son and all my hopes for him would one day be rewarded by deceit and ugly words. Four months ago, I gave the boy a monthly salary generous enough to allow him to save toward his twentieth birthday. This money, every satang of it, he has used for evil purposes.

I began to notice, a month or so ago, that he was becoming somewhat less careful in his work than usual, and making peculiar errors, but it was not until Meng Chu reluctantly came to me with the truth that I realized why my son had little strength for work.

How could he stand before me, lying in my face as he asked if he might put his money into a bank instead of leaving it in our safe? I cannot help but realize that he intended from the first to behave deceitfully, and that is the most painful aspect of it all. How little regard he must have for me . . .

Meng Chu knocked on my office door one evening soon after Weng Khim had left for the Chinese school, and her eyes were red with weeping.

"Whatever is wrong, child?" I asked, filled with alarm, for Meng Chu seldom cries.

"It isn't me, Papa . . . I have something to tell you, something bad. I don't want to, but—I must! You know, I'm the one who lets him in at night, and he—Weng Khim—he comes home drunk every night, Papa. I don't want to be a tattle-tale, but to see my brother like—like that, I just can't bear it any longer . . ."

My mouth was dry as ashes, and it was all I could do to find breath enough to say, "You have done the right thing, Meng Chu."

She turned and fled then, to spare not herself but me, for there was no way I could hide my pain from her.

Weng Khim slouched into the office with an expression in his eyes I had not seen there before. Clearly, he had abandoned a no longer useful pose and stood ready to confront me on ground we had never occupied before.

"So the little brat came to you with stories!"

"I don't see it that way at all, Weng Khim. It is the duty of brothers and sisters to protect each other, and that is why Meng Chu told me . . . what she told me, to protect you. I gave you eight hundred baht a month so that you could save toward your twentieth birthday. Or is it that you want to be a common soldier?"

He did not answer, but his eyes were hard, his mouth set resolutely.

"Well? You want to eat brown rice, live like a peasant? After the way you've been raised, I doubt whether your stomach or your muscles are equal to life in the Thai army."

"I shall begin to save money," he said, "when I have bought something I need more than freedom from the draft."

"And what is that?"

"Fun!" he replied, with a silly, insolent smirk. "The kind of fun other boys my age have and consider their right, Papa. I want to go out with my friends after work and enjoy myself. Frankly, I don't know why that should frighten you," he added sarcastically.

"Frankly? Frighten me? What the hell is the matter with you? You are talking to your father, Weng Khim, and I have news for you—it's all over! All this filthiness you have learned from your fine friends. From this day forward, you will sit at your desk and attend to your responsibilities like a man instead of shambling through the work with a brain numbed by whiskey and the kind of women that crawl around those places—"

He compressed his lips angrily, but made no response. Instead, he turned and stalked from the room, slamming the door behind him.

A boy of Weng Khim's age feels strongly the need of women. That is natural, but the girl we would have him marry he does not want. What does he know of women? Those with grace and dignity of spirit are seldom the ones who inflame young men's passions. Why it is so, I do not know, but that great accident of nature has blighted many lives, including my own.

That evening, I knocked on his bedroom door. After waiting a moment for some response, I entered to find him stretched out on his bed reading a cheap Thai novel. He did not look up.

"Son, do you want to get married? I realize that—well, at your age . . ."

"Sure I want to get married. But to someone I love, Father, and I doubt if you could choose such a girl."

"So my eye is that bad, eh? You talk as though I've offered you a hunchback whose face is covered with boils! Your sister seems happy enough with the spouse I chose for her."

At that, he put down his book and looked up, surprised. "You chose—I mean, didn't Chui Kim and Seng Huat know each other before?"

"No. It was my idea from their first meeting. Do they seem so miserable to you?"

He looked away, trying to digest this unexpected information.

"Khim, why must you make everything so difficult for yourself and for us? At least you could try to understand why Rose is the kind of wife I want you to have. You could ask yourself, 'What good reason has my Papa for encouraging this?' But no, you refuse to think in such a way, you prefer to think that your Papa only wants to boss you around. Am I wrong?"

Weng Khim answered me by picking up his book and turning the page. What could I do—strike him? I knew that there was nothing I could say now to reach his heart, and beating him could only destroy the slender thread left between us.

For two days, we did not speak to each other, though I was aware that he had gone to Meng Chu and threatened her. This did not worry me, for his feeble tantrums are no match for the ferocity of his mother where her baby is concerned. It was on the third morning after our sad confrontation that I came down to breakfast to learn of the disaster that has struck our household.

"Where is Weng Khim?"

Mui Eng did not look up from the pot of rice gruel she was stirring. "Not up yet, I suppose. Does he have an early errand today?"

"Mama," Meng Chu said, meticulously separating the shell of her boiled egg, "Weng Khim never came home last night. Go see for yourself."

"You knew it would happen!" a small, mocking voice whispered inside my brain. "The bond is broken, Suang U! You knew it a week ago—why pretend before them?"

"Hah—he's probably with some girl!" I said gruffly, ignoring the small voice, and no one dared to look at me. "Well, the hell with him, I'm starved."

It was the most ghastly meal of my life. I ate twice as much as I ordinarily do, joked with Meng Chu and Bak Li, and was scrupulously polite to Mui Eng. I knew that I looked like a death mask and sounded like a clown, but what did it matter? None of them looked at each other until I had left the table, stuffed and nauseated. I went to the bathroom and vomited, then worked the next fourteen hours without stopping, worked like the adding machine Meng Chu urged me to buy, ceaselessly, without rest or reason, unaware of fatigue or hunger.

Two days later Weng Khim returned briefly, while I was out.

Mui Eng moved slowly, heavily in the deepening evening shadows of the bedroom. She wrapped a fresh *sarong* about her pale, fleshy body in preparation for her bath, took a towel from her closet shelf, then turned and sank onto the bed, buried her face in the pillow and shook with sobs.

I stood motionless before the window, letting the hot, foul breath of Yaowarat Road and all the discordant braying of its traffic envelop me as the woman wept. I felt no desire for quiet, for a cool bath and fresh clothing, for hot tea and a newspaper, for any of the comforts a man welcomes at the end of a hard day. With refreshment comes the desire to renew efforts, eat good food, laugh with friends; I wanted nothing more than to stand at the window until the city sucked me once and for all into its corruption and had done with me.

"He took two or three suits of clothing . . . when I asked him . . . why, he wouldn't say a word . . . then when he was gone, I went upstairs, and—" Here she broke down completely and wailed, "My jewelry box, Suang U! He had forced it open and taken my best necklace, my wristwatch, a ring . . . Oh, husband!" She turned her swollen, mottled face up to me, and I stared at her in horror. "Oh, what terrible things did you say to him?" she asked, shaking her head in misery and bewilderment, and letting the tears run down her puffy cheeks from eyes that showed more of her than I had seen in all the years of our marriage.

"It will solve nothing to lie there and cry," I replied at last, unable to believe that our son had gone this far to humiliate us.

"Whatever he has done, he is our son," she said, pulling herself up and wiping her ravaged face with the towel. "Oh, my son, my boy! At the first hour of his manhood he has disgraced us with evil women— I know it is that . . ."

"Shut up and quit dramatizing yourself. The important thing is to find him, not revile him!"

"Find him?" she shouted angrily. "Where do you suggest we look?"

"We will go to the Chinese school first."

The Chinese master teaches in an ordinary storefront and has his lodgings above. When we arrived, the class Weng Khim had attended was still in progress, so we waited outside, avoiding each other's eyes and listening to the drone of voices repeating his meticulous phrases. After a few moments, he noticed us and signaled to one of the boys to take his place.

Without a word, he led us up the dark, narrow stairway to his rooms, unlocked the door, and bade us sit in his study while he prepared a pot of tea.

"Now, what may I do for you?" he asked kindly, pouring fragrant pale tea into three cups.

"I am the father of Tan Weng Khim."

"Yes, of course, I remember you."

"Does he come to the class?" I asked, knowing that my face burned with shame.

"No, he has not come for sometime . . . I thought you knew."

"How many days has he been absent?"

"Days? I am sorry, sir, but it has been months since the boy was here. I should say about three months—yes, he left at the same time as his friend Huang." Then, realizing that his words had stunned me, he smiled sympathetically and added, "I see that I am the bearer of unwelcome news. I am so sorry, Tan Suang U. Your son told me that he had too much work to do at home and would not be able to study any longer. I thought nothing of it at the time, for Weng Khim studied with me longer than any of my other boys, and it seemed reasonable to me that he would end his studies about now."

"Does he have any friends who are still in the class?"

"One or two, but you know, very few boys stay with me as long as your son.

"May I trouble you to call those who know him?"

The master nodded and excused himself, returning with two frightened-looking boys.

"I am Weng Khim's father," I said, finding it difficult to meet their eyes.

"He has not been home for three days, and I thought you boys might know where he has gone."

One of the boys, visibly relieved at not finding himself the subject of this meeting, cleared his throat and said, "Sir, Weng Khim has not been in the class for a long time—"

"We know that. Have you never seen him since?"

"Well, a few times, but he mostly hangs around with Huang."

"Where does this boy live?"

(Could it be the same, I wondered . . . the Huang with the birthday party those many years before? That father I have met; worse the shame. But then, it would be his shame as well.)

I learned Huang's address and we excused ourselves, our faces scarlet with embarrassment before the patient Chinese master.

"Tan Suang U," he said with a slow smile, "many a boy has strayed in the season of his youth and returned home to make his parents proud. Do not think that your Weng Khim is a bad boy."

It was not the same Huang, I was relieved to learn. This Huang is the son of a prosperous grocer whose shop was still open when I went there early that evening.

"Huang, eh?" The heavy, cynical face of the man arranged itself into an unpleasant smile. "Him you can see at two in the morning when he gets home, or at noon when he wakes up."

"He is your son?"

He did not reply, but turned to make change for a customer and wrap a half kilo of dried shrimp in a piece of newspaper. This is a man who has given up hope, and that I will never do.

Mui Eng's face questioned me anxiously. I shook my head without speaking and went straight to my office. Still, I could hear her irksome weeping, and wondered that she mourns so loudly the son whose bad habits she has always been willing to shrug off.

The next day important customers kept me home, men I could not send away. That was yesterday, and this noon I hurried again to the grocer's, only to find that the boy Huang had left an hour before.

Why must it be my only son who causes me such pain, Mother? The girls have given no real trouble, and my son-in-law Seng Huat is a fine young man. It is painful to reflect that his father can have done no more than I in raising a son. There is no sense to it all, no justice. Tomorrow I shall go again to the grocer's shop. Huang cannot avoid me forever.

—

LETTER #75   FIFTH MONTH, TENTH DAY
30 JUNE 1963   YEAR OF THE HARE

I AM deeply ashamed that my son has brought dishonor upon our family, and ashamed that you must learn of it from me. Sadly, there is no news in this letter but of further dishonor. I humbly apologize to you, and to the memory of my father and our ancestors. I can only pray that you will grieve with me and find it in your heart to forgive.

I waited in the grocery store for two hours that morning, until at last Huang came pelting down the stairs from the family rooms above, whistling cheerfully and smoothing back his long, wet-looking hair with pale, delicate hands that could never have done a man's work. When he spied me, sipping tea at a table near the front of the shop, he hesitated for a second, then swaggered toward me as best he could through the jostling crowd of his father's customers.

He recognized me, and I him, for this boy, I realized at once, had been in our home before. I had not liked the look of him then—furtive, somehow, and with the bad complexion that speaks of bad habits.

"I need your help," I said simply, as he approached the table. "Where is my son?"

He grinned insolently, dropped into the chair across from me, and propped his feet on another. "Who knows?"

"You do. I want to find my son and speak with him."

"Why, old man? So you can run his life? No way."

It was all I could do not to slap his sneering, pimply face. "It is clear that I cannot run his life," I said calmly, "but I am still his father. I want to know how he is, what his—his wife is like."

"Wife?" he cried gleefully, untangling his skinny legs and sitting up. "You can't be serious!"

"He is with a girl, isn't he? My daughter-in-law . . . is she pretty? Who are her parents?"

Huang stared at me in disbelief, then threw his head back and broke into a raucous braying that turned every head in the shop (except his father's). "Daughter-in-law? That's great! A Thai whore ten years older than he is! She won't hang onto him that long, Papa, don't worry!"

My eyes felt as though they must explode with the pressure behind them. How could a boy of less than twenty years speak so cruelly? My son has fallen into a vile pit, and this boy leans over the edge to jeer at him . . . my son thinks he is in heaven, but Huang knows exactly where he is, and finds it funny.

"Where did my son meet her?"

"Phanni? She's easy enough to meet. She's a partner in a bar we go to. I used to go around with her myself—" He cocked his head to one side for a moment and assumed a more reasonable expression. "I told Khim, honestly, I told him this girl was not for him." Then he shrugged and said, "But Khim is crazy about her, and for a guy who never even had a woman before, Phanni would be—you can imagine."

"Where does she live?"

"She rents a dump on Soi King Phet."

I walked until my legs ached, but I could not find the house, for there were many small lanes laced behind the main street. Hundreds of shacks ranged out in every direction, tottering over catwalks above a swamp of stagnant water and putrefying garbage. When it grew dark, I dared not go on.

"You'll find him tomorrow!" Mui Eng said hopefully, carefully setting a heavy pot of rice on the edge of the sink and then tipping it slowly to let the scalding water drain off. (This is the Thai way—they boil rice as we boil yams.) "And when you find him, promise him anything to get him back home—anything! I want my son back."

"He wants the girl."

"Aow! He'll be bored with her before you even find him. A prostitute!" she spat out, shaking the rice pot fiercely over the charcoal until the rice had settled again into a thick, even layer.

"You don't understand, you are thinking like a Thai. The Chinese have taken prostitutes as wives for a thousand years, Mui Eng, and we don't know this girl. She may not be so bad, and if we offer her a decent life—who knows? It may not be the worst thing . . ."

"You are mad!" she cried, turning on me like a dragon. "Do you think this girl will be another Nang Kim Leng, bringing her husband good luck and a fortune? You are full of stupid fairy tales your mother told you when you were a child! This is real life, Suang U—a Thai whore, a slut from some filthy slum. She will take every cent she can, and drag our name through the mud! I know what they are . . ."

"This is our only way to get the boy back, Mui Eng. Think!"

"You will never convince me that a Thai whore will turn into a virtuous wife for our son, and then you tell me to 'think'! Go to him, then, if you will not listen to reason. Tell him whatever you like, but—" Her shoulders sagged, and she seemed suddenly to cave in. She leaned against the sink and closed her eyes, then covered her face with her hands. "I am against it, I tell you . . . it is not the way, not the right way at all . . ."

In the morning I set out again, and this time I found the house. My heart sank when I saw the dilapidated shack my son preferred to his own home. After standing a moment before the door and composing myself as best I could, I knocked.

"Go 'way," came a woman's voice, thick with sleep. "Not taking anyone today . . . go 'way!"

"I am here on business!" I shouted. "Open the door!"

"Not today!" the voice retorted angrily, "now go on, get the hell out of here!"

"I am not here on your business, young lady. I am—I am the father of—Witthaya, your lover!" Silence. "If you don't open up this door I shall kick it down!"

A long, exasperated sigh was followed by a word I had never heard a

313

woman speak, then the sound of bedroom slippers shushing from bed to door. The girl opened the door a crack and peered out suspiciously, then closed it again and lifted the hook from a chain that held it fast and stepped outside, squinting in the sunlight. She closed the door again and leaned against it, folding her arms across her chest and fixing me with a hard, calculating stare. This, then, was the temptress who had stolen our son from us—this brown, plump, disheveled girl whose hair stood out in stiff tangles all over her head. Patches of orange makeup streaked her face, and her eyes were so clotted and smudged with color that she appeared to have been brutally beaten. But in spite of it all, I could see that under more favorable circumstances Phanni would be a good-looking girl indeed. Her upper garment was made of some filmy stuff, now wrinkled from sleep and revealing an impressive amplitude of bosom. Below that, she wore a flowered *sarong* which, instead of being folded and belted about the waist, was draped low about her hips in a precarious fashion. "Is my son in there?"

"Uh-huh."

"Come to the door, Weng Khim!" I shouted in Chinese, avoiding her curious eyes. "The least you can do is tell your Papa what—what you intend to do . . ."

For a moment there was no answer, and I stood staring at the shabby door, paralyzed with shame.

"Go home, Papa!" he shouted finally. "I'm not going with you!"

"I don't like talking to a door when I have come to see a son—anyway, what makes you think I want to take you home?"

Silence.

"Let me call him," the girl whispered, grinning now and obviously amused. She opened the door a crack and called in a wheedling tone, "Khun Witthaya? Come on now, I won't let your old Papa hurt you!"

(So she will take care of the little fellow! My heart twisted with grief and disgust.)

"How long have you known my son?" I asked, forcing my eyes to meet hers.

"A few months, I guess."

"What good is he to you? I should think you could have found a boy with more money of his own to spend."

She studied me critically for a moment, absently patting her tangled

314

hair into place. "He—suits me," she said slowly. "If he could support us, I guess I'd quit working."

"Quit?"

"Sure, why not? I mean, anybody would rather have a good husband than live like this, wouldn't they? And, well . . . I like your son a lot." She accompanied this remark with a coy smirk, and suddenly Weng Khim appeared behind her, a spare ghost compared with the brown and buxom girl.

"Why did you come here, Papa?" His cheeks were gaunt and there were dark circles beneath his eyes. I was shocked at the change in his appearance.

"Because you are my son," I replied, struggling with the lump growing in my throat.

"I am never going home, Papa."

He also spoke in Chinese, for we had never used Thai with each other.

"What will you do for a living? Or do you intend to let this girl support you?"

He closed his eyes and smiled peculiarly. "I'll look for a job one of these days . . . any Chinese company would be glad to get a boy with as much education as you've pumped into me. Or maybe you'll make sure I don't get a job—then I'll tend bar."

"You think you could live on the salary you would get tending bar? Not with expensive tastes like yours. Or hers."

The muscles of his jaw flexed with anger. "You don't know that! You don't know anything about me!"

"Then you do as you please," I said, frightened by his intensity. "I shall not trouble you again."

I turned and all but fled, leaving them in the doorway. The grim-faced, bitter boy and the plump, blowsy girl whose reaction to a scene she could understand only by instinct was to laugh, shrug, and shuffle back to her bed.

But I knew that Weng Khim had in him none of this Thai girl's ability to shrug and forget, and that is where I have him, Mother. For Weng Khim is Chinese, and he will never believe, as Phanni surely does, that sex and rice can be enough.

I shall wait.

315

PARENTS LOVE their children and fear for them. It is our greatest weakness and their greatest weapon. In sum, I have accepted the girl Phanni into our home, lest I lose my only son.

Of course, almost no one agreed with my decision, least of all his mother. If she were in my place, she insists, shouting and sobbing, no Thai prostitute would set foot in our house, shaming us beyond endurance before the eyes of the whole neighborhood. But she is not the head of this household, I am. She is free to tear her hair and weep on her bed, knowing that I bear all responsibility for the decision. In spite of her tantrums, I believe that she is grateful, in one way, for she did not have to sacrifice her pride. That, too, I took upon myself.

It is my opinion that Thai society is unfair to women like Phanni, for if they try to leave prostitution they find it impossible to do so. They are forced, by the very people who most deplore it, to return to the streets or starve. There are no other jobs open to them—none, that is, which pay anything near what they can earn by selling their bodies.

I would like to see such women given the choice of occupations other people have, and this is my opportunity to put my beliefs to the test. Phanni may not like the way we live. She may grow tired of us and leave—or she may do well and become a credit to the family. But only by taking her into our home can we know, and if she does leave, my son may choose to stay. It is a gamble, but it is the only way.

Weng Khim's life will not be ruined by this experience, if things turn out as I suspect they will. With the girl behind him, his life can go on as if she never existed. After all, he is a boy. It isn't as though one of our girls had ruined herself.

I went once more to the little house in Soi King Phet. Weng Khim was still asleep after a night at the club, but Phanni came to the door dressed in tight red pants and a thin yellow sweater. Her hair was piled to an incredible height, shining with lacquer, and her face looked altogether like someone else's.

"Papa!" she cried, breaking into a cheery smile. "What a nice surprise—how's business?"

"Er—fine," I replied, astonished at my reception. "Is he—does he have a job?"

"At the club," she replied. "He's a 'boy,' you know what that is? He really likes it. I'll wake him up for you—"

"No, wait, I—what about your monthly income? Is it enough? I know a girl like you wants to look pretty, buy nice things . . . and what about your old customers, now that you and—that is, now that my son lives here with you?"

"Who tells them? They don't know who I go home with."

"A friend of mine told me that 'partners' earn extra money after work."

"A 'friend of yours,' eh?" she grinned mischievously. "Well, sometimes I tell Witthaya to go on ahead—the nights we're short of cash, you know. Don't look so shocked! We need the money, and what do you expect me to do—take in washing?"

"You told me you might consider giving up this life if Weng Khim could support you."

"I know, but I'll bet you never paid him as much as I earn. Anyway, it isn't a bad life, and what I really like best is dancing. It's like . . . in my blood, you know? If I couldn't dance every night I wouldn't be a happy little girl. As for all the rest, it's a hell of a lot better life than my mother ever had. Or my sister, for that matter."

"Where are they?"

"Starving on a rice farm up in Udon. I saw my sister last month, and she looked about a hundred years old. She's twenty-five, she's got eight kids, and do you think she called me dirty names when I threw a hundred baht on her kitchen table?"

I understood, but I knew that Mui Eng never would.

"What if I offered you the chance to live in our home? You could dance every night with my son, turn on the radio or buy records you like and play them on our phonograph."

"You got a phonograph?"

"Nobody would bother you, Phanni."

She glanced quickly over her shoulder, for noises from within announced that "Khun Witthaya" was up and about.

"You are a funny man," she said. "I never met anybody like you before. I've had a lot of young guys, you know, and their fathers—well, they never made me an offer like—I mean, they made me some offers all right," she laughed quietly, "but not like this. One old guy sent his son to college in America . . ." She gave a shrug so slight that it was more nearly a shiver and said, "America is more interesting than Phanni, no? I never even got a postcard. But I got the last laugh on the old bastard, because the kid came home with a big blond wife. I know, I saw them at the movies once . . . Laugh? Right in the old man's face, I did. He was there with them, and the *farang* broad asked him to introduce us. Another one sent his kid off to be a monk—ha ha! I shouldn't laugh, though. He's still a monk. That was four—no, five years ago. Not very flattering for Phanni, eh? But I made money on both of them, and the blond and the temple can have them, for all I care . . . The Chinese pay the most . . ."

"You've had other Chinese boys?" I asked, and she gave that quiet, throaty laugh of hers again and said, "Why not? All kinds."

I glanced quickly to the house on the left, where a pair of old ladies were locking their door and setting off for market with baskets over their arms. They showed no interest in my presence but waved to Phanni as if she were any housewife. She waved back and smiled, "You expected them to throw rocks at me?" she grinned. "You're a funny man. Sure, I've had Chinese boys—Thais, Indians, and *farang* too. I can speak pretty good English! The *farang* pay, but they don't pay off, you know what I mean? One old guy bought his son back from me for thirty thousand baht—how do you like that? But I blew it all playing poker, in a month . . ."

What fearful candor! She is different from anyone I have ever met.

"Your son doesn't make any money, you know, but he's cute. He makes me laugh. What are you thinking of," she asked then, cocking her head to one side and eyeing me suspiciously, "asking me to go live in your house? You and your wife have some plan cooked up, maybe?"

"I know what you're hinting at," I replied with a smile. "I read that story too, the one where the parents take in the prostitute and then concoct some situation to make her look bad in the boy's eyes. But you won't be any heroine in a novel, Phanni, if you come into our home. My wife and I have no time to scheme against you."

"You want your son back so much that you are willing to do even this."

"Yes."

She was silent for a moment, considering. "Witthaya told me there is another girl, a girl you want him to marry."

"I do not know that you have any idea of staying with my son for the rest of your life."

She looked down and began to pick at the buttons on her sweater. "I'm not sure," she mumbled, caught off guard for once.

"If you mean to stay with him, it can be arranged. We are Chinese. With us, your past can be lived down. Our ancients said that a bought woman could bring a man special luck if she changed her ways, and that such a woman could do anything she set her mind to."

"You—you're just trying to confuse me."

"No. All my life I have heard tales of great women who were once—what you are now."

She grinned self-consciously and said, "You think I could work? I mean, sell stuff?"

"It is said that no one was ever born knowing how to do more than eat and cry."

At that moment Weng Khim stuck his head out the door. "Oh, it's you. I'm not coming home, Papa, not without Phanni. My mind is made up."

"All right."

Startled, he looked quickly at Phanni, who laughed and said, "Go home now, Papa, and we'll let you know." Before she disappeared into the shack, she turned and threw me a glance full of mischief and—something more dangerous. This is the way she must look at the young boys who fall under her spell.

I hurried home, thankful that I am not susceptible to such eyes. Work is my minor wife, money our offspring, and it is better that way—how much better, I never realized until these dreadful days came upon us.

After two weeks, there was still no word from Weng Khim and Phanni, and I could not restrain myself from visiting the shack on Soi King Phet again.

"We haven't decided yet!" Phanni said angrily, when she opened the door and found me there. (I doubt if she has ever bothered to control her emotions in her life.) "I thought it over, but I know the women in your house would treat me like dirt. Why should I live with that? Here at least no one looks at me as if I were a disease."

"You are wrong, Phanni. No one will behave rudely to you in my house."

I argued with her for almost an hour, and at last she agreed to try. When I returned home, my heart was lighter than it has been for months. The fate of a parent today, rejoicing that his son has agreed to bring home a prostitute.

Mui Eng and I prepared the largest bedroom for them, and put Bak Li with Meng Chu, which naturally displeased her.

"The house is so little now, Papa. It's only since Chui Kim and Weng Khim left that we have any room to turn around in."

"A bedroom is to sleep in!" Mui Eng snapped. "You and Meng Chu will have room enough for that. Now make up your mind to it and stop complaining."

"Oh, Mama, you're no more pleased about this mess than I am. A fine 'sister-in-law,' ten years older than Elder Brother and a you-know-what besides."

"You both shut up!" I said. "This is our investment in getting Weng Khim home with us, and it is not too great to bear. Behave decently to the girl, and don't make this all harder for your Mama and me than it already is, Bak Li. You don't have to be her best friend, but I won't allow you to drive them both away after I have humiliated myself to get them here. And don't you ever, ever mention her . . . background. You give her the respect due any elder sister-in-law."

"If I have to *wai* her, I'll be sick."

Meng Chu, who had been listening with half an ear while typing a letter for me, interrupted to say, "You needn't *wai* anybody, Bak Li. We are Chinese, we'll act like Chinese. All you have to do is call her 'Elder Sister.' So? You go to work, I go to school, and we'll go on speaking Chinese at home as we've always done, except to her."

Mui Eng, mending socks in her favorite chair, leaned back with a deep sigh and said, "Rose . . . poor Rose. I don't know what we're going to do about her."

"Rose?" Bak Li looked at her mother quizzically. "What does she have to do with anything?"

"She is promised to your brother," I replied for Mui Eng. "I arranged it many years ago with Uncle Kim. But never mind about that now, it will be three years before we must face that problem."

Kim's words of caution that long-ago day came back to haunt me. I slipped the memory quickly back into its dark corner. "Uncle Kim is a very old friend, Bak Li, and even if he is angry at first he will forgive me. If he had a son, I don't doubt he would do as I have done."

"But I do not agree with what you are doing!" Mui Eng cried out suddenly, tears coming to her eyes. "Whatever you say, I do not agree that it is right to debase our home!" She covered her eyes with a red sock and began again the weeping of which I have become so deathly tired. "I am only a wife . . . my heart is breaking, but that is my affair . . . who cares for my feelings?"

Bak Li, who lay sprawled at her mother's feet, rose and stood behind Mui Eng, patting her shoulder sympathetically and glaring at me with such disrespect that I left the room.

What a peculiar woman my wife is. Whatever she has once learned to believe, she clings to unreasonably and forever. It is not within her powers of intellect to accept any deviation from the rigid ideas that rule her life. The children all think I am the more old-fashioned one, simply because their mother curls her hair and smears makeup on her face, but I have changed my mind about many things since I was twenty years old, and Mui Eng is still the spoiled child she was when I married her.

Ang Buai, on the other hand, reacted to the news characteristically.

"You're certainly in a mess," she announced simply when I went to see her yesterday. "I want you to know that I believe you are doing the right thing. I don't say it will work out, and it may even make things worse, but you have nothing to lose, considering where you stand now, that is. You know, Mui Eng and the girls are so sure they won't like her. I wonder if any of them has considered how Phanni is going to feel about them?"

That thought had not occurred to me.

—

PHANNI HAS been in our home since I last wrote to you, and to tell you the truth I am sick at heart. I can only hope that it is not long before she either leaves us or decides to live as one of us, and may I say before I go any further that I have never sufficiently appreciated the manners of my own girls. If only Phanni would try to emulate her young sisters-in-law, if only she would realize that the way they look and behave is the standard of this house, but to this day, she has shown nothing but contempt for us and our ways.

We all rise at five and work together to ready the shop and bakery for the day's business. Customers begin arriving not long after six, and while we and some of our employees have our breakfast in the back, one person always remains in front, for a successful business puts its customers before its stomach. Some stores do not open until eight, but I have always found those two hours profitable, for many customers like to stop here on their way home from the market, which opens at four.

Phanni rises at eleven.

"I don't know how much longer I can stand this," said Mui Eng peevishly, shaking her finger at Phanni's permanently unoccupied place at the breakfast table. (The place is always set, a silent reproach.) "Won't get up in the morning like decent people, and won't go to bed when she should at night. The television is on until the station closes, and then she turns on the radio. And Khun Witthaya, he goes right along with whatever she wants!"

"I hardly get any sleep anymore," Bak Li pouted, joining the daily lament. "And poor Meng Chu can't study with that radio blaring away, you know."

"Don't worry, Papa," Meng Chu said with an affectionate grin, "I'm not going to flunk out of school because of Phanni's radio."

Bless her.

At first, Weng Khim did not help in the bakery as before. In fact, he did nothing the way he ever had before.

"You earned your salary then," I said when we were alone in the office early one morning. "Now you don't, even though you've got everything going your own way. Haven't you heard that government slogan, 'Work is Wealth'? Even the Thai are beginning to believe that, Weng Khim, and even more should a Chinese boy like you."

He said nothing.

"Your sisters have been washing Phanni's clothes—did you know that? Bak Li works all day, Meng Chu goes to school and does all my correspondence in the evening. Both of them are up at five every morning, and besides all that they do that lazy girl's laundry!"

Weng Khim turned away angrily, but he was ashamed and I knew it.

"We have no washgirl now, your mother and sisters do it themselves, and if Phanni had any sense of fairness she'd offer to do their laundry instead of throwing her things and yours into the family hamper and lounging in front of the radio all day listening to soap operas."

"She has never worked, Papa. She's not used to getting up so early."

"M-m, and she isn't trying very hard to get used to it, is she? Not that you've been up on time once since you came home. You're pale from lack of sleep, Weng Khim. Look at yourself in the mirror. You're a merchant, not an owl, and you should be teaching her to behave like a merchant's wife instead of—of toddling after her like a baby!"

I stopped there, frightened by my own anger, so long suppressed. But to my amazement, when I got up to go over to the bakery the boy set his jaw firmly and trudged after me. Thus began a strange day, for it seemed we were competing with each other with every fiber of muscle and brain, setting each other ever greater tasks, more errands, longer rows of inventory and figures to be checked, goading each other on to work harder than either of us had worked in the days before he left us. At dusk, we gobbled our food wordlessly and fell into bed exhausted. Phanni wandered aimlessly about the house and out onto the sidewalk with the little radio that dangles from her wrist by a strap, and the next morning Meng Chu informed me that the girl had gone to bed long before her usual hour.

I paid the unavoidable visit to Kim one month after Phanni came to us. Why did I wait so long? He knew, of course, for news of her arrival on Yaowarat Road was everywhere within hours. But I knew that Kim would understand better than anyone the depth of my sorrow. There was no hurry.

He greeted me with a sympathetic smile. "Be with you in a minute— I want to get a couple of beers out of the cooler."

"Have you finally come to un-betroth them, my friend?" he asked, reappearing with a bottle of beer in each hand.

"Beyond the main facts, there is nothing much to say, but I haven't come to ask you to release my son from the promise I gave. I've got him home now, and I believe that when she finally gets tired of us and leaves, he will not follow her."

"Pretty bad, eh?"

"Terrible. And lately, I notice a difference between them. It could be my imagination, but—Mui Eng and the girls are starting to give her a fair share of the work, and I see Weng Khim look at her, then look at his sisters . . . he's seeing her in a different light, you know? She's not so glamorous anymore. Anyway, no one talks to her, and Phanni is a friendly girl, whatever else she is, so that hurts, I know it does—that may be the worst of it for her, the silence. And the Chinese, of course. She doesn't understand us when we speak to each other. That and having to wash Weng Khim's work clothes will get her out of our hair before much longer, you'll see."

Kim laughed. "Well, I'll wait awhile then. You know, if anyone else had known about the betrothal, I'd have broken your neck! But no other suitors are kicking down the door, so . . . it's all a shame, Suang U. I want you to know how sorry I am."

"Don't—please! I was a fool, and if you're a true friend you won't contradict me for saying so. But I think everything may work out all right yet."

"I hope so, for all our sakes. Rose is upset, of course. When she saw you come in, she ran upstairs."

"Someday I'll make it up to her. Kim, I promise you that."

At home, the laundry battle continued. Bak Li put a large rattan hamper into her brother's room, and if Phanni put anything of hers or Weng Khim's in another hamper, Bak Li quietly plucked it out and tossed it back where it belonged. Eventually, Phanni had to lug the hamper out into the back yard and, clad only in a towel, wash all her clothes and Weng Khim's the next day or go naked, after an argument that I am sure the whole neighborhood heard (and discussed the next evening in the corner coffee shop).

This was followed by the battle of the lights. Suddenly, our household would be plunged into darkness at ten o'clock, our usual bedtime. Now, this is not unusual in Bangkok, where modern conveniences still have a way of becoming irksome inconveniences at the most inopportune times, but the fact that every other house on the block was brightly lit left no doubt in Phanni's mind that subterfuge was involved.

This annoyed her more than anything, more than the silence or the Chinese or Weng Khim's laundry, for it deprived her of both television and radio. But if there is one thing Weng Khim cannot bear it is nagging and complaining, having grown up with Mui Eng, and so he began to avoid her.

Mui Eng knew nothing about the mysterious blackouts, nor did Bak Li, and so at last I came to Meng Chu, whom I had suspected from the first.

"Why did you do it?" I asked sternly. (For whether it accomplished the hoped-for result or not, it would not do to show approval of such methods.)

She only shrugged and grinned, and continued making notes on a piece of paper.

"Doesn't it interfere with your studying?"

"I bought a bedside lamp with a battery."

"But Phanni isn't stupid, daughter. She can certainly understand how to change a fuse—"

"Yes, if she could get at it," said Meng Chu, looking up from her homework with no trace of guilt in her eyes.

"Ah, yes, and the fuse box is on a shelf outside your bedroom window! Er—what about Bak Li? She seems to know nothing of the matter."

"Why should I tell her everything? She can't keep her mouth shut."

More days passed, and one early morning Kim came to the office with the presents we had given, as a sign of betrothal.

"Here—I'm sorry. Chaba is getting fed up, nagging me about it. Anyway, it isn't fair to Rose herself."

"Please, Kim, he's young! Things between them are even worse than when I last spoke to you!"

"Oh, don't start that again. So what if he gives her up? He'll probably find himself another just like her, especially now that he's seen what you do about it . . ."

"I swear to you," I said angrily, "if it should ever happen again, I would cut him off forever."

"An only son? Why, anyone who knows you would laugh in your face to hear you say those words, Suang U. The boy is your life!"

"Is he? I wonder now . . . but no matter, please keep the presents, and if he fails me again I will gladly accept them and beg your forgiveness."

Kim threw the bag onto my desk, sat down, and looked at me in a way that made me uneasy. "Suang U, have you thought at all about my daughter? She knows what's going on, and she feels humiliated. You know, this mess affects her as much as anyone, and she's changed, my friend. Rose is not the girl she was six months ago. I don't know how many times we've heard her say that if she ever marries Weng Khim she'll chain him to his desk by day and his bed by night . . . those are her very words, and——"

"There, you see? You say she's furious, yet she speaks of marrying him!"

"Hasn't it occurred to you that she may care for the boy? She always has, though he's treated her no better than he treats the laborers in your bakery." Then, recovering some of his usual good humor, he added, "Knowing my Rose, if they do marry there'll be an end of that soon enough!"

He returned home with the bag of jewelry in his hand, but the fates seem to defy me at every turn. For Phanni has begun dragging herself out of bed at eight every morning and even helping Mui Eng in the store. Why? I am not so heartless as to thwart any honest attempt on the girl's part to make Weng Khim a decent wife, but there is something odd about the way she looks at me, at all of us since the improvement in her behavior. As if she had some good joke up her sleeve . . .

"If they can live together," Mui Eng said with a deep sigh, turning back the covers of our bed with a deft flip of her wrist, "then we may as well consider it our fate!" She scooped up each pillow in turn and shook it down with her strong arms, plumped it and propped it against the headboard exactly as she has done every night of our married life together. "Don't let your head burst with anger and regret over the boy's karma—or our own, Suang U. It would be a waste, and foolish vanity . . . Have you nothing to say? I should think you would be glad that I am accepting it! I still don't like the girl, but she is trying. I'll say that for her. Oh, and by the way, this morning she waited on two men who seemed to know her. She chatted with them for a few minutes, sold them some toothpaste, and then went to wait on old Ah Lim, and they left. I didn't hear what they talked about, but she kept her eyes lowered, there was no—you know, nothing . . ." It was Mui Eng who had railed and wept, lamented the prospect of living under the same roof with an "evil woman"; now she shrugged her shoulders and spoke of karma while I burned with rage that no one saw, hating myself.

Confusion and shame overwhelm me, for I lied to myself, to Mui Eng and Kim, to you. To each of you, I told a different tale, believing none. You must have wondered whether I was mad, with my scribblings about women in ancient fables who left lives of shame, bringing honor and riches to the families wise enough to call them daughter. I curse myself for heaping upon my loved ones foolish lies and pompous words . . . "Here is my opportunity," I wrote, "to put my beliefs to the test" . . . when all I ever hoped for was that Weng Khim would tire of her, would one day turn from her painted face and lacquered hair disgusted with her and with his own lust. If only it had happened that way, you see, I would have gladly accepted harsh words from my wife, the resentment of my son, the jeers and mocking faces of my neighbors. If only I could have had my own way at the end of it all, none of that would have mattered. And I was so smug, I rejoiced when I saw the tedious rhythm of our days robbing her eyes of their mischief, her step of its joyous, languid swaying, so sure that one morning we would wake to find that she had fled in the darkness to rejoin her own kind, to drowse behind the crumbling shutters of the dark and squalid hovel in Soi King Phet.

Pray, my Mother, that your son and grandson have not both brought ruin upon this family, and shame to our ancestors. And pray that my grandsons will not call a prostitute their mother, though I have done nothing to deserve a happier fate. While a shred of hope remains, I cannot give in, as Mui Eng already has, and accept this as our fate. Something in the girl's eyes gives me hope that she will leave, at last.

LETTER #78
18 JUNE 1964

FIFTH MONTH, NINTH DAY
YEAR OF THE DRAGON

IT IS said that there is good in every person, that even a lazy man will hurry to do the work he enjoys most, that a liar will be truthful to

327

protect those he loves. A murderer will sometimes confess a motive for his crime so understandable that we suspect we might have done the same in his place.

We all admit now that, in the beginning, Phanni was a less than welcome guest in our home, but as the months passed by and she learned to conduct herself more suitably, even Bak Li no longer avoided her, but spoke with her on several occasions in an ordinary and courteous manner. All the more reason why we have reacted with more astonishment than anger at the terrible thing she has done.

Phanni left our home in the dark hour before dawn several days ago, taking with her a great sum of money, a considerable part of Mui Eng's silver, and anything else of value that she and her friends could carry away quietly. She had drugged our food or drink somehow, for we slept like the dead. Meng Chu, as she told us later, had found herself unable to study past nine and had gone to bed fearing that she was coming down with the flu.

At noon on the previous day, I had taken from the bank money with which to pay our employees on the day following. That night, I put it in the safe in our bedroom, as always, together with some money a customer had brought in after supper, a considerable sum long overdue. Also in the safe were items of jewelry belonging to Mui Eng and the girls, worth not less than fifty thousand baht.

How long did we work for what she stole in less time than it takes a man to eat one bowl of rice? How many days did we rise before the sun, and still were hard at work long after it had set? But the greatest cause of pain has not been her perfidy, or even our loss; it has been Weng Khim's unreasoning defense of the girl.

We gathered around the breakfast table in awful silence, each afraid to meet another's eyes and see his own anguish mirrored there. I myself trembled at the knowledge that strangers had crept about our bed while we lay drugged. How easy it would have been for them to kill us as we slept!

"We are in a bad way, children," I said at last. "I cannot understand—"

"You cannot understand?" Weng Khim exploded, his face contorted with rage. "I should think even you could understand how hard it was for her to—to breathe in this damned jail! How can you blame her?"

Meng Chu was the first to find her voice after this appalling outburst. "Elder Brother, you know very well that none of us ever said an unkind word to her. We minded our own business from the day you brought her home."

"Yah!" he jeered, his voice shrill with bitterness, "you were just wonderful to her, weren't you? Peering at her over your almighty books like she was some kind of insect, some kind of bug that had crawled in here . . . the hell with all of you! Not one of you has ever cared a thing for my happiness!" Then he leaped up from his chair, threw his napkin on the floor, ground it with his foot in a pathetic display of temper, and fled. I was reminded, for the first time in months, that Weng Khim is only seventeen years old.

Mui Eng called the police after we had finished breakfast, and they were quite decent, surprisingly. They found the key still in the safe lock, for the thieves had not bothered to remove it, and when Mui Eng told them that she has always kept it in a box in her lingerie drawer, including the night of the theft, they had no further doubts as to Phanni's guilt. Nor, apparently, had they any strong hope of locating her, much less our jewelry and money.

"By now," the officer said politely, not looking up from the notebook in which he was scribbling, "I'm afraid the jewelry settings have been destroyed and the stones passed on to someone who knows nothing of the theft. Even if we should find them, the jeweler couldn't help us—anyway, sir, identifying jewels is almost impossible, you can appreciate that."

They were efficient and treated us kindly, but they told us nothing beyond what any fool could readily see. We had been fearfully victimized by a prostitute our son had brought home with his father's own blessing. One police sergeant about my age threw me a quick, sympathetic look as he left, as if to say, "Have courage, old fellow—it's hard days for our generation." It was the best thing the law did for me that dreadful morning.

There is nothing else to say and no point in elaborating, though it would be easy for me to ease the fullness of my heart by pouring out its bitterness to you. Forgive your poor grandson, if you can. Perhaps I should be ready to turn him out, to let him follow his depraved lover, but I am moved to tears every time I look at him, bent under a terrible load of guilt and self-disgust. The rude and awful things he says, his tantrums, his unswerving defense of Phanni—all that is nothing but pride and the pain of betrayal. I look into my boy's eyes and grieve that one so young must bear this. That he brought it on himself only makes this hard lesson more of a torture. Why do men say, "So-and-so brought it upon himself, at least . . ." as if the pain of a failure were mitigated by one's own contribution to it? It is quite the other way round! But I myself had never recognized this simple fact before. Had I ever looked as deeply into my son's heart as I have looked these past few days, I wonder if we might have been spared—but it will do no good to punish myself further.

I pray that this ugly blot upon our family's honor may be erased by the subsequent deeds of this confused and angry boy, for what he shall be, I yet insist, remains to be seen, and I shall do everything in my power to turn to good account this terrible experience.

LETTER #79   NINTH MONTH, THIRD DAY
8 OCTOBER 1964   YEAR OF THE SNAKE

THE POLICE have not found Phanni or her fellow conspirators, and Weng Khim no longer seems to mourn her. But he is more silent, almost grim in his attention to the business. If I had not promised myself to stop making predictions about my children, I might say we paid a hundred thousand baht for the manhood of our son.

Meng Chu knocked briskly at the door of my office.

"Papa, are you busy?"

"No, no—come in, child. I was just about to quit for tea."

She set her schoolbooks on a corner of the desk and pulled up a simply carved corner chair that had belonged to Mui Eng's mother.

"I graduate in two weeks, you know," she began, running her tongue over her lips rapidly as she does when bad news is imminent. "What I want to ask you is, if I work in our store after graduation, will you give me as much money as you give Weng Khim? Of course, I would expect to do the same work."

"But Weng Khim needs money for the draft," I exclaimed, taken completely by surprise. "What do you girls need money for? I think I

330

have been quite generous with you."

"That isn't the point. I don't want to come to you like a child for a handout every time I want to buy something, and besides, I'd like to start saving toward my marriage. Who knows whether I'll marry a rich man like Seng Huat? Although that really isn't the point either, because even after I marry I'd like to have some money of my own."

"I must tell you that I consider your attitude rather unsuitable, Meng Chu, but at any rate you are too young to think of marriage."

At that she burst out laughing. "Too young? What else have you ever talked about since we girls turned twelve but—" (and here she made a solemn face) "'when you are a wife' . . ."

Irritated by her mockery, I opened my ledger again, slowly ran my pencil down a row of figures, and began to make notes on a pad of paper.

"You can't fool me, Papa," she said mischievously. "You forget—this is Meng Chu, not Bak Li, and I know you aren't doing anything!"

"Ah, Meng Chu, you are a terrible daughter!" I said, grinning in spite of my best attempt at a frown.

"Did you know that Bak Li has a boyfriend?"

"Eh?"

"You know perfectly well what I mean. Stop trying to act as though you never heard the word."

(What daughter in our village would not have been beaten for speaking once to her father as this child always speaks to me?)

"His Thai name is Surasak—nobody calls him by his Chinese name. I don't even know what it is, though I'm sure he has one. He's the younger brother of the girl who owns the beauty shop where Bak Li works. He has a job in a bank and an interest in the beauty shop too, she told me. He earns more than two thousand baht a month, and he isn't more than about twenty."

"M-m, not bad, but why must he call himself by a Thai name? If I were his father, I would forbid it. It is one thing to deal with Thais and another thing to—"

"Yes, yes, we all know, but Surasak doesn't have a father. His father died when he was a little boy and he lives with his mother who by all accounts is something of an old dragon."

"Meng Chu," I said, "I certainly hope all these Thai friends of yours at the school are—girls."

331

She was startled at the sudden change of subject, and somewhat annoyed. "Really, Papa, must you be quite so obvious? Sometimes I think you're really a—a bigot!"

"Why? Just because I am not as impressed with these people as you are?"

"I didn't say I was impressed."

"Oh but you are, you definitely are . . . or you wouldn't always be defending them."

"I try to be fair."

"Daughter, I have already lived here half my life, and outside of four or five unusual men, I have seen Thais able to achieve nothing but the growing of rice. They import almost everything else they need, and look what happens when they have a few years of famine. Thousands of peasants from the Northeast descend on Bangkok to beg in the streets until the rains begin. And then they return to their farms to plant rice again, with never a thought for the next time, and everyone in Bangkok is glad to see them go. They prepare themselves for nothing, hope for nothing, accomplish nothing!"

"And this, in your estimation, is a fair assessment of 'the Thai people'? How do you think they feel about the million Chinese who live in Bangkok and control all the money?"

I slammed the ledger shut and leaned back in my chair. "Why must you talk like an editorial in *Thai Rath*? Meng Chu, understand this, please. I am grateful for the opportunities I've enjoyed here. I do not mean to disparage the source of my own success. But why aren't these people able to use the opportunities I have used? They're not stupid people, but sometimes I wish I could shake them all by their collars, tell them, "You can be as rich as any of the Chinese if you would only learn to use what your country offers!"

"So you think they don't?"

"No, they don't! The Thai who has a little money, what does he invest it in? Nightclubs! Massage parlors! Factories are too boring, too slow to show a profit. But that's how fortunes are built, Meng Chu. Getting rich can be a long, slow, boring process!

"Do you think I want to see this country go on forever with its nose on the ground? Why should I want that? You ask me whether Thais like to import so many things. I say yes! Otherwise, tell me why they

332

buy canned peas from America when the markets in Bangkok are full of fresh vegetables, why they're in debt for television sets and refrigerators and cars from Germany, handbags from Italy, and electric fans from Japan. Don't tell me these things can't be made here, because I know they can! But Thais are obsessed with the idea that foreign goods are more desirable. When we bought your mother's car, I wondered why no one was assembling cars here. Now they do, but the Mercedes-Benz is still the only 'prestige' car, Meng Chu, and they don't put those together in Bangkok. Now, go on—it's your turn."

"No. I won't bother to try."

"Oh, I know I'm not supposed to criticize—I'm supposed to keep my mouth shut because I'm an 'outsider,' but I am a person who must speak his mind honestly. I know there are Chinese merchants here who are crooks, and I don't defend them. How about that? I admit that there are those who take advantage of Thais in every way they can, who squeeze every satang out of everyone too stupid to know whether or not he is being cheated. But they are in the minority. Yet, when Thais lump me in with the worst of my people, then I am supposed to smile and shrug my shoulders, and gladly take the blame for every swindler in Bangkok who pays the alien tax—the last generation of the great, greedy Chinese money-grubbers!"

She laughed in spite of herself. Fathers and their children, trying to talk with each other. Heaven help us.

There are polite ways to speak of these things, but I am too old and too disgusted to learn all that now, and not interested in the euphemisms Meng Chu and her friends use for the troubles that afflict us today. "Urban development" is their name for the ever increasing squalor that is Bangkok, higher and broader and filthier and more crowded every year; "rising expectations" the new excuse for wanting everything you see whether you need and can afford it or not.

I can love my children, argue with them, and attempt to guide their steps, but I cannot protect them from the times in which they must live. Whatever I may think of it, this is their world and not mine, and who is to say they will not make a better peace with it than their father made with the world of his own youth?

THIS DAY your son has good news and bad, and the good news deserves to come first: Weng Khim has agreed to marry Rose.

You know that the boy does not easily admit defeat, nor was I interested in further humiliating him. He searched for Phanni for two weeks without any more luck than the police, and at last he ceased haunting the nightclub and calling on his old disreputable companions for news of her. But while he continued to work here with the silent, almost grim determination I mentioned in my last letter, he retained the spare and ghostly look I had first noticed on Soi King Phet.

After the first few days of Phanni's disappearance, Weng Khim and I worked together, ran errands together and returned home together. Now and then, he would go off on his own for an hour or two, either early in the morning or in the evening, but I was careful not to inquire about his private hours. He even went with me to Kim's a few times, where he was friendly and polite to Rose, and once when I heard them laughing together over a film they had both seen, I had to struggle to suppress tears of joy. As it was to turn out, our troubles were nearly over—but for one regrettable scene.

"Mama, is Weng Khim gone already?" Meng Chu asked, setting her schoolbag down on the kitchen counter and taking her place at the breakfast table.

"M-m, he had to go to Thonburi this morning, Meng Chu."

The girl laid a small white paper envelope on the table, the kind pharmacies use. "Do you and Papa know what this is?"

Mui Eng took her place at the table and set a bowl of dried spiced pork before me. "Looks like a packet of pills," she said, scarcely glancing at the little envelope.

"I found it on Weng Khim's dresser when I went in his room this morning to get a book he borrowed from me. I have to turn the book in at the library, or I wouldn't have gone in there."

"So? For a long time he's kept his pills up there—aspirin, I think, and some capsules when he had a cold."

I picked up the little envelope and studied the English label, which of course meant nothing to me.

"This is the kind of medicine people take for infections, Papa. But particularly for—the women's disease."

Mui Eng's eyes bulged. "Meng Chu, for shame! What are you saying?"

"How do—how can you be sure of that?" I stammered, unwilling to believe her and shocked that she would know of such things.

"I can read English, you know. The serious thing, Papa, is that this medicine may not keep the disease from returning, and if Weng Khim is infected he should be seen by a doctor. That's why I'm willing to be the family tattle-tale again."

"He may have bought it for something else," I insisted. "Read the label to us in Chinese."

"It's possible," she said, "but I don't think so. You must ask him, Papa."

She could have misunderstood, I tried to tell myself, but as she translated the information on the envelope, my heart began to sink, and there was the boy himself, so pale and thin in spite of the food his mother pushed at him day and night. He had lived with a woman who scarcely heeded the faces of her many lovers. How many among them had pale cheeks and hollow eyes from unspeakable diseases? And suddenly I felt a chill of fear, remembering Rose . . . what if he were to infect his wife, his children?

That evening, I waited until Mui Eng and the girls had gone to bed, then asked Weng Khim to share a pot of tea with me in the kitchen. He looked pleased, settling himself at the table with the sports section of the newspaper. I watched the water boil, and steam rise up the yellow, grease-stained wall I have meant to repaint for so long. Our house had been, no doubt, a disappointment to Phanni.

"You don't look so good lately, Weng Khim. Are you sick?"

I measured two spoonfuls of our best tea into the pot, then added the scalding water carefully.

"Nah, I'm all right," he replied without looking up.

"Your mother says you've had a packet of some sort of medicine on your dresser for weeks. You know how she is. She's sure you're sick, you don't want to tell her . . ."

"Oh?" He frowned intently at a photograph of a Thai boxing champion clapping his gloves above his head and beaming through a row of false teeth. "Yeah, there's some aspirin in there, I guess . . ."

"You're a liar!" I said, my voice breaking on the word, and Weng Khim shut his eyes tightly, as if struck. "Do you think your mother and I—your sisters—do you think we are all stupid in this house? Why didn't you go to a doctor if you have the woman's disease?"

"And humiliate myself further? The medicine is there for anyone to buy."

"And have you cured yourself, doctor?"

He made no reply, but continued to hold the newspaper open on the table before him, staring at it miserably.

"Tomorrow you will see a doctor, and you will keep seeing him until he says you're cured. Why, you act as if this disease were your private property instead of a filthy curse that you might pass on to your innocent children!"

We sat in silence then, sipping the best tea in the house. "Khim," I began when several minutes had elapsed, "have Mama and I refused you anything since all this—this mess began? We took that girl into our home, and if your sisters didn't act thrilled to have her here, what did you expect? I haven't said a word about what happened since— since she left, but I am going to tonight. What did I do? Did I let them treat her badly, call her a whore or—"

"They wouldn't do that."

"No, they wouldn't. Khim. We did our best, I think we all did our best. I don't know, I don't understand . . . no man ever gave his son a better start in life than I gave you. Of course, nowadays it's a sin to remind a boy what he owes his parents, but you got an education, a start in life I'd have done anything for when I was your age. What I want to know is, if being a father according to my understanding of the word father is no good anymore, what am I supposed to do?"

He dropped the newspaper onto the floor and turned sad eyes to the screen door, then stared out into the darkness as if hypnotized by some creature crouched there.

"How can I be a good boy, Papa?" he asked in a small voice, sounding very young. "I'm so—confused . . . this house, it's like a queer little world of its own." He glanced away from the door then, and his eyes darted about the room as if noting each familiar object: the refrigerator, the Japanese clock ticking above it on the wall, the straight wooden chairs my adopted father bought for us before our wedding, the worn brown and yellow linoleum on the floor that once was new and shiny, Mui Eng's pride and joy.

"When I was a little boy, school always seemed like another world— the Thai school, I mean—like another planet or something. Here we spoke Chinese, and you expected us to behave like kids in that place where you grew up—Po Leng village? Well, in the Thai school they told us we were 'new people,' whatever that is. I think its good that we kids know both languages, but—in business, Papa, where you think I speak Thai like a Thai, you know? Actually, I have this—this accent. They laugh, like the kids used to laugh at the Thai school, only kids laugh right in your face and not behind your back . . . well, that part isn't so bad, maybe, but what it means is that a guy has to be two or three kinds of persons, you know? No—please, don't say anything, not yet . . . I am telling you tonight, and I want to tell it all, because if I don't now . . . that is, I don't much care tonight, but by tomorrow morning whatever pride I have left will keep me from ever telling you.

"There just isn't anybody who can please everyone. I always tried to conduct myself in the old ways at home, to please you, but the harder I tried the less you seemed to notice me, because you expected it. The only time you really noticed me was when I forgot myself enough to act like myself. Outside our house I tried to be a 'regular guy' and act like other kids my age. Oh, a lot of the Chinese boys are like me, crazy to find a way out . . . they drink, they go around with girls—everything. They see the Thai boys doing anything they want and it's tough to be sixteen and work all the time and know that two hours after you've gone to bed all those guys are out there having a good time.

"I act too much like a Thai to satisfy my parents, but to a Thai I'm still—*chek* . . . I'm a *chek* with a Thai education. Papa, do you understand what I am trying to say to you?"

How to reply, when my throat ached with stifled sobs? Never had I heard my son speak so many words together, or guessed that he was capable of such anguish. Was I alone to blame, and my profound hopes for my only son no more than shackles he cast off in despair? I could blame "society" instead. Even Meng Chu might allow me a reprieve for such a modern idea. What does it matter now?

"Can't you say anything. Papa? Can't you do anything but . . . look at me like that?" His mouth began to wobble dangerously, and after a

337

brief effort to blink back his tears, he began to weep unashamedly. "Oh, Papa, it's always been 'Weng Khim, you must do this, you're expected to do that . . .' I'm the big deal son, the hope of the ancestors, but when there's anything good going, who gets it? Meng Chu! The third stinking daughter whose guts you hated until she got old enough to suck up to you with her straight A's and her flattery and—and every time I've gotten into trouble it's been Meng Chu who made sure you found out what a bastard your only son is!" He folded his arms on the table and laid his head on them, shaking with sobs, and I sat, frozen with horror, as the hatred so long controlled poured out of him.

"Once in my life, Papa," he sobbed, "I made you do something you didn't want to do, after all the things you made me do, but I still lost, didn't I? Weng Khim never wins, that's a fact of life . . ."

"Who told you to take that medicine?" I asked, desperate to end this tirade.

"Phanni," he replied, lifting his head and sniffling into the handkerchief I gave him. "She laughed, she said it's nothing to get the disease once in awhile."

"And you grieved for her . . . Weng Khim, all females are alike inside their clothes. Why couldn't you have married a clean girl and satisfied yourself with her? I asked you before you left home if you wanted to marry."

"I wanted Phanni . . . I wanted her the first time I saw her, and I got her," he said. "It was the only time in my life I ever got what I wanted the way I wanted it and on my terms. And she showed me how to be happy, how to forget . . ."

"But any woman could have given you that, and happiness with a woman can take many forms. A fresh young virgin like Rose, for example . . . she could bring you other pleasures."

"I don't believe it," he replied, still sniffling and noisily blowing his nose.

"How do you know, eh?"

He managed a grin and replied, "Uncle Kim isn't likely to let me try her out."

"No, but you could try marriage. If it doesn't work out, what will you have lost? That will be my concession, Weng Khim."

"You mean you would let me divorce her?"

"Do not ask me to say that. I tell you only that I am willing to be—flexible."

"You never knew me, Papa. You've never seen me as I really am."

"I see you as you really are, Weng Khim. I see you as my only son."

LETTER #81
2 MAY 1965

FOURTH MONTH, SECOND DAY
YEAR OF THE SNAKE

OUR TROUBLES with your grandson had scarcely ended when new troubles arose from a most unexpected quarter. What evil deeds stalk my past lives, that I should suffer so from the perversity of these children? In my youth, good fortune blessed me in many ways. Now it appears that the balance is due. The ancients said that ill fortune never makes a single visit, and my life gives me no reason to dispute their wisdom. Second daughter, Bak Li, has brought more shame upon your son.

Weng Khim's affair has left sores on my heart which will never heal, but I must not allow myself to think about it, at least not yet. This I know instinctively, as a dentist knows that an infected tooth must not be pulled, but drained first of its poison.

Two weeks ago Bak Li woke up ill and did not appear for breakfast. Mui Eng looked in on her. The girl improved, days went by, and though Bak Li looked better Mui Eng herself looked terrible. Then one evening I entered our bedroom to find my wife weeping on the bed. The words she told me you will have guessed, and there is no reason to elaborate on them. No tears or angry words passed between us, only dull, resigned misery on her part and, on mine, the frantic hope that the secret might be kept.

"How many months along is she?"

"More than two."

Even from the first, awful moment I had no intention of castigating her, or shouting at the girl. I knew that any show of anger would bring further shame upon us, for our neighbors have a thousand ears.

Bak Li opened the door of my office tentatively, then stood holding onto the doorknob as if she might turn and flee at any moment.

"Come in," I called out irritably. "Do you think I am going to beat you?"

She scurried across the room and crouched on the edge of a chair like a frightened cat. "Oh, Papa!" she sobbed into her hands.

"Ah, none of that now! Does the boy know?" She shook her head miserably. "Well then, you go tell him, and let me know what he says. Today!"

Surasak did not tell Bak Li to do anything sinful to solve her condition—he was not without human feeling entirely. But he did tell her that he could not yet afford to marry . . .

"Quit your bawling now, girl, and tell me every word he said!"

"I don't know why he can't afford to marry," she blubbered. "He earns more than two thousand baht a month, Papa!"

"That is not such a fortune as you seem to think, Bak Li. You children are extravagant and spoiled, and I wouldn't be surprised if two thousand baht lasted you only a week! I've seen eighteen-year-old boys spend more in one evening at a nightclub."

"Surasak is not—not like that. If anything, he's a little stingy."

Talking to Mui Eng was of no use, for she could think only of keeping the matter from the neighbors and was unable to see the importance of a plan that would provide for Bak Li's future and the child's. But Ang Buai learned of the crisis from Meng Chu and entered the house the following day as we were finishing supper, and immediately there seemed to descend on our household an atmosphere of order, reason, and grim humor.

"Hope you have plenty of dessert!" she grinned, poking her head through the doorway.

Mui Eng rushed to set a place for her. "Brown coconut pudding— your favorite," she said, unwilling to meet her younger sister's eyes.

"Look, let's not waste time," Ang Buai said (and cocked her head at me with an expression that said, "or pretend Bak Li is not pregnant and blushing into her soup across the table"). "Pay for the whole wedding and get it over with!"

Everyone at the table sat up a little straighter, stunned by her candor.

"If Bak Li has to be a bride without any gifts from the groom," she continued, "that's the least of her worries. And as for yourself," she said, reaching across the table and lifting Bak Li's chin gently, "accept

340

the fact that you've been a bit of a fool, but remember—when you are an old, wrinkled grandmother, if this is the worst moment you have to look back on, you will have lived a better life than most people."

And so it was done, but Surasak set the price of my daughter's honor so high that I could not help entertaining certain suspicions about his motives.

He declared that he could not live as a married man in his sister's house. Perhaps, then, I would be willing to take over the payments on a new one he had recently bought . . .

"It would be Bak Li's, too, of course," he added quickly, his sharp eyes shifting about nervously, for we both knew that Thai law recognizes only the husband as owner of his home. He demanded nothing—he didn't have to—but at least I got him to agree to have only a Chinese wedding, without a marriage license from the government.

Thirty thousand baht, Mother! How much have I spent on my children's follies that might have been spent for their good? We haven't so much cash available in our business, and this new blow is a grievous one financially, though I would not have you think us in peril of losing our home or the bakery.

The quietest wedding of the year took place with only four elders in attendance. One hundred people were invited to the reception, half attended, and Meng Chu related afterward that that was a blessing, since Surasak had grudgingly agreed to provide the food. (And there was, as Ang Buai had inadvertantly predicted, no gift for the bride).

"The poor guests," Meng Chu laughed sadly, "Bak Li was right about his being stingy. You never saw such dreadful food in your life—what there was of it. And you told her they couldn't live on two thousand a month? He could live on two thousand a year!"

Yet Bak Li seems to like him well enough. What can I say, except that her mother's blood is strong. For it was Mui Eng, you will remember, who made our own marriage possible, by making her affections too plain. As for me, I was in love with a dream, a dream that never became reality in any part, and when I recall the love I once felt for Mui Eng it is the dream that I think of, not the life we have shared since the hour my proud step-father blessed us in Nguan Thong's house on Sampheng Lane.

Bak Li is pretty, but I have never seen Surasak look at her as a man looks at the woman he loves. Well, Ang Buai is probably right—she is better off than she might have been, and if this is the worst thing that ever happens to her she may indeed consider herself fortunate.

Chui Kim was furious when she learned of our latest crisis, and I arrived home from visiting Kim one evening to find her berating the sister who had so recently been her closest companion.

"I think it's disgraceful!" she all but hissed, matronly virtue outraged. "Having to buy your child a father, and he gets a free house out of it besides—goodness, how could you do this to Papa, after all he's been through with Weng Khim?"

"You are acting ridiculous, Chui Kim," the sullen girl retorted. "Anyway, what do you care about Papa? You were glad to take everything you could get when you married Seng Huat."

"Don't you dare talk to me like that! Are you going to keep on working?"

"I will have to."

"But you've never taken care of a house or had to cook any meals. Mama does all of that. How will you manage?"

"I can get some girl, probably—"

"Some girl! That Surasak of yours will never allow it, you can be sure. And Mama says his mother may be living with you."

"Maybe. I don't know, it might not be so bad. She can watch the baby while I work, and Surasak's sister has promised me my old job back. It's near here, you know. I can come home sometimes . . ."

Bak Li's mother-in-law moved into the house before the young couple had been married a month, and her presence in no way eased the already strained atmosphere.

"She's so dirty, Mama, you wouldn't believe it!" Bak Li complained to Mui Eng on one of her frequent visits. "And if there are more than three kinds of food on the table, she keeps talking all through the meal about how we're on our way to the poor house."

One of our girls from the bakery goes over to do their laundry every morning, but Bak Li does all the cooking. Not because she wishes to spare her mother-in-law the trouble, but because she dreads having to eat anything the old woman has touched.

"She never uses soap, Mama, not even to wash clothes. 'It wears them out too fast,' she says!"

Even so, Surasak himself is not as miserly as Chui Kim and even I had feared. He is willing to pay for good food and even for the little washgirl from the bakery. It is only in the matter of a personal allowance for Bak Li that he is adamant.

"He says I must earn that myself," she pouted to her mother on another occasion, "and that makes me furious. After all, it was our family who paid for the house we live in!"

"Ah, but you aren't the one who paid for it!" Mui Eng said sternly, shaking her finger in the girl's face. "'Our family,' indeed! . . . it was your Papa and I who paid for it, and you can very well earn your own spending money after the baby is born."

Before long I will be a grandfather, which is not so bad, though I wish of course that it were Rose's child and not Bak Li's.

That is one of the great pleasures life has to offer a man—a son's son. I console myself with the certainty that Weng Khim will soon be pronounced cured, and in a year I may have a little one to admire and enjoy; and I should like to see the man who has earned that pleasure with more difficulty than your son.

LETTER#82   SIXTH MONTH, SEVENTH DAY
5 JULY 1965   YEAR OF THE SNAKE

I HAVE been so beset by family problems that, for too long, I have written nothing of important events transpiring in my adopted country.

A few months ago, Field Marshal Sarit Thanarat, the political leader of Thailand and a man of great power, died. A squabble of immense proportions followed his death, for the "family" of this field marshal included nearly two hundred "wives"; each had, at the very least, a house of her own, an expensive automobile, and a claim on his will. They are striking girls, of course, many of them beauty contest winners, and they were only too glad to cater to the lusts of a sick old man in return for lives of luxury they would not otherwise have known.

The world knows by now that this nation, most of whose citizens are poor farmers, supported all of this extravagance and debauchery with

343

years of toil in their rice fields far from the conveniences and entertainments of Bangkok. Even I, who consider myself a son of China, feel embarrassed for Thailand

In his lifetime, the field marshal was known as a hard worker, an innovator, and the only man who could lead Thailand into what is called the "developed" world. Soon after his death, however, the secrecy which had shrouded his administration began to dissipate, laying bare facts both ugly and embarrassing to the Thai nation. The people have responded with slightly shocked disapproval (for whatever they hadn't known before, they suspected) and also with laughter. Sarit raised the standard of living of poor Thais, one journalist wrote—at least two hundred of them. And it is true that even the brothers and sisters of these young women, were educated and some sent abroad as the indirect result of Sarit's carnal appetites.

He was not, by the way, such a very old man in years, but what women did not take from him, whiskey did. If this was the leader considered most able to "develop" the nation, what is the true meaning of such "development"? An equally serious question, it seems to me, is whether Sarit's example is to be followed by his successors and accepted as inevitable by those they rule.

Everyone is obsessed with tales of the Sarit regime, and one cannot stop in at a noodle shop for lunch without hearing some new revelation being celebrated at the next table. The newspapers you can imagine: the coy smiles of this actress or that beauty queen smirk from every page, over reports of the millions spent on beach houses and jewels, automobiles and trips around the world. Worse are the interviews. In one, the reporter asked Miss A how she met the field marshal, whether he was charming, and was it true that her bathroom fixtures were gold-plated. Then, Miss B was asked whether she "truly loved him." The next day, Miss B hotly denied having ever known the field marshal or given such an interview, and swore to fight the defamation of her character in the courts. Two days later another report appeared, wherein Miss A alleged that Miss B had "chased after him like a dog after a mail truck," whereupon I determined never to read another line on this distasteful subject again.

Meng Chu brought home a thick magazine printed by a clever group of journalists: *The Times and Lives of Sarit's Minor Wives.*

Who could resist paging through its blaring headlines and eyestopping, enormous photographs! Neither Mui Eng nor Meng Chu, nor any of the servants who passed it back and forth feverishly over the next several days.

"Just think, if Chui Kim had entered that contest years ago," said Meng Chu, "Papa might have ended up the field marshal's father-in-law!"

"And I suppose you'd have liked being his sister-in-law," I rejoined. "One day he might have turned an eye on you, and how would you have liked that, eh? It is better to be the wife of a poor man and make do with the simple pleasures of life. But then, I don't think those girls ought to be dignified by calling them 'wives' . . . well, enough of this talk. You are the only daughter I have left, and your Papa hopes to see you marry a good man when you have finished your studies."

She smiled. "You still consider marriage the only proper topic of conversation for young ladies, don't you?"

"I do feel that way though I admit that the world has changed, Meng Chu. It will never be as it was when I was comfortable in it."

"I look at Auntie," she said thoughtfully, "and at you, and I feel that I have something of both of you. It is not bragging," she added, turning her frank gaze on me. "It is what I truly feel, a responsibility I suppose you'd call it—as if I cannot fail, with both of you counting on me."

It is painful to recall that I fought the girl's going on in school. She will finish her education, and I have no desire to pursue a match for her until then.

Weng Khim and Rose's betrothal was a festive occasion indeed. The week before, Chui Kim made a few unpleasant remarks having to do with the disappointment she felt on her own betrothal day, but I paid little attention, for this celebration honors more than an imminent marriage and after all Weng Khim is the only son of this house.

We invited all our friends and business associates to a fine dinner. Seng came, of course bringing his cheerful wife and the two eldest children. I felt proud and happy, and if any man raised an eyebrow about certain recent unfortunate events in my household, why should I care? Who in this gathering, I asked myself, had escaped every consequence of sin and sorrow in his lifetime?

Seng took me aside as he was leaving.

"Your spirits seem to be up," he said, "and I'm happy to see that, but to tell you the truth—you still look like hell, old man. Why don't you put your butt into a beach chair at the seaside for a week or so? The bakery won't fall apart without you."

Strangely, the same idea had occurred to me, if not quite in Seng's blunt terms. (He has grown rather coarse over the years, but he has also become an observant and sympathetic man. Can you believe it? I may say that, of the three of us, Tae Seng least resembles the boy he was.)

Rose fluttered about, flushed with excitement, laughing and joking with everyone. I must admit that her voice does have an unusual "carrying" quality to it, one might almost say strident . . . but no matter, she is a fine girl and not at all bad looking.

When all the guests had left, Mui Eng and I, Meng Chu, and Weng Khim cleared the litter of dishes and food from our kitchen table, put away the remains of the feast, and sank exhausted into our chairs to enjoy a cup of hot, fresh tea. Weary and happy, we reviewed the events of the day, and it was an hour to savor, to tuck away and pull out later in less happy hours. If I have learned anything during this past year, it is that the absence of sadness is good enough to call happiness, and the best memories are made of simple pleasures fully indulged and consciously appreciated.

"I think Uncle Seng's idea is super," Meng Chu ventured.

"What—he told you?"

"Of course!" she laughed. "He told me to nag you about it, and I am happy to oblige him."

"We had a good time there, at Hua Hin," I said, averting my eyes as certain memories drifted by. (I am grateful that Meng Chu has never asked to make a trip there with her friends. She is now the age of those girls in the scanty bathing suits.) "If we're going, why don't we all go? Ang Buai, too. Meng Chu, you go tell her to lock up that money tree of hers and get a little sea air with us, eh?" I began to feel almost jolly. "It will be a celebration of Weng Khim's marriage!" I said, smiling at Weng Khim. "Rose must come too. I'm sure I can get Uncle Kim to agree."

Other advantages of such a trip had occurred to me since Seng had cornered me some hours earlier. The betrothed couple would have time together . . . it would be easy enough to close an eye once in awhile. For

346

whatever I may have told Weng Khim, I fervently hope this marriage succeeds. You may disapprove of your immoral son's plotting, but they will marry soon, and if moonlight on the sands of Hua Hin can make that loud, eager, formidably healthy girl look more desirable to my son's eyes, I will be profoundly grateful.

Everyone agreed at once that we ought to make the trip, but no one could agree on where to go, or how many days to stay. When Meng Chu suggested returning to Hua Hin, Weng Khim protested loudly, declaring that Bang Saen is "more fun nowadays," though how he knows that I cannot imagine. Ang Buai showed up the next day to say that the beach at Bang Saen is filthy and the crowds terrible. Pattaya, she insisted, is the only place to go. A heated conversation ensued until, at last, none of the celebrants were speaking to each other.

"Now listen to me!" Mui Eng said at last, "This trip is in honor of Weng Khim and Rose, and his wishes ought to be respected. That is only fair."

And that night, before she turned out her bedside lamp, she said, "We'll drop Weng Khim and Rose off at Bang Saen and go the next twenty miles to Pattaya where the water is clean. Who's to know if we don't tell?" She laughed, then, at the expression on my face and said, "I could read your thoughts right through your forehead, Suang U! You scarcely tasted your dessert for plotting . . . you are a strange man . . . well, good night."

Later, unable to sleep, I kept hearing her words. "You're a strange man," she had said, and I wondered—ah, yes . . . our wedding night, upstairs in the little house on Sampheng Lane. How her eyes had twinkled with mischief when I suggested that she take a nap.

I stretched out on my left side, propped my chin on my hand, and studied her sleeping face for a long time. She looked so peaceful lying there, like a fat baby bloated with rich milk and dreaming of nothing.

LETTER#83
29 JULY 1965

SEVENTH MONTH, SECOND DAY
YEAR OF THE SNAKE

FOR MORE than an hour, I have sat with my pen in hand staring at the paper before me. In the past few years, scarcely a letter has reached

347

you from me that did not carry news of trouble or death, shame or sorrow, and you must shake your head with wonder that men save and struggle as they do to make new lives in a new land, only to find that tragedy and calamity beset mankind everywhere, and prosperity is no weapon at all.

In the past, even when I was overwhelmed by shame and trouble, I took up my pen and gladly performed the duty of an affectionate son. This day, for the first time, I dread writing to you. For I must tell you to prepare your heart for the saddest news I have yet had to share with you.

We rented a hired car with a driver for our trip to the beach, because our own automobile was not big enough for all of us. In high spirits, we packed our bags, five baskets of food and even a huge beach ball Rose had thrown to Weng Khim with a screech of laughter as she breezed into our house early that morning.

Before we had traveled ten kilometers, I was uneasy about our young driver, who sped through traffic in a fearful manner. But, as everyone teases me about my cautious ways, I tried to assure myself that he had made this trip many times before. Later, he could not be found, so I do not know if that was so.

Thirty kilometers from Bangkok, he pulled out to pass the car in front of us, and even I, who do not drive at all, knew at once that the truck approaching us in the opposite lane was coming near far too quickly, and our car speeding too fast . . . out of control, lurching, careening wildly . . . and then came the moment of terror, and before the scream that rose from all my being could reach my throat, all was blackness, pain, and confusion.

Mui Eng, my wife of twenty years, is dead.

At the moment I regained consciousness, emerging from the nightmare I was soon to find true, a composed and kindly young nurse laid her hand on my arm and studied my face sympathetically.

"You are in the Chonburi Hospital," she said quietly. "You were brought here after—after your accident. Are you in pain?"

I shook my head feebly, for though all my body ached dully I was certain that I had suffered no real injury.

"You are a very lucky man. You were thrown clear of the car and landed in a pond near the roadside. Some little boys fishing nearby dragged you up the bank and stayed with you until the ambulance came."

"The others?"

"I am sorry . . . your wife did not survive. But your children and— is it your sister-in-law? Yes? All of them are doing fine. The youngest girl has a broken arm, but she will be all right. I know it may be of little comfort," she added, averting her eyes from mine, "but it was a miracle that only one of your family was lost. I-I know, I was with the ambulance. I will leave you alone now. You see that little button on your headboard? If you need me, you press it, but I am going to give you a sleeping pill now, so you should get some rest."

She left me alone then, alone with twenty years of my life, and I struggled against sleep as a thousand half-forgotten incidents swarmed about in my throbbing brain like vicious wasps.

I closed my eyes and saw Mui Eng at seventeen, opening the kitchen shutters on Sampheng Lane in the chill mist of a Bangkok dawn. The shutters opened, then quickly closed with an echoing sound, opened again, slammed again, while the young Mui Eng, grinning foolishly, popped in and out like the doll on a German clock I saw once in a department store on Ratchaprasong Road. Each time she bobbed through the shutters, she tossed out a jade bracelet pinned inside a soft, pink lady's towel. Then, suddenly, the shutters opened to reveal Mui Eng at thirty, scowling and fat. Again it opened, and she was older, puffy and a little gray at the temples. "My money!" she shouted, her face bloated and flushed with rage, "My father's money!" The shutters slammed again, and this time when they burst open I screamed and sat bolt upright in the hospital bed, for her face was brutally smashed and covered with blood.

I shook my head violently and groped for the bell. My pajamas were drenched with sweat, and I trembled as if in the delirium of a fever. But then a new feeling washed over me as the drug began to take another kind of hold on my mind, and I sank back gratefully against the pillows. Soon I was unconscious.

When I was awakened many hours later, it was Ang Buai I thought of first, for in the gentler dreams of my deepest sleep she had led me from the wreckage of the car, comforted me beside a still pond, and cool breezes had blown about us under a mild blue sky.

The next day I was pronounced well enough to be out of bed, and it is not possible to describe the sense I had of being a different man. I felt, as I dressed and prepared to leave my room, that nothing could ever be the same again—not our home or the business, not even my children, and certainly not myself. But I had no premonition about our future, mine or the children's, nor did I make any attempt to think beyond the present.

I could not bear to look at her, and turned away in sorrow from the terrible remains of Mui Eng, grateful for the time- and mind-consuming duties that awaited me. We had made no plans for death, for we were young and accustomed to the best doctors and hospitals in Bangkok, and accustomed to having money enough to pay for them. But the modern world mocks our prosperity, for there is no medicine to prevent mindless use of the powerful automobiles which maim and kill so many. The foolish boy who drove Mui Eng to her death escaped, as so often happens in such cases, and I call down a curse upon him, though I know it is a sin to do so.

It was Meng Chu who suffered the broken arm, and because of it she missed several days of school. Many of her friends came to visit her, and she greeted them with becoming gravity. Only at night did I hear her cry, alone in her room, but I did not go to her then, for her relationship with her mother was deep and strong and I had had no part in it. They were nothing alike, these two, but the early days of Meng Chu's life, when she was a sickly child to whom no one paid the least attention, whose own father scarcely acknowledged her existence, those days had formed a bond between them that never weakened and they had shared many simple pleasures and quiet, comfortable hours.

Meng Chu's friends also attended the temple ceremonies, and I must say they seem a nice enough group, young and fresh-faced, and unfailingly polite to me. But one young man has given me an unwelcome sense of foreboding about her future. He brings roses, and looks at her in a disturbing manner. He is Thai, and is called "Winyu."

"Who is that one?" I asked her one evening as we walked home from prayers at the temple.

She looked up, startled, then lowered her eyes to the white cast that still covered her left arm. "Just a friend. He is studying at the university to be a teacher. His younger cousin is in my class."

"And what else?"

"What else? Well, let's see. His name is Winyu Thiploet, he lives with his mother in Thonburi in a rented house. She makes candy and sells it and they are poor, but they used to have orchards in Chantaburi. When his father died, she sold the orchards so that he could go to the university and, in a few months, he will graduate and they will live happily ever after."

"You know everything about him,"

"You seemed to want his life history, so I gave it to you. Knowing his cousin's, it is not unreasonable that I would know his. Anything else you want to know?"

"You know why I ask."

"Yes." She paused and cleared her throat as she always does when she has said as much about a subject as she intends to say. "What are you going to do about the funeral, Papa? We don't even have a crypt. I realize you are—upset, but you must make up your mind soon."

"Yes. I know, but I don't want to put her down at Saraburi, Meng Chu. That's the logical thing to do, but think of Cheng Meng Day, having to go way out there. Will you all understand if I say I don't want to leave the city anymore?"

"Then have her cremated, Papa."

"What—like a Thai?"

"Many Chinese cremate their dead now. It isn't as if we lived in a village and had a proper cemetery. Here, we must drive fifty miles to honor family graves, and land keeps getting more scarce. You know it doesn't make any sense."

"I will have to think about it carefully. I—such a thing never occurred to me. I have to see my friends—"

"Only what you think matters. Go off by yourself for a day, think it over, and we'll all abide by your decision. But don't go out and have tea with some old crony who will make you feel like a traitor to the homeland. That is one thing I will not respect, if you let your mind be made up for you because you are afraid to disappoint others."

"I never let anyone make my mind up for me!"

How clever she is.

"I shall see your aunt first," I said, though I knew that Ang Buai would agree with this idea at once, she who has always been more sympathetic to convenience than to the traditions of our people.

Once, at a funeral all the family attended, she expressed annoyance with our custom of burning paper possessions. To honor the dead man, she said, the family would have done better to donate money to a hospital than to burn little television sets and cardboard Mercedes-Benz automobiles. I asked whether, then, she disapproved of giving food to monks at dawn, but she surprised me by replying, "Since it hurts no one, it probably does some good." As for paying homage to our ancestors, she approved of that as well. "Gratitude is never old-fashioned," she pronounced solemnly, but her eyes sparkled so mischievously that I began to wonder at what point in the conversation she had abandoned principle in favor of amusing herself at my expense.

Most of the young, educated people Meng Chu brings to our home appear to have left what used to be called "faith" to the peasants, turning wholeheartedly to the embrace of "science." Evil spirits and ghostly signs, however, still seem to fascinate everyone, and if the thrillers I spy under their textbooks are any indication I might venture the opinion that superstition dies harder than piety.

While we grieve over the death of our wife and mother, we are grateful to see Weng Khim and Rose draw closer together. She has performed every duty of a faithful daughter-in-law since the tragedy. I hope that Kim will not ask us to delay the wedding. Of course no one would blame him, for no man wishes to see his daughter married in mourning, but it will be three years before the marriage can take place if he and Chaba will not consent to have it now.

I dreaded writing this letter, and now that I have come to the end of it I am only sorry I did not write sooner, for I feel at peace. My children do not yet understand the power of custom and habit to heal the wounds life inflicts. I write to you, for it is my duty as a son. I carry out meticulously the solemn responsibilities involved in my poor dead wife's funeral, and I seek to fill my days with the performance of the thousand trivial tasks that are a part of our tradition of mourning. Why do I do these things? To honor the dead and the living, and more than that, to survive with dignity. The poor in China learned long ago that if life is hard and the future at best undependable, dignity as least is beyond no man's purse.

WHEN I did go to see my friends, and ask their advice in the matter of cremating Mui Eng, they were not only opposed to the idea but shocked that I would consider it.

"Mui Eng died on a journey," I explained to Seng and Kim. "Why take her on another? What is the point of tormenting her spirit further? Anyway, I can't find a place near Bangkok. There's no land left for cemeteries."

"Maybe you're afraid of joining her by way of upcountry traffic," said Kim, and set a steaming bowl of beef *masaman* curry between us. The table was laden with all the house specialties, at Chaba's insistence, and she hovered near me all during the meal. She, who has never been at a loss for words, was curiously upset by Mui Eng's death. On the day we returned from Chonburi she was at the house waiting for us, red-eyed and silent, having cleaned the house and filled the kitchen with food enough to last a week, but said less than a dozen words before she fled, refusing to accept our thanks with more than a brief, tearful bob of her head.

She has become extremely thin, a poor advertisement for her own good food. Perhaps Mui Eng's death affected her so strongly because she feels her own life to be in jeopardy, though Kim has said nothing about her health to me since he complained about her love of hot peppers many years ago.

"So," I said, "you think Mui Eng is impatient for me to join her in the land of the dead? I doubt that! And the more I listen to all of you, the more I agree with Meng Chu."

"You!" Seng exclaimed. "You of all people, shaming the rest of us on every holiday for neglecting some detail or other that no one but you and the gods remember!"

I accepted the jibe with good grace and said, "The world has changed for us, Seng. I admit that I have been a nuisance, behaving like an old man before my time, but I too have learned. We Chinese used to send our dead back to China, so that people in our village would bury them in the earth beside their ancestors. Later we sent them to Chantaburi, to Saraburi . . . why? Chantaburi is no land of ours."

"I shall have her cremated because it is the sensible thing to do, and if any man has words to say behind my back, tell him that I observe our customs to the limit of what is reasonable, for the Chinese are a reasonable people. But to drive a body fifty miles to bury it because we would bury it in China if we could? There is no reason to that."

I spent many baht on the little paper possessions for her funeral. Meng Chu looked them over the day they were delivered, with evident disapproval.

"Burning all this stuff, Papa! It's ridiculous, don't you see that? Sometimes, you even see little people," she said with a shudder of distaste, "a reminder of the days when real people were sacrificed along with the dead. Is that a custom worth remembering?"

"In this family we have never had the little people, not even in your grandfather's time. But these other things," I said, indicating the neat rows of delicately fashioned chairs and tables, beds and chests, "they mean something to me that I cannot explain to you. And I can no more leave them out of the ceremony than you can pretend to appreciate them. Let us each be as we are, and respect each other."

"I agree, but—I have been giving this some thought, and there are other things we could do in addition to this. I've often heard you say that you felt sorry for children made homeless by fires in the city. Why not donate money where it can do good, instead of burning it all up? Or do you honestly believe Mama will use these things in the spirit world? I can't believe you do."

"But it is the custom, to honor our dead in this manner—"

"But why can't we honor the living? I loved Mama with all my heart, but this is not love, not to me!"

"Meng Chu, we have saved money already by deciding not to buy a funeral plot or a crypt. Shall I let it be said that I begrudged your mother even this? And don't be so certain that money given to charity here reaches the hands of the poor. You have only to read the newspapers to learn that that is not so."

"Then help a Chinese charity, if you think that's safer."

"I do."

In the end, we sent gifts to a Chinese foundation which aids the poor and disaster stricken, and also to a Chinese hospital. I confess that it gave me a sense of real satisfaction, not only because it was a good thing to do but because Meng Chu looked so happy. She is the only person in the house with whom I can discuss these things, for Weng Khim is always out somewhere with Rose. I am sure he feels responsible for all that has happened, even his mother's death.

"Papa, do you think you will marry again?" Meng Chu asked.

"What? Indeed, I don't know what you can be thinking of."

"You are young, Papa, and you haven't got a paunch like all your friends. You will be considered a great catch, especially after I've married and gone."

"I do not expect to marry again, to tell you the truth. On the contrary, I worry about you marrying . . . You do plan to finish school, I hope."

"Of course! After all, I'll be graduating in a few weeks."

"And then?"

"And then that will be it, at least for awhile."

"Why, dear? Am I to beg you to go on with your studies, after all?"

She smiled. "That would be ironic. It's just that I don't think the time is . . . right, not now."

"It isn't that boy, I hope—the tall, dark, Thai schoolteacher who brings roses!"

To lose this daughter whose birth I cursed, and whom I now depend on for so many things—how shall I bear that? She is so clever, Mother, so warm and loving, and she is truly all I have left, for Chui Kim and Bak Li are absorbed in family problems of their own. I was about to write that Weng Khim and I are now too far apart to ever be as we were, but the truth is that we never have been close, in the way that Father and I were close. He comes to the supper table, sits down and eats and rushes out again with no more than a perfunctory exchange of words.

Only Meng Chu comes home with a funny story to tell me, or asks my advice about something she needs no advice about, or she starts an argument that ends in teasing laughter. She lifts my heart.

I have decided to work in Mui Eng's store, for that is all I care to do now. I shall turn the bakery over to Weng Khim and Rose and what remains of the import business to my colleagues, for Weng Khim is not interested in it. The old trucks and the car will be sold to pay bonuses to our employees, and those Weng Khim cannot use I will place with my friends. If this is a rash decision on my part, at least no one shall suffer for it.

I am so weary of striving, Mother, and eager for peace. The rhythm of the days in Mui Eng's little shop holds that promise. I hope you are not disappointed in a son who is satisfied with so little.

LETTER #85   ELEVENTH MONTH, FIFTH DAY
27 NOVEMBER 1965   YEAR OF THE SNAKE

"AM I to marry her off, then, with a mourning band on her wedding gown?" Kim twirled the last inch of beer in his glass and stared at it morosely. "It doesn't seem right to me, especially after, you know, after all of that . . ."

"I want to see them married, Kim. Three years, think of it! It is a long time. Surely Rose does not want to remain betrothed for three years."

"Don't you think I know what is in your mind? Grandchildren! Or—pardon me, grandsons. You aren't seventy years old, Suang U. There is plenty of time."

In the end, he relented, and the gossip that ensued did not trouble him, for though it is difficult to persuade Kim to do what he would rather not do, he is curiously immune to criticism once he has done it. Often, over the years, I have thought him a weak-minded man, yet Kim married a Thai and worked hard to build the reputation of his fine restaurant, which, if it is still patronized mainly by workingmen, is an extremely profitable concern. It may be only that his strengths are not the ones we Chinese most admire.

Rose wanted to wear a pink gown, for pink is the color brides favor here, and she was sullen for many days after I forbade the wearing of color. This is a wedding to honor Mui Eng as well as the living elders. I explained to her one evening at tea that it would shame the memory of her mother-in-law if she were to conduct herself as if the tragedy had never happened.

"Then what color do you expect me to wear?" She pouted like a child, thrusting her lips out. "I am dark, and pink is the only color that doesn't make me look . . . muddy!" Then she folded her arms across her chest and began to sniffle most unbecomingly.

"How about white?" Meng Chu asked, laying a sympathetic hand on Rose's shoulder. "It's the *farang* bride's color, white for purity, and you could wear a white hat and veil, too. Why, you would look wonderful in white, Rose, and you'd be the most modern bride in Bangkok besides! You could carry a bouquet of white orchids. Why, all the guests would be speechless!"

Rose brightened instantly. "I saw some white lace on Phahurat Road," she said, grinning sheepishly and brushing a tear from her cheek. "It's fearfully expensive, but—I deserve it!" She laughed, and Meng Chu laughed too.

"Never mind the expense!" I cried, almost laughing myself with relief. "We will gladly buy it for you, and the bridesmaids' dresses, too!"

The imported Swiss fabric she chose cost one thousand baht per meter, and for a dress which needed two meters she bought five. I was bewildered but said nothing, and it was not until I saw the material she sent over for the bridesmaids' dresses that I began to understand. Even I could see that it was terrible, cheap stuff, in a shade of green which could not possibly become anyone. When Meng Chu came home from school the afternoon it was delivered, she held it up with both hands for a moment and, with a burst of laughter, dropped it in a heap on the kitchen table.

"Papa, you are seeing a hitherto unsuspected side of your new daughter-in-law. Beware!"

"I don't understand, I'm afraid, but it is quite awful, isn't it?"

"Oh, it's awful all right . . . and it will ensure that Rose stands out from the crowd."

"Meng Chu, what is she doing with the extra three meters of that Swiss lace?"

"Doing with it? Nothing. She's going to keep it as a—memento."

"That seems rather mean-spirited to me."

"Yes."

We invited only fifty guests—our relatives, close *sae* brothers, and a few business associates, and no one dared behave as wedding guests generally do. It was, for different reasons, a wedding only slightly more cheerful than Bak Li's, in spite of Rose's spectacular white gown. Weng Khim's sisters, in the cheap, bilious green cloth that not even Chui

Kim and all the dressmakers in her shop could render fashionable, expressed the mood of the occasion more nearly.

The bride and groom do not occupy Weng Khim's old room, for Rose made it clear immediately following the betrothal that she would not set foot in the room he once shared with Phanni. No one blamed her for that, and I had three rooms added on above the bakery, which pleased her, so they have an apartment of their own, now, and new furniture too. She is well aware of the fact that I greatly desired this marriage, and the implications of that for her. I must admit that I am a little disappointed in her. Weng Khim once complained that she was a "vulgar girl," and I am now forced to admit (only to you) that his words were not altogether unfair.

She insisted that they must be "alone," but she also insisted on a pair of servants, husband and wife. You see, young women today understand "alone" to mean untroubled by parents, whether his or hers. Only servants are truly welcome, and I would not be surprised if they are treated better than parents.

Of your four grandchildren, only one remains at home, and I wonder how long I will have her, for Winyu is here several times a week. Meng Chu insists, of course, that they have never been alone together, but she cannot hide her feelings for him. I sicken inside when I see the way she looks at him, and I have no weapon left but the last, most shameful one.

"Your sisters, your brothers, everyone has gone off and left me. Now I suppose you will, too. Well, there it is, that is what a father means to his children nowadays, just an empty sack to throw away."

"Auntie is alone, too," she said in a no-nonsense tone of voice. "Why don't you ask her to move in here?"

"Move in here?"

"Marry her."

"What?"

"Of course. You need little children, Papa, and someone to fight with when I'm gone. A new life, if you will."

"I don't want to listen to such talk. I have enough on my mind, and—what are you saying, anyway? The memorial dinner for your mother is weeks away, and you would have me running to her sister's house and proposing marriage."

"About the dinner, Papa," she continued as if the subject of my marrying Ang Buai had never come up, "have you made up your mind about the food?"

"Yes, it must be vegetarian. No meat at all."

"That's a good idea. Let's have the caterer make up some of those chickens and ducks for centerpieces—you know, the ones they sculpt from vegetable fat."

"Frankly, I detest those things, It is—impure, improper to my mind. What is the point of a vegetarian dinner if the first thing one notices on the tables is a flock of counterfeit ducks?"

She stared at me for a moment, then collapsed into a fit of giggles. "You're right, Papa. We must neither take life nor mock it. I'll stop by the caterer's tomorrow on my way home from school and tell him: no counterfeit ducks!"

The caterer was furious, for it denied him the chance to impress potential customers with his skill in fashioning poultry to feed the eyes. Meng Chu had to promise him that we would tell all our guests it was our own fault that the decorations were so simple, that his suggestions had been marvelous, and so on. A temperamental artist, this sculptor of vegetable fat.

Besides the feast at noon on the day of the cremation, there were gifts to be prepared for the guests. Thais give a book printed for the occasion with a picture of the deceased as a frontispiece and, sometimes, a short biography preceding the text, which may be anything from classical Thai poetry to a treatise on good health practices. We gave the customary white face towels tied with black ribbon, each bearing the words, "On the occasion of the funeral of Mui Eng Sae Lo."

The Thais, and many Chinese too, often show movies or hire a stage troupe to entertain at their funerals, and I discussed with Ang Buai and Meng Chu whether we ought to have something of the kind.

"I think it's insane!" Ang Buai snapped. "Why a funeral should be conducted like a district fair is more than I have ever been able to understand. Oh, people are bound to say that you are stingy if you don't have something, I suppose, but if the decision were mine, I wouldn't."

"I agree," Meng Chu said. "I don't want a lot of strangers crowding the temple grounds to see a movie, laughing, and throwing candy wrappers around while we mourn Mama. It's wrong, and I don't care who else does it."

I had had similar thoughts myself and was relieved to learn their feelings. There will be no one at Mui Eng's funeral more important than those of us who truly mourn her, after all, and if anyone else has unkind things to say, that is of no importance to us.

I hope you are glad to learn that I shall act in these matters as my own conscience and judgment guide me. It was you who taught me to have confidence in myself, to respect my own judgment, and if I have made any positive use of that lesson in my life it is due to your loving counsel.

I shall write again before long to tell you what my life is like with only half the responsibilities I have been accustomed to, responsibilities I sought so eagerly for so long. This morning I walked through the bakery and saw four or five unfamiliar faces at the old machines. Weng Khim said nothing to me about hiring new people, but then, there is no reason why he should. It is I who will soon be an unfamiliar face in the bakery, as much a ghost as my adopted father, or old Nguan Thong. Perhaps it would be better if I were to live away from here altogether.

LETTER #86
30 JANUARY 1966

FIRST MONTH, TENTH DAY
YEAR OF THE HORSE

THE PEOPLE of our neighborhood, I learned recently, find my letters to you a great source of amusement.

"Did you know," they whisper to any newcomer who will listen "that for twenty years Tan Suang U has written to his mother in China, and he has never received one letter in return? He must be getting, you know . . ."

Well, they are quite wrong, and I am not getting, you know . . . Nobody today understands about families, real families. Nobody knows, or cares, what old people need. "Filial piety" is nothing more than a term studied in school, a description of an old-fashioned pastime.

All I can do for you is send a little money now and again, and write my letters. I like to imagine the expressions that pass over your face as you read them, how you look when you're surprised, or glad, or concerned. And I try especially hard to imagine how you must have changed over the years.

There is one person who does try to understand why I write these letters, and oddly enough it is Winyu the schoolteacher, who hopes to marry my Meng Chu.

"I wouldn't be surprised, sir," he said the other day, "if you wrote those letters to yourself as much as to your mother. They are probably a good outlet for your feelings, especially about those things our generation doesn't understand very well."

This is what you get these days, for sending your children to a university.

"You see," he continued, "I realize that the Chinese take their responsibilities toward their parents seriously. I can understand why you would continue to write to your mother all these years though she never answered. It doesn't seem strange to me at all."

"And how do Thais feel about their parents?" I asked, grudgingly pleased at the wisdom of his words.

"Oh, the same in many ways. But they don't show their feelings in the same ways. You see, Thai parents let their sons depend upon them. The Chinese and the *farang* don't understand why Thai parents encourage that, but they do it because they see dependence as a form of love. The Chinese raise their sons in just the opposite way—your son knows that he must one day be willing to provide for you."

"Then you think we are too hard on our children?"

"I don't think that, though some Thais do. I think it is a kindness to a boy to encourage independence, and I believe that if every Thai boy had to rely on himself more and on his parents less, we would have a stronger generation of men. Anyway, our fathers can't be with us all our lives, can they? Eventually, we must face life alone."

"Why don't you sound like a Thai?"

"I'm not so unusual, sir," he smiled. "But I'm not afraid to borrow an idea, if it's a good one."

"Well, you're certainly different from most of them."

"Most of 'them,' eh?"

Meng Chu hadn't come into the room since he arrived. She had left us alone, purposely, no doubt with the hope that we would become friends.

"Some people say," the young man continued when several silent minutes had passed, "that eventually the Thais and the Chinese in Bangkok, a million and a half of each of us, will intermarry in such numbers that there will be only one, integrated group. What do you think of that?"

"I think you have a lot of gall, that's what I think. What do you expect to see, five thousand Chinese daughters carried out of Yaowarat Road each night in chartered buses?"

He laughed and said, "No, sir, not as long as all the bus companies are owned by the Chinese!"

I had to struggle to keep from laughing myself.

"I know what I am," he said quietly. "I know exactly where I stand with you, too. I'm not Chinese, not even a Thai with money. I'm just a middle-class Thai schoolteacher. But the things you believe about Thai men are as unfair as the old saw that all Chinese are greedy chiselers, if you'll pardon the expression. To be content with what you have, when it isn't much—is that so bad? We 'peaceful Thais' have been invaded, not by armies or bombs but by things—which are so much more dangerous—and by what is called progress. So far we haven't handled it all very well, but that is changing. You see, my generation is different from my father's in one important way: we are preparing ourselves to deal with the world as it is, not as we think it ought to be. We're ready to deal with the tricks and deceptions that can masquerade as 'progress,' and for that matter, with people like you, sir. I don't mean to be disrespectful, but it's the truth, and I don't want to get along with you at the cost of disrespect for myself, or merely for Meng Chu's sake . . ."

"Wonderful! Just leave my daughter here and go away, and you won't have to get along with me for anybody's sake!"

"I believe that you and I could come to respect each other."

"Don't kid me—you don't like the Chinese!"

"That isn't so. I like everybody, Chinese included. It's an old Thai failing, you know. We're too agreeable. What I do not like is the fact that you came to my country and got rich in my country, and now you sit there and tell me I can't marry your daughter. And you tell your son that he has to marry a nice Chinese girl. You, personally, I rather like, but your attitude toward your place in our society I frankly detest. Since

I plan to marry Meng Chu—please let me finish—I intend to tell you a few things about myself, because you ought to know what kind of person I am, even if you disapprove of me. It isn't right for her to marry a man who is a stranger to her father."

"You said it, not me."

I am not struck dumb by his golden tongue, even if she is.

"Well, I care about my work," he began, clasping his hands over his knees earnestly, "about teaching, very much. To you, I guess I seem like a dangerous radical, but I'm not at all. I want to see the country move forward, but not in a great hurry and without consideration for the consequences. I care for peace, and I want my students to develop sound attitudes toward the unpeaceful world they live in. But it isn't easy, you know . . . I tell my class that the ideal man in today's world would have the moral principles of the *farang*, the diligence of the Chinese, and the heart of the Thai . . ."

"So nobody else has a heart."

"That isn't what I said."

"Then what is the 'heart of the Thai' supposed to mean?"

"The love of peace, contentment with little concern for others, and a sense of moderation. Our new generation is more aggressive, which is good, but we must see to it that the old Thai values are not lost. I myself am not the Thai who will compete with a Chinese millionaire in the Bangkok business world ten years from now, but I may have been his teacher."

"Oh, I've seen your aggressive new generation, all right. Running in and out of bars, going to the horse races, loitering around on street corners making lewd comments to the girls passing by . . ."

"Really, sir," he said with an amused expression, "do you really think the country will stand or fall because of rude boys on street corners? Those are minor problems compared with the strides our society is making in most areas."

I have never met anyone like him. He isn't like other Thais, whatever he says, but he isn't like the Chinese or the *farang* either. He can be polite and argumentative at the same time.

"The Chinese people," he had said several days earlier, when Meng Chu was also present, "are gradually being assimilated into all the societies they have entered."

"Nobody is going to assimilate me!"

"Papa, it's not something you decide to do," she laughed. "It happens in the normal course of history."

"Your idea of normal is different from mine."

"Excuse me, sir," Winyu interjected, "but wouldn't you rather see people marrying each other than fighting each other?"

"A remark," I said, "which proves that you know exceedingly little about the state of marriage. My children are very stubborn, Winyu. Meng Chu has devoted most of her life to arguing with her father. She's a great champion of your people, and she's been calling me a bigot for years. You haven't said anything she hasn't said before."

"I'm sorry if I—"

"Ah, don't apologize! Anyway, it seems to be the fashion nowadays for children to insult their parents. Meng Chu has been breaking me in slowly."

"I respect you sir, and so does she. But Meng Chu doesn't mean to insult you when she asks to be respected as a person. She only wants you to accept her as an intelligent, feeling human being. Does that have to mean disrespect?"

Children want so many things. Who can keep track of all their "needs"? And why don't I remember having such "needs" as a child? When children get into trouble nowadays, there are only two possible reasons for it: either the parents meddled in their lives and didn't leave them alone, or the parents didn't give them enough attention and they felt left alone. Meng Chu tells me that good parents should be consistent, uncritical, supportive, and understanding with their children. That is what they teach her in school. I can't wait until she has four children of her own. I want to go over there and find out how that works.

After Winyu left, I tried to talk to her about her future.

"So you are going to go ahead with this. I know I have nothing to say. After all, I'm only your father, not an intelligent, feeling human being . . ."

"Oh, please. If by 'going ahead with this' you mean, am I going to marry Winyu, then the answer is yes, I am going to marry Winyu."

"You think you know him well enough?"

"I doubt it. I don't know myself very well, either. And I hardly know you at all, though I've lived with you all my life."

"That answer is my reward for sending you to school all those years. Try a few plain words for a change: do you think you can be happy with that man?"

"We think we can be happy," she replied. "We have a more intellectual than emotional relationship."

"Ah! We are 'assimilated,' we are 'intelligent and feeling,' we are 'more intellectual than emotional'! You know a lot of big words, Meng Chu, but what do you know about life?"

"Papa, would you have Thailand like America, where the races hate each other, and resort to shooting and rioting? Pride of race is nothing but an excuse for jealousy and hatred, and this country is sick with the same disease, only the symptoms are milder. People from the countryside are looked down on in Bangkok, and everybody looks down on the Northeasterners—they say they aren't 'real Thais,' but Laotians. We Chinese aren't the only minority, you know. There are Muslims, Vietnamese, Indians, hill tribes . . . if we can't start doing better at getting along with each other, we're all in trouble."

"So you are going to risk your life on him."

"What marriage is not a risk? Chui Kim's husband is a good man, but being Chinese doesn't make him so, any more than being Chinese makes Bak Li's husband less of a stinker. You know you can't stand the sight of him yourself, Papa, don't try to tell me otherwise. I'm going to marry Winyu because we think we can be happy together. We may be wrong, and if we are . . . then we'll think again."

"Think what again?"

"I wouldn't stay married to a man for the rest of my life if I could see the marriage going sour."

"So you think marriage is some kind of arithmetic problem you can do over again if you get it wrong the first time?"

"Exactly! That's a very good way to put it, Papa. If I get it wrong the first time, I fully intend to do it over." She turned from me angrily and said, in a sad quiet voice, "What did you and Mama ever have that was worth hanging onto in that marriage?" I felt as though I might faint. Instead, I turned abruptly and walked out of the house.

Ang Buai was sitting at her kitchen table eating a big dish of her favorite brown coconut pudding.

365

"Mmph!" she said with her mouth full of pudding, waving me into the kitchen.

"Swallow first."

"M-m, thank you. Sit down—have some pudding." She wiped her mouth with a paper napkin and said, "You look awful. What's wrong?"

"Your youngest niece is going to marry Winyu the schoolteacher."

"So?"

"Is that all you can say . . . So?"

"She's old enough to get married. What do you expect me to say?"

"Ang Buai, he is a Thai schoolteacher."

"Well, who did you expect her to marry, an ice cream vendor?"

"I'd rather she did. At least all the ice cream vendors are Chinese."

She put her spoon down carefully on the plate beneath her bowl, propped her chin in her hands, and stared at me. "Suang U, men are walking in space and you would rather have your brightest child marry a Chinese ice cream vendor than a Thai schoolteacher? When are you going to catch up with the rest of the world?"

"She'll have nothing but trouble!"

"Leave the girl alone, Suang U. You can't make people happy. If Winyu makes Meng Chu miserable, it won't be because he's Thai instead of Chinese."

"Wait! Wait until you hear the rest of it. If it doesn't work out, she's already planning to get a divorce!"

"Would you rather run her life, and then feel responsible for every sorrow in it? Do you want to choose a husband for her yourself, and then maybe he turns out to be a drunk, or he beats her, or they can't have children together? Do you want to bear all that guilt?"

"It is a parent's duty, especially a father's."

She rose from the table with a deep sigh and said, "If you don't want any pudding I'm going to clear the table. I think you're being very foolish."

"If she marries Winyu, they will get nothing from me."

"Do you really mean that?" She stood before me with a pudding bowl in each hand.

"You're damned right I mean it."

"In that case," she said, crossing the room and dropping the bowls into the sink carelessly, "Meng Chu is lucky her auntie is still around!"

366

Then she left the room, slamming the door behind her and leaving me sitting there, alone in her kitchen.

This is what I get from the one person I hoped would understand how I feel. There is something worse than being lonely, it appears. Being humiliated and lonely.

—

NOT CONTENT to support the lovers in every way imaginable, Ang Buai has gone so far as to offer them a choice between a plot of land and an automobile as a wedding gift!

But proud Meng Chu refused, saying that she could not accept anything so extravagant.

"It isn't that we're ungrateful, Auntie, but Winyu will never take anything from the family, under the circumstances."

I couldn't help but laugh at that. "You can bet he'd like a new car," I said, ignoring Ang Buai's pointed look. "What did you expect him to say? He has to refuse, at first."

"Anyone would like to have a new car, Papa," she said angrily, "but he won't humble himself. You don't know him. Auntie, if you want to give us something, make it a small gift, maybe some pots and pans."

"How is the job search going?" she asked, letting the pots and pans pass.

"Oh, all right, I suppose. Winyu is sure to be offered a teaching post when he graduates, but that's only a thousand baht a month. Of course, it will be more when he has his master's degree, and I won't have much trouble finding a bookkeeping job. That's another thousand or so."

"Two thousand baht a month—there's a fine income," I said. "How do you think you can live on that, eh? Why, your Mama's shop here brings in three thousand even when business is slow, and that's nothing. I tell you, you'll never keep your bellies filled to the end of a month."

"Winyu is as frugal as I am."

"Frugal. There isn't a person in your generation who knows the

367

meaning of the word. What are you doing about your betrothal, by the way? Or is that old-fashioned?"

"You're quite right. A wedding is enough."

"Will there be no betrothal gifts?"

"One small gift, to remember the day. But no show of wealth for the sake of the wedding guests."

"Wizardly boy, Winyu. He gets a free wife, and you leave your father's house with nothing but pots and pans. But I give you my blessing in spite of it, because I know you would only run off with him and cover my face with shame if I didn't. He hasn't even sent an elder from his house to ask for your hand. What do they think of you over there? Perhaps they are not so happy to have their son marrying the daughter of a *chek* merchant!"

"As a matter of fact, Winyu's mother is coming to see you this week, and she's the only elder he has. I want to ask you one favor: don't ask her for anything. I mean, if you expect them to come up with anything approaching Chui Kim's wedding gifts, we'll have to live in sin, and you won't like that."

"Meng Chu," I retorted angrily, "every coin that passed from Seng Huat's family into this house I used for the jewelry she wore the day she left us."

"I am simply telling you that we want nothing from any of you—no house, no car, no money. All I want is—is to feel that you are not displeased with me."

"You go against my wishes, you even reject the gifts your adoring aunt would heap on you, and then you tell me not to be displeased. I have to be happy about the situation on top of everything else! Well, soon enough I will see how well you live on—love."

"Stop it," Ang Buai said quietly. "What kind of father are you, that instead of rejoicing in your child's happiness, you poison the air with your selfish, bitter words? Does nothing matter to you more than having your own way? I should think you'd have learned better by now."

"You are telling me, then, that I have had my own way before? When? Weng Khim shamed himself, Bak Li shamed me, and now this!"

"This is no shame, Suang U, and you will be a sorry man if you drive Meng Chu away. Why don't you accept the children as they are, and look forward to your grandchildren?"

"Grandchildren, eh? How will these two keep from starving to death when the babies start coming?"

"That won't be for quite awhile, Papa."

"Hah! At your age, the babies come easily."

"I'm going to take the pill, and it's guaranteed."

"'The pill'?! It is a terrible sin to take that medicine. How can you even bring yourself to speak of it?"

"Sin, Papa? The pill does not take life, it only prevents life."

I did not know where to look for shame. A girl not yet twenty speaking of such a matter as if she were discussing the color of her wedding dress or the food to be served at the bridal dinner.

Perhaps the real reason she plans to take these pills is that in her heart she knows that Winyu, without money or standing in the community, is no fit father for her children. I do not understand why this generation marries at all, when they have abandoned all that is meant by marriage.

"Stop looking at me like that!" she said suddenly. "Nobody today is ashamed of planning a family."

"What is 'planning a family'?"

"How many children to have, and when—it is the only reasonable thing to do."

"It is a selfish approach to life, it seems to me."

"On the contrary, it is one reason the *farang* nations have prospered. They encourage family planning to ensure each person a good life, not just life for its own sake."

"M-m . . . I'm curious to know what your partner in the good life is giving you as a token of his esteem. Or is that a secret?"

Meng Chu smiled at her aunt and said, "It's no secret at all. Auntie already knows! He gave me a beautiful necklace, Papa, gold with a pendant of diamond chips surrounded by pearls. I chose it myself."

"Close to the heart," Ang Buai added, beaming. "Meng Chu didn't ask for a ring, like the others."

"We shall see," I said, disconcerted by this unexpected generosity on

Winyu's part, "what your feelings are in a year. I have little faith in any young men today, even some of the Chinese. I have seen them, I know what they do after a few months of marriage."

I thought of Seng, who still loves his nightclubs and seeks pleasure in the massage parlors, wasting thousands, eagerly giving in to temptation whenever possible. On the other hand, Seng stays jolly on heavy wines and rich foods, while Suang U chews the crusts of old dreams and is discontent, so who is the wiser man?

"When is the wedding to be?"

"We aren't sure yet. There must be a water-pouring ceremony, the Thai way, but there won't be much of a wedding dinner. We're thinking of doing a small buffet ourselves, four dishes or so. Little steamed fish puddings, fried meat and peppers, and—"

"I will die!" I shouted, unable to believe my ears. "My daughter's wedding feast, with poorer food than I allow on my own supper table? Why don't you be really frugal and buy a barrel of dried fish from the market? You can give all the guests plastic spoons and let them dig right in!"

Ang Buai covered her mouth and rocked with silent laughter.

"You must have a proper table," I said. "At least, that."

"No! The purpose of the wedding dinner is to share our happiness with our friends, not to impress people."

"Share your happiness, eh? Will there be any presents for the guests after the feast at which nobody gets anything to eat?"

"Papa, please at least try to understand. We don't want to go into debt to make our wedding fashionable."

"I agree that it is foolish to go into debt at the beginning of marriage," Ang Buai said, "when a young couple should be trying to put money aside."

"A lot they'll put aside on their income. In five or six years, maybe they can go out to a movie."

It gives me a headache to argue with these women. Why can't they realize that this is no time for marriage, without money or the certain prospect of any? But no, they rush to marry and then postpone having children, which is against all reason, and Ang Buai grins like an idiot and gives her blessing to it all.

What would Winyu's mother be like? I was curious to see a Thai woman who would come asking for the hand of a Chinese merchant's daughter for her son . . . or was she, perhaps, hopeful of certain advantages?

I did not have long to wait, for Winyu's mother paid the promised call within the week.

Frankly, I was amazed when a very attractive, immaculately dressed woman entered my office. I had expected, I was forced to confess to myself later, a betel-nut-chewing hag with dark, leathery skin and the glittering, avaricious eye of an upcountry beggar in the marketplace.

"Thaokae is aware of the reason for my visit," the tall, stately woman said quietly, keeping her eyes firmly rooted to mine. "I am the mother of Winyu."

"Ah . . . yes indeed. I—please sit down, won't you? Have a nice cup of tea with me and we'll, er, talk about the young ones. I have wondered for a long time how you—what you think about all this."

She accepted the cup of tea gracefully, then smoothed her skirt with her free hand and said, "I do not know . . . one gives in on so many things and then . . . Winyu said that I must see you, tell you that . . . that he loves your daughter, and wishes to marry her. He does love the girl, and I think she is a very charming child."

"Yes. My daughter also, er, seems . . . that is, you have a fine boy there. Winyu is a fine boy indeed."

"We are poor," she said slowly. "Thaokae is perhaps dismayed at that. I would not have come to you, except that Winyu was so sure you would respect your daughter's wishes."

"Indeed I will. To keep her from running off with him."

The woman drew back slightly, offended. "I do not believe you need worry about that. Winyu takes his position as a teacher seriously. He has a strong sense of duty. But he is not planning a very suitable wedding, if I may say so. What do you expect, in accordance with your customs?"

"Nothing," I muttered. As if it mattered, when nothing is all they have.

"I am poor, but I have saved—"

"No no, please—you must leave it up to them," I hastened to say, embarrassed.

"Thaokae does not like my son. I can tell."

"I believe that they are too young. And let us be honest with each other; your people are very different from ours. No, I do not think there is a good basis for marriage there. But then, my notion of marriage is hopelessly out of date, or so I have been assured."

"You know, it seems to me peculiar that you find the difference between our people an important consideration. I do not. Thai and Chinese, we are cousins, and I have no difficulty in accepting a Chinese daughter-in-law. When we lived in the countryside, there was a Chinese merchant in our town, and we were all fond of him. He married my sister, and they have been happy together."

"Then you have no objection to this marriage?"

"My Winyu may have a chance to study abroad; his grades have been excellent. I don't mind his marrying a Chinese girl. I would be less happy were he to bring home a *farang*. I do not say that I would send her away, or behave unkindly to her, but I would be happier to see him married to a girl who has grown up here. When people are young, and fall in love, they do not think of being old together. But it is in the long years when people are old together that what is called 'background' matters, when to be happy is to know the meaning of life, and of death . . . for the Thai, for the Chinese, that is not so different."

"You are a very wise woman."

"I will tell Winyu that we have spoken," she said, and rose to leave.

Suddenly Bak Li burst into the room, pregnant and round as a rain barrel, disheveled and red-eyed from crying.

"Oh, Papa!" she wailed, "I'm so miserable!" And she bolted across the room toward me, oblivious of the tall, dignified woman who cast her eyes discreetly downward and closed the door behind her.

"It's Surasak's mother!" she blubbered, sinking heavily into the chair the older woman had sat in a moment before. "She's awful!" She pulled a crumpled handkerchief from her pocket and sobbed into it wholeheartedly.

"Do you expect him to throw his mother out of the house? He would not be much of a man if he did."

"I know, but she whines and complains all the time, and she's so dirty. Oh, you can't believe the things she does, she even goes through the neighbors' garbage looking for old tin cans. The house is full of them, piles of dirty, rusty old tin cans, and I have to wash them or we'd have rats all over the place. If she wants a cup of coffee from the shop at the corner, she takes one of her wretched cans down there and brings the coffee home, because they charge her a few satangs less! And she wants me to do it, too!"

"It is only that you do not understand her, Bak Li. You do not know what it is to have been really poor. Many people never recover from it. But that is not the point. You chose this man, you left your parents to be his wife. Now I see you fat and healthy, wanting for nothing. All the rest, I am afraid, is . . . too bad. You never asked my advice when it might have done you some good. By the way, did you know that your younger sister is to be married?"

"To that Thai?" she sniffed.

"She too has found a husband of her own choosing. And she will have to endure the consequences, just as you must. Weng Khim and Chui Kim alone have earned the right to come in here and complain about their marriages. Now—I suppose you have come to ask for money."

"N-no, I have enough. And don't worry," she retorted stiffly, stuffing the wrinkled handkerchief back into her pocket, "I won't come troubling you again."

"Come, come, child, I am not casting you out into the street. To tell you the truth, I have been thinking of you all lately, of how I can . . . but never mind that now."

"I don't understand."

"Not now, I have nothing to tell you now. Go home and don't worry. Your Papa will think of something." Then I rose and patted her shoulder, embarrassed for us both and saddened more than I would have her know, poor child.

How to explain to her what is in my mind, how to explain to any of them? I have a notion to give up even Mui Eng's little store and move across the river to Thonburi. And leave them to their own lives, with capital. Shall I give an equal share to Meng Chu? She has brought me less shame than Bak Li, if no less heartache. I must wait and see what comes of that marriage.

Bak Li's husband is really a terrible fellow, as mean and grasping as his unfortunate mother, "modern" only when it came to violating my daughter to meet the mortgage on his building. I am grateful now that the Thai marriage license was avoided.

373

For a couple of years, Weng Khim had thrashed about like a fish in too small a pool, learning almost too late that outside the pool he could not survive at all, but it is Meng Chu who defies me triumphantly, knowing herself to be free as her brother can never be. Education has made modern woman clever and competent, but it has also made her selfish. If only I didn't love Meng Chu so . . .

I am tired of it all, and I long for a little place far from all that I have known. Meng Chu wants me to marry Ang Buai. That is unimaginable. We are too different, and anyway I am too burdened with failures and disappointments now. Marriage is not a cure for anything.

I read somewhere that every generation surpasses the previous one, that it is unavoidable, and logical. How opposite from the beliefs and customs of my youth. Confucius taught that the world progresses only toward calamity when children do not follow the ways of parents and ancestors. Weng Khim wept like a child and asked me how he is to survive between two worlds . . . what about me? Does he realize that I studied all the years of my childhood for a kind of manhood I was never permitted to have?

When I was young, I too was stubborn, and even ran away from home to a land I knew nothing of. I had to do it, and felt that I could not survive if I did not. Perhaps my children feel that way about their own dreams. Meng Chu loves Winyu, and that is everything to her . . . love, the invisible tyrant responsible for ten times as much misery as joy in this world.

Tell me about love, Meng Chu, but not yet. Tell me later, when you have tasted more of the dish.

Soon the last of them will marry and be gone, and Mui Eng has escaped forever into the Land of the Dead. I often imagined, while they were growing up, of the day the last child would marry, and the reality of that day will mock my daydreams bitterly.

What shall I have to reflect upon the day my youngest marries? Weng Khim, broken by his own folly into an imitation of a man; Bak Li, married in haste to a scoundrel I would not have spoken to on the street; Meng Chu, running into the arms of a penniless Thai schoolteacher; and Mui Eng, a broken corpse lying in a ditch beside the Pattaya Highway. The day I looked forward to with such arrogant expectations has dawned as a day through which to survive, and nothing more.

Chui Kim, alone, seems blessed with a beneficent karma. Smug and self-righteous with her handsome, forthright husband, she has no sympathy for her brothers and sisters, and little enough for me.

—

I HAVE informed the children of my intention to close up Mui Eng's shop and move to Thonburi. Meng Chu alone had any comment to make, and that was critical.

"Papa, marry Auntie!" She cried in an exasperated tone of voice. "She cares for you, and I know you care for her, if you could only swallow your pride. The worst thing you can do now is to stick yourself off somewhere in Thonburi, away from all of us."

"What, is a daughter her father's matchmaker nowadays? Since you are well aware of the fact that your aunt and I have never carried on a conversation for longer than fifteen minutes without disagreeing, I cannot understand why you continue nagging at me to marry the woman!"

"The only thing you've seriously disagreed over is my marrying Winyu."

"Oh, child, it goes back years . . ."

"You have nothing to lose by asking her, and all of us would be pleased."

"In the first place, if she refused me I'd never be able to look her in the eye again. In the second, what would people say if I married my sister-in-law before your mother's ashes were cold?"

"Do you hold the opinion of gossipy neighbors in higher esteem than your own happiness? If they have nothing better to do than criticize you, that's their problem, not yours. Besides," she added, quickly lowering her eyes, "Auntie would not refuse you, of that I am sure."

"Let me live as I must, Meng Chu, not as you think I should. None of you understands what I need now."

"All right, Papa. Have you sold the trucks yet?"

"No, two are left. I'm leaving the good delivery truck and the car for Weng Khim and Rose."

"Then you're serious."

"I am serious."

"Where will you go?"

"I have my eye on a place."

"What's it like?"

"Not much. Two up and one down, small, deep in a quiet lane with undeveloped land in back. Undeveloped! Listen to me. It's a swamp."

"I just don't know what you think you'll do with yourself in a place like that."

"Work. I'll set up a shop like your mother's, but even smaller."

"Then why move?"

"Because I am fed up with this place, with these people, and I want to know how people live in this city beyond Sampheng Lane and Yaowarat Road. And another thing—your Mama. I need to get away from her kitchen and her favorite chair and her dishes. Everything here is hers. There is nothing in the house she didn't buy, touch, wash, sit in, or walk over, and it's driving me crazy."

"I hadn't thought of that at all . . . I'm sorry."

In spite of all the bitter words that still echo through these rooms, there are memories . . . In the room where we slept, her old sewing machine crouches in a corner, under a dozen socks no one will ever mend. In the kitchen, her battered chopping block still hangs on a hook above the sink, bearing the signatures of a thousand breakfasts, lunches, teas, and dinners. I hate the sight of the damned thing, and haven't the heart to throw it away.

I sit down to dinner and am surrounded by empty chairs. Here Bak Li sat, there Weng Khim, there Chui Kim, and across from me . . . my wife. Only Meng Chu remains, and in a few days five empty chairs will mock me at my solitary meal. How could Meng Chu have failed to understand? To survive, I must find a place where the kitchen table has no stain from nail polish Mui Eng once spilled on it, a house without memories of children with the measles playing checkers in bed, laughing so loudly that I heard them in my office below; where there are no baby shoes on the closet shelves or old shopping lists in the kitchen drawers ("Remember the batteries" read one, in Mui Eng's familiar, tiny, neat characters).

I heard Meng Chu come into the house, throw her books into a chair, and set the tea kettle on to boil.

"Papa! Come out of there and have tea with me!"

The tears that came suddenly to my eyes appalled me, and I waited for them to pass, hoping she would not come in after me.

"Good to see you around here for a change," I said, sauntering casually into the kitchen five minutes later with two or three business letters in my hand.

"Mm-m, good to see you too. Guess what. Winyu has a job! At Sathit School, which is very good. Of course, he will have to study at night to finish his master's degree." She paused to pour the tea and straighten my place mat. "There now, drink and refresh yourself. And here comes a bigger surprise: I have a job too! Keeping books for a monosodium glutamate tycoon from Taiwan. Well, my dear, he was very impressed to learn that I can speak English and Thai, in addition to Mandarin and Teo Chiu, of course. You see, Papa?" She wrinkled her nose comically. "An educated daughter is a fine thing! But the important thing is that we won't have to worry now. We can live all right on our combined income. I never thought that man would offer me so much money. I'll be making a lot more than Winyu, at least until he finishes his degree."

"How much were you offered?"

"One thousand eight hundred! If I worked for the government, I wouldn't make even a thousand, but if I do well in three months with the monosodium glutamate man, I'll get two thousand."

"Not bad at all. Perhaps I judge too hastily, but I am surprised that you look forward to working toward someone else's profit. The goal of my generation was always independence."

"What choice do we have? Winyu has to teach in a government school because the private ones pay even less. After all, he can't start his own school."

"Yes, but what confuses me is why a man whose parents had a business of their own—orchards, you said—why a man like that would want to shackle himself to the government for a pittance."

"M-m, that would be hard for you to understand. All I can say is that everybody's different. If he had stayed where he was instead of coming to Bangkok, your daughter would never have met him. Sad for her, if not for you."

"He'd have five children by now, and you'd be content to marry some nice Chinese boy of your father's choosing."

"You know better than that."

She is so like me, so determined to take life on her own terms, afraid of nothing, least of all the criticism of others, for no one can judge us more harshly than we judge ourselves. I came to realize, as I listened to her, that my leaving this house is another sign of that quality in myself, for to stay here would be to wander forever in the wreckage of the years, and life is too precious for that.

I have begun to go through the place, dividing everything among the children. I shall take only my clothes, and they will not fill the bench of a pedicab. Now I shall see, dear Mother, who comes to visit me, and whether any of them will miss me as I have missed you.

LETTER #89   FIFTH MONTH, SECOND DAY
20 JUNE 1966   YEAR OF THE HORSE

MENG CHU is a married woman, and soon I shall be a resident of Thonburi, a dweller among banana palms at the end of that inviting, quiet lane, a whole kilometer's distance from the clamor of the city.

Now that the monsoon season is here, my inviting, quiet lane is deep in muddy water, rendering those cars which dare to intrude a distinct menace to the hapless pedestrian.

Weng Khim and Rose went to see the house with me last Saturday and were appalled.

"This is impossible!" Weng Khim grumbled. "My slacks are filthy—look!" He slapped at his cuffs irritably and glowered at a retreating Toyota taxicab. "Papa, this place is the middle of nowhere. Where will you get any customers?"

"Why, they're all around you."

He ran a disparaging eye over the modest row of houses on either side of the lane and sneered, "A bunch of truck farmers!"

"Yes, but I wish to live in peace and quiet, as they do."

He and Rose exchanged a meaningful glance, and after they had spent five minutes in my little house, we returned to Yaowarat Road.

I haven't moved yet because the lease arrangements on the old house are not complete, so I spend my days pottering about in both places and having a fine time. I no longer have the least reservation about my decision.

Meng Chu often goes out to Thonburi with me to help me clean and ready the place, Chui Kim and Bak Li only occasionally. I do not think that Weng Khim and Rose will visit it again unless I die there.

Meng Chu's wedding day passed uneventfully. I did not attend, of course, but this time I felt no compunctions about heeding my own custom. Chinese people do not attend a daughter's wedding, and that is that. With each passing day, I find it harder to recall why I used to argue with them over such things, but that is in the past, and not worth the time it takes to wonder at it. And I did not mope about feeling sorry for myself on her wedding day, as I threatened to in my last letter.

"It was lovely!" Ang Buai pronounced cheerfully as she entered Mui Eng's nearly empty store. "Packing again? Why don't you take some of that kitchen stuff with you instead of giving it all to the girls? They don't need it and you will."

"Don't want it, that's all. Tell me about the wedding."

"Fun! Mostly because of Winyu's friends, Suang U. They're very nice boys, and there was none of the nonsense that went on at Chui Kim's wedding. They brought musical instruments and everyone sang. They didn't serve any liquor, by the way, and that was a plus in my estimation."

"None? At a Chinese wedding they'd never have got away with that. Besides, I thought the Thais drank themselves silly at weddings."

"You're never satisfied," she sighed. "Times have changed, and the younger, educated Thais don't want any brawling at their weddings. But they do like music, so the money goes there instead, unless they are lucky enough to have friends who can supply it free. Meng Chu and Winyu had plain food and no one minded, because they didn't go expecting a fancy dinner. Some of Winyu's classmates chipped in and bought them a small refrigerator, which ought to serve them better than a lot of fancy dishes and ugly vases. What's your gift?"

"What's yours?"

"All right, me first," she grinned. "They wouldn't take property or a car, so I gave them an electric fan. I would have given them a television set, but believe it or not Winyu and his mother have one, a gift from a relative last New Year's Day, and Meng Chu's friends gave them a stove. Sensible kids, aren't they? It's almost frightening. Odd, I think, given the fact that we've all considered them a spendthrift generation. You'll have to eat your words, my friend, because this is the most down-to-earth generation of kids that ever lived. Now—what did you give them?"

"Not a damned thing."

"You are awful."

"He's so proud, what makes you think he'd take anything from me? Before you criticize me, though, here's something you might like to have a look at . . ."

I crossed the room and took four small, blue leather folders from a bureau drawer. Bank books.

Ang Buai leafed through them quickly, then looked up at me with a startled expression.

"What did you do, wipe yourself out?"

"Not quite."

"This is—very generous, to say the least."

"M-m. I want you to keep Meng Chu's for the time being. Their damned pride, for one thing. Besides, I don't want this to look as though I approve of the marriage."

"You're an old fraud," she said, grinning.

"If they won't use if for themselves, they may use it for their children."

"Weren't you paying attention?"

"We'll see about that nonsense. And who knows? Maybe having a little money will encourage them."

"So you still think you can manipulate everybody with cold cash. Well, never mind that for now. I've been to many of my Thai friends' weddings, and Meng Chu's was one of the loveliest, in its own way. She looked lovely in the Thai wedding dress, by the way."

"She wore a Thai wedding dress? Had she no shame before his Thai relatives?"

"Shame, indeed! Meng Chu has a Thai education. She's a Thai citizen and a subject of the Thai king. I don't know why you persist in this 'what village did your grandmother come from' business. It doesn't become you!"

"Perhaps," I retorted, stung by her words, "you have it in mind to marry one of them yourself."

"How dare you say that!"

"Ah, indeed! So I touched a sensitive nerve . . ."

"It is not your business to ridicule me!"

"Ridicule you?"

"Oh, just—shut up!" she said through clenched teeth, then grabbed her handbag and flounced out of the house.

That is Ang Buai for you, and Meng Chu would have me propose marriage to her—a woman who cannot carry on a conversation for ten minutes without losing her temper. But she could not have been very angry, for I saw her thrust Meng Chu's bank book into her bag before she reached the door—she had presence of mind enough to take care of essentials.

I set out the next morning to deliver my gifts to the other three in person. My reception was different in each house.

"Papa, you're a darling!" screeched Rose, baring all her teeth, "to give us all this money. Now we can expand the bakery!"

Weng Khim showed less emotion, and mumbled his thanks almost inaudibly.

"How do you know your neighbors will sell?" I asked him.

"Oh, we wouldn't expand here," he explained. "The landlord wants this property back, didn't I tell you? Sorry. Well, we have a chance to buy across the street. I mean, we have the chance now, since getting this money. Funny, we were only talking about it yesterday, and now we can do it . . ."

Strange, it seemed to me, the way he took to the change in his fortunes, as if it could hardly matter to him either way. It is fortunate for him that Rose has enthusiasm enough for both of them when it comes to the business.

Chui Kim received me demurely by comparison with her effusive sister-in-law but, I felt certain, with more real pleasure.

"This is very good of you, Papa." She smiled and held my hands, and I felt very happy. Chui Kim has begun to lose, I am happy to say, the irritating smugness she displayed in the early months of her marriage. "But I'm glad Seng Huat is not here. I don't want him to know about it, because he would invest it in something or other . . . I think he's what you call over-extended. He's a good man, but he can't stand to see money lie in the bank. I want to keep this in case of an emergency; it isn't that I want to spend it on myself."

"I understand, and don't worry. I won't tell him. There is merit to your idea."

"Thank you. I love Seng Huat, but sometimes he scares me. Or perhaps I'm just too used to my cautious Papa!"

Bak Li had the same idea about the money, if different motives.

"Papa, you should never have come without calling or sending a message," she whispered, lest Surasak's mother hear her from the next room. "Don't you know he'd take it all? Please, don't make me tell him about it!"

"No, I won't make you tell him. In fact, I would feel better if you put the bank book out of sight, or left it with me."

I stayed for lunch, an awful meal the old woman presided over dressed in a blouse and wide pants so dirty that their original colors were not to be guessed at. She whined on endlessly.

"Look, look!" she cried, pointing a bony, trembling finger at a bowl of fried shrimps. "Expensive, like gold! But what does she care? Does she bargain in the market? Bah! Whatever price they tell her, she's happy to pay it, drops the money into their hands and laughs. And chickens—eeh, she comes home with a fat chicken in her basket every day . . . every day is a feast in this poor house!"

"Surasak likes chicken," said Bak Li, her jaw rigid.

"So you have to give it to him? Tchah! We did well enough before you came along. You think it's shameful to eat dried fish and pickles and a bowl of rice gruel, but I'll bet your papa has got by on less, eh?"

Her shrewd old eyes caught and held my own, and I felt sick. She goes on like this every day, I thought, at every meal. I should not have been so hard on Bak Li the day she came crying to me. Well, she has the bank book now.

When the old woman finally tottered off grumbling to herself, I said, "Old people are often like that, you know." Bak Li looked up from her plate and tried to smile at me, but her lips quivered and the tears streamed down her plump cheeks.

382

As I walked off down the street, I thought of you, and knew that I had not believed my own words of comfort. To excuse the old crone because of age would be a lie, for I am sure that Surasak's mother was a hag at twenty.

—

YOU SEE a new address above, for your son is now a resident of Thonburi. I have met almost all my neighbors—that is to say, all the Chinese, many of whom have lived in this very lane for forty years. They are a thrifty, honest lot who gather in the coffee shop at the end of the lane every evening to enjoy each others company. The comforts of their homes are few, and no television aerials roost on these modest roofs.

Their talk is of China, many old stories and some new, or of the current news. They are the easiest people to talk with I have ever met. Checker games are picked up each evening, games that began decades ago, yet they accepted me without suspicion—if not without curiosity.

"You're new," the owner of the coffee shop declared with a friendly grin, "down at the new store, right?" (The "new" store is twenty-five years old.) "Married?"

"My wife died recently."

"Oh . . . I am sorry." He polished a glass slowly and set it before me. "Any children?"

"Four. All married."

"What, at your age? Oh, ho! No one would think it, my friend. Don't you have a son you could live with, instead of building your own nest down here?"

"Yes, but I like it here. I can manage."

He inquired after my *sae* and a few other details of my personal life, then launched into what appeared to be a well-rehearsed speech on the difficulties of raising ten children, for ten he has, all ages. Soon the place began to fill up and he left me to wait on his old customers, who had finished their suppers and were ready for the evening routine of gossip and checkers.

"You ought to have one of your children here with you," insisted one fellow who had been filled in on the salient features of my background by our host. "To be alone here is no good. The neighborhood is quiet, sure, but so are the thieves. Some night you'll go home to find nothing."

"I have nothing in there that would tempt a thief."

"No radio? No refrigerator or television set?"

"No sir, not so much as an electric fan."

And that is the truth, for all that I gave gladly to Weng Khim, all the luxuries Mui Eng needed to make her life bearable.

"I don't think even the poorest thief will be tempted by what I have," I said, whereupon another fellow sitting nearby said, "One cannot be sure . . . almost anything can be sold. You know, a young fellow like you ought to find himself another wife."

As the conversation developed, it appeared that marriage was this man's solution to all the world's problems, but I cannot agree. Happiness can mean many things. In my case, it is time to recover from sorrow, and the peace that comes with freedom from striving.

"Are there many of us here?" I asked.

"Chinese? Not many real Chinese . . ."

"Where are all your sons?" I asked, puzzled that I had seen no young men in the place.

"This is the old duffer's retreat. The young ones go up the street, where pretty girls wait on the tables."

The regular customers continued to meander in, two or three at a time, as dusk clouded the narrow street and lamps began to flicker in open doorways. What a gentle tempo life has here, compared to Yaowarat Road.

One new arrival began to shuffle a deck of well-worn cards on a tabletop dappled with old cigarette burns. "A cop told me today there are only two hundred people left in this district to pay the alien tax this year," he said with an expert flip of the deck. "What do you think of that?" Then, turning to me, he asked, "Where did you live before?"

"Yaowarat Road."

"Many Chinese there," he nodded. "Must be a lot more than two hundred paying the alien tax over there, eh?"

"Not really. Many are Chinese sons who were born here. It seems a Chinese neighborhood because we have kept many of the old ways, and the temples are there . . . but it is changing. Go to one of the temples on Yaowarat now and look at all the dark young women who pray to our gods. Who are they? One parent is not Chinese, that's certain. We used to marry our children to our friends' children, but now—they have other ideas."

Several men nodded in commiseration.

"In the old days, few of our children went to the Thai schools, but now they all do," I continued. "They want the kind of lives their Thai classmates have—or the lives they think those children have. But your sons, they are probably no different, for they have lived even more among Thais than mine."

My guess was correct, as it turned out, for many of their sons have married Thai girls and live as Thais. But if their children are far from the large Chinese neighborhood, they are also far from the nightclubs and massage parlors of the city, from most of its vices. The two exceptions are gambling and fortune telling, which flourish and thrive here.

Since my coming, visitors have been infrequent. Meng Chu comes faithfully every other Saturday to clean house, do my laundry, and cook a few things that will keep several days. She is careful not to ask after her brothers and sisters. Winyu came only once, for he must not only study and teach, but correct his students' homework, and his Sundays seem to be busier than other men's Mondays.

"Papa, I still can't get over this place!" Meng Chu exclaimed. "Look at it—everything in a mess, no decent food to eat. This just doesn't seem like you."

"I eat all right. I make boiled rice and pork in the morning—that doesn't require any special talent. Then I have noodles from a wagon at noon, and some sort of stew for supper. You know, I'm not a fussy eater like the rest of you."

"Do you ever think of the bakery, since you left?"

"Why should I sit and chew over what is past?" I returned irritably. "Weng Khim and Rose are doing a fine job there."

"Won't you consider living with them, Papa?"

"With them? Tchah! Don't you think they could have brought that up when I moved here, if they wanted me so badly? Oh, no . . . they turned their noses up at this and told me I ought to stay in your mother's shop, but did they ever say, 'Stay near us, Papa! We'll worry about you over there, Papa!'? Hah! It doesn't work anymore, the parents with the children."

"Why, that isn't so!" Meng Chu exclaimed. "Winyu's mother lives with us and we all get along fine. Every morning Winyu and I do the washing up and sweep the house while she starts her candies, and then we all hurry off at about the same time."

"A man washing up and sweeping floors? Those are a woman's duties. I never heard of a man doing such things. What if the neighbors should see him, eh? Just because you work, you shouldn't expect him to get down on his knees with a scrub brush."

"If he didn't help, Papa, we'd all be in trouble. But it depends on the day, too. Whoever has extra time at home does extra housework, and sometimes Winyu has a whole morning free. Then he does many things, but I can never be late at the office, so I seldom get to return the favor. My boss is very firm about punctuality, and I don't take any chances. You always used to say that a new sprout needs more care than an old tree, and this job is a new sprout. I want it to last."

"Last for what? It isn't your business."

"It certainly isn't!" she laughed. "That would be nice, but it isn't worth dreaming about."

Ang Buai came to visit me yesterday afternoon, and by the time I reached the coffee shop last evening, I was amused to see that all the old men were eyeing me with curiosity.

Who was she? My wife's sister? If she was single, what was I waiting for?

That's all they ever think of. One of them, who's at least sixty, had a marriage broker find him a buxom thirty-year-old widow, and another married a divorced woman with three children. Lonely old men, Mother, and sad.

386

I HAVE lived alone for three months, and I too am becoming a lonely old man. Even writing to you does not help much.

The society of the coffee shop I can no longer bear, and the other place, where the young men congregate, is more depressing. All day they lounge about, teasing the waitresses with bad jokes and gambling, and some of them have more education than my own son. They cannot find a job, they say, or they are waiting for a place at the university. All this talk is nothing more than justification of plain laziness. One hears it even from the sons and grandsons of the Chinese. Some of them, I have discovered to my horror, are addicted to heroin, and many nights their lamps flicker in the darkness among the trees behind my house, for they go into the swamp to commune with their evil sickness.

Youths of twenty or so ought to be the strength of a nation. Whenever education can no longer be pursued, that is the time to go to work. But they scorn the work they can get and, I am told, refuse all jobs that are far from Bangkok. I should think that would be a positive factor from a young man's point of view, a chance to see more of his own country than he might otherwise, but the crowded streets of the capital exert a stronger fascination than the countryside, where there are no television, running water, or girls with the citified beauty they are used to.

Winyu told me that his classmates in the university are scarcely more eager to live outside Bangkok.

"If they go out there to work, their chance to earn a higher degree is lost. Even so, some of them would go if their parents didn't prevent them. I have a friend who trained to be a *nai amphoe* and wanted to live in the South, but his mother made such a fuss about it that he's never gone more than fifteen kilometers from home."

"They need teachers out here too, I should think."

"Of course they do, desperately, but conditions are very bad. Imagine—one teacher for seventy or eighty children, often without books and sometimes without paper or pencils."

When Winyu did accompany Meng Chu to my new home, he brought his books and studied while she hurried through her work, then fell asleep with his face on an open book just before supper time, poor fellow. It is quite obvious that he gives his utmost to the goal he has set.

I have thought of going to visit the others—to see how the bakery is doing, whether Chui Kim's dress shop is thriving, how Bak Li is managing with the house full of old tin cans . . . but it is not the business of elders to go visiting. They ought to come to me! Then, occasionally, it would not be improper for me to return a visit or two.

Meng Chu has tried another angle of attack in her campaign to marry me off. She will do all the arranging, she says, if I will consent. Incredible! I told her that no man would agree to such a plan.

I have repaid Ang Buai's visits, though, and I enjoyed myself pretty well over there. She has two servants living with her, but what are servants? I think she is as lonely as I am.

"You're wrong there," she said when I broached the subject. "I put on a pretty dress every morning, make up my face, and get my mind in order. "Ang Buai," I say to myself, "today is an important day in which good things will happen!" And I don't let trivial matters put wrinkles on my face."

I wish I had the ability to enjoy life alone, but in spite of what she says I believe that it must be a special talent, one that I do not possess.

⸺

LETTER #92   Lo Buan Chai Heng Bakery
23 October 1966   Yaowarat Road
         Ninth Month, Tenth Day
         Year of the Horse

HERE I am again, on Yaowarat Road. But this is a different house. Weng Khim's new enterprise is across the road from the old bakery, and our old pieces of furniture in these rooms do not disturb me.

It was not loneliness that drove me back. Fire struck the quiet lane in Thonburi and while it did not reach my own house it came close enough to frighten me badly, and my old dread of fire is scarcely diminished because I survived.

The fire started in a warehouse full of tinned vegetable oil, and might have done more terrible damage had it not been brought under control fairly soon. All that night, I dragged such possessions as I had out behind the house and piled them in a heap. But so did my neighbors, and after a few hours it was difficult to tell what belonged to whom. Those people who carried their belongings into the street instead were less fortunate, for many "volunteers" who stopped to lend a hand disappeared into the night, their arms loaded down with the choicest items. A few good souls did help, and stayed to comfort the homeless, but crowds of onlookers lingered until dawn to do nothing but gloat over the spectacle of destruction and loss.

By dawn, when the fire had been conquered, the stench and smoke of it still hung about us. I dragged everything I could find back into the house again, exhausted by the night's efforts, then dropped into a chair to stare witlessly out my doorway at the ruins of my idyllic surroundings. Between charred stumps and the blackened skeletons of houses, people wandered about aimlessly. Women wailed and picked through piles of their own and their neighbors' belongings. Some children played and laughed in the street, but others wept and were afraid, and there would be no breakfast until someone went to fetch soup and rice from the main road, a kilometer's walk. A few families who had lost everything were preparing to go to the temple nearby, where they could sleep and eat until such time as they could weave their lives together again.

Then I saw a stranger approaching, running, stopping briefly to shout something to the owner of the no longer existent coffee shop, running again, coming nearer . . . could it be Weng Khim?

It was not Weng Khim. It was Winyu, breathless and waving both arms above his head as he drew near my house.

"I—I read about it in the newspaper at breakfast!" he cried hoarsely, bursting through the doorway, catching me by the shoulders, and lifting me out of my chair as if I were a puppet. He smiled, gasping for breath. "But you're all right, and that's all that matters!" He set me down in the chair again, still a puppet, and dropped onto the floor beside me. "Well, you really scared me to death, old man," he said shakily, mopping at his face with a handkerchief. I only hope Meng Chu hasn't seen the papers yet. Whew! This place is really a mess."

"I just got everything back in here," I said gruffly. "Of course it looks like a mess."

"Yeah, well I'll put it to rights, don't worry."

"So you were scared to death, eh? You should have been here last

389

night, watching the fire crawl down the street. Say, aren't you supposed to be teaching?"

"It's all right. I had only one hour to teach this morning, and I got a friend to take my class for me."

He rose to his feet and stood, hands on hips, frowning at the piles of debris that filled the room. I was weary beyond caring.

"You just stay there, let me handle this," he said, than scooped up a great armful of bedding and staggered up the stairs to my bedroom.

All was silent but for the ticking of my alarm clock somewhere, and the cries of householders in the street, sounds which echoed dizzily and then faded away as I dozed off in my chair.

"You're alive! Wake up, you bad boy, scaring a poor girl with your nasty headlines!"

I woke with a start and looked up into the face of Ang Buai.

"Wha-? Aow, what are you doing here?" I shook my head and lifted a hand to shade my eyes. The sun was already high, streaming though the doorway behind her.

"I thought you'd got yourself a free cremation over here."

"What a ghastly thing to say!"

"M-m, yes . . . but the newspapers made it sound as though the whole neighborhood had burned to the ground."

"Newspapers must sell themselves. The kind you read, anyway."

"The ones you read are a bore," she retorted, seating herself on an overturned washpan and crossing her legs neatly.

She looked extraordinarily out of place in a crisp, pale blue suit and white high-heeled sandals slightly the worse for the trip from the main road.

"You came alone?"

"I called Weng Khim, but—he has an important customer coming in at noon. I'm supposed to file a report when I get home." It hurt, as she knew it would. "But Meng Chu says she'll be here tonight, and tomorrow we'll come together in my car. At least as far as the main road. It's a hell of a walk in here, by the way. If they don't clear your road soon, you may lose your most faithful but laziest visitor."

"Why should Meng Chu bother to come out here, as long as she has a telephone?"

"Now, now, none of that. You must have had a damned good scare last night."

"Why must you use swear words?"

"I only use them when they suit the circumstances; I don't choose the circumstances . . ." She glanced up at the ceiling. "I hear strange noises."

"Winyu is here."

"Ah, ha. You really ought to know his mother better, Suang U. Then you'd understand why he's such a lovely boy."

"Lovely boy? You've really fallen for the old Thai charm."

"Let's not go through that again, shall we? And the old Thai charm has a lot going for it, besides. It's—refreshing."

"I don't want charm."

"That's no secret. But you have certain . . . attractive qualities." She blushed furiously. I felt a sense of rising panic, and she chose that moment to hurry upstairs to see Winyu.

At dusk, Weng Khim appeared with Meng Chu.

"Well, Papa," Meng Chu began, thrusting her chin forward in preparation for ordering her father about, "now will you listen to reason?"

"The *farang* say that life begins at forty, Meng Chu. I read it in a magazine. That gives me almost a whole year to get ready for the prime of my life, so don't treat me like a doddering old crock!"

"Papa," said Weng Khim, "stay with us for a little while. Until you can make other plans. This is no place for you."

"How do you know that, eh? Little enough you've seen of it! It's quiet here, and peaceful. And cheap! Yaowarat is a stinking madhouse."

Let him coax me a little, I thought to myself. Of course I am lonely, and fed up with the company of old men living on gossip and failed dreams. I want to live with my son, to share his life and lend my strength to his business. As for Rose . . . the hell with her! I deserve this much, and they owe me more.

But it is Rose, after all, who runs this household. What is a man to do when the daughter-in-law he chose himself, chose because she was hard-working, cautious, shrewd, and fervent in her appreciation of the uses of money—what is a man to do when that daughter-in-law welcomes him into the home he provided for her with an expression on her face more suited to the discovery of a cockroach in the rice bin?

"Well, Papa," Weng Khim's thin voice jabbed feebly into the silence of the dinner hour, "it will certainly be to our advantage to have your help with the books . . ."

"Nonsense!" Rose flashed her formidable array of teeth in what passes for her smile. "Why, you already have me to help, and now you want to drag your poor old Papa back into business? You lazy boy!" She gave a snorting laugh and turned a glance on Weng Khim which stopped a mouthful of soup halfway down his throat. "I have a much nicer idea. Instead of fuddling his head with figures . . . money and all that . . . I think it would be perfect to have Papa supervise the trucks, see to it that the orders are straight and the drivers minding their jobs. No one is more particular about those things than Papa, isn't that right, Khim?"

Weng Khim coughed politely into his napkin, and nodded.

All day, while he is away, she never looks at me. I must admit that she is a diligent girl. The place never ran more smoothly. But there is an air of grim efficiency here now that I am not at all sure I like.

When her husband returns from his business calls in the afternoon, Rose is like a fish thrown back into water a moment before certain death, leaping about ecstatically, grinning her great shark's grin, dominating and devouring him ruthlessly. That she loves him I have no doubt, but it seems to me a terrifying love. I can imagine now what the days of Phanni were like for her, if she loved him then as she does now.

How did Rose ever come to be as she is? Kim and Chaba are gentle people, diligent but also warm and loving. It is as if a pair of sparrows had hatched a hawk.

—

LETTER#93
16 NOVEMBER 1966

LO BUAN CHAI HENG BAKERY
TENTH MONTH, FIFTH DAY
YEAR OF THE HORSE

I AM disgusted with myself for having allowed my loneliness to obscure my reason. I have nothing here. Only the shadow of a son, and a daughter-in-law who frankly despises me.

"What's wrong with her lately?" one servant grumbled to another, undisturbed by my presence in the room. "She was never this bad before."

"M-m, she's been a real bitch lately," replied her companion. "Yesterday she threw all the ironing I had just finished down into the yard from her bedroom window, how do you like that?"

But the cook, who has been here since Weng Khim was a boy, came directly to me with her tale of woe.

"Sir, she never stops scolding me about money." she blurted out, a skinny little woman with sparse gray hair pulled back into a thimble of a knot. 'How you love to waste money you don't earn!' she says to me. 'Two days and we're out of rice—we may as well buy it by the sack!' Well, sir, I tell her we always did buy it that way before she came, but that makes her madder than ever, and she says, 'Then stop buying meat! We can live well enough on fish!' So I say, 'Fishes and shrimps cost too.' And it's true, sir—you can't touch shrimps for nothing nowadays, sir!"

Poor old thing. What could I say? I could only shake my head, embarrassed, and congratulate myself on the money I kept for myself, money which now rests comfortably in the bank, money enough to buy my freedom from the foolish dream of a home with my son. It never occurred to me that Weng Khim's fervent dislike of the girl years ago might have been based on good sense. Why didn't it? It is a thought worth pondering.

In my loneliness on the quiet lane in Thonburi, I could pretend that they were all too busy to visit their papa, too successful for free afternoons. Now I have destroyed all my illusions, and perhaps it is for the best. But I gave Rose a beautiful wedding in a Swiss lace gown, while all of us wore mourning bands; nothing was too good for her. Why should she despise me so? Or perhaps the suspicion I mentioned earlier is the answer—she despises me for the months Phanni slept away the mornings on Weng Khim's pillow.

If Rose has deprived me of any work in which I might take pride, she has also deprived me of honest sleep, and a man who has always worked hard, long days has never learned to court sleep. Now that my days are spent largely in idleness, my body is not ready to sleep when I want it to, and so I lie awake and worry. That is how I happened to hear them through the thin wall of my bedroom the night after the little cook came to me with her unhappy tale.

"Khim, you've just got to keep him out of my papers! He was in there again this morning, I'm sure he was."

"Oh, Rose, what do you expect? He ran the place for twenty years."

"And some of our employees are going to him now for orders, or haven't you bothered to notice?"

"They worked for him. They're loyal, that's all."

"So you're willing to crawl back into your corner and wait for Papa to pat you on the head once a month and say, 'good boy!' He despises you, can't you see that? I want you to be happy, Khim. I make you happy, don't I?"

"Yes, Rose."

"I feel as if I didn't even exist, with him here. All the old customers . . . I was getting their confidence, you know? And now every time they come in they head straight for him. It galls me, being treated like—like nobody."

"I'm sorry."

"You're sorry, but you're too scared of him to stand up for your own wife."

They have a new car, a new air conditioner, and what Rose spends on makeup alone would put pork on the dinner table every day.

"People should only eat what they need," she says. "It's out of style to be fat, anyway. We're not common laborers, using up five thousand calories a day!"

I looked up this word calorie in the dictionary. It is too complicated to explain, but the main idea is that rich food has more "calories" than poor food, so that Rose's common laborers are the people least likely to get five thousand of them in one day. We have always known that wealthy men grow fat, and why. New in the world is the idea that the rich ought to show their wealth by means of fancy clothing worn over skinny bodies.

I have come to live in an age where the rich choose to starve and children are admired for leaving their parents. When I was a boy, a dead father was shown more attention than a live one receives today. I must live in my son's house as a guest—I ask you, does a father want to be treated as a guest? To be alone is terrible, but it is not so terrible as to be a guest in a son's house.

It is possible that I stressed the money-getting aspect of life too much with Weng Khim, for he talks of nothing else. You and my father spoke of money only when necessary, and whatever we did at home was shared, not one going here, one there, each pursuing his private goal. But I am a hypocrite to say these things, for what did I share with Weng Khim besides work? When he was a small boy I drilled him in sums and calligraphy, but you taught me ideas as well: the words of Confucius, and the beauty of what Meng Chu would call our "culture."

We had time for many things in our village, and every man adhered to the ways of his ancestors without question. No man would conduct his life differently from his neighbor, or wonder whether another way of life might be more satisfying. This neighborhood is larger than our village, and as all men in Po Leng were farmers so all men here are merchants. But no one bothers about his neighbor, and each one does as he pleases. A man in Po Leng was closer to a distant cousin than a Yaowarat merchant is to a brother in his house.

I visit Chui Kim frequently to escape Rose's sulks, and a busy place it is, no less so than the bakery.

"Oh, I am so tired!" she said with a great sigh, pulling a tidy knot onto the end of her thread and biting it off neatly before she folded a newly hemmed skirt on her lap.

"But you are doing well. I am proud of you. Now, what are your plans for the money I gave you? Or haven't you thought it over yet?"

"Land, Papa. I'm glad we had only a Chinese wedding, without the Thai license, or I'd have had to get Seng Huat's approval to buy it. Meng Chu keeps scolding me about that—the more fool she! We're as married as anybody else, and she'll find out how much good a license does her."

"Yes, it is less trouble in many ways to avoid that, to follow our own customs, though none of my children would believe me until their own mistakes proved me right—except for you, dear. But this business of taking out a license to marry is absurd. In the old days, the Chinese believed that a man who had abandoned his first wife could never prosper, and that was a wife's greatest protection. Say a fellow went to a neighboring district to find work, and stayed ten years. He might return home with a wife and five children after all those years, but if he had married in his own village and his first wife still lived, the second wife from the other village would become her servant the day she arrived. And believe me, Chui Kim, she did not complain. She respected her husband for doing his duty. Stranger than that, a betrothal was considered as binding as a marriage, so that if the man had only been betrothed to the first woman, she would still be considered the mistress of the house. That was because the parents had agreed to the match, and parents had that kind of authority then. These customs are imbedded in the soul of our people, even now, so that you will never see a Chinese man cast out the old cow for a frisky calf!"

"Oh, Papa," she chuckled, "you are awful."

"Go on and laugh, then, but it is so. Let me give you one piece of advice, Chui Kim. Land is a good investment, but secrets about money are no good in a marriage."

She frowned and began to wind the thread around her finger thoughtfully. "Why must I tell him everything? He knows I have some money of my own, but he never mentions it. I guess he respects my right to it."

I wondered at that. Perhaps she is right. We do not always agree, Chui Kim and I, but what a joy to talk with her, after Rose.

Sometimes I visit Bak Li, but she is busy with the baby now. It is a girl, and bears another man's name besides, another *sae*. I am not much interested in it. I long for a son's son, but what part of him would I have in this house?

Perhaps I should go to stay with Chui Kim for a while, for I am growing bitter here, and it is not good. Everything Weng Khim and Rose have, all the money they spend so freely, where did it come from? Even if they cannot respect me as the head of the family, I should think they would be grateful for my generosity.

But there, you see how bitter I have grown? I am sick of myself, bored with my own whining. Forgive me, please. I wish them well in spite of everything.

In Po Leng, have parents and children come to this? I close my eyes and try to picture our village in the year 1966 . . . It is very difficult.

LETTER #94
26 DECEMBER 1966

DUEANGPHEN DRESS SHOP
SURIWONG ROAD, BANGKOK
ELEVENTH MONTH, FIFTEENTH DAY
YEAR OF THE HORSE

LONELINESS IS a clever enemy, the more one tries to defeat it, the wilier it becomes—lurking in odd corners, springing out where it is least expected. I have lived in Chui Kim's house for a month, long enough to know that I shall not stay. No one ignores me, there are no sullen faces here, but their way of life is foreign to me and I cannot feel comfortable with it.

The day I left their home, Weng Khim and Rose both pleaded with me to stay, but the day before I had heard yet another conversation between them. This time I was trapped in the kitchen, unbeknownst to them, while they argued outside the door, and I dared not move for fear they would hear me.

"It is just as well, I suppose," I heard Weng Khim say with a dispirited sigh. "Damn that fire in Thonburi . . . I haven't had a night's peaceful sleep since. One lousy year of freedom, and bang! here he was, pushing up the thermostat in our refrigerator. I admit that you were right—but don't keep nagging me about it, all right?"

And the next morning . . .

"Why do you have to leave us and live with Chui Kim, Papa? Everyone will talk . . . I mean, how does it look? All your old cronies will think—well, you know—living with a daughter and all . . ."

"Are you afraid of losing face, then?" I asked, fastening the lock on my trunk.

"I'm worried about you, too, of course. But let's face it, Papa, you could go back to that place in Thonburi if you wanted to. You liked it over there, didn't you? Why do you have to look at me like that?"

"Forget the neighbors and my 'old cronies,' will you? It's clear that I'm going of my own free will. Everyone you know is too busy with his own affairs to care where I go or what I do, and as for my friends, they are few and getting fewer. Since I left the society, who do I see? Kim and Seng, and I can see them whenever I want to."

"You want me to run you over to Chui Kim's? Unfortunately, I have an errand in the other direction . . ."

"Never mind."

The atmosphere of Seng Huat and Chui Kim's household overwhelmed me. This is a house of women! Seamstresses, servants, clerks, all are women, with Seng Huat in firm control. He is an expert salesman, perhaps too expert. How can that be? He is not extravagant in his habits and he works hard, but he is so adept at dealing with the *farang*, who increasingly patronize the place, that he has begun to act like one of them. He watches *farang* films on television, then goes out to the theaters to see even more. Nowadays he even hugs his wife in public whenever he feels like it, or worse, so that one scarcely knows where to look.

Seng Huat is exceedingly thrifty, but I never hear him grumble about the cost of good food on the table. He smiles all day long, at me, at everyone, and his customers obviously like him. Chui Kim has nothing to complain of, that's certain, nor need I worry for a moment on her account. Not like our poor Bak Li, whose future worries me greatly. I do not trust Surasak to give her any happiness. Nor do I believe that he is capable of loving any woman, though the blame for that, I fear, lies with his mother and not himself.

The girls who work here are irritating and foolish. I never noticed it when I used to visit Chui Kim, but they giggle like a pack of chimpanzees at anything that strikes their fancy. A dress pictured in a magazine pleases them, so they crowd around it giggling and hissing at each other through their fingers. What is the matter with them? Their conversation I cannot bear, and when a customer joins in it is worse.

"I believe the skirt could be shortened another inch," the young lady whined in a high, affected voice. "Who will look if it's this long?" She turned and glanced over her shoulder into the mirror to study her stocky bare thighs, though the dress already revealed more of them than most men would consider tempting.

"You really want to catch the boss's eye, don't you?" her companion asked, then tittered naughtily, which was followed by a chorus of titters from three little girls on their knees with pin cushions.

"Idiot!" the first replied archly. "He has two kids and a jealous wife. I prefer the widower across the street. No kids and a couple of million under the mattress."

Are you shocked?

Another day a pretty young seamstress came to work arm in arm with a young man, stuck to his side like one cooked noodle to another.

"Shame on them!" I said to Chui Kim when they were out of hearing. "Do newly married people nowadays have to walk arm in arm?"

"Why, she isn't married to him, Papa," Chui Kim said, turning to me from the pattern she was cutting. "Arm in arm—tch tch!" She laughed and shook her head, amused.

"Even if they were married," I persisted, "why do that in a public place? Do they have to announce the situation to a thousand strangers?"

"A thousand strangers who couldn't care less, Papa."

"Now, now, you aren't old enough to talk like that," Seng Huat said to me, leaving the customer he was waiting on with one of his clerks. "No wonder you give me the evil eye every time I pinch my wife—"

"Husbands and wives used to keep a decent distance in public. In fact, when I was young a man went out alone on festive occasions, or sent his eldest son. A wife never appeared with her husband except when absolutely necessary. Why do wives show up at all these things now?"

"I don't know, I never thought about it," he replied. "But weddings and parties are not only for men, and people our age are considered pretty old-fashioned if the wife stays home."

I determined to ask Meng Chu about this when she and Winyu visited us the next day. And I did, but it was Winyu who answered my question.

"I believe it is because today women are more, well, equal is the only word that says it . . . not an expression to your taste, I'm sure, but—say a married man is invited alone to a party. Will he behave like a married man?" He grinned at Meng Chu. "Or will his wife greet him with a big frown at midnight because she wonders the same thing? Unmarried girls at parties always have an eye on likely prospects. Ah! The look on your face is priceless! But many young men, excluding present company of course," and he nodded an exaggerated wink in Seng Huat's direction, "are not above taking advantage of the situation. So you see, wives believe that if they are good enough to go to work at dawn, they're good enough to party at dusk."

Everyone laughed at that, including four or five customers who had gathered around to hear him expound.

Winyu's words made sense to me, whether he realized it or not. I suppose I am getting used to his peculiar sense of humor. The young women who frequent Chui Kim's shop prove everything he said, for it is true that they think of nothing but husbands. Their garish makeup, painfully plucked eyebrows and indecent clothing, the meager food they starve on to assume the gaunt proportions their fashions demand—all are ritual sacrifices toward the all-consuming goal of trapping a man.

Twenty or thirty years ago, Seng Huat would have made a decent living and no more in this business, when fathers sought husbands for their daughters and young women were not required to approach every eligible male with the savageness of cobras cornering a rabbit fallen haplessly into their nest. What have women gained, I ask you?

Expensive cloth rolls off the bolts as if it were newsprint. Chui Kim and the girls can scarcely cut and sew fast enough to keep up with their customers' demands for those tight little skirts and all the other paraphernalia they must have. The cleverest of the girls cut and sew, the others do minor jobs such as fastening buttons and stitching hems. Seng Huat enjoys presiding over this assemblage of females. I told him frankly that I would go mad. He only laughed and said that looking at pretty girls all day is good for the soul. But he mollifies Chui Kim by declaring often that she is "still the best-looking woman in the place!"

It is an honest business, I suppose, an honest enough occupation that does not break any moral law. But I could not be comfortable, knowing that the money I earned in my shop was spent for nothing but vanity. How can Seng Huat and Chui Kim stand those endless, stupid conversations in the sewing and fitting rooms, the constant emphasis on things which should not even be spoken of? Even to you I would not reveal some of the things I have heard in this place, and my ears burn with shame a dozen times a day.

I taught our children to work hard and to be fair with their customers, but I never said, "This business is honorable, that one less so . . ." if I spoke such words now, they would be amazed, I am sure, to learn that the old man might well turn down money if its source offended him.

I suppose that what bothers me most in this shop is that all the things I disliked about Mui Eng have been developed to a fine art here:

extravagance and disdain for good taste are catered to, declared respectable and even necessary for "happiness."

I should not be so lonely that I have to shift from one to another of my children's homes, irritated, and, no doubt, irritating—turning up a refrigerator thermostat here, frowning at the indecency of a girl's new dress there . . . what business is it of mine if Weng Khim's electric bill is too high, or Chui Kim's customers choose to wear no skirts at all?

To hell with all of them.

Not that I had any plan to spend a month with poor Bak Li, her girl child, her whining old mother-in-law, and Surasak the spoiler of men's daughters. I shall go to Meng Chu, I think. For rest, and for time to get up the courage to begin again. My lamentations have probably convinced you that Suang U has quit, has given upon life, but that is not so. All my unhappiness has gone into these pages, for which I apologize and offer, if you will accept them, my thanks. I have stepped back from each letter, studied my own mewling and misery, and gradually a new sense of purpose has begun to dawn.

Do not be afraid for me, or sad. I have more to say, but the time is not yet right. My thoughts and prayers go with this letter, and my promises to write soon, and of happier things.

LETTER #95
11 FEBRUARY 1967

SOI SABAI CHAI*
THONBURI
FIRST MONTH, THIRD DAY
YEAR OF THE GOAT

TODAY I write from the home of Meng Chu, Winyu, his mother Khun Surang, and—myself.

This place has given all that I asked of it, peace and time. Khun Surang doesn't bother me much, for she is always puttering about with her candy, with the deep bubbling pots and shimmering wide pans of mysterious concoctions she sells. (Not bad, some of them.) She has a cheerful disposition, and there is a difference, somehow, between the

*The author indulges in a play on words. The word *soi* means lane; *sabai chai* means content, at peace, happy. Tan Suang U has at last come to live in a place of peace, and joy. *Trans.*

Chinese and the Thai style of cheerfulness. Winyu's mother is content in herself, and whatever anyone else does or says she remains—herself, slow and patient and yet dignified, which was the quality I noticed first the day she visited me in my office.

The neighborhood is full of "old" Thais, many of them with her easy, relaxing ways, and there are no "mini-skirts" on Soi Sabai Chai.

Meng Chu treats me as she always has, with exasperated affection, even though she knows I have given great sums of money to her sisters and brother, and does not suspect that there is a share left for her. When Bak Li came to visit the other day, she brought up the subject. (Since my days in Weng Khim's household, I am no longer ashamed of snooping. You are no doubt amazed at this, but surely snooping is no great sin).

"What did Papa give you?" she asked bluntly. "Weng Khim got more than us, you know."

"Be glad with what you've got, sister. Something for your children's future, that should relieve your mind . . . for us, it doesn't matter."

"I just want to know, that's all," Bak Li retorted, miffed. "I got thirty thousand, and it's all in the bank. He'll never get his hands on it."

"Aren't you afraid of what will happen if he finds out?"

"If I were, I wouldn't have done it. What about Winyu? I suppose he knows."

Silence.

(Perhaps she was thinking, "My share has gone to Weng Khim . . .")

"He knows. How's Chui Kim?"

"She's kept her mouth shut about the money too. Seng Huat knows she got it, but he's—not like Surasak."

"I asked how Chui Kim is, not how her money is! Bak Li, is that all you ever think about?"

"I have to think of myself and the baby, Meng Chu. Don't come over all smug with me. Just wait until you have children!"

I wonder what Winyu and his mother, Khun Surang, do think about it. Ang Buai has invested the money in government bonds. Next year, she says, she'll give them the interest as an ordinary New Year's gift, if I haven't yet told them the truth.

Meng Chu returns from work each afternoon with a big smile and, often, a little surprise for me. Yesterday it was a bag of our competitor's *chan-ap*, of all things, which made me laugh. She will do anything to wring a laugh out of me. It is beyond my understanding that she can behave as she does, believing that I have taken her portion from her and given it to Weng Khim, while he, who has been given so much, never even comes to see us.

Winyu, observed in his own home, is surprising. He does nothing but work! And he is constantly surrounded by mountains of paper and books, his students' and his own.

"I remain astonished," I said to him the other evening, "at all this work of yours. I never saw a Thai—"

"Now stop that!" he cried, giving a sharp downward slap of his hand to *Primary Education in the Provinces: An Overview.* "You never spent a day on a Thai farm. You ought to sometime, instead of comparing every Thai with the laborers in your bakery."

He was right, and for the first time I apologized to Winyu sincerely for my thoughtless words.

I cannot live here doing nothing. Already I feel that I am— shrinking. I want to work, but there is no room here to start any kind of business. And I suppose I do want to get married, Mother . . . though I have not got up the courage yet. That is why I scoured the neighborhood for a shop I can rent while living with Meng Chu. There aren't many nearby, for most of the houses here are just that, houses where people have lived for forty years. But I have found one, and now I feel truly content. Meng Chu and Winyu do not pinch each other, his mother is a nice lady who does not begrudge money spent on proper food, none of them is extravagant with money, and there are no giggling girls here staring at their behinds in long mirrors. Are my needs, then, so difficult to meet? Bah! I have been made to feel like a freak, and I am no freak.

My own bank account is more respectable than any of the children suspect, and recently I sold the land I bought last year in Thonburi. There is money to spare, then, for a new venture. Rose and Weng Khim will take a sudden interest in Papa when they realize that the well is not yet dry, and I will enjoy that.

I went to Winyu's mother with my plan.

"There are no shops for rent that I know of," she said, shaking her head slowly, "but—wait, I have friends who mentioned a few months

403

ago that they might rent their ground floor if they could find a tenant. They both work, but they need the money. I could ask."

"May I go with you?"

"Why not?" she smiled.

This excellent lady took me to her friends, and the transaction was completed with few words.

"If you only want the front downstairs," the landlady said with a shrug, "all right, yes, why not?" This strange, friendly little person repeats everything she says two or three times using different words. "But downstairs, we will need the kitchen, a place to cook, room to eat our food . . ."

"No problem there," I said, trying to hide a grin.

"And you will only sell things in the daytime, before dark, never at night?"

"I promise you. Dawn until dusk only. I will sell canned food, the kinds of things people discover they've run out of just before supper. You approve?"

"Yes, of course, why not?"

"The only thing that worries me is, I won't have anyone to guard my stock at night—"

"No no! She shook her little head fiercely and said, "This street is safe! I know every family, all the children, the whole neighborhood. No one would steal from you and—we are here, no?"

I left with a light heart. Canned foods, candy bars for school children who pass by—nothing perishable. Enough to amuse myself with.

After supper, I asked Meng Chu to come outside with me onto the small front porch.

"You know about the money I gave the others, don't you?"

"Bak Li told me. No, that's a lie—I knew before."

"Are you angry with your Papa? Sorry, maybe, that you invited him to live in your home?"

Meng Chu, who was sitting on the step below me, turned and looked up at me anxiously. "No, Papa, I never had such a thought! I married against your wishes, and—and you still care about me, I think, and—and that's enough for me . . . "

"And Winyu?"

"He knows. His mother heard Bak Li—who didn't? She's always

404

had the biggest mouth in the family."

"What did Khun Surang say?" I asked worriedly, distressed to think that this woman I so admire might think ill of me, and certain that she must.

"Winyu's mother? She didn't say much about it. You help us out a lot, you're always out buying food. She doesn't think you should do even that, it you want to know the truth. I guess she thinks you have nothing now, and she doesn't realize that you've always lived modestly, even when you had the business. She—she feels sorry for you, Papa."

"Indeed!" I replied indignantly. "And what do you think about my—my situation?"

"I don't know. It seems to me that you gave away too much."

"And if you learned that there was plenty left, enough for you too—"
"Don't—"

"Let me finish, Meng Chu, and tell you what is in my heart. But first, tell me what you would do if you had money, lots of money, mine or anybody else's."

"If I had money . . . well, I suppose would go back to school."

"You can go back to school, Meng Chu."

"No. Keep your money, Papa. I know you must have some from selling the land in Thonburi, maybe twenty thousand, but I don't want any of that. And Winyu—" She laughed. "He wouldn't touch it, he's so determined to prove to you that we can make it on our own."

"He has, you both have, and in more ways than I can bear to think about. Meng Chu, the two of you have had thirty thousand baht in the bank ever since your marriage—or rather, it was in the bank until your aunt invested it in government bonds on your behalf."

"Oh, Papa!" she cried with an anguished expression, "Take the money and lease a big store and marry Auntie!"

"For once in your life, will you stop trying to boss me around?"

"I tell you Winyu won't take it."

"Who is he, to tell me what to do with my money?"

"We know who we are," she laughed. "I'm not so sure who you are anymore!"

Two days later Winyu came to me.

"It isn't right," he began, swallowing nervously. "I am—touched, and very grateful, but it isn't right. How can we accept that kind of money from you while you sit in a little shop selling candy bars day after day? I will tell you frankly, we need some money, about five thousand would clear us. But no more."

"You are fools, Winyu. Putting off children, scrimping and saving and worrying yourselves to death, and for what? I have plenty of money, and I don't have to sell candy bars for a living whether you take thirty baht from me or five thousand or the thirty thousand already in your name. Damn it, give me the pleasure of seeing you do something my way for a change."

"There is one thing we will do . . . I don't know if I should call it 'your way,'" he laughed, "but—my mother too wants a grandchild. We won't have more than two, though, even if they turn out to be girls."

"You need money to raise children," I said, praying already for boys.

"Not thirty thousand baht."

"Oh, ho! You tell me that in five years."

"Then maybe I'll bother you from time to time," he said, with a grin, "but I don't want the whole chunk right now."

I would like to think he will give in, but I know he won't. How can I understand this man? He makes a joke of everything, even when he is serious, or angry. I know now that I sadly misjudged him, Mother, but how could I have judged him fairly? What Thai did I ever know, besides the few I employed, what Winyu accurately called "a few laborers in a bakery"?

I wrote earlier in this letter that I came to their house for peace and time, but I have found much, much more. Winyu's mother, a poor old Thai lady who sells candy in the streets, feels sorry for me. My bakery produced in an hour ten times the candy she sells in a month, and she feels sorry for me! That is something to think about, and when I have thought about it long enough, I believe that I shall be ready to live the rest of my life.

Letter #96
17 June 1967

Soi Sabai Chai
Thonburi
Fifth Month, Tenth Day
Year of the Goat

IN THE past six months I have learned two astounding facts. One is that money is not the most important thing in life; the other is that what we believe does not necessarily reflect what we are.

For all that you taught me, I paid least attention to lessons which were unspoken, but which were my real food and shelter through out my childhood. I took understanding and sympathy from you without question, but I never learned to give them to others.

Weng Khim stopped by my little store today to ask whether I need anything. Ever since I divided one hundred and twenty thousand baht between them, he and Rose have connived to discover how much is left, and how to get at it before I have the decency to drop dead. He seems more sure of himself lately, less frightened of his wife, and I felt this morning that I was seeing the real man at last, though I would be hard put to describe the emotion that revelation produced.

"Is there anything you need, Papa?" He smiled self-consciously and stepped into the store with a furtive glance behind him. "Rose and I don't understand how you can get by living like—like this," he said, indicating my surroundings with distaste. "We'd be glad to let you have a little cash every week. I mean, it wasn't our idea for you to give everything away."

"Oh, I'm quite all right. I have enough to get by on. Selling these few things keeps me from getting too bored with myself."

"But living with them . . . doesn't it bother you to eat Winyu's rice?"

"Had I gone to them with empty hands, I suppose it might. But I contribute my share. You might say that if the rice is Winyu's, the fish is my own."

"What do you mean by that?" His eyes glittered with suspicion.

"I am not destitute, you know."

"But you can't make more than thirty baht a day in this dump."

"Weng Khim, you do not know that this 'dump' is my only source of income."

His eyes widened. "How much is left? If you're just—stashing it away somewhere—"

"I have no intention of discussing it with you."

"But if you don't want to start a new business, why don't you put more money into the bakery? Rose and I are thinking of adding a line of soda crackers."

"Soda crackers? What are soda crackers?"

"Little white salted crackers. People like them now, the imported kind sell very well. Aren't you interested in the business anymore?"

"No."

"But if we had just a few extra pieces of machinery, we could do it."

"You can afford to buy a few extra pieces of machinery without coming to me."

"No, I can't! Bank rates are high, the cost of living is high. A hundred baht doesn't buy anything. It's not like before, Papa. Our profits aren't higher than they were five years ago, but our overhead is tremendous. And the money we got from you is almost gone."

I said nothing.

"Well, at least think it over," he said angrily, and was gone.

My son! I held the infant Weng Khim in my arms and whispered into his tiny ear that money was a worthy god, business happiness, profit pleasure. Sometimes he faltered, and he never had real talent for it, but patiently I picked him up each time he stumbled and pulled him along. I taught him never to break the law, but to know where its joints are, and where it bends most easily. I wanted so badly to see him become a good businessman and somehow, in spite of himself, he has become a remarkably astute one, for all his extravagance. He lied when he said profits had not increased in five years. He is not only astute, but ruthless, shallow, greedy, and selfish. Everything he is today, he owes to his father.

He asks whether I am ashamed to live with Meng Chu and Winyu. I am ashamed of a few things, but none that would ever occur to him. I will tell you and no one else that I am sometimes ashamed of my defeat, ashamed that I failed to live here as a true Chinese, and raise a Chinese family. I could not shelter them from the thousands of daily experiences which made them another people, another race. There are so many of us Chinese here, yet the Thai have won. And it was never a contest anyway, but I pretended that it was for the sake of my selfish pride.

If there is a better man than Winyu Thiploet, I have not met him. I was of the opinion that a good heart was not money in the bank. You couldn't buy a bowl of rice with sympathy, I used to say. But two baht worth of rice with love at the supper table is a feast, and I know, because